Burial Ground

by

Stephen B King

The Wild Rose Press, Inc.
PO Box 708
Adams Basin, NY 14410-0708
Visit us at www.thewildrosepress.com

Publishing History
First Edition, 2024
Trade Paperback ISBN 978-1-5092-5372-2
Digital ISBN 978-1-5092-5373-9

Published in the United States of America

Dedication

To my family, who not only put up with living with an author, but actively encourages me. I love you all.

Book 1
The Abyss

"I don't suffer from insanity.
I enjoy every minute of it."

~Author Unknown

Chapter 1

Firelight Burning Bright

Tammy Reynolds felt relaxed as she sat on a makeshift seat made from an old red gum tree log. It seemed solid enough so long as she or any of the other three girls sitting on it moved slowly. They were laughing and joking, and occasionally the log rocked and threatened to crumble or drop them to the grass, which only added to the fun-filled atmosphere.

Tammy sipped from her fourth can of pre-mixed vodka, lime, and soda and had a warm buzz glowing inside her. That was helped by the toasting feeling on the front of her body, which radiated from the leaping, dancing flames. She was pretty sure she wouldn't get *too* drunk, as she had been eating the sausage rolls, tiny triangle sandwiches, and mini pizzas placed neatly on aluminum foil trays brought around regularly. Sarah's mother served them. You could hear her making her way around the fire as people said, "Thank you, Mrs. Morris," repeatedly. Tammy had to admit the food was lovely and welcome. She hadn't eaten dinner before the party and hoped Mrs. Morris' offerings might help her avoid driving the *porcelain bus* later that night, which she certainly thought she could have done on an empty stomach. Tammy was spending the night there, sharing her best friend's bed, as they had done many times over the years. Being the good friend she was, she was determined not to get too untidy. Tammy had volunteered to help with the morning clean-up and didn't want to wake up with a severe hangover.

It was Sarah's nineteenth birthday, and as it fell just before the start of the fire ban season, yet still in the warmer time of year, someone had come up with the idea of having a bonfire party. As Tammy looked around at the fifty or more people present, she noted everyone was having a great time, so the idea was brilliant. It was a cold night, and the bonfire flames reached ten or more meters into the night sky, sending out waves of warmth and tiny sparkling embers in the chilling breeze and warming the teenagers present.

The Morris family owned a fantastic twenty-acre block with amazing views of the rolling hills and a lovely home in Roleystone, situated in the eastern hills of Perth. Tammy knew they were well off, unlike Tammy's own family. The Reynolds had a three-bedroom brick and tile house in Belmont, with just one bathroom, unlike the Morris' three and a half bathrooms spread over two stories and a mezzanine, and completing the picture were three stables for the horses.

Tammy became friendly with Sarah only because of the scholarship she had won years ago to go to Saint Bernadette's Catholic School, where they had become best friends. Tammy's parents would not have been able to afford the extraordinarily high fees for her to attend such a prestigious school without the sports scholarship she had deservedly won.

Tammy was a natural athlete. She was one of those fortunate individuals who excelled at every sport she tried, and the prestigious school welcomed her with open arms. Once there, Tammy worked hard and excelled at most subjects, but sports were her passion. Specifically, she loved all forms of running. Sprinting or long distances were equally the same for Tammy. She was a shining track star and had won many medals for the school. While on the cross-country running team, she and Sarah became acquainted. It quickly advanced to a close friendship deserving of the title *best friends,* or *besties,* as they called themselves. They became almost inseparable ever since.

They shared a quirky sense of humor, including a fanatical love of everything related to a famous American sitcom TV show. They would annoy their friends by continually copying sayings from the show. They recited phrases such as: "Not that there's anything wrong with that." "No soup for you," or "Again, with the complaining?"

Their best impression, which made them giggle hysterically every time they performed it, drove one of their friends to anger. Her name was Belinda Newman. When either friend saw her, they would put on a heavy Brooklyn accent and say, "Hello, N-e-w-man," dragging out the "N-e-w" part of the name, as the star did when he greeted his neighbor. Both girls almost fell about laughing each occasion, and the more Belinda complained, the funnier it was to Sarah and Tammy. With fierce promises to each other, they vowed that whoever had a daughter first would name her Rochelle, with a middle name Rochelle so that they could immortalize the featured play, *Rochelle, Rochelle.*

Despite their different upbringings, they were extremely close. Some girls at school spread a rumor that Tammy and Sarah were lesbians. Both were pretty, fit, and lean. They wore short hair and were *touchy-feely*, particularly with each other, as was natural with girls in team sports. So, their over-closeness seemed evident to those who didn't know Sarah and Tammy well. They were confident that no two girls could be that friendly and always touch each other unless they were gay. Although this perspective often had more to do with jealousy than observational skills, Tammy thought. Some girls might have gone to the principal to complain because the jealousy could have been interpreted as bullying. Or worse, the girls could have lost their tempers and fought the ringleaders who spread the rumors. Instead, Sarah and Tammy did the opposite; they played up to it.

At sixteen years old, it became a joke between their true friends, and the girls often held hands when they walked, dirty danced with each other at parties, and even pretended to kiss each other in greetings. They allowed themselves to get caught making out to fan the flames of rumor ever higher. That's how they were; everything was funny, but some things were more comical than others. The rumor of them being lesbians was, to them, hysterical. As the rumor mill spread, Tammy and Sarah laughed at how stupid some people could be. To them, laughter was what life was for, and that people thought they were gay if anything, brought them closer.

To some at school, the rumor made the pair more

popular because bisexuality was considered fashionable. Some made it clear that if Tammy or Sarah wanted to, they would be more than willing to participate too. One or two, tired of their overtures being ignored, asked if they could join in, to which both replied, with gleeful smirks, they were exclusive. They would giggle hysterically about the proposition when they were next alone.

To their detractors' chagrin, Tammy and Sarah's group of friends grew more extensive, as to be the friend of a bi girl was seen to be the height of coolness. This was especially true for the girls who were closeted gay and lacked the courage or practical experience to come out. They seemed to feed off Tammy and Sarah, not caring if the rumors were true but hoping they were. Tammy and Sarah maintained a neither confirm nor deny attitude, content to let people draw their own conclusions.

****

One Saturday night, just over a year before the party, Tammy was invited to sleep at Sarah's. They had spent the afternoon riding Mr. Sloan, Sarah's horse, which she had been given for her thirteenth birthday and adored every day since. After dinner, the girls showered, went to Sarah's room, and watched two episodes of their favorite show. They were in a giggly mood when Sarah suddenly became serious and said, "Hey, Tam, you know I love you, right?"

"Yeah, I know that, stoopid. What's up?"

"Do you ever think about trying it? You know the lesbian thing?"

"Not that there's anything wrong with that," they both said in synch, then spent two minutes giggling at their perfect timing. When they calmed down, Tammy realized how warm Sarah's hand was as it rested high on her bare thigh. They both only wore long T-shirts and panties, having gotten ready for bed after their showers, and suddenly Tammy looked at Sarah in a different light. Sarah tilted her head to one side, which made her look even cuter than usual, as the light from the bedside lamp glittered off her hair. Tammy found her voice first.

"Not really, no. Why?"

"Ah, well now, if you had said a more definite *no*, I'd believe you, but you are saying *not really,* so I reckon that kind of means you have. It's okay, Tam, cos, umm, I have too."

"Really? With anyone I know?" They giggled again though Tammy knew who Sarah thought about. She needed time to process it because, deep down, she *had* wondered the same thing on more than one occasion. Usually, those intimate thoughts occurred at night, while in bed alone, as her fingertip caressed herself.

"With you, stoopid. Who else would I have the hots for?"

Tammy felt staggered that her best friend would have the nerve to admit her desire. Tammy could never have been *that* brave. She tried to hide her innermost feelings with humor. "Let me repeat, *really? You want to make love with me?*"

"Yeah, well, it's not like I've stopped thinking about boys. It's just with people believing you and I are getting it on. Well, it got me thinking about what it would be like. So, umm, I just wanted you to know the thought of that isn't, like, horrible to me."

"Wow, kiddo, I don't think anyone has ever propositioned me in quite so lovely a way before. *The thought of sex with me isn't horrible?"* They laughed again, but this time, when they stopped, it was as if they were drawn together like magnets.

They kissed. When their first kiss ended, they parted and looked at each other, neither saying a word. Finally, they kissed again, with tongues moist and touching, hands exploring, learning, and loving, with neither feeling anything like it before.

****

It had only happened once, although Tammy would have loved to do it again, as she had been in love with Sarah for years. Tammy only truly realized how deeply she loved Sarah as they lay wrapped around each other's naked bodies in the afterglow of the biggest orgasm of her life.

Tammy was mature when Sarah insisted it shouldn't happen again. They understood that their friendship was paramount. If they became lovers, their friendship would inevitably change, and neither wanted to risk that because Tammy acknowledged that any change might be for the worse, not the better. They agreed they had experienced something extraordinary and felt their relationship was better for exploring it than never having tried it. Sarah insisted she didn't want to stop because she hadn't enjoyed making love with Tammy, quite the opposite. Sarah realized she could become addicted. Plus, acting gay was one thing, but she didn't feel ready or willing for the whole world to know she was a lesbian. And then, what about their parents? If they found out, might they stop them seeing each other? No, it was better if what they had experienced was a one-and-done; wonderful, but too good to be repeated.

At a party the following weekend, Tammy and

7

Sarah hooked up with two boys, and they moved on so willingly that it was as if they both had a point to prove. They never spoke of their evening of passion again. While they stayed the best of friends, they never felt the need to try sex with each other for a second time. But occasionally, like the night of Sarah's birthday, while sitting by the roaring fire, Tammy looked at Sarah and remembered how her body responded to Tammy's touch, how she tasted, and how beautifully Sarah moaned when she came.

****

Tammy snapped out of her daydream. She realized that her sexy thoughts were caused by too much vodka. *Or maybe, not enough*, she mused. Her can was empty; ergo, it was time for replenishment. The combination of the drinks, mood, and thinking about the time she made love with Sarah made her feel just a bit aroused; she realized and smiled. *Not that there is anything wrong with that.* She grinned.

She approached one of the big, ice-filled cold boxes of drinks when Greg grabbed her by the hand. He dragged her to the makeshift party-hire dance floor near the DJ and forced her to dance with him. Not that it took much force. Greg was just about everything a girl could want in a boyfriend. He was tall, fit, blond, and delicious looking. Only one teensy little thing spoiled the image, which was his surname. How could anyone take him seriously when his last name was Brady? He had been teased about being one of *those* Brady's for years, but he was such a good-natured guy that it didn't upset him. Greg always said it was better to have a name people could remember than one they could too easily forget.

Greg loved to surf, and his hair was bleached from

long hours in the sun and ocean. The muscles under the gaudy red and blue Hawaiian shirt he wore stood out as he danced. Tammy felt herself getting more turned on as she admired his body after her earlier thoughts about Sarah. Tammy watched his lithe body move to the music, and her thoughts became more erotic. *If Greg plays his cards right, he could have me six ways till Sunday later tonight.* Her cheeks flushed as she imagined him taking her.

An hour later, Tammy had drunk another two cans and danced non-stop with Greg. They drifted back into the shadows, away from the glare of the fire and party lights, which Mr. Morris had set up, and they kissed like school kids. The escalation had started with Greg touching Tammy between songs. Greg put his arm around her while they waited for the next one to play. Then it progressed to touching her sides and hips as they *dirty danced.* Tammy loved how his caresses gave her unspoken promises of naughty things to come.

Greg whispered how hot she looked in white jeans, which showed what a great ass she had. In reply, Tammy giggled sexily, danced away, glanced over her shoulder, and winked. She loved the attention and wanted to reward him, so she turned her back to him, bent slightly, and shook her tush.

Their mating ritual had begun. The touches and looks between them became urgent as they became more intimate. Tammy slowly licked her lips while leering at him, and he openly stared at her breasts as she shook them. Not that she was well endowed there, she did way too much sport, but Tammy knew it was amazing what a padded bra and tight T-shirt could do for a girl.

The school where she first met Greg was a long way

behind Tammy. She now worked as a doctor's receptionist but still played competitive soccer and did cross-country running with a club called the Western Harriers. She wanted to work her way up to triathlons, and while Tammy didn't see herself as a slave to sport, she loved being fit. She always ate healthily, ran four times a week before work, and didn't carry an ounce of fat anywhere.

She thought that Greg realized he had won the lottery with her, making Tammy feel special. They had known each other for years but had never been an item. One or the other had always been in a relationship when their paths crossed. He mentioned, while hugging her between songs, he thought the night would end up as just another drunken one with the boys. He hadn't believed there would be a single girl there worth staying sober for until he saw her. Tammy took it as a compliment and one which should be rewarded.

Greg kissed her for the first time during a particularly sensual slow song. While hugging Tammy's body, his tongue entered her willing mouth, and his hands cupped around her bottom. She moaned into his open mouth to let him know she liked it while he used his hands to grind her lower half against him. Tammy could feel his hardness pressed against her tummy, which turned her on more than she thought possible.

Tammy wanted him desperately, but she didn't want people at the party to see her rutting like a dog in heat. She lifted his hands back up and shook her head at him. Like a typical nineteen-year-old male, he pouted for not getting his way. Tammy laughed and mouthed, "*Not here*," to let him know she was willing, just not in public. He nodded and danced away, then slowly worked her toward some trees during the following two songs. He guided her farther toward the darkness, never stopping touching or fondling her body.

She was breathless with desire when they reached the darker area of the property behind an ancient oak tree. Greg kissed her with a hunger she hadn't felt for around seven weeks when her previous boyfriend Brad broke up with her after an argument. Tammy responded to Greg's ardor by slipping both hands inside his shirt, loving the feel of his bare skin and the defined muscles of his back. Before she could stop him, he undid the button of her jeans during a particularly long tongue kiss. Tammy knew he did it to distract her so he could slide his hand inside them. She didn't want to stop him then as his fingers eased under the elastic of her lace, see-through panties, over her hairless mound, and down to her velvet wetness.

"Oh God, I want you," she moaned as she gently bit his ear. "But not here, Greg. Take me somewhere private. Have you got condoms?"

"Yes, I do, but why not here?"

She pushed him away with a hand on his chest and stared up at him. "Seriously, Greg, really, are you kidding me? Right here? You want to do me up against a tree at my best friend's birthday party, where anyone can see us?" she asked incredulously.

"Okay, okay, I get it. Where can we go?"

"Anywhere quiet, dark, and private, Greg, I don't care. Have you got your car here? Let's go parking somewhere. You live around here, don't you? For God's sake, you must know a place; we're in the hills. Trust me, Greg; I want you as much as you want me." And she did. Tammy couldn't remember the last time she felt so horny.

"Yeah, okay, I know somewhere. The old gravel pits are close."

"Good, we can only be gone an hour or so. Sarah is my best friend, after all. I'm supposed to be spending the night with her. Grab some drinks from the ice box, and I will see you at your car. It's the black sedan with the red flames on the wheel arches, isn't it?"

Greg nodded eagerly and raced off to raid the ice box for drinks while she watched him go, softly shaking her head as she grinned. As horny as she felt, Tammy had to smile at how malleable guys were when they thought they would get to screw a girl.

Five minutes later, they were in his car, and Tammy stared at him in the dash light glow while he drove just a little too quickly. *He is a good-looking guy,* she thought, knowing soon she would be naked for him, and she hoped he would like what he saw. Her hand rested on his thigh, and she loved the firmness of the muscle beneath as he changed gear. Slowly, unable to resist it, she raised her hand until she fondled him through his denim jeans.

"Slow down, tiger," Tammy said softly, her voice husky with passion. Tammy gripped his length and squeezed it. "We do want to get there in one piece, don't we? There's no rush. You're going to get lucky; I guarantee it."

He eased his foot on the accelerator, and she rewarded him by undoing his button and zipper. *Turnaround is fair play.* Tammy remembered where he had put his hand earlier as she opened his jeans and felt him through his boxer shorts.

Within a few minutes, which felt longer for them both, Greg drove through a broken gate that looked as if the hinges had been rusted wide open. The place seemed deserted, and she watched as he backed his car into a corner of the long disused blue metal gravel pit. He stopped between a few small hills, shut the engine, and turned the lights off.

He switched the interior light on as he turned to her, but she shook her head, so he turned it off again. Simultaneously, they clambered over the back of the front seats and, within moments, were kissing frantically while Greg pulled at her clothes. Between hungry kisses, Greg helped Tammy wriggle out of her jeans and panties and tossed both onto the front seats. Her T-shirt and bra were already on the floor, and he worked her into a frenzy of need.

Tammy spread her legs for him, willing and ready while he attacked her body. She pulled his shirt off and helped him push his jeans and boxer shorts over his behind as he knelt on the floor between her spread thighs. She gazed at his hardness in the moonlight streaming through the windows as it sprang free from its confines and licked her lips in anticipation.

After as much foreplay as either could handle, she lay back in the corner of the seat, panting and ready. She watched as Greg ripped open the packet and fitted the condom. She licked her lips and lifted herself a little to help him enter her.

Then, they heard an approaching car scrunching across the gravel. They froze, and Tammy could feel her heart crashing inside her chest. There was no reason for her to feel petrified, yet she did. Thankfully, Tammy was grateful she had made Greg turn off the interior light, making it hard for them to be seen, especially as Greg's car was black. Tammy couldn't explain, but she felt terrified and trembled, clinging tightly to Greg. Visions of past horror movies flashed through her mind, and she regretted leaving the safety of the party and her friends.

"It's okay, Tam. It's probably just another couple looking for some privacy," Greg whispered in her ear. But she could tell he was scared too, as his voice quavered. His penis shrunk inside her, and she felt it slide out.

The other car drove into the depths of the pit two hundred meters or so away. She heard the engine switch off and saw the headlights extinguish. Slowly Greg turned away from Tammy and perched on the seat, his jeans around his ankles. They peered above the dash to see what the occupants in the other car did.

In the distance, two shadows exited the large station wagon leaving the doors open so the interior light stayed on. The two shapes stopped momentarily and looked around, seemingly in no hurry. Tammy thanked her lucky stars that Greg's car was black and wouldn't be easy to spot at the distance they were away, but she still felt icy cold with fear. The two men seemed to look around, then walked to their car's rear and opened the tailgate. The next moment they had what looked like shovels in their hands, which they put down on the ground and then leaned back into the car again.

"What the fuck are they doing?" Greg whispered, not sounding as scared as Tammy felt, more as if he were interested. Tammy didn't answer. She was still too frightened to move.

The shapes stood up again, with what looked like pickaxes by the moonlight glinting off the blades. They backed away from the vehicle and used them on the ground, the muffled clangs echoing across the landscape.

Firstly, they used picks to break up the surface, then shovels to dig. The men appeared to know what they were doing as if they were well-rehearsed and worked solidly for around ten minutes without a break. By then, they had dug quite a long and deep hole.

Tammy and Greg sat still, watching silently. Tammy wanted to put her T-shirt back on as she was cold but couldn't find it, so she folded her arms across her breasts and shivered. She was so fascinated with what the men were doing that she worried she might miss something vital if she moved. Suddenly, the two men stopped. Though she couldn't positively state they were men, Tammy assumed by the shapes that they were. The *men* walked to the back of the car and leaned in the rear compartment again.

Tammy gasped and put her hand over her mouth to stifle the scream which threatened to break free. They dragged a large bundle out of the car, dropped it on the ground, and rolled it into the hole.

"Maybe they're farmers around here, and they are burying a dead animal," Greg whispered.

Tammy knew it wasn't that. She didn't understand why it was rubbish, yet she knew it was. It was a corpse; no one could tell her overheated imagination differently. "It's a dead body," she hissed back. "Oh my God, they're murderers."

"Settle down, Tam; this is real life, not a movie," he insisted, but Tammy didn't think he sounded convinced; she thought he was as afraid as her.

The men grunted as they shoveled gravel back onto whatever they had buried. It took a lot less time to fill the hole than create it. Before long, they had roughly smoothed the excess gravel out, leaving a mound indistinguishable from the ten thousand other small bumps over the surface. With one last scan around, they put their tools away and closed the rear tailgate.

"We need to get out of here and get the police," Tammy whispered, reaching down to the floor, trying to find her panties. They would not be having sex that night; making love with Greg was the last thing on her mind.

Her movement shook Greg out of his lethargy. He grunted in agreement and started pulling his jeans and boxer shorts up. "They'll be gone soon. Then we will take off back to the party and phone the cops, but I reckon they will laugh at us when we do."

The two men climbed into the wagon and started it up. At that distance, to Tammy, it sounded like a diesel motor, but it could have been petrol with a faulty exhaust. Either way, in the still night, it was deafening. They turned the car in a wide arc to head back the way they had come. It was at that very moment that Greg and Tammy's luck ran out.

Perhaps it was the moonlight glinting off chrome or the windshield. Maybe the sweeping headlights as they turned caught the car in its sight. Whatever it was, Tammy knew the men had seen their car when the other vehicle lurched to a halt. Their parking spot had been discovered.

Suddenly, the other car started again, spraying pebbles as it slewed across the loose surface. At the gate, it skidded to a halt, so it sat sideways across the narrow driveway. There was no way that Greg could get past it, and Tammy realized they were trapped in a gravel pit with the two men who had just buried a body.

"Oh, my God. They've seen us," Tammy screamed.

Greg sounded nervous, his voice near breaking point, as he replied, "You sit tight, Tam. I'll go and see them. I'm sure it's not what you think it is." He lifted off the seat to get his jeans up the rest of the way, not realizing the condom was still in place. He yanked open the rear door and stepped out. The interior light came on, which momentarily blinded Tammy. When she could see again, Greg was twenty meters away, quickly approaching the two men who had gotten out of their car and were walking toward him.

She felt helpless and terrified. Tammy's intuition was on hyperdrive, and she knew they were in a lot of trouble, despite Greg saying otherwise. She looked around for her clothes. As she struggled to find her panties to put back on, she noticed Greg's keys dangling from the ignition. She clambered back into the driver's seat. As her fingers closed over the key to start the car, she suddenly realized it was futile, with the other vehicle blocking the exit. With a sinking heart, Tammy knew that wasn't the only problem. Greg drove a powerful V8 manual shift car, yet Tammy had only ever driven an automatic. The one time she tried a manual, it had been a dismal failure when she stalled it repeatedly. Filled with embarrassment, she vowed never to do it again, despite her father lecturing her to mark his words. *"One day, Tam, you will regret you've given up so easily."*

Guess what, Dad? she thought. *You were right, as always.* Tammy looked up to see what was happening and screamed. The three people had come face to face, and one swung some sort of weapon: a club, tire iron, or spanner; Tammy didn't know what, but it looked heavy. It hit Greg squarely on the side of his head with a sickening *clunk*. He fell to his left, rolling on the ground, clutching his head in his hands, and the two men stood over him and hit him again. They were both armed with the same type of weapon, and the sounds of the metal hitting his head and body made Tammy want to vomit.

She fumbled the door open and screamed at them as she half fell out. *"What are you doing? Leave him alone."* They stopped hitting Greg's now still body and looked in Tammy's direction. Then, they rushed toward her. In a blind panic, Tammy turned and ran into the darkness, screaming as she went.

Chapter 2

Run Rabbit Run

Tammy's bare feet hurt horribly within fifty paces of running on the gravel surface, but there was nowhere to hide so she could rest them. The men were too close for her to do anything but run, which she did in a blind panic. She headed toward the boundary in her desperate attempt to escape Greg's attackers, and she realized too late that she had somehow to scramble up the slope of the gravel pit as there was no other way out. Effectively, she had boxed herself into the corner unless she could climb the incline. She heard footfalls and muffled breathing behind her, the men's boots scraping on the gravel. Then came a gruff, gravelly voice calling out to the other, "Go and bring the car around and get up the other side and wait for her. I'll go up here. She ain't gonna get far."

Tammy tried hard not to panic, knowing she could die if she did, but staying calm was not easy. Tammy took a few precious moments to look over her shoulder and was pleased to see she had put some distance between them. She was almost at the pit's side wall, which seemed to be about a forty-five-degree gradient. Tammy realized climbing straight up was impossible, being far too steep, especially with no shoes to protect her feet. To the right would mean heading back toward the road, so she needed to angle to the left toward what looked like a line of pine trees which she could vaguely make out atop the hill.

As she took off, Tammy heard a chilling voice call to her from behind, "Run, little rabbit, run. We're going to get you, little rabbit; I can see you. One slip and you're mine, don't you worry." His tone terrified Tammy to her very core. The murderer spoke in an evil, horrible voice, and it took all of Tammy's willpower not to vomit. Fear made her tremble along with the cold, which caused her to lose her breath. She risked one last look to see where her pursuer was and seeing him only meters away sent further chills down her spine. He had gained on her. Then she did feel like a startled rabbit as she began her run diagonally up the side of the gravel pit wall.

Tammy's heart rate skyrocketed from the adrenalin caused by her terror, and she knew if she didn't try to calm herself, she would fall over with exhaustion when it became depleted. She needed to focus on her breathing and footing, or she would slide down and land at the man's feet. *Calm down, calm down, calm down* became her mantra, and she felt it helped. Using the dim moonlight, Tammy put her head down to watch her footing. She became like a machine as she had trained and knew without looking that she had found her rhythm and was pulling away from the man intent on murdering her.

The next second, a rock hit her back, and she stumbled, the pain sudden and severe. She lost her grip and almost slid back down the slope. Another stone hit her arm and bounced off into the night as she scrambled to regain her footing, her bleeding toes digging into the shards of gravel. As frightened as Tammy felt, she knew her only hope of survival was to ignore the stones hitting her and keep running. Tammy's stinging feet found purchase, and she was determined to ignore anything he threw at her. Five more pebbles hit her, and others whizzed by into the night as she felt the rush through the air and heard them hit the slope above her.

Eventually, panting for breath, Tammy reached the top rim of the pit. She turned back with hands on knees to see where her pursuer was and heard him clambering up the slope, though he seemed a long way back. Her fitness had won out, plus he had lost ground when he stopped to throw stones. She bent at the waist and sucked air into her burning lungs as she tried to remember her coach's instructions about getting her breath back. In her position, she could see her feet and the blood on their sides, which made her realize how painful they were. The adrenaline rush had masked the pain, which now rammed her like a tidal wave hitting a cliff, and Tammy almost fell to her knees. She turned toward the distant pine trees, eerily standing out in the moonlight, and took off at a limping jog.

At her current pace, she could run all day. They would never catch her on foot if she did, but they would be on her quickly if she panicked and got out of breath. She looked up, trying to guess where the other man would come from if he drove up ahead of her, but it was useless as she had no idea of the layout of the roads surrounding the gravel pits because she didn't live in this area.

Tammy concentrated on where to place her feet as the terrain was no longer gravel but tufts of grass and possible hidden rocks. Suddenly, she ran straight into a hip-high, three-strand barbed wire fence. It had rusted from prolonged use of stopping animals from wandering too close and falling into the pit. The top strand gave way under the weight of her pin-wheeling body, and Tammy felt the barbs rip into the meat of her thigh as she fell heavily, banging her head on a rock that jutted up from the ground.

She lay on her back, staring at the stars, wanting to stop running and go to sleep, on the verge of passing out, and visions from her childhood swam through her mind. She was vaguely aware of the warmth on her forehead. *I'm bleeding from head to toe,* she mused. *How much blood have I got to lose?* Tammy slowly drifted toward the beckoning darkness. *I can rest, just for a bit, just for a little while.* She raised her fingers and touched the lump, which helped wake her up with a jolt that hurt with a sharp stabbing pain.

Every part of her body hurt. She could tell her feet were a mushy mess. Her lungs were ready to burst, and she had several bruises from the stones thrown at her, and her thigh had a long gash from the wire fence. She was aware of the blood which poured from it as if from a tap, and now, to complete the list, her head was bleeding too. *Maybe he's given up chasing me?* She was close to slipping into the void which beckoned her.

As her hunter struggled for purchase on the slope below, Tammy heard his boots sliding on gravel. Then the sound of a muttered curse woke her from her malaise with a start. *He's nearly on me; what was I thinking? I don't want to die!* Tammy somehow found the strength to climb to her feet and started toward the tree line again at a limping gait. The thought which kept her going was remembering how the men had beaten Greg without warning or mercy. They would undoubtedly do the same to her if she gave them a chance. If she could get away, find a house with a phone, and call the police and an ambulance, maybe she could still save Greg.

Tammy entered the trees and glanced back and, by the moonlight, saw the man climbing over the fence. *Typical,* she thought; how *come he didn't run into it?* She looked around her. It was dark outside, but under the tree canopy, it was inky black. She could faintly see a rough-looking trail between the trees, possibly, she wondered, formed by sheep or cattle if this was farmland.

Deep inside the wooded area, Tammy had to slow down to see where to place her feet. She could ill afford a trip that sprained her ankle. At least the ground was softer, she noticed, with the bed of pine needles. She zig-zagged around some trees to help distance herself from the chasing man. With a new sense of fear, Tammy suddenly realized that changing course to put trees between her and the man chasing her had caused her to lose her sense of direction. All she could do was keep running and pray she was heading away from the second hunter and not straight toward him.

After what seemed an eternity, Tammy became aware of a light ahead and instinctively ran toward it as the filtered glow helped show the branches and pinecones which littered the ground. *Perhaps the light was coming from a house,* was her hope. They would have a phone, and she could be saved. The trees thinned out as she broke through the last of the bushes. She realized it wasn't a house but a streetlamp on the side of a road.

Shit, shit, shit, she screamed inside her head as she stopped and once again put her hands on her knees and took huge gulps of air into her tortured lungs. Then

Tammy saw something that made her gasp in sheer terror, and the blood remaining in her body turned to ice water. Around a hundred meters to her right, a car was parked facing her. It was a big vehicle with headlights turned to high beam, illuminating the road as far as she could see. Then she noticed, deep in the forest, to the side of the car, a powerful torch beam arcing through the trees and bushes, obviously searching for her. One man was behind her, somewhere, and another with a powerful flashlight was to her right. The road was illuminated, so that was out, which left only one course open to her. Tammy sighed, turned away from the light, and took off again, hoping that by running parallel to the road, she wasn't heading toward the first man waiting for her in the stand of trees.

Tammy was soon out of breath again and stopped for a moment. She was shocked at how ragged her lungs sounded. *What if they hear me panting?* Tammy forced herself to take several deep breaths and exhaled each slowly. She could hear the men stumbling around and saw flickers of torchlight between the tree trunks. Tammy thought they were a hundred meters or so away. Now she watched *two* jiggling torch lights heading her way through the trees, and they seemed to be tracking toward her.

Please, God, she thought, *help me get away from these maniacs, and I promise to be good for the rest of my life. If only I had grabbed my jeans,* Tammy cursed, knowing if she had, she would have had her phone, which was in the hip pocket. If she had, she could have called the police. *If, if, if…*she muttered to herself. As she ran and found her rhythm once more, despite the agony. Tammy permitted herself to daydream. She remembered a saying her dad always had about the word, *If.* He often said when she dared to wish *if* she had something or other. "If your mum had wheels, she'd be a bike, and I could ride her more often." Tammy and her sister would say he was gross, but now she wished more than anything that her dad was there to help. The thought saddened her because Tammy loved her mother and father dearly and wanted to see and hug them again.

To her relief, she burst through the trees and noted the road curved away. The car's headlights were now out of sight, hidden by the trees. Tammy moved to the edge of the bitumen surface, put her head down, and as freezing cold as she felt, despite sweating, concentrated on finding her perfect pace while trying her best to ignore the increasing pain from all over her body. For the first time since the horrible mess started, Tammy felt she had a chance to live through the night.

Time passed. How much Tammy had no way of knowing, but the stand of pine trees was well behind her. She was running between what looked to her untrained eye like two farming paddocks when she heard a car engine behind her coming up the road fast. Was it the men chasing her or someone who might be able to help? Tammy knew she could not take a chance, so without a second thought, she angled off the tarmac and dove headlong into a culvert that seemed to be designed to carry flood water away from the road. Suddenly, she was lying in six inches of cold, brackish, and muddy water. It took all her willpower to keep still so she could hide.

Please, bugs, don't crawl on me. Please, bugs, don't crawl on me, Tammy thought repeatedly, and then, without consciously allowing the thought, the word *snake* flitted into her head. *Please, snakes, don't bite.*

Please, snakes, don't bite. Tammy had found another mantra.

Tammy heard a clicking noise, an incessant vibrating, and worried it was some sort of bug, or worse, a rattlesnake right next to her face. It took every ounce of her willpower to keep still and calm. Suddenly, she remembered Australia didn't have rattlesnakes, and relief flooded her freezing-cold body. Tammy realized the noise she could hear was her teeth chattering. She was bitterly cold, lying in icy water, making it much worse. As the car approached, Tammy felt scared beyond belief. Before, when she was running, she had some control. Now all she could do was hide and hope they didn't find her. Tammy was soaking wet, tired, and in pain. Blood from her many wounds stuck to her skin. She was cold, scared witless, and miserable.

After what felt like an eternity, Tammy heard the slow-moving car pass by and was aware of a sweeping torchlight scanning the side of the road. She exhaled, trying to keep quiet, and realized she had been holding her breath. Tammy poked her head up to look in time to see the car pull into the shoulder fifty meters ahead. Her heart leaped in her mouth as she feared they must have seen or heard her ragged breathing and were returning to finish the job. To have come so far and get caught was unfair, and Tammy felt despair in her chest.

Tammy knew she was finished and was in so much pain throughout her entire body that she no longer had the spirit or energy to run farther. She lowered her head to her arms and cried softly, waiting for the blow which would end her life, which she was sure was coming. Tammy felt so exhausted that she was past the point of caring. But the car performed a turn and passed her a second time before gaining speed, heading back the way it had come. Stunned, she cried earnestly, sobbing with relief, shivering with the cold, but so glad to still be alive.

Chapter 3

Return to Duty

It had been a tumultuous four months for newly promoted Detective Inspector Sam Collins since being pulled out of the Swan River by a Tactical Response Police Officer. Drug dealer Jimmy Mallory shot Sam in the shoulder, and Sam could have died if he hadn't been spotted in time. Sam suffered hypothermia due to the extended period in the water while trying to save a young couple, Nicky and Didi, from the underworld dealer.

Sam spent three weeks in the hospital while he recovered from the effects of hypothermia and surgery comprising reconstructive operations on his shoulder. The .357 magnum bullet had caused considerable damage, though Sam's intervention had saved Nicky and Didi's lives.

After healing from surgery, Sam underwent physiotherapy to rebuild the muscle tissue before he could use his arm again. Though he never admitted it for fear of being downgraded in rank and losing his operational duty status, he felt he had lost a reasonable amount of movement and strength in the joint. Sam had always been fit. He worked out regularly and jogged most days of the week before the shooting, and he hoped he had hidden his limitations well enough that the full use of his arm would return in time.

Since his recovery, Sam could predict a change in the weather. Depending on how much rain or humidity was headed their way, he would feel anything from a dull ache to screaming pain. During those times, Sam liked to think of it as a bonus of being shot. He had always possessed a positive mental attitude, which most people liked about him. He was well known as a glass-half-full man rather than a glass-half-empty and was respected for it.

Much to his disgust and everyone's amazement, because Sam was always one of the most level-headed people they knew, he had developed a phobia for water. There was no doubt in Sam's mind that the *psychological hiccup*, as he liked to think of it, was because of time spent during the tracking down and eventual shootout at the marina where Mallory's boat had been moored. Sam had spent an hour and a half in frigid river water late at night, which had been the only way he could get to the drug dealer's boat and stop what would have been the brutal slaying of two wonderful people. Sam always smiled when he thought of Nicky and Didi, even though Nicky had been a self-appointed vigilante, and it had been Sam's job to catch him.

As protocol demanded when a policeman was shot, Sam worked with a police-appointed psychologist, Dr. June Faraday. Besides the trauma of the gunshot wound, Sam suffered tremors anytime he was near a bathtub, and he found it almost impossible to get close to the ocean. If he went over one of the bridges which spanned the Swan River, he had to close his eyes to avoid sweating and trembling fits. Driving a car over a bridge with eyes closed and suffering from the shakes was far from ideal for anyone, especially a police officer.

Initially, showering would reduce him to a blubbering mess, which annoyed and angered him, but he was powerless, at first, to stop it. Sam worked diligently with June, a wonderfully rotund married woman with seven children and a husband who adored her. After three weeks, his phobia eased until Sam could bathe and swim in a pool again. The ocean and river were tougher to beat, but eventually, he felt no more than a sinking stomach and a sense of despair.

During the four months that Sam was off work, he received a commendation for bravery and promotion to Detective Inspector. He received extensive positive publicity and was labeled a hero. His new public status saw him enjoy invitations to celebrity events, and his time was taken up with social functions, much to the chagrin of his then-girlfriend, Zoe. She ultimately left him because she did not enjoy the spotlight which had been thrust upon her boyfriend or the numerous women who wanted to take him away from her. Sam took the breakup in his stride; he had no desire to settle down with Zoe or anyone. He was not short of offers from attractive women who wanted to spend time with him, and he loved his new persona.

Sam could have returned to work a little earlier than he did but elected to take a few days additional leave as he wanted to attend the wedding ceremony of Nicky Pantella and his bride Didi. He felt that once the ceremony was over, he could draw a line under that episode of his life, get back to work, and focus on the following case, or cases, which his new rank would bring.

Behind the scenes, his meteoric rise to prominence was lauded by some and ridiculed by others. Notably, the people at the top determined to watch his progress, as they hoped he could one day progress to become an Assistant Commissioner. With his high profile, it was believed Sam would be an asset to the force's image. He had not only solved the Domin8 case, captured a serial killer, and halted the murder of Nicky and Didi. Though he disagreed, he was also credited with ending *the Northbridge Vigilante's* reign, which the *higher-ups* were delighted with. His detractors were, in general, cops who had been around a long time and could never rise to his lofty new rank. Often that was due to bad habits, poor attitude, or laziness. The tall poppy syndrome was alive and well in the West Australian Police Department, and some took delight in undermining Sam behind his back at every opportunity.

****

Sam arrived at Superintendent Brandis' office at nine a.m. on the Monday following the wedding. He was there to discover what his next posting would be. Brandis held the Head of Operations and Personnel role, and he alone, Sam thought, held Sam's future in his hands. Sam felt ready and wanted to get back to work. Four months had been long enough, and he was bored. His phobia was better, if not almost back to normal, and while not entirely cured, it was manageable and sufficient that Dr. Faraday had signed him fit and ready for active duty.

His shoulder was as good as it could be, his mind was clear, and he was excited to find out what was in store as he started the next chapter of his life.

He was shown into Brandis' office by his middle-aged assistant, Dorothy. Brandis stood when Sam entered and held out his hand to shake, which Sam did warmly and firmly. "Welcome back to work, Inspector,"

Brandis said warmly. "I can't tell you how good it is to see you on your feet and ready for action. You had us worried for a while, and we don't want to lose you. Take a seat, please. How's the shoulder?" he asked genuinely.

Sam sat down and placed his hands on his lap. "Oh, it's fine, sir. Bit of an ache if it's going to rain, but no loss of mobility," he lied. Which was not the first lie he had ever told a superior officer, and he doubted it would be the last.

"And how are you getting on with the lovely June Faraday?" he asked with eyebrows raised, though Sam was sure the superintendent would have seen June's report, which cleared him for duty.

Sam smiled broadly, "Well, excellent. Honestly, I didn't feel guilt or remorse over Mallory's death. As for the water phobia, it was the stupidest thing, but I can drive over the Narrows Bridge now without breaking into a cold sweat. June and I believe everything is one hundred percent normal. Thanks for asking, sir."

"Sam, I know you've probably had it all up to the eyeballs by now, but I wanted to tell you personally; what you did by going into the river that night to rescue the hostages was outstanding work. We need more officers like you, and you should know you are being watched by..." He raised his eyebrows toward the ceiling and continued, "...by the suits upstairs. They see a bright future for you, and so do I."

"Thank you, sir," Sam replied, squirming imperceptibly as he knew he had, deliberately and knowingly, let the man known as the Northbridge Vigilante off the hook for five shootings. While that was not something a police officer should do, he genuinely believed his decision was justified because the homicides were of the worst possible types of criminals. Worse, Sam knew that any form of arrest would have led inevitably to the death of Nick Pantella in jail at Mallory's instigation. Pantella was undoubtedly an otherwise good man with a dreadfully tragic past who had already ceased his vigilante ways when Sam first met him.

Smiling, Brandis mistook his squirming for embarrassment, Sam thought. "Okay, I get it. You've had enough people telling you how good you are. Right, let's get down to it, and let's get you back to work. I'm sending you to the Major Crimes Squad; your new partner will be Sergeant Jenny Markham. I've grabbed her from Organized Crime. Have you met her?"

"Once or twice, yes, sir, she seems very capable." Sam felt happy about the change in subject.

"Your old boss, Felix, has given her a good reference and thinks you two will be a good fit. She is a no-nonsense officer, and I'm inclined to agree with his recommendation. She will meet you in your new office at ten-thirty. Before then, you need to go down and be allocated a new weapon; your last one was never recovered and is probably rusting away in the river. Make sure you fire a few rounds through it and get a feel for it, then go and meet Bob Young. He's your new boss. I've spoken to him about your first job; he has something interesting to ease your way back into the saddle. It shouldn't be too much of a strain for your first outing.

"He will give you the full details, but once you settle in and pick up Jenny, go to Fiona Stanley Hospital and see one, um, let me see what it says in my notes...oh, here it is, one Tammy Reynolds."

"Yes, sir. May I ask why?"

"Of course, you may. Apparently, she has quite a story to tell, which we need to investigate. It may be nothing; she may have had some sort of drug-induced psychosis from a party she was at on Saturday night in Roleystone. Someone may have put something in her drink, or maybe she got drunk or dabbled with drugs and hallucinated about everything since. She was found yesterday afternoon wandering deliriously around the hills naked, suffering some horrendous cuts and bruises, hypothermia, and dehydration. When she woke up this morning, she remembered things and told the doctors she was chased by two men who killed her boyfriend. As I say, it might be nothing or a serious crime. Check her out, see what you think, and report to Bob. He's your Detective Superintendent at Major Crimes." He stood up and held out his hand to shake so Sam knew he was dismissed.

"Thank you, sir," Sam said and left. He was very keen to get back to work.

He signed for delivery of his new Glock at the weapons section, a spare magazine, holster, and ammunition. He then went down into the basement to the shooting range. Like all Glocks, it performed well, didn't jam, and had a smooth action. He fired fifty rounds with reasonable groupings. He was far from a marksman but shot well enough on most occasions. *Sadly, the last time out, I missed my target completely,* he mused regretfully, thinking if he had been accurate, he wouldn't have been shot himself.

At ten a.m., Sam arrived at the Major Crime Squad offices and introduced himself to Superintendent Bob Young, whom he knew only by reputation. People spoke highly of Bob, especially his subordinates, which was the only thing that mattered to Sam.

Two years previously, The Major Crime unit switched to having two Detective Superintendents working in conjunction to split the workload rather than just one who had managed the department since its inception as the Serious Crime Squad. Each year had brought a significant increase in the rate of murders and serious crimes in Western Australia, and the original staff had been overwhelmed. A study commissioned by senior government officials demonstrated that the workload linked with unreasonable expectations of clean-up rates had caused errors, including three notable wrongful convictions. There had also been two reported corruption cases, and in some instances, innocent people were framed for crimes they did not commit by overworked detectives.

After the report was presented to the government, a shakeup followed, including recommending increased resources. More officers were employed, and senior rank officers received promotions to manage the influx. The focus then became quality in investigations over quantity. In the Major Crime Squad, each superintendent had twenty detectives of different ranks under him. Both units shared civilian data entry staff and forensic and specialist support personnel.

To Sam's knowledge, there hadn't been any retirees or transfers, so he assumed his and Jenny Markham's appointment increased the total number of officers in the squad, which he felt was unusual, and suggested the position had been created for him.

"Good to meet you, Sam," Bob said with what looked like a genuine smile. "Welcome to the squad. Grab a chair. So, you're the blue-eyed boy of the modern police force?"

"Um, thanks, sir, I think." Sam supposed this type of teasing would be expected with the publicity he had received, but he was just as happy to stay out of the spotlight.

"It's okay. I'm just kidding. I've read your file, and you've done outstanding work and have justified your promotion. You are among friends here; however, you may have to earn your stripes with some of the others to overcome what some may think of as *preferential* treatment."

"Preferential treatment, sir?"

"We've been ordered to make room for you and your Sergeant, Inspector. Generally, we take applications and choose who we want and only pick the cream of the crop, but we've been ordered to take you. I think you could be on the short list for a ride upstairs, and there will be some in the department who will resent that. Just giving you a heads up is all."

"I don't want any preferential treatment. All I want is to do my job, sir."

"That's just as well, Inspector, because you won't be getting any from me, but you won't get a hard time either. How well you do here and how far you go is in your hands, not mine. And, Sam, if you are good enough and you do make it, I won't object to calling you sir one day."

Sam was impressed. Most other senior officers would have resented his appearance, but Bob Young seemed fair, though, of course, only time would tell if it was an act or not.

"Right. I will show you around in a minute. Your Sergeant is due here soon, so for the moment, we will wait for her so I don't have to do it twice. Meanwhile, let's go through this case, such as it is at the moment."

He opened a manila folder and began the briefing. "Tammy Reynolds, aged nineteen, works in a doctor's surgery as a receptionist in Rivervale and has no record, juvenile or adult. Ms. Reynolds lives with her parents in Belmont. She was found yesterday afternoon, naked, delirious, covered in blood, and hiding in some bushes in the Roleystone hills. When approached by a farmer, she tried to run away screaming, 'Please don't kill me,' then passed out, and he called an ambulance. She was taken to Fiona Stanley Hospital extremely dehydrated. She also suffered from hypothermia, numerous cuts, and abrasions, including nasty gashes, one to her leg and another to her forehead, both infected. She won't be walking anywhere anytime soon as her feet were badly bruised and cut with parts of her skin worn away as if she had been running through the hills bare-footed."

"Has she said anything other than 'please don't kill me,' sir?"

"Yes, but I will come to that shortly. Apparently, Tammy disappeared from a bonfire birthday party the night before at her best friend's home, several kilometers from where she was found. Her friend, Sarah, was shocked because she had just vanished, and was supposed to be spending the night with her. They figured she had gone home or off with a boy, even though it was out of character. We only have this second-hand from the girl's parents at the hospital with their daughter. They phoned Tammy's friend, Sarah, and got the story from her.

"When she woke up this morning, Tammy was hysterical and had to be sedated, but before they knocked her out, she said her boyfriend had been murdered. The problem is that it conflicts with what the parents say because she broke up with him seven weeks ago. Go and check it out, talk to the parents, and go to the friends. See if there is anything to this and speak to the girl when she wakes up. If it's some sort of drug or alcohol-induced hysteria, hand her over to uniform and get back here. There is a mountain of cold cases we look at until something else fresh comes in for you. Ah, your Sergeant is here," He waved through the window at someone behind Sam's back. "Good, let's go."

Sam nodded thoughtfully, not wanting to make rash judgments, but the facts sounded interesting, and he was sure Tammy Reynolds had a story to tell. He thought it a challenging case to start after four months away.

They left the office, and Sam re-acquainted himself with Jenny Markham. She smiled warmly as they shook hands. The Super showed them around and introduced them to the officers who were in at the time, along with the data entry staff. Sam had been given an office to befit his new rank, while Jenny would have a desk in the general area with all the other detectives.

When they were finished, they were herded back into Bob Young's office for one last lecture. "Right, listen closely, you two. Here is my card with my mobile number, which is on twenty-four-seven, got it?" They both nodded in unison. "Good, now, I know you are both very accomplished officers; you wouldn't be here if you weren't. However, this is Major Crime, and we can't afford any more cock ups, understand? We have the eyes of the world upon us ever since the reshuffle. So, if you are not sure about something, for God's sake, ask me or one of the others who are senior to you. Are we clear?"

They both replied, in unison. "Yes, sir."

"Well done. Okay, what are you waiting for? Get going—oh, and one last thing. I want a briefing every morning. Got it?"

****

When they were in the elevator going down to the car park, Jenny broke the silence and said, "Is it okay if I tell you, right now, I'm crapping myself here?"

Sam laughed. He liked her instantly and turned to her. She appeared to be in her late thirties and solidly built. No one could ever say she was beautiful, but neither could they say she was ugly. Her brunette hair was shoulder length in what Sam remembered being called a bob cut. She wore little makeup and was smartly dressed in a business suit and sensible shoes. *All the better for running after criminals,* he thought.

"You'll do fine, Jenny. Felix speaks very highly of you."

"Well, that's rather the point, Boss. And, just quietly, he isn't the only one who speaks highly of you. I'm not dumb. I know I only got this gig because they needed to give you a partner to fast-track you, and they didn't have a spare sergeant. But let me tell you; I'm not complaining. Major Crime is like a dream come true for me, so, just so you know, I'm with you a hundred and ten percent."

"That's good to know, Jen, but let's get one thing straight, okay? I don't give a flying fig about fast-tracking my career or any of that stuff because I can't control it. All I care about is the job and getting the right result, and if we are both singing off the same page of the hymn book, we will get along fine."

"Oh, I think you will find we are, Boss. Like you,

I'm not married except to the job, and it's mainly because if I'm on a case, I work all the hours under the sun. As you'd know, it's hard to keep a partner when you do that. I'm gay, in case you didn't hear it on the grapevine."

"No, I hadn't heard. It's none of my business, and it doesn't bother or affect me in any way, so you won't hear any poor-taste jokes from me, Jen. To each their own, I'd like to think."

The lift opened, and they were in the underground car park. They went to the office and picked up an unremarkable near-new sedan that had been allocated to them. Sam drove and pulled out into the traffic, heading toward the hospital, so it was a good four or five minutes before he resumed the conversation. "I'm glad you told me about your orientation. Even though it's none of my business, I appreciate your honesty. I think we'll make a good team, Jen. You being a lesbian is not an issue with me, and by the way, neither should it be. I must say, though, while I accept gay people don't walk around with a sign on them announcing their orientation, I never would have picked it of you."

Jenny thanked him, shrugging the conversation off as if now it was out in the open, nothing was left to say about the subject. They spent the rest of the journey discussing the mysterious case of young Tammy Reynolds.

At the hospital, they asked for and received the use of an interview room the hospital management had set aside for the police. Knowing where the parents would be, Sam requested they be brought to the room for privacy. They waited a few minutes, and a late middle-aged couple was brought in, looking very nervous. Sam took pity on them, understanding they must be concerned for their daughter's well-being and possibly scared for her mental health. He held out his new ID card, courtesy of Superintendent Brandis. Jenny did the same.

"Mr. and Mrs. Reynolds, I'm Detective Inspector Collins, and this is Detective Sergeant Markham. We are from the Major Crimes Squad and are here to investigate your daughter's allegations. Please have a seat and tell us what you can before we go and speak to her. Don't worry; we will get to the bottom of all this."

Mr. Reynolds held out his hand to shake while his wife burst into tears. He put his arm around her and said, "Settle down, Jules; Tammy will be right." He turned back to Sam. "I'm George, and this is Julia. Thank you for coming. We're at our wit's end with this."

"That's understandable, but I promise we will investigate what transpired and find out what happened to her. I don't want you to worry. She's not in any trouble so far as we can see. Your daughter, Tammy, went to a party, yes?"

"Yes, it was at her best friend Sarah's parents' home in Roleystone; it was Sarah's birthday; Julie dropped her off at about seven-thirty. She was going to spend the night there so she could, you know, have a few drinks and not worry about driving home. It's such a long way; a cab fare would be out of the question. The young have trouble affording stuff like that at the prices they charge, don't they? So good old Mum and Dad's taxi gets a workout, but at least you know your kids are safe, don't you?"

Sam nodded enthusiastically and warmed to what he thought of as a loving mother and father.

"I was going to pick her up yesterday afternoon

when she gave me a call when she was ready, but she didn't phone. Tam had offered to stay back and help clean up afterward, so we didn't expect a call too early. The two of them have been as thick as thieves for years, and you should hear the way they laugh with each other. Anyway, I was getting a bit worried by the evening when we got this call from the hospital that our little girl had been brought in.

Jenny asked, "Did her friend's parents not contact you when she wasn't there to spend the night when the party wound down?"

"No, and I phoned them this morning, and they were very upset. Her friend, Sarah, thought she had changed her mind and went home. But if you want to know what I think, I reckon she thought our Tam had got herself a new boyfriend, and that's why she wasn't worried. Well, we were all young once, weren't we? The party didn't finish 'till after four in the morning, and then they couldn't find her. They said they didn't want to worry us in the middle of the night. Sarah tried to call her mobile phone, but it rang out, apparently, so they assumed she was home with us. They did say she was drinking well early on, so thought she might've called for a cab when she got a bit under the weather. Meanwhile, of course, we were none the wiser."

"I see," Sam said. "Now, what about this boyfriend of hers she says was murdered?"

"Well, that's what's odd because she broke up with him about six or seven weeks ago, and he wasn't part of her crowd. She met him through work, so she wasn't with him that night, as far as we know. That's another reason we think she went off with a new boy she met there. Plus, of course, his name is Brad, not Greg."

"Sorry, who is Brad, and who is Greg?"

"Greg's the one she said was killed, but she never told us about any Greg. She didn't have secrets from us, so we didn't know who she was talking about. Brad is the boy she stopped seeing a few weeks back. He was a bit too moody and possessive for her. She's more your, well, free-spirited kind of girl."

"Perhaps it is someone she met at the party then. Please forgive me for asking this, and understand it's just a routine question, but has Tammy ever dabbled in recreational drugs, that you're aware of?" Sam asked with his most disarming smile.

Mr. Reynolds stood up immediately, angry at the question, which was to be expected. Sam and Jenny remained seated, knowing he would calm down if they kept smiling. "For your information," he said, pointing his index finger at Sam, "She wouldn't do stuff like that, and I'm not just saying it because we're her parents. I know you think she wouldn't tell us if she was using, but I tell you, she would have. Tammy was very much into her sport and believed in a healthy body and mind. She didn't smoke, hardly ever drank, and would never put anything poisonous in her body. She was training for a triathlon. There's no way she would have done anything like that, and the only thing we can think of is maybe someone put something in her drink."

"I see," Sam replied, nodding. "Well, thanks for being so frank with us, Mr. Reynolds. It's time, I think, for us to go and try to speak to her. Before we do, though, can you please give Sergeant Markham the names and phone numbers of Sarah, her parents, and her ex-boyfriend, Brad? We better make sure he is out of the picture. Jenny, you take care of that, please? I will check with the doctor to see when we can see Tammy."

"Well, if you hang around, Sarah and her mum are on their way here. You can talk to them soon. They should be here in half an hour or so. They rang to let us know. Young Sarah is distraught, by all accounts."

"That's excellent and will save us some time. Thanks."

At the nurse's station, they were told the doctor looking after Tammy would be along shortly, and the patient was sleeping comfortably. Her vital signs were stable, but the lab's blood screening results had not returned. While Sam and Jenny waited, they compared notes.

"What do you think of the parents?" Jenny asked.

"Honest, salt of the earth people who love their daughter, and it sounds like she isn't into drugs. Of course, someone could have put something in her drink and got her away from the party. Unfortunately, that's a real possibility. But you know what? It seems to me it's not that type of crowd, just on first impressions."

Jenny nodded enthusiastically. "They remind me of my own parents, and yes, I'm getting the same feeling. A nineteenth birthday party in Roleystone doesn't shout drugs to me. But open mind, at this point, obviously."

The doctor arrived. He was a young migrant from India or Pakistan who spoke exceptional English and introduced himself as Doctor Ngala after they showed him their IDs. Sam realized his name was more likely African. He asked how the patient was and when she could answer some questions.

"Well, it's difficult to say. She lost a lot of fluids and blood and was clearly in shock when she came in. It will be a long time until she can walk again without pain. Her feet were badly cut up. It looks like she has been running on broken glass or sharp stones, so we need to keep a good eye on infections. Her hypothermia was mild, and her other injuries were mostly superficial. The cut on her thigh was infected, but we think we got to it in plenty of time and have stitched it up. She's had over twenty stitches to various cuts, but none of the cuts are in and of themselves very bad. There are just a lot of them. Her high temperature, from the infection and a combination of hypothermia and dehydration, has caused her to be delirious. We've got her on Valium to calm her down and help her sleep. I think she has suffered some sort of mental trauma or shock. When she wakes, hopefully, the antibiotics will have kicked in, and she should be more lucid. If you like, I can take you through to her. I was about to go and check on her anyway. If we can wake her gently, you can try talking to her, and we can see how she responds. If she responds badly, we will have to sedate her again. I'm not sure what this girl has been through emotionally, but whatever it is has terrified her."

"Thanks, Doctor. In your opinion, is the story of her boyfriend being murdered the truth or part of her delirium?"

"You must understand, whether a murder occurred or not, to her, it's genuine. She is one hundred percent sure she witnessed her friend named Greg being killed; therefore, in her mind, she did. Something has upset her deeply, but beyond that, I can't speculate if it is a psychotic episode or a fact. Shall we go through to her?"

"Yes, thank you, but one last thing. You've taken blood; obviously, we will need it checked for drugs or excessive alcohol, and if you would be so kind as to arrange a sample that can be sent to our forensic people. We will need it for evidentiary purposes."

Chapter 4

Reliving the Nightmare

Tammy was awake, though, to Sam, she appeared drowsy, almost close to death. Her face was pale and gaunt, her short hair stringy and sweaty, and she sported a large gauze bandage on her temple, which looked swollen. Sam thought he could be forgiven for thinking she was an old woman rather than a young, vibrant one.

Jenny and Sam held back while the doctor checked her vital signs and spoke to her in a gentle, soothing voice. Tammy's eyes turned wild, and she jerked her head from one side to the other, searching for them when he told her the police wanted to talk to her. The doctor spent a few minutes reassuring her she was safe and in the hospital. Tammy nodded, and Doctor Ngala beckoned them over. Sam motioned subtly for Jenny to go first. Sam felt a woman questioning her might be gentler than him. *After all,* he reasoned, *this may be some sort of rape allegation.*

"Hi, Tammy, I'm Jenny, and this is Sam; he's the Boss," She winked at the girl to build rapport. "We are from the Major Crime Squad, and we would like to talk to you about what happened to you if you feel up to it. If not, we can come back later."

"Yes. Ummm, I need to tell you about Greg. He may still be alive. Do you know if he's been brought into a hospital? What day is it, and how long have I been here? I feel so groggy, and it seems like everything is muddled in my brain." Her voice was weak, and she seemed confused yet agitated.

"It's Monday lunchtime, Tammy. You went missing on Saturday night. Can you remember what happened?"

"Oh my God, I've lost a day. He must be dead by now." She burst into hysterical tears.

Jenny sat on the side of the bed and took the girl's hand in hers while Sam pulled up a chair behind so Tammy didn't see him towering above her. Sam was impressed with Jenny's manner and silently agreed with Felix's assessment that they were a good pairing. It was usual for the junior officer to take notes while the senior detective led the questioning, but he took out his notebook and pen. Without a doubt, Sam decided Jenny should be the one to lead this part of the interview.

"Can you tell us about Greg, Tammy? What's his last name?" she asked softly.

"Brady. I knew him at school." She murmured after sniffing and choking back her tears.

Sam groaned quietly. The use of a TV character's name was suggestive of a hallucination. Sam believed Greg Brady couldn't possibly be a real name.

"Greg Brady? I bet he copped a few jokes about his name at school." Jenny smiled at Tammy, who nodded back, her tears slowing. "He did, yeah, but he always said it was better to have a name people would remember than one easily forgotten. That was how he was; Greg was one of the nice guys."

"So, I'm guessing at the party you and Greg, what, you hooked up after all this time?"

Again, Tammy nodded and whispered, "We danced

for a while, and I really fancied him and him me. I broke up with my boyfriend a few weeks ago, and well, you know." Tammy shrugged, and Jenny smiled, encouraging her to go on. "We snuck away from the party; I don't think anyone saw us, out to his car, just for an hour, we thought, to be alone, you know, so we could..."

"Yes, Tammy, I get the picture. I was nineteen once too. Why wouldn't you? Good looking guy, is he?" Tammy nodded again, but the tears started in earnest, and Jenny waited until they subsided.

"So, okay, you both snuck out in his car. What sort does he have?"

"A black sedan, a big one, I don't know the make."

"I see. I'm guessing a V8 sedan, a manual, I bet? Is it a late model one or one of those old ones?" She smiled and winked.

Sam sat back in his chair, marveling at Jenny's superb way of questioning Tammy. It was just two girls chatting, and he knew she would get more helpful information far quicker than he would, with his sledgehammer, male manner."

"It's fairly new. It looked it anyway, and Greg has a good-paying job. Oh God, I hope he's still okay."

"So, what's the story, Tammy? You went back to his place?"

She shook her head, "No, like me, he lives at home. He said we could go to the old gravel pit close by. We were, you know, in a rush, and I didn't want to be away too long; Sarah is my best friend."

"I'd have been in a hurry myself; don't you worry. So, you made it to the gravel pits, okay? Where did you park?"

Her eyes clouded again, and she sobbed, "I had to get him to slow down. He was driving too quickly. We got there, and he drove through the open gate, then turned to the right, reversed it back, and parked between some small hills, kind of in the back corner but not quite."

"So, being a manual, I'm guessing you guys got into the back seat?" Tammy nodded. "There's no need to go into those details; they're private. What went wrong, Tammy?"

The tears came afresh as she sobbed with remembering. It took several minutes before she could continue. When she calmed down, Tammy was still distraught, but it seemed like she wanted to try her best. Between sobs, she told them of the car coming and how they appeared to bury a body, or at least something which was the size and shape of a body.

Sam sat up straight and paid more attention. He joined in and asked gently if she could remember any details of the other car, but she couldn't other than some sort of station wagon or big four-wheel drive which sounded noisy, she explained.

"Go on, Tammy, love. What happened next?" Jenny asked gently.

"When the men went to leave, they saw our car somehow, and they parked theirs, so it was blocking the gate. I knew straight away that was so we couldn't get away. Greg got out of the car to go and talk to them and told me to stay put and not to worry. I was trying to get dressed, but when they got level with Greg, they started hitting him with something metal. Oh God, it was awful."

Once more, Tammy broke down, and Sam

instinctively believed it was no hallucination; it was real.

"Did you see what sort of something, Tammy?" Jenny held one of Tammy's hands and stroked her lower arm with the other. *Obviously,* Sam thought, *she is trying to calm her down.* Again, he was impressed with Jenny's manner and ability to get the witness to recall details she would rather forget.

"No, it was so dark, and they left their lights on, so when I looked toward them, I was a bit dazzled, but I thought it was something metal, like a pipe or a tool or something. Oh my God, the sound as they hit him over and over again: it was horrible." Tammy frantically sobbed, trying to catch her breath, and her eyes darted between them, seeking understanding.

Sam's heart went out to Tammy. He couldn't help but try to soothe her, "It's all right, Tammy. You're safe now, and none of this is your fault. Take your time; you're doing really well."

Tammy dropped Jenny's hand and hid her face in the bedclothes, and cried a soulful, agonizing cry which screamed of heartbreak. It was three minutes later before she could continue.

"Greg fell to the ground, and they stood over him, hitting him over and over. I got out of the car and screamed at them to stop, that they were killing him. Oh God, help me."

Sam and Jenny waited and exchanged glances. Sam knew Jenny believed Tammy as he did; there was no way this was some drug-induced fantasy. Sam completely understood the horror of what she had been through.

Tammy looked up at Jenny. "Once they heard me screaming, they saw me. Then they ran toward me, obviously to kill me too. I ran away from them. Should I have stayed to help Greg?" she pleaded.

"No, Tammy, you did the right thing. If you'd stayed, you'd be dead too. You would be buried in the pits alongside Greg, and we would never know." Tammy nodded at him, looking grateful, her eyes bloodshot as she wept some more.

Jenny looked at Sam, then hugged Tammy, pulling her head to rest on her shoulder to soothe the sobbing girl. Sam stood up and pointed at his mobile phone, letting Jenny know he would call it in.

Once in the passage, Sam dialed the dispatch number and introduced himself with his name, rank, and badge number. "What is it, Inspector? How can we help?"

"I need a patrol car to go to the disused gravel pits in Roleystone. Sorry, I don't know exactly where that is. Look for a black late model sedan, make unknown, owned by one Gregory Brady, and please do a registration check for me."

"Really, Inspector, Greg Brady?" The bored-sounding radio operator had probably heard them all over the years she had done the job.

"This is not a wind-up. We have reason to believe he has been murdered. His body may be in plain sight, buried in the gravel, or in his car. Please have them call my cell when they have checked it out. This is extremely urgent."

"Yes, Inspector, sorry, but the name threw me."

"Yeah, it did me too. There is a chance this young man is not dead, so let's turn the sirens on, okay?"

After giving his phone number, Sam ended the call, then crept back in quietly. He listened as Tammy recounted her mad run through the pits and the forest to escape her hunters. The last thing she remembered was lying in a ditch after the car had passed her.

Poor kid, Sam thought. *She must have been in shock by then and passed out. Then when she woke, she would have been disorientated and delirious.*

He left again to go and find Tammy's parents, leaving Jenny to get anything else that could be useful. He found them by the nursing station. They stood up as soon as they saw him, frantic for news.

Sam led them away to a quiet corner. "Your daughter has been through a horrifying ordeal. My sergeant and I don't believe she imagined it or had drug-induced hallucinations at this point. She's been very brave, and if she weren't so fit and determined, she could have been killed by the men she says murdered the young man she was with. She tells us she left the party with Greg Brady, and while they were parked in his car in a secluded area, they witnessed two men bury something they thought was a dead body. Those two men attacked and killed Greg, but she was able to get away. You should be very proud of her. She will need a lot of emotional support and possibly counseling to get through this. She's an amazing girl."

"Thank you for being straight with us, Inspector. Our daughter *is* amazing. She was at school with Greg Brady, I seem to remember. We met him once, I think. Is he *really* dead, do you think?"

Sam shrugged. There was no evidence other than Tammy's words, but his instincts were that he couldn't imagine the young man surviving the beating Tammy described. "It would appear so, Mr. Reynolds, but we will get back to you once we've had a chance to investigate further."

"Can we go in and see her now?"

"Of course. Tammy isn't delirious now but is still distraught and probably suffering from shock. My sergeant will be finished with her anytime now; she's just trying to get any last details that may help us find Greg Brady and the men who attacked him. Naturally, we will need a full statement from her, but we have enough to make some preliminary inquiries for now. Just give her lots of love, which I'm sure you will. She blames herself for not staying to help Greg out, but we've tried to tell her that if she had stayed, she would have been killed too. She really is an exceptional girl. We will be in touch very soon."

"Thank you for understanding and being straight with us, Inspector."

"That's no problem at all. Look, a couple of other things occur to me. If you want my advice, firstly, don't leave Tammy alone. One of you should be with her nonstop for a while. Secondly, once the press gets a hold of this, they will be all over it, so if there is somewhere she can stay away from the limelight until she feels up to facing the newspapers and TV reporters, it would be a good idea.

"If you think it's necessary, then, of course, we will. We have other family she can stay with,"

He looked at them as they wrung their hands. Sam had to try to ease their worry. "Look, it may not be as bad as I'm saying. Different people react to trauma in different ways. She seems to be a very strong-willed young lady, but sometimes we all need professional help. I had to have some myself recently, so please don't think it's a sign of weakness. That's why we have professionals. I will get Victim Support Services to get in touch; they can recommend someone who specializes in this sort of thing. I can tell you are a very close, loving family, and that's what she needs more than anything else right now." He handed them one of his cards and added, "This is my mobile number. If she remembers anything else, no matter how small she thinks it is, please call me any time, night or day."

"We will, and thank you again for being so understanding."

"No problem at all. Now, let me just confirm your contact details." He took out his notebook, jotted down everything he needed, and led them into Tammy's room. As soon as they saw their daughter, they rushed to her, and Tammy burst into tears, followed by her mother.

Jenny slid out of the way to let the three of them be together. She turned back at the doorway as she and Sam were leaving and said, "I will be back to see you soon, Tammy. You get better, okay? And listen to me, please. You've done an amazing thing here. We are all proud of you."

Once outside the room, Jenny said, "She is one amazing girl. How tough would it have been to run out of a gravel pit and through the bush naked and with nothing on her feet? Not to mention with two psychos chasing her."

Sam's mobile rang, and he answered it immediately. "Hello?"

"Is that Detective Inspector Collins?"

"Yes, it is."

"This is Constable Billy McGillivray here, sir. We were asked to check out the gravel pits for you, for a body and a car belonging to Gregory Brady?"

"Yep, what do you have for me, Billy?

"Well, a bit of bad news really on two fronts. Firstly, we are here at the pits now, and it's as quiet as anything. No cars to be seen anywhere, and certainly no dead bodies lying around. Secondly, I'm sorry to tell you, but Greg Brady died in a car accident when he came off a blind curve on the side of the hill on Brookton Highway early yesterday morning."

Chapter 5

What's wrong with this picture?

Sam tucked his phone in his jacket pocket and turned to Jenny, confused. "Well, either we are both crap at reading people, or there is something strange going on here, and I mean really strange with a capital S. Question for you, how sure are you Tammy told us the truth?"

"Why are you asking, Boss?" Jenny looked startled.

"Humor me. Tell me what you think."

"Well, okay. I think Tammy is an honest girl. Sure, there may be details she has forgotten or won't face emotionally yet, but so far as my read of her is, Tammy is telling the truth or as much as she can right now."

"Yeah, that was mine too. So, what would you say if I told you they found Greg Brady's dead body in a burnt-out car wreck at the bottom of a ravine on Brookton Highway? At this stage, they think alcohol and speed caused him to lose control on a blind curve early yesterday morning."

Jenny stared at him for a long time. Eventually, she said, "Nope. That can't be true; it just doesn't feel right."

"There is no sign of a body or disturbance at the gravel pit. It all looks all normal. Uniform has been and checked the place out."

"Boss, she's just not that good a liar. No way. And I do not believe she was high on something and imagined it. There was far too much detail for that."

"Well, let's not get emotional. Instead, let's workshop our way through this. She leaves with him, as she says, and they are both drinking heavily. They are heading for somewhere to have sex, but he is driving too fast. Let's face it; most guys would think of doing it with her. She's a good-looking girl. He loses it on a curve in the road. She's thrown clear, but he rides it all the way to the bottom and dies in the fire. It fits the facts."

"And, in being thrown clear, her clothes and shoes are ripped from her?" She stared, disbelieving.

"Maybe he was diddling her with his fingers while driving?"

Jenny looked incredulous. "So let me get this straight in my head. We both thought this girl was a good, honest young lady who was so concerned about her fitness that she didn't do drugs. She broke up with her boyfriend seven weeks ago and is desperate for a good time. She lets a guy, who has been drinking not only drive too fast, but wait for it, it's a stick shift, and they are on a steep road with lots of turns. So, she takes her clothes off so he can play with her between changing gears? Really, Boss, what's wrong with this picture?"

"Tammy isn't that kind of girl, is she? I got the same impression but needed to hear it confirmed from you, too, as you spent more time with her than me."

"Nope, she isn't. No way, José. She would have a good healthy appetite for sex with a good-looking young man, but I cannot see her in the way you describe."

"Okay. Let's workshop it the other way and see if it makes any more sense. She is telling the truth, and these two killers return to the quarry when they can't find her. They grab Greg's body and bundle him in his own car.

They then drive him to Brookton Highway and send him over the cliff in the car to make it look like an accident. Does this remind you of a famous eighties TV crime show episode?"

"Your oblique reference to TV cop shows, I assume, is to illustrate how unlikely this scenario is, then yes, I agree. By the way, Boss, my dad watched those shows and was addicted to them. I wouldn't have thought you were old enough," she smirked.

"Reruns, Jen. There are always reruns on cable. You should check it out sometime. Those shows are where I honed my interrogational skills. Back to the case, though. Why not just leave the body there and get out? What were they trying to achieve by taking all those chances and staging a car accident? Unless…"

They both realized it simultaneously and, word for word said together: "The body they buried there."

"But surely, they would have been better to go and dig it back up again? Wouldn't you?"

Sam nodded in agreement but raised a finger to make a point, "Well, maybe they did, but then again, maybe they couldn't."

Jenny looked at him quizzically, clearly not understanding him.

"Look. I've not been to this gravel pit, so I'm no expert. I imagine it all looks pretty much the same, acres and acres of gravel everywhere you look. Maybe they didn't know where they buried it. It was dark, after all. How would they know where it was if they didn't mark the spot somehow?"

"Oh my God, I think that's it, Boss; that makes sense." She smiled and nodded in agreement.

"Well, let's not get carried away. Maybe our girl is

just a very accomplished liar, or Greg put something in her drink to get her away from the party. One thing's for sure, we've got a lot more work to do, so let's keep an open mind."

"Excuse me, Inspector Collins?" one of the nurses poked her head around the corner and asked.

"Yes, that's me." He turned toward a young, dark-skinned nurse who smiled at him.

"You asked to be notified when Mrs. Morris and her daughter arrived. They are waiting for you in the same room you used before.

"Thank you, nurse."

They hurried down to the lower floor and the interview room. They quietly entered and introduced themselves to mother and daughter, who seemed on the verge of nervous tears.

"Sarah," Sam began, "Tammy is doing fine, but she's been through a tough time. What can you tell us about Greg Brady?"

She blinked rapidly to clear the tears before more fell. Sam noticed Sarah had extraordinarily long eyelashes. "Thank you for telling us; I've been so worried. Greg was a school friend. He was in some of our classes and was at my birthday party on Saturday. I saw them dancing together; it looked like they were having a good time. Why do you want to know?"

"I'm sorry, but he died early Sunday morning in a car accident on Brookton Highway, not far from your home. Can you tell us the last time you saw him?"

"Oh my God, he's dead?" She stood and clasped her hands over her face, and her mother reached and put a hand on her arm to calm her.

"He was such a nice guy," Mrs. Morris whispered as

her daughter burst into tears. To give Sarah time to recover, Sam turned to her mother.

"Did you know him, Mrs. Morris? I'm sorry to seem heartless, but this is a very serious matter we are looking into, and we need information fast."

"I knew of him through the girls, but I don't think they socialized regularly. I met him several times and thought he was a nice young man. He was one of their school friends at the party on Saturday night. The last time I saw him, he was dancing with Tammy. That was around ten or ten thirty, I suppose."

"Sarah, this is important; when was the last time you saw them? Please, think carefully," Jenny broke in.

"As Mum said, he was dancing with Tammy. Umm, they were getting close. He was kissing and feeling her up, and umm, she looked like she was enjoying it. I was dancing myself, but the next time I looked, they'd disappeared. I think it was a bit after eleven."

"So, you weren't overly concerned when she didn't come back because you thought she had returned to his place?" She nodded and looked toward her mother.

Mrs. Morris stared at her with a very disapproving eye. "Sarah, she's only nineteen!"

"Yes, Mum, exactly. She's nineteen. What do you think? Nineteen-year-olds don't have sex? She lost her virginity when she was sixteen." Sarah raised her eyebrows at the police officers as if to say, *Mothers, seriously!*

"Sarah," Sam jumped in, not wanting it to turn into a domestic argument, "tell us about Tammy. I know you are best friends. Is she truthful? Does she take drugs? Would she make up stories to hide the truth of a situation? And please, it's most important you tell us everything."

Sarah looked defiant with hands on her hips, shaking her head. Then she took a deep breath, sat down, and rested her elbows on the desk. "Yes, no, and most definitely hell no. We are talking about Tammy Reynolds. She'd no sooner take drugs than convert to Judaism. She is always, are you listening? Always truthful. Even if it means she's going to get in trouble. At school, she would take the blame for protecting a friend for something she didn't do. That's how special she is."

"Thank you, Sarah. That was very much the feeling Sergeant Markham, and I got when we spoke to her, but the fact is we have two very conflicting scenarios regarding Greg's death, and we needed to hear it from someone who knows her well."

"What happened to her? Why didn't she come back to the party? Was she in the car accident too?"

"At this point, we don't know for sure, but I can say if what she told us is true, she's been through a horrific experience and is lucky to be alive. Please understand that we can say no more than that. We must look into what she has told us and what the technicians discover about Greg Brady's accident site."

"Tammy has been my best friend for seven years, and she's like a sister to me; in fact, she is closer than that. I know for her not to come back to the party to spend the night as we'd arranged meant something happened. Yeah, at first, I thought it was because she shacked up with Greg, but I only thought so because she hadn't a boyfriend for a couple of months. But, really and truly, if she had done that, she would have at least called to tell me because she would have known I'd worry, and I'd understand her wanting some fun in her life."

"Can you tell us how far the old gravel pits are from your house?" Sam asked suddenly.

She did a double take. "The gravel pits, why do you ask?" Sam didn't reply. "Four or maybe five minutes or so. Oh, now I get it. They went there for a quickie in his car. He was all over her on the dance floor, like a fat kid with a doughnut; they were both into each other."

"Sarah!" her mother said.

"Oh, Mum, come on. Please. She likes sex. Who doesn't? And Greg's a hunk of a guy, err, was, I suppose. Jesus, I can't believe he's dead." Sarah shook her head and blinked back tears.

"Sarah, what sort of a driver was he? Did he like to drive fast?" Jenny asked, and Sam mentally applauded her. It was an excellent question; by changing the subject, Sarah wouldn't have time to gloss over the truth.

"I don't know. I've never been in a car with him, but I've never heard anyone talk about him as if he's an idiot when he drives. Unlike some others, I could mention. So, I think he was okay. He drives a powerful car, but what guy his age doesn't? Greg's a surfer, know what I mean? He wouldn't want to risk losing his license because that would mean he couldn't go surfing. Plus, he had a great job as an apprentice plumber and needed his driver's license for work."

"Sarah, you've been a great help and a good friend. Thank you," Jenny said.

"Here is my card; it has my mobile number. If you can think of anything you think might help, please call me," Sam said, holding it out to her.

"Help with what? You haven't told us what's going on?"

Sam and Jenny looked at each other. What could they say that made sense? Sarah would take Tammy's side no matter what. That much was obvious. *But then again*, Sam thought, *maybe it is worth getting her opinion early if only to give more weight to pursuing an investigation when the Boss tries to stop us for lack of evidence.* He decided to go with his instinct. After all, she would find out as soon as she spoke to Tammy anyway.

"All right, please understand we cannot go into too many details, but Tammy says that while they were getting intimate at the gravel pits, they saw two men burying what they thought was a dead body. Greg was attacked and killed by them, and those same men chased her most of the night on foot to kill her as well. But the preliminary report from the accident investigation team is that Greg died in a car accident on Brookton Highway early Sunday morning. You can see why we're confused."

"Oh, my God. Poor Tammy," Sarah whimpered. Her mother gripped her arm again for comfort.

"So, there is no doubt in your mind she is telling the truth?" Jenny asked, knowing what the answer would be.

"Of course not. Why would she lie?"

And there it is in a nutshell. Sam thought, *exactly why would she lie? Unless she was delirious or dazed from the accident, she did have that wound on her forehead.*

"At this early stage, we just don't know enough, but we will be checking the facts very seriously, don't worry. When we spoke to her, we felt that she was telling the truth, but having such opposite scenarios is such a bizarre situation. Oh, by the way, when you see her, remember she has been through the wringer. I would ask you not to mention to her about the car accident. She's got enough on her plate for now. I think it best to let her get over one thing at a time, don't you?"

Mother and daughter agreed. Sam and Jenny took their leave, walking out to the car very much deep in their own thoughts.

****

Back in the car, Jenny turned in her seat to Sam, "If you don't mind me saying, Boss, I think you're like a magnet for odd jobs. You got the killer in the Domin8 case, then with *the vigilante*, you helped bring down Jimmy Mallory and saved two innocent people. I think I'm going to enjoy working with you. This one is the weirdest yet."

"Things are only weird until we understand them, Jen, but yeah, this one is odd, to say the least."

"Very Zen Buddhist, Boss. So, where are we going now?"

"I think we need to look around this gravel pit for ourselves, don't you? While I'm driving, get on to Accident Investigation. See what they've got to say about the crash."

It took over forty-five minutes using the GPS in the car to get to the gravel pits on Smokehouse Road. As they drove slowly down the gravel driveway, Sam noticed no nearby residences could provide witnesses. It was hidden well amongst the hills. As they approached the gate, Sam pulled over, not wanting to drive over any potential evidence, just as Jenny ended the call with an Accident Investigation officer.

"They are emailing me the report, which is still open at this point, but the short story is inconclusive, as you could probably guess. Now they know Major Crime is looking into it, you can bet your bottom dollar they will check more closely, but the guy seems cruisy about the whole thing. The car was burnt out at the bottom of the hill on a spot in the road where there wasn't a crash barrier. That alone I find strange, but also there are no skid marks or braking marks, which means he drove straight through the gap without hitting the anchors and all the while with a naked girl in the car. If that's what happened, obviously, they didn't know about Tammy. If she was there when the car crashed, she was gone by the time they found the wreck."

"Can they tell if the fire started before it left the road or after it hit the bottom?"

"If you want to know what I think, Boss, they wouldn't have bothered checking it out if we hadn't stuck our noses in. I mean, what do they think they are looking at? A nineteen-year-old driver in a V8 sedan, driving in the middle of the night on a country road. They knew he had been drinking and thought he had fallen asleep at the wheel. They told me they found some bourbon and cola cans and vodka spritzers. Pretty open and shut, you would think, unless there is anything that hints otherwise. My take on the investigator is that he had already made his mind up. Booze, speed, and inattention on a winding hilly road. I suppose he sees hundreds of those sorts of accidents, especially in the hills. A young bloke driving a car which was too powerful for him, and without the experience to handle it."

"Hmmm, you said spritzer cans. Greg wouldn't drink that, so it does suggest Tammy *was* in the car. But maybe that's what those two guys wanted us to think.

The clincher will be what the Medical Examiner says. Let's have a look around here and check with them next."

"There is one thing they said which is interesting, however. They found a mobile phone under the passenger seat. So that could verify Tammy's story. She said it was in the hip pocket of her jeans, assuming it was hers, of course. Yet the officers didn't find women's clothing."

As they walked through the gate. Sam squatted and tried to see any tire tracks, but it was loose gravel, with the odd weed poking through here and there. He could see ruts but no tire definition. Being careful not to tread in any of them, just in case, they carried on.

Firstly, they turned to the right and headed toward some small hilly mounds where Tammy and Greg had supposedly parked. It was easy to find by her description, but there were no signs anything had happened there, just gravel and more gravel. Wheel ruts crisscrossed all over the area, and it was obvious it was the sort of place kids might sometimes come to hoon around, or as Tammy and Greg had done, to have hot and heavy car sex.

Sam scanned the area three hundred and sixty degrees. He could see three burnt-out car wrecks at odd spots, and the vegetation was trying to reclaim its land, with tree saplings, enormous weeds, and bushes all working on getting a foothold here and there. The section they stood in appeared to be a large oval shape of around six hundred meters, funneling down a narrow path between giant hills at the far end. Where it went then was anyone's guess. To more gravel. he assumed.

"That looks like the pine trees she said she ran toward," Jenny said, pointing up to the quarry's rim.

"And she ran up the slope in bare feet? My God, she should be in the Olympics, not working at a doctor's surgery."

The lip was around eighty to a hundred meters higher than the ground they stood on, and there seemed to be no clearly defined path she could have run up. *But,* Sam thought, *in the darkness, she wouldn't have been able to see a safe way up, even if there was one.*

"Unless we can find something which gives her story a bit of weight, they won't give us the resources to send searchers and trackers out here to check," Sam shook his head in frustration. "Again, maybe that's why those two guys returned and got the body and car, so her story would be seen as just that, a story. If there's enough doubt, it will stall, if not halt, the investigation and have us think she was drunk or dazed from the accident. Pretty smart when you think about it."

They walked around the pit looking for any signs of recent digging, but as Sam had surmised earlier, they were walking on a mixture of gravel and weeds on undulating ground. They couldn't see anything which said freshly dug grave to them. Similarly, they looked for blood drops where they assumed Greg Brady had been beaten. But, if there had been blood spilled, it had been raked over, and the sun had long since dried out any moisture.

"Maybe we could bring Tammy back here and recreate where they were in the car. Possibly she could remember where they were burying, whatever it was. What do you think, Boss?" Jenny asked as they walked, scanning the horizon.

"I think that's an excellent idea, but I somehow think she won't want to come anywhere near this place anytime soon, and I doubt her parents would be keen either." Sam shook his head.

"But surely, if it means the difference between being believed or not, I think she would be busting a gut to help prove she wasn't imagining it."

"To be fair though, Jen, it's easy to say that when you didn't go through what she did to escape. Look, I think it's a great idea, and I'd be happy to bring a shovel myself and dig if we can't get a search sanctioned, no problem at all. But she's been through a lot, assuming she is telling the truth, of course. Even though she may want to help, she may be unable to get through those gates without suffering a massive panic attack, which wouldn't surprise me. I wouldn't even contemplate it without her, her parents, and her doctor agreeing she should."

"Yeah, I guess you're right. I didn't think of that aspect." Jenny looked down at her feet as she walked.

"You know, I'd like to look at a detailed topographical map of this area and mark the house where the party was, the car accident site, and where she was found wandering around. This is inhospitable terrain, and if those guys made a mistake, it could be crashing the car too far away from where she was found. There's nothing to see here, unfortunately. Let's go and look at the crash site for ourselves."

As they walked back to the car, Jenny called the accident investigation officer back and asked for specifics of the crash site location and told him they were going for a look themselves as they were in the area. The officer was unhappy to have a Major Crime Detective inspection looking over his shoulder.

"Sergeant, can I ask what's so special about this

case? Everything seems straightforward to us," he asked.

"Hang on a sec," she said and queried Sam, who beckoned for her to give him the phone.

"This is Detective Inspector Collins. Who am I speaking to?"

"Senior Constable Joe Pike, sir."

"Look, Senior, we are not jumping all over your case, well, at least not at the moment, but we have some information that conflicts with your findings, so we need to be very careful and make sure all the I's are dotted and T's are crossed. For example, could this accident have been staged to hide a murder? Have you had forensics look at the wreck?"

"Inspector, there seemed no need for that. Everything looked kosher to us. The one thing which could be deemed a bit off was no marks on the road indicating he hit the brakes, but that is consistent with the driver falling asleep at the wheel."

"Yes, I see. Rest assured; we are not inferring you have done anything wrong. When you found the wreck, were any of the doors open, indicating a passenger could have been thrown clear?"

"One rear door was open, but both front doors were closed."

"Hmmm, did you find any clothes inside?"

"Clothes, sir? The car was burnt out. If there had been, they would have gone up in flames."

"Point taken. What about the driver's window? Was it open?"

There was the sound of rustling paper before he answered. "Yes, it was. Why is that important?"

"Look, Senior. Do us a favor, would you? I appreciate how busy you are but trust me; you don't want this to come back on you if some smart lawyer gets involved. Can you have a second close look at this wreck, and I mean a real close look, and search for anything, anything at all, that seems off-kilter to you. Here's the thing: a woman says she was with him before the crash, and she gives an entirely different story about his death. So, either she was with him and thrown clear, and her story was imaginary, or she wasn't. Now if she wasn't in the car then, Senior, your driver was already dead when the car left the road, and trust me, you don't want that coming back on you if your report says differently. And, to me, the driver's window is important for two reasons, one, would he likely fall asleep if he was driving at speed with the window down? No, I don't think so. And secondly, if the accident was staged, the window would have to be open so it could be steered through from someone outside the car while it was being pushed over the cliff."

He sounded morose as he grudgingly answered that he would go over it a second time, including dusting for prints on the steering wheel and window frame where hands would be if the vehicle were pushed. Sam returned the phone so Jenny could get directions to the wreck site.

Back in the car, they turned the navigation back on and saw it was about nine kilometers from where the car was wrecked.

"I've got a question for you, Jen. Let's play, *just suppose.*"

"Oh, goody, I love those games." She grinned back at him as the air conditioning cooled the car's interior.

"I've got a theory as to the answer to the question I'm going to pose, but I want to see if we're thinking along the same lines. Just suppose they do come here to have sex. Either they do, or they don't, but for whatever reason, they leave here with her undressed. Maybe she is drunk or high, or it seems like a fun thing to do. Maybe she passes out or something, and he needs to get her to the hospital. Whatever. The why isn't important. They leave together and drive onto Brookton Highway. This is what we are supposed to think by the killers, right? So, the question is, why did it take nine kilometers to have the crash? Also, where are they going? It's nowhere near the house, so they aren't going back there. It's heading away from Armadale Hospital, so they aren't going there either. And finally, the big question: why no skid marks? If there is something wrong with her, which explains why she isn't wearing jeans, how can he fall asleep at the wheel?"

"Yeah, I get where you are going with this. You think it was the closest place on the road where this type of accident could be staged; there were no convenient ravines any closer."

He nodded, "That's right. Let's go check it out." He put the transmission into drive and pulled away from the pit.

Chapter 6

Investigating the Investigation

As Sam had suspected, there was nowhere between the gravel pit and the crash site which looked like a good spot to stage a fatal car accident. Other than running the car at high speed into any of the thousands of trees along the side of the road, he believed this was the best candidate. Sam knew that didn't prove it had been staged, but he and Jenn shared the same feeling of unease at how the case was developing. The accident must have been faked if they accepted that Tammy was being truthful. Nothing else made sense.

Sam parked twenty meters away from the taped-off area, which showed where the car had gone down the steep slope, and looked around from the road. The shoulder was gravel, and while there were car tracks in a straight line to the side of a white roadside marker, there was nothing else to indicate a fatal accident had occurred.

They stood, both silently surveying the view and looking down the hill. The drop seemed innocuous to Sam, more of a steep incline than a cliff ravine though it was strewn with varying-sized boulders, which would make a mess of a high-speed collision. The slope was scattered with occasional trees, low scrub, and outcrops of moss granite rocks, which the area was famous for.

The charred area, where the car had come to rest, lay sixty meters away.

"You take the left side, and I will take the right. Maybe they missed something which was thrown clear," Sam said.

Jenny nodded, and they walked slowly down toward the spot ten meters apart, looking from side to side for any debris missed by the investigator, tow driver, and clean-up team. When they reached the bottom and looked back up to the road, following the car's tracks, they both shook their heads at the same time before Jenny summed up their feelings when she said.

"Call me a skeptic, but this does not look like a fatal crash site. I would think most cars that came down here that didn't catch fire, the driver would be able to walk away from. Maybe hospitalized for cuts, bruises, concussion; those sorts of injuries, but what on earth would have killed the driver? Of course, that presupposes the car didn't roll half a dozen times, but if it did, we would have seen indentations and scarring on the ground, surely."

"I agree. Maybe we need to see the wreck for ourselves. But first, come on, let's go to the morgue. I'm guessing with the report from Crash Investigation; they would have recommended an autopsy would not be necessary. We need to insist they perform one."

"Wouldn't they do one anyway, being a sudden death?"

"In an ideal world, yes, you'd like to think they would. But with a body badly burnt from an accident where the crash report says the driver was a nineteen-year-old, and speed and alcohol caused the accident, then probably not. What would be the point? Especially if they have an enormous caseload and are short-staffed, which they usually are, then they probably would just agree with the accident report and sign off on it.

"The problem we have is if we can't get any evidence, we may be ordered off the case, and I have to say, so far, this reeks to high heaven, but that's all. Everything is circumstantial, we have no corroborating evidence, and the real issue is it's one young alcohol-affected girl's word against probably a seasoned police crash investigator. If I were in charge and just had the reports to go by, I would probably discount her version too. From that perspective, this does not justify a Major Crime full-blown investigation."

Sam stopped at a quaint roadside café for lunch. They sat at an outside table and admired the view across a forest valley. While they ate fresh home-baked meat and potato pies, they chatted. Sam asked about her time with Felix Milanski with the Organized Crime Squad, and they joked about his completely strait-laced, old-fashioned ways.

"He was always good to me, though," she replied. "Unlike many bosses I've had before, who either take the piss out of me for being gay or try to convert me as if all I need is one good man to show me the error of my ways, and I'd change."

"Yeah, but I bet Felix wanted you to settle down with a nice girl rather than be footloose and fancy-free. He hated that I played the field after my marriage ended, and still does, in fact. The last of the great monogamists is our Felix."

"What do you know about our current boss, Sam? Do you really think he might tell us to drop this?"

Sam noticed Jenny had a tiny dribble of meat gravy

on her chin, which he pointed out, then watched as she dabbed it away delicately with a napkin. "I don't know much about him at all," he began when she had finished, "except a few guys I've met who work there speak highly of him. Like everyone, he has a budget to juggle and must justify his resources, which is understandable. Let's face it the only reason we think this case is all wrong is because we've interviewed the girl and believe her. Bob Young hasn't, and as it's our first day on the squad, he might not be disposed to trust our judgment, especially in the light of the accident report. We need to find something, Jen, and I'm hoping the pathologist can tell us if Greg was alive when the car crashed or was already dead. Otherwise, I think we might be sunk."

"You'd think if what Tammy says is true, if he were beaten to death, it would be easy to spot even if the corpse is badly burned, wouldn't you? I certainly wouldn't want to be the one to tell Tammy we don't believe her after what she has been through."

Before Sam could answer, his phone rang; he eagerly answered it, expecting it to be the Crash Squad calling back. "Sam Collins," he spoke into the phone.

"Bob Young, Inspector. Well, hot shot, congratulations. You've broken the record."

He sat up. The derogatory term instantly fired his temper up. "What record would that be, sir?"

"Well, most new detectives who join us usually wait a couple of days before their ego gets the better of them, and they start upsetting the other departments, but you did it before lunchtime on day one. Well done, Inspector."

He counted to ten, not wanting to upset his new boss on his first day by completely losing his temper. "Sorry, sir, I really don't know what you mean. Are you referring to the Accident Investigation detective?"

"You mean there could be more than one police officer you've upset?"

"No, I meant I had no idea I upset him. Curious that he should complain to you. Very strange. Now I wonder why he would do that."

"Well, before this investigation of yours turns into an interdepartmental World War Three, you better come in and tell me what the hell is going on, don't you think?"

"Yes, sir, do you mind if we make one stop on the way in just to check something out? That way, we can lay everything we have out for you."

"Be back in my office by two-thirty. Oh, and Inspector? Don't piss anyone else off before then, please."

"No, sir. We will be on our very best behavior, I promise."

He hung up the phone and turned to Jenny. "We have to go. The idiot at the crash investigation has complained about us for questioning his judgment. It seems like we may well be out of a job if we can't justify what we've done. Oh, hang on just a sec before we go."

Jenny looked crestfallen, but he was gone before she could respond. Sam went back inside the café and grabbed a free tourist map of the area from a rack on the wall. Back outside, he handed it to Jenny. "It's not topographical, but while I'm driving us back, I want you to get a hold of the guy who found Tammy and get him to tell you roughly where he found her on this map. Let's hope my gut feeling is right, and it's too far from the crash site for her to have walked half-naked and barefooted."

Sam was in a hurry to get to the morgue before facing his new boss. He was desperate for anything which would give weight to their argument that Tammy had told the truth and the accident investigation was slipshod at best and negligent at worst. He went as fast as the speed limits would allow getting there as quickly as possible. While he drove, Jenny got a hold of the hospital and wrote down the details of the farmer from them. She called the home number he had provided and tried to speak to him, but he was out on a tractor, according to his wife. Fortunately, she was accommodating in pinpointing where her husband found the young lady wandering around, *in a state*, as she called it. "Thanks so much for your help. I appreciate it very much," Jenny said and hung up.

Jenny made a mark on the map with a blue pen she took from the inside pocket of her jacket. "Without looking at the terrain or at least a satellite image of the area, it's impossible to say conclusively. But from the look of this map, unless Tammy is a superwoman in disguise, I can't see any way she got there from the crash site barefooted. But I can see how she got there from the gravel pits; it is in the direction she said she took."

"Okay, good work. Now we're getting somewhere. Next stop, pathology."

By one-forty-five, they were sitting in front of the senior pathologist for the Coroner's Office, Ray Bryant, and the accident report was on the desk between them. He was shaking his head as he said, "Based on the Traffic Investigation Report, under normal circumstances, we would see no point in doing a full post-mortem. We would do an ID check, fingerprints, toxin screens, etcetera, and submit our report to the coroner's office. If they requested further investigation, we would naturally schedule it, but generally, they would accept our findings. In my experience, in a situation like this, unless there is pressure from the family or some doubt as to the veracity of the accident report, and this does seem pretty cut and dried to me, we would just release the body to the family."

"Doctor Bryant, can I tell you the situation we have? Please don't misunderstand. I am not impugning the accident investigation report or your office in any way, shape, or form. To be fair, if I had prepared that report, looking at a nineteen-year-old P plate driver in a V8 sedan and alcohol affected at four a.m. on a twisting road, I might well have come up with the same findings. The body was badly burnt, too, in the resultant fire. But there is a problem here, despite everyone's best intentions."

"What sort of problem?" He sat on his chair, tenting his fingertips together.

"We have a statement from a witness who says she was with him that night and saw him get hit over the head several times before by two men wielding some sort of metal weapon. She was chased by his attackers but escaped, mainly due to her fitness level; she is quite a remarkably fit young woman. Now if what she says is true, and we have no reason to doubt her, then it only leaves two possibilities. Either the killers came back, took the car and the body, and staged the accident to hide the murder, which is what we think happened. Or the second possibility is perhaps the victim wasn't dead but woke up, found his girlfriend gone, and drove the car nine kilometers to search for her, before crashing. Perhaps he passed out because of the wounds. Either way, we think, but we can't prove it at this point. He was beaten severely, which ultimately led to his death, and the car accident was after it."

"I see. That's a serious statement to make. What exactly are you proposing I do for you?"

"Doctor, without upsetting the applecart, which we don't want to do, you have to think this girl will not keep quiet if we tell her we don't believe her version of events. Then, once the young man's family finds out from her what she says happened is contrary to the report, all hell will break loose. The press will have a field day, and who could blame them? And then, all of us who might be seen to have not investigated properly could be in strife. Is there any way you could have even a cursory look at the body and see what you think? Maybe, just maybe, now knowing there is a second, even remote possibility of a cause of death, something might suggest itself to you, which would then warrant a closer look. Only then perform a full autopsy if you feel the report differs from the facts."

He looked at them thoughtfully. Sam thought he weighed whether the risk of an angry family making waves was worth the inconvenience versus the potential political fallout of checking further now. "Do you think what we do here is simple? Just a quick look, and we can tell how someone died?"

"Oh, no, far from it. Please, I don't mean any disrespect. I know what you guys here is phenomenal work, but for argument's sake, if there was no smoke in the lungs, am I right in saying that would infer he was dead before the fire?"

Bryant shook his head negatively. "Absolutely it would, but we'd have to look inside the lungs. That's hardly a cursory look."

"Okay, I see. but the wounds to the head, even though the body is burnt badly, could just a quick look suggest he was beaten with, say, a spanner or metal pipe as opposed to the head wounds he might receive in a car accident?"

"I see where you are going with this. You think if we saw anything obvious, from a cursory look, that looked like it might conflict with the report, then it would be worth performing a full postmortem. But, if it all looked consistent, then at least we can say, well, we did consider other possibilities."

"Exactly, Doctor, and I think we could all live with that if the proverbial hits the fan at a later date."

"When would you like us to schedule this?" he asked, opening the page of his diary.

"Well, here's the thing, Doctor. I had a similar conversation with the investigator regarding the crash report, and he took offense and complained to my boss that we were interfering and impugning their evidence. Really though, all I'm trying to do is investigate another theory and, truth be told, save his career if he missed anything. We are on our way now to a carpeting session from my Superintendent."

He sat for a few minutes, thinking, before nodding to them. "Inspector, you were recently wounded while on the job, and you weren't on duty at the time, is that right?"

"Yes, I was shot by Jimmy Mallory." He felt a twinge in his shoulder, which he did every time he spoke about the wound.

"That's why I'm going to help you. I read about it and think you went above and beyond your job description. I'm not the slightest bit interested in potential comebacks and fallout because we have followed protocol here. But, if I'm going to do anyone a favor, it may as well be you. Give me your mobile number, and I will go and have a look myself and give you a call shortly."

"Thanks so much for your understanding, Doctor."

On their way to the car Jenny, having kept silent during the whole process, said, "Boss, I have to say, I've learned a lot from you already today. How you handled that situation was impressive. You're good."

"Thanks, Jen. Let's hope he finds something which will save our bacon."

They arrived at Bob Young's office with five minutes to spare and were waved in immediately. "Well, now, it's the terrible twosome. Come in, sit down, and tell me why you're trying to give me an ulcer on your first day."

Jenny knew enough to know this was another situation where she should speak only when spoken to, so she sat perfectly still but tried to let her body language show that she was not nervous and was in complete agreement with her partner.

"Sir," Sam began, "let me start by saying I don't have an issue with the crash investigator. He's looked at a scene where the victim was a P plater, driving a V8 on a winding road early morning, with alcohol in the car. For him, it's a no-brainer typical fatality, and I get that. He looks at crashes every day; let's be honest, it would be a shitty job. Plus, if something walks, talks, and quacks like a duck, it probably is a duck, right? But when Jenny and I interviewed Tammy Reynolds, she said she was with the driver, and he was beaten to death by two men in a gravel pit. So, we have a totally different story and one which we tend to think fits the facts far better than the accident report. I asked him if he could have a second look, just to make sure he hadn't missed anything, and I suggested it may go in my report if he wasn't helpful. I pointed out if it later turned out he missed something when asked to re-check his findings now, it wouldn't look good."

"Okay, talk to me. Tell me what you think as well as what you know. This sounds intriguing." He sat back in his chair, put his hands behind his head with fingers interlaced, and listened with eyes closed while Sam outlined everything that happened but left out his visit to the pathologist, choosing to hold that ace up his sleeve. He finished by laying out on his desk the map with locations marked with red ink circles around Jenny's original blue crosses to show the implausibility of her trekking that far. Bob opened his eyes and took a close look at the conflicting scenes.

Once he looked at the map, he turned his gaze to Jenny Markham and asked, "Sergeant, what do you think? And don't just agree with your partner because you think you should. I want free thinkers here in Major Crime, not lap dogs."

"Sir, the truth is my opinions were even stronger than the Inspector's, and his playing devil's advocate stopped me from going hollas bolas. I must stress, and I am *not* saying it because he is here. I've found the inspector's reasoning and investigative techniques exemplary. We know the two of them were at the party together from both the host and her mother. Tammy says they left to have sex, and my take on her is she is an honest and truthful young lady who has been through hell."

"Okay, I'm glad you said that Sergeant, because I think so far you two have done some extremely good work, and I'm impressed with your deductions. Now, how can we progress this case further without making an enemy of the Crash Investigation officer?"

Breathing a sigh of relief, Sam decided now was the time to play the medical examiner card, "Sir, I've begged and pleaded with the pathologist to have an informal look to see if anything doesn't look quite right with the body. If we're lucky, I think it will be self-evident now he knows what to look for, and it will give justification for a full postmortem. If they don't see something, we will need a full forensic look at the car wreck, which will rustle feathers."

Bob nodded and looked from one to the other two or three times, weighing them up. "Okay, listen up. We are Major Crime here, and while I don't like big egos and piss-poor attitudes on my team, if we need to ruffle feathers or kick butts, I will do it. Whoever's ass I am kicking will know all about it, trust me. I'm satisfied you haven't gone out of your way to upset another department, and I find this moron's attitude strange at best and questionable at worst. I like the fact you've used kid gloves with the medical examiner's office, and in general, I like your work ethic. Of course, you realize this is going to be a forensic nightmare searching for one dead body in a gravel pit the size of a small suburb, don't you?"

"Yes, sir," Sam replied, "That was why we wanted as much corroborating evidence as possible before calling out the corpse sniffer dogs and ground penetrating radar. It's a huge area to search."

"All right, you keep going the way you are, and I will back you all the way. Just find me something to go on other than a possibly hysterical girl's words. I will talk to the Commander of the Accident Investigation Team and see what they are playing at, see if they can give us a second opinion, and look at the car rather than just assume. Keep me posted on all developments. Not that I'm looking over your shoulders, but if this goes the way I think it might, you will need a lot of support."

Just over an hour later, Sam got the phone call he was hoping for, "Inspector Collins, it's Ray Bryant here."

"Thank you for getting back to me so promptly, Doctor."

"Look, I won't beat around the bush. I've authorized a full postmortem on the body of Gregory John Brady. Having performed a preliminary assessment, I found the cause of death is inconsistent with a vehicular accident and subsequent fire. Naturally, I can't go into specifics at this time. Suffice to say I'm inclined to agree at this early stage with your initial theory as to cause of death being multiple blows to the head with a blunt object."

Sam couldn't help himself: once he thanked the Doctor and got off the call, he stood up, clenched a fist, and yelled, "*Yes, Jenny, we've done it.*"

Chapter 7

Validating Suspicions

With the pathologist's confirmation that the cause of death was as Tammy had described and not a car accident, Bob Young confirmed Sam's case was officially a murder investigation. Tammy's assertion that they had witnessed the burial of a body at the gravel pits, or at least something which resembled a dead body, now had to be given credence. It didn't enter Sam and Jenny's mind that it could be anything but a corpse because they theorized why would the two men murder Greg and attempt to kill her if it was simply a dead animal?

Sam had to rely on Superintendent Young's authority to make several things happen, which he did with a speed that impressed Sam. The gravel pit had to be treated as a crime scene and preserved as a matter of urgency. Bob accepted they had already lost valuable time and potentially forensic evidence, but that couldn't be helped under the circumstances they had had to deal with. A patrol car was dispatched to secure the site and maintain a guard overnight to ensure that, if there was any evidence, it was protected from removal or contamination.

Because of its location, a local hire company was commissioned to provide three lighting towers, so the area was lit effectively. This would soon grow to seven once the scale of the site and the difficulty of creating enough light over such a large area was assessed. They were also asked to deliver a large tent or marquee to provide shelter as well as portable toilets.

The police mobile and tactical command center was to be dispatched early in the morning, as well as a senior forensic pathologist with assistants, a corpse sniffing dog, and a ground penetrating radar unit. The remaining equipment and support personnel to help in the search would also arrive with the command caravan. Depending on the scale of the operation, more people would be seconded as required. At that point, they had yet to learn how many people would be necessary until the site had been professionally assessed.

To thoroughly search the entire area for evidence, fifty senior trainee police recruits and their tutors working with the forensic officers would be called in. The operation would provide valuable practical training for their future careers. They would be spaced arm's length apart and walk the length and breadth of the pit, scouring for any helpful evidence.

Bob Young brought in two other Sergeants to work under Sam's authority to assist in interviewing neighbors. This surprised Sam as he thought detectives would be sufficient, but Bob explained he wanted experienced officers to conduct the house-to-house interviews because of the time which had already lapsed. Initially, a five-kilometer radius was drawn around the pit on a map to provide a starting point. They would be briefed to ask about the specific night in question, along with more general ones about people seen going there regularly, including those using the area for trail bike and four-wheel vehicle driving, or sexual liaisons, as Tammy and Greg had, or other similar pursuits.

Notably, he arranged for forensics to attend the Accident Investigation Holding yard with a tow truck to pick up the wreck. They would take it back to their lab so it could be microscopically searched for evidentiary clues to help identify the two offenders who had staged the accident.

By five o'clock, all arrangements had been made for the search for the body, which was very much like looking for a needle in the haystack to begin in the morning. As officially it was the end of their shift, Bob Young asked Sam to stay for a few minutes to chat with him without Jenny being present after they had stood to leave his office. She waited patiently in the general office, making up the incident board with such information and pictures they had rather than just taking off without saying goodnight to Sam.

"Sit down, Sam," Bob said.

"Thanks, sir," Sam sat relaxed and crossed one leg over the other.

"It's after hours, officially, so call me Bob. It's still day one for you but a great start to your transfer to Major Crime, so how do you feel about heading up this case all the way through to its conclusion now that it's grown legs?

"I'd be disappointed if I couldn't." He smiled.

"Hmm, look. There are two schools of thought concerning you. Number one is that you are a good copper and deserve the promotions you've received. The second is you've been lucky, and those people resent the ride you've had. What do *you* think about your meteoric rise through the ranks?"

"Bob, it's not for me to judge my own performance.

I just do my job as well as I can. To be honest, I don't lose sleep worrying that some people are jealous of my success. But what annoys me is those who criticize weren't up on an apartment block roof without a gun arresting a serial killer or floating shot in the Swan River while trying to stop another. Of course, no one mentions I've been a cop for twelve years and conducted hundreds if not thousands of successful investigations."

"Well said. All right, it's been a good first day for you. You've shown good instincts, followed them, and been shown to be right when others had the opposite belief. Your sergeant seems to like and respect your judgment, so that's a plus too, but here is my only reservation, and this is not a personal attack. This case has the potential to be a forensic nightmare, and you could be bogged down in technical minutiae while collating evidence that may not be your strength. That's not a criticism, but in my experience, some guys are fantastic at the technical stuff. In contrast, others are great gut instinct followers who want to be investigators rather than directors."

Sam considered Bob's statement, which he believed was made with the best intentions, not malice. "I must admit I don't enjoy going through reams of paperwork and technical jargon, but it comes with the job. No matter how much forensic evidence they turn up, Bob, two men out there have murdered someone, assuming it is a body that has been buried. We have no idea who or why, but they didn't stop there. After burying the body, they killed Greg Brady, chased, and terrorized Tammy Reynolds, whom they wanted to make a third victim. Next, they staged a car accident to hide their tracks. Bob, I have a bad feeling that because of their ruthlessness, maybe they've done this before. I want to nail them and nail them hard. Especially having met Tammy Reynolds, I believe she is a genuinely nice girl who has been through hell. So, for my money, bring on those forensic reports of the burnt-out car, the two bodies, the gravel pit, and let me put these two murderers away."

"All right, it's yours, and I've got your back. Mark my words, you will have your detractors if this turns out to be a big case, the kind of case every copper dreams of cracking. But, Sam, I want you to talk to me constantly and keep me up to speed. I don't want things spiraling out of control. I don't mean you are to ask me to make your decisions for you, more that I want you to advise me of what you decide to do before doing it. Get me? Tell me if anything looks like it might turn curly, so I can go into bat for you if required."

"I will, Bob. I'd appreciate the benefit of your experience and being a sounding board for me, so you can let me know if I'm going off track."

"Okay, that's good. Tell Markham she has seniority over the other two sergeants joining you tomorrow because she is heads-up. I have already informed them of this. One piece of advice I have for you, Sam. Felix Milanski tells me you are an exceptional doer with the best instincts he's ever come across, but to progress, especially in a big case, you need to be a good delegator. Then become a good analyzer of the data your detectives bring you. Point taken?"

Sam nodded thoughtfully, realizing for the first time how true that was. Sam had to admit it could well be a weakness of his. He had always been a hands-on investigator with an excellent mentor in Felix. Sam knew he would need to learn to take a step back and trust those under him to do their jobs, which was a sobering thought indeed.

He must have looked concerned because Bob said, "You'll be fine. I have faith in you; I would have taken the case away from you if I didn't. Now go and prove me right."

"Thanks, I will. If you don't mind, Jen and I have one more job to do, so we will get off. We need to break the news of the car crash to Tammy. I've also printed off a Google Earth shot of the pit; I want to get her to give us a rough idea of where they saw them burying the body and narrow the search area down a bit."

"No worries, and the map is an excellent idea. The command center and searchers will be there by eight. I suggest you go straight there. I might drop out mid-morning and see how it looks and get a feel for the location. In the interim, remember all these people will look to you for guidance and leadership. Respect is earned, never given by rank alone."

"Okay, Boss. See you there tomorrow. Goodnight."

****

Sam found Jenny finishing her work on the whiteboard, now showing pictures of Greg Brady and Tammy Reynolds, downloaded from their Facebook pages, Sam guessed. A layout of the pit and several notes, like *STATION WAGON*, were the only relevant information they had on the two offenders.

"Good work, Jen. Are you ready to go back to the hospital? I know it's after hours, but we need to bring Tammy up to speed and see if she has remembered anything else.

"Yep, I'm good to go, and I'd like to be there to tell her the news. I feel a bit like she's a kid sister." She grabbed her bag and jacket, and they headed for the lift.

"Once we're done, if you like, you can drop me home in the city at my apartment and take the car home, then pick me up in the morning if that works for you." He pressed the button for the car park exit.

"Yeah, that works for me fine. What did the big white chief want? Anything I should know about?"

Once the lift doors opened in the car park, he replied, "Well, he wanted to know if I thought I felt I was up to retaining operational control. By the way, I didn't get a chance to thank you for your support earlier. I appreciated what you said, Jen; thanks."

"Nah, no dramas. I wouldn't have said it if I didn't mean it, just so you know. What do you mean keep control?"

"He was concerned there would be a lot of forensic information on this job and thought someone with more technical knowledge might be good. He also thought I might be more of a doer than a delegator, and he makes a good point there. I will need to rely on you, Jen; you will have seniority over the other two sergeants coming on board in the morning, so I want you to coordinate the house-to-house interviews. The only thing I can say is to be careful not to go off on a tangent. Look at all sides before you decide, remembering we will be held accountable for them. Oh, and one last thing occurs to me. These two guys are cold, calculated murderers, watch your back and don't take any chances."

"I'm glad you said we, and not you, would be held accountable, but I take your meaning; I will watch my impetuosity. And yes, I take your other point. I'll watch my back."

"Everyone will scrutinize us carefully because

we're the new kids on the block.'

"So, there's no pressure then," Jenny grinned. "Well, we better impress the heck out of them, hadn't we?" Sam laughed at her optimism; he liked her and again thought he should thank Felix for recommending her.

****

At the hospital, Sam checked first at the nursing station if Tammy's parents were in attendance with their daughter and were told just Mr. Reynolds was. Sam asked if one of the staff could discretely ask him to step outside for a moment.

As soon as he saw them, he asked, "Hi. Is there any news?"

"I'm afraid there is Mr. Reynolds. While we haven't performed a formal identification, we believe it was Greg Brady found dead in his burnt-out car at the bottom of a hill on Brookton Highway. The accident investigator believed he had been killed in the motor vehicle accident, which contrasted with what your daughter told us." Sam held up his hand to stop him from interrupting to defend his daughter. "We now know that to be false. The accident was staged to make it look like that is what happened, and Greg was killed in the manner Tammy reported."

"I see. Poor Greg. Thank you for coming to tell us, not that we ever doubted her word."

"Sergeant Markham and I didn't doubt her, either. We would like to pass that information on to Tammy and ask her one or two more things if you think she is up to it."

"Tammy's feeling a lot better than she was earlier, that's for sure, ever since Sarah came and spent a couple of hours with her. She cheered her up no end. Those two girls together, well, it's remarkable to watch them, especially when they take turns quoting from their favorite TV show. She has just finished her dinner and ate well, too, so yes, come through. She is awake. I will take this opportunity to go for a walk, stretch my legs, and grab a bite myself if you don't mind."

"It's great to hear she's perked up a bit. She's a strong girl. You must be very proud of her," Sam said warmly.

"You've got no idea how proud we are of our girl and how glad we are she survived," he said with a serene look before heading off for a walk.

"Oh, Mr. Reynolds," Sam called out to his retreating back, "Her phone was destroyed in the car smash. I know girls her age feel naked without one, so you may want to consider getting her a replacement while she is cooped up here."

He turned back and nodded. "That's a great idea," he muttered, and Sam noted his voice was breaking up. Mr. Reynolds held his thumbs up before passing around the corner. Sam thought the father was close to tears, so he wanted to escape. Sam realized just what a strain it must be for loving parents in this situation. Everyone thinks about the victim, but what parents go through is often horrendous.

"Not sure he likes us very much," Jenny suggested and shrugged.

"Oh, I think he likes us fine, but the family has been through the wringer, and he probably just wants some alone time. I can't blame him for that."

They entered Tammy's room and simultaneously said, "Hi, Tammy." She was sitting up in bed, propped against a mass of pillows. The TV was silently showing a movie, and a deck of cards was on the tray where she had been playing with her father. Sam took the only chair leaving Jenny to sit on the edge of the bed.

As they had discussed in the car, Sam was happy to let Jenny run with the questioning as he saw they had a connection. Jenny asked, "Are you okay if I invade your private space and sit up next to you?"

Tammy looked apprehensive when she answered, looking from one to the other. "Sure, feel free. What have you found out so far?"

"You look a lot better than the last time we saw you. Tammy, how are you feeling?"

"Good, thanks. Apart from being stiff and sore and the pain in my feet, head, and legs, so not so good, if I'm honest. My feet are a bit of a mess, a bit like chopped liver, but honestly, I'm just glad to be alive. Have you found Greg? Is he all right?"

"Yes, we have, and I'm very sorry to tell you, but no, he isn't all right. Your fears were correct, Tammy; Greg was murdered."

Tammy lowered her head but didn't cry; maybe she had no tears left. She shook her head a few times before lifting it again, her eyes blazing with defiance. "Fucking bastards," she whispered.

"Yes, they are. I completely agree with you. We need to ask if you have thought of anything else or remembered any other little details which could help us. In particular, we need to know as much as you can recall about the car. It's sometimes the tiniest of things which witnesses don't believe will matter which can mean the most."

"The only thing I remember thinking at the time was

it sounded like a diesel, but I never got a clear look at it because it was so dark. I'm so sorry; I wish I could think of something else."

"Tammy, if you feel up to it, could we do a little exercise? I do this occasionally; a relaxation technique which can help people recollect something they otherwise might not."

"Sure, anything at all to help catch those monsters."

"Okay, that's great. Let me hold your hand, and then I want you to lie back on your pillows, close your eyes, and relax. If you feel uncomfortable at any time, you can open them. Meanwhile, I will take you back mentally to when you were looking at the car in the darkness in the pit.

She reached out her hand, snuggled back into the pillows, closed her eyes, took a deep breath, and said, "Okay, I'm ready."

Jenny held Tammy's right hand with her left and softly stroked from the back of her hand to her lower arm. She began in a soft, low voice, "Tammy, you're perfectly safe here, relaxing in your bed. There is nothing to be frightened of, it's just you and me, and we are chatting like old friends. Do you feel safe, Tammy?"

"Yes, when I'm with you, I feel safe."

"Good girl, Tammy. You are doing well; you are comfortable and relaxed. I want you to remember when you were in Greg's car. You were driving to the gravel pit. You were laughing and joking. Both of you were happy and excited to be alone. Can you remember?" Jenny said, her voice soft, almost hypnotic.

"Yes, I asked him to slow down; he was driving fast. I touched him to reassure him he didn't have to hurry." Sam noticed Tammy was smiling; she obviously had fun

96

with Greg during the ride.

"Good girl. Now Greg has driven in through the gate and parked the car back into the corner near those little hillocks. You are now with him in the back seat, having fun, and about to make love with him. Can you remember how you felt?"

"Yes," she replied in a dreamy voice. "God, he's so fit and handsome, and I love his straggly blond hair; he's got me so hot for him. I'm watching him put on the condom; I can't wait for him to be ready."

"Good girl, you're doing well. Now, another vehicle drives in, and you both stop what you're doing and look. Can you see the car?"

"Only the back of it. It's driving away from us, big and dark, and it sounds clunky."

"When you say clunky, do you mean the sound of the engine or that it rattled and clunked when it hit bumps and holes in the gravel?"

She was silent as if she were listening in her mind. Sam was very impressed with Jenny's technique; she had gotten Tammy to return to be in the moment and thought, for yet another time on their first day together, they made a good team. This was her show, and he was very content to sit and listen, confident she would get everything useful from her.

"Both, there are some rattles and squeaks, but the engine sounds loud like a diesel, or the muffler has a hole in it. Dad's car sounded like it once, he had to replace the muffler, and he moaned about how much it cost."

"Look at the back of the car for me, Tammy. Can you see it? Study it for me, and tell me what do the taillights look like? Are they round or square?"

"Oblong…one brake light isn't working on the

right."

"You're doing fantastic, Tammy. I'm so pleased with you." Still softly stroking her hand, Jen continued, "Now can you look at the number plate, where the white light is?"

She shook her head, slowly at first and then more firmly. "There is no white light. I can't see the number plate."

"That's okay, Tammy. You are being such a big help here. You said it was a station wagon. Do you mean a station wagon style or a bigger four-wheel drive-type wagon? Can you see that for us?" There was a long pause, but Jenny was happy to wait, still stroking her hand.

"It seems high off the ground. I think it is four-wheel drive…something is sticking out the sides…it has those sort of side steps."

"Okay, wow, Tammy, you are helping us enormously. Can you see anything else?"

"No, it's too far away now. They have parked. They are opening the back, getting shovels out."

"Which way does the tailgate open, up and down or to the sides?"

"It's half and half, up then down."

Jenny glanced at Sam. This was significant and greatly reduced the possible makes and models. "Can you tell us anything about the two men?" she continued.

"It's dark. They are too far away. One man is bulkier than the other but similar heights."

"Okay, so now they have finished and packed up. They are driving back toward the gate, but they see Greg's car and are parking across the driveway. Are they facing you?"

"Yes, at an angle but pointing toward us. The headlights are on."

"Okay, so the headlights are on. What shape are they, round or square?"

"Sort of oblong. They have left the lights on. They are walking toward us. Greg has got out and is going to meet them. He told me to stay in the car. I'm so scared."

"It's okay. You are here with us. You are safe, and you have nothing to be scared about. Can you see the front number plate?"

Her voice became more strident; she was trembling. "No, the lights are too bright, dazzling me."

"That's all right, Tammy. It's fine. You're safe. Can you see the two men as they walk toward your car? Can you see anything about them at all?"

"Not really. I stopped looking; I searched for my knickers because they were on the floor. I see one of them hit Greg with a spanner, and now the other one is hitting him with something too...*Oh my God, they're going to kill him. Leave him alone.*" Tammy shouted, and Sam stood concerned for her.

"Open your eyes, Tammy. It's okay. You're here in hospital. You're safe."

She sat up suddenly, crying, and Jenny hugged her. Sam sat down again quietly and made notes in his book. *Older, four-wheel drive. Rattles, squeaks, possibly diesel, side steps, the driver's side brake light, and the number plate light are not working. Dark color? Taillights and headlights are oblong shape, and rear doors open up and down, not side to side.*

"Tammy, you've done so well. You've been such a big help. Thank you for facing up to that. I know it was tough." Sam said, and Jenny agreed.

"He's right, Tam. Seriously, well done. You're amazing."

"I'm sorry I can't remember more. I tried my best."

"It was dark. You did better than most would, Tammy. Are you up to one more job for us?"

"I'll try. What is it?"

Sam passed Jenny the picture map they had of the quarry and his pen. Jenny smoothed it out on the tray and said, "Can you look at this map and try to show us where the car was parked roughly, when they buried the body, in relation to where you were parked? We will start searching tomorrow, and any help narrowing the area down would be fantastic."

"Gee, it looks so different. We were parked somewhere around here, facing this way. I think they were, I don't know, a hundred and fifty meters this way, so somewhere around here, maybe?" She marked a circle on the map.

"Again, brilliant work, Tammy, and will help us a lot. Thank you. Now we need to tell you the circumstances around Greg being found, in case you hear it or read about it in the papers, okay?" Sam said.

"Why, what do you mean? Wasn't he at the pits?"

"No, he wasn't. Once they stopped searching for you, they went back and picked Greg up and his car, then staged a car accident a few kilometers away. We believe their motive was so no one would believe you. They went to an awful lot of trouble, and we think that is because they didn't want us searching for the body."

"But you believed me?"

"We never doubted you."

She had tears in her eyes again as she nodded to them. "Thank you," she whispered.

"Tammy, do you think if I had someone bring in a picture book of different cars, you might recognize something else and help narrow down the make or model?" Jenny asked.

"You can try, but I really don't think so. It was so dark. It wasn't much more than a shape to me. I'm sorry."

Sam broke in to give his support. "There is no need to be sorry, Tammy. You've given us a lot of good information, which will help narrow it down. It was dark, so don't give yourself a hard time. You've already done so much better than most witnesses we get. One of my sergeants will drop by with a book for you to look through in case you see something which strikes a chord."

"Okay, but, umm, could you drop it off, Jenny? I feel comfortable with you."

"Of course I will. You try and keep me away." Jenny smiled at the poor girl lying in the hospital bed.

Sam stood up to leave and said, "Well, you sleep tight, Tammy. We will stay in touch with you. You've got Jenny's and my number if you think of anything, anything at all. It doesn't matter how inconsequential you might think it is. To us, it could be massive. Goodnight, Tammy. I hope your feet get better soon."

"Night-night, Tam, see you tomorrow," Jenny added.

Back at the car, Sam handed her the keys. If you drop me at the Grosvenor in town, I live only a couple of hundred meters from there, and I can walk. I'm going to grab a steak. Want to join me, or do you have plans?"

She stared at him pointedly, "Boss, I'm a middle-aged gay woman married to the job, and it's midweek.

No, I don't have plans, and a steak sandwich at the Grosvenor sounds like a plan because otherwise, by the time I get home and shower, it will be baked beans on toast and bed for me."

He laughed, "Yeah, I get you. Come on, then. It's my buy. Oh, and it's after hours, so call me Sam."

Chapter 8

The Grid Search

True to her word, Jenny Markham ordered the steak sandwich and a club soda to wash it down while Sam had the fish of the day with two beers. It was inevitable that they talked about the case.

"It occurs to me, Jen, the offenders either now or used to live around the gravel pits somewhere. Possibly quite close by. Otherwise, how did they know the pit was even there? Plus, there's the site of the accident. How did they know that curve in the road existed with a steep hill by its side? It can't be a fluke, and they found it by accident. At some point in time, these guys lived in or near Roleystone, so when we perform the house-to-house, we need to be mindful we could well be interviewing the murderers. If the residents haven't been there for more than five years, we want to know who the previous ones were and talk to them too."

"Hmm, good point. Once we've got the interviews nailed down, we can do vehicle checks on all owners and families and any who own four-wheel drive wagons."

Sam shook his head. "Not to rain on your parade, but this area is predominantly hobby farms and some bigger station properties, so I assume pretty much everyone will have some kind of four-wheel drive vehicle."

"Well, hopefully, forensics will turn up something from Greg's car; we may get fingerprints or DNA. One of the men had to drive it."

"That's right, Jen. Hopefully the fire didn't destroy everything. Then, of course, there is the buried body. Once we find it, the evidence could open other avenues, especially when we identify it. I will also go to the press tomorrow morning and ask for help with anyone seeing Greg's car driving to the crash site. Theoretically, if someone saw it, they may have seen the wagon behind it. Early morning on Brookton Highway, it's unlikely. Still, we won't know if we don't ask the question."

After a silence, while they both ate their main courses, Jenny asked, "So we've talked about my love life or, to be precise, the lack thereof. What about you, Sam? Who's waiting at home for you?"

"No one steady now, and I'm enjoying being single. I was married early and am in no hurry to repeat the mistake."

"No kids?"

"Thankfully, no. What about you?"

"Eleven-year-old boy, Josh. He lives with his father, which is better for him with the hours I keep. His dad fought me for custody when I left him for another woman. That relationship didn't work out for me. Far too complicated, too much baggage, and once the feeling of excitement and newness wore off, we didn't have too much in common. The Family Court Judge was sufficiently old-fashioned enough to agree with him that a heterosexual man working normal hours would make a better single parent than a lesbian policewoman. And look, he was probably right. We can't have a gay mother permitted to bring up her son. A straight father, it was felt, would be a lot better for his wellbeing."

"I'm sorry to hear that, Jenny. It sounds cruel."

"Oh, it's all right. Thanks anyway, but I'd rather be alone and true to myself than continue to have lived a lie. It wasn't his fault. He was, and still is, a good man and didn't deserve what I did to him. I fought my inner feelings for years and tried to conform for him and Josh. But I was miserable, though I didn't know why until I met Megan. I thought I was just in a rut with him and life in general. Who knows, maybe I was. Being unhappy, I was no good as a mother and even worse at being a wife."

"Do you mind if I ask a personal question? I'm genuinely interested."

"Sure, go ahead. I'm used to having the mickey taken out of me in the force. I'm the butt of all the lesbian jokes, but so long as it's not said in spite, I can take it."

"Well, you won't get malice from me. My question is, when you were married and you realized you were attracted to other women, was it like being bisexual and you enjoyed both? Or did you know you were gay, and sex with your husband suddenly became horrible?"

"That's a good question, Sam." She pushed her plate away, leaving half a plate of fries. "In my case, I only ever had one boyfriend, and he became my husband, so I never knew any better. I never had an orgasm with him, but that didn't mean sex with him was awful, either. I know a lot of women don't orgasm from vaginal sex. It was just how I thought normal was. But then, when I fell for Meg, and we made love for the first time. Oh my God, it was amazing. It was only then I realized how bad it was before. Suddenly my world was rocked."

"So how come it didn't work out?"

"I just wasn't ready for it, even though I thought I

was. I had too much going on. I was fighting to keep my son, my ex was heaping guilt on me from every which way, using family and friends against me, and poor Meg copped the lot. One day I wanted to be with her, and the next, I wanted to go back home and try to pick up the pieces. The sad thing is if we met now, it would be brilliant, but you know what they say, you can never go back once it's gone wrong. Besides, Meg is now happy with someone else. She's a schoolteacher and works in the country now. Megan was Josh's teacher at the time. That's how we met. I didn't know it, but she saw something in me; I was ripe for seduction, and that's what she did. Hey, that's life." She took a long drink of water to hide she was upset with remembering, but she failed; Sam could see it.

"I really am sorry, Jen, that sucks. Let's change the subject. Can I tell you I think you were fantastic with Tammy earlier? Was that some sort of hypnotic trick?"

"Not hypnotism, no, not really. It's more a deep relaxation thing. My father is a psychologist, and he taught me. If someone wants to remember, and you can get them relaxed enough to relive a situation, it helps them think of details that they took in only on their subconscious level. It's a party trick of mine, but it comes in handy in situations like today. The touching is important though I don't know why, but it works for me."

"Well, Felix was right on the money. We make a good team. I like working with you, and you have some extraordinary interviewing skills."

"Feeling's mutual, Boss." She smiled at him before adding, "And now it's time to get home. What time shall I pick you up in the morning?"

"If seven is not too early for you, it would be great. I'd like to be on-site by eight."

"No, all good. I'd like to get my teeth into this case, too, and I do want to make my mark in Major Crime. I'll see you at seven out the front of your apartment block. It's that yellow tower block just down the road, isn't it?"

"Yep, The Swan View Towers. See you in the morning. I will be outside in the drop-off bay."

****

He poured himself a tumbler of Scotch on ice back in his apartment, went out onto his balcony, and stared across the river into the night, where he did his best thinking. On impulse, he took out his mobile phone and called his old mentor, Felix Milanski. He answered on the fourth ring. "This better be fucking good, Sam. We are watching a romance movie, and I've had to put it on pause."

Sam laughed heartily, knowing that while Felix would undoubtedly be watching TV with his wife of nearly forty years, he would welcome the interruption from a rom-com. His gruffness was just his way. "Sorry, Felix, I was just ringing to thank you for recommending Jenny to Bob Young. She is amazing, and we are a good fit."

"Yeah, I knew you would be. Jenny Markham is married to the job and gay, so she won't fall for your irresistible charms and want to jump into bed with you. She is also a fine Sergeant, the best I've worked with at interviewing suspects, especially female ones. You can trust her and rely on her judgment. She will be good for you. I've only eighteen months until retirement, so what do I care?"

"You are so full of shit. You do care, and that's why

you recommended Jenny so I could have every chance to make it in Major Crime. You care about the job and the people who work for you; you're not fooling anyone, old man."

"Well, that just shows how dumb you are and how I've had you fooled for years. Now is there anything else, big shot Major Crime Inspector? Or can I go back to watching this scintillating movie rather than listen to your bullshit?"

"Goodnight, Felix, and thanks again."

Felix hung up first. Sam knew Felix wanted to create the illusion he was grumpy when, deep down, he would be pleased Sam took the time to phone to say thanks.

****

Sam and Jenny were in the Mobile Response HQ before eight. It was a fifth-wheel caravan with offices, satellite, phone and radio communications, computers, and an incident board. It had a pull-out awning with a table and fold-up chairs which were set up underneath it. It had been delivered to the site, towed by a Ford F Truck, and set up. With them were sergeants Roger Kincaid and Beverley Maddison, and they were going over the detailed map, drawing up lists of houses and properties to visit and questions that would be asked.

The homes in the area were houses with acreage properties, from a minimum of five acres to twenty-five, with the odd one being a full-sized farm. Some had horses, others were orchards or small holding hobby farms, and a few ran sheep. They had drawn a five-kilometer circle from the pits and were going to use that as a starting point. They would go ten kilometers and then fifteen if they had no joy. Of course, going farther out encompassed hundreds of houses, and should they need to go that far, they would get uniformed officers to help. For now, though, by staying within the five-kilometer limit, they felt they could handle it themselves.

Sam had the detectives sit with him at the outside table for his first briefing. He decided not to pull punches remembering what Bob had told him about respect being earned, so he thought it best to address the elephant in the room immediately. "Thanks for joining us, we've not met before, and I'm told there may be some animosity toward me within Major Crime because of how I have been promoted. All I ask is you give me a chance to prove myself; I have twelve years as a detective, so it's not like I got off the banana boat yesterday." Sam noticed the new pair shifted uncomfortably in their chairs, so he knew he had started on the right track.

"I've got no issues working with you, Boss. You did a fantastic job with the *Northbridge Vigilante,*" Roger replied.

Beverley nodded earnestly in agreement. "In my opinion, anyone who says anything negative about the job you've done is simply jealous. I promise you have my respect."

"Okay, thanks for that, you two. Just do me a favor. Please remember the person you may interview today could be the killer. So, don't probe too deeply and put yourselves at risk. Today is more about eliminating suspects from the list. If you have any suspicions, we go back as a team for in-depth questioning with a warrant. Are we on the same page here?"

Everyone agreed. After Sam asked them to check in with him regularly, the three detectives took off to make a start while Sam stayed to oversee the search.

****

The cadets arrived on a large bus with two instructors from the training academy in Maylands. Sam asked them to form a line starting at the gate a short distance from each other. Keeping the line moving slowly, they scoured the gravel, putting into evidence bags anything they found after photographing it in situ and marking where it had come from on the ground with a stake and on a large-scale map with an X.

By ten o'clock, the forensic van had arrived along with more staff in another vehicle, and Sam showed the man in charge, Lewis O'Bannon, the approximate location pointed out by Tammy on the map. They agreed that distances can be deceiving at night, so while it would provide a starting point, they might need to search farther afield radiating out. A series of string lines were pegged out so a full grid search could begin, and within half an hour, they were ready to start.

Bruno, the trained German Shepherd, was brought over by his handler while the ground penetrating radar unit started in an adjacent grid square. Dogs had been used for years to find bodies and human remains; however, they were not foolproof. So, the dog would be moved from square to square, and the radar unit would follow to ensure he didn't miss anything.

Two specialists from the tactical Response Group had been asked to search the side of the pit where Tammy had made her desperate run for freedom, and Sam's radio beeped to life as they reported they had found blood stains heading up toward the pine trees but no trace of the man who had followed her. This discovery put her version of events beyond all possible doubt. Standing down in the pit, looking up at the trail she took, he was once again in awe of her fitness and desperation to escape the two men who chased her. Sam liked to think he was fit, but he seriously doubted he could have successfully climbed the incline in daylight fully clothed, let alone in darkness and naked.

****

Just before eleven, Bob Young arrived and walked around with Sam discussing his tactics and could find nothing he felt had been missed until he asked Sam what he had done to arrange food and drinks for lunch for the number of officers on site.

Immediately, one of the data entry techs from the mobile HQ was dispatched to scour the local shops to contract a supply of sandwiches, pies, and bottled water. At the same time, Bob organized the mobile canteen to arrive in the afternoon.

As Bob pointed out to a crestfallen Sam, this was a big area to search and protect the integrity of. In his opinion, it would require personnel to attend for at least a week, so food and drink would be an essential part of providing for the staff. Sam had been so busy organizing the search that he hadn't thought about feeding everyone. He was saved from further embarrassment by a shout from the dog handler and barking, which signified Bruno had found something. The handler led Bruno away, and the radar unit was brought over, and within minutes confirmed something was buried there. Bob Young left, leaving Sam back in charge but asked to be notified as soon as there were any developments.

The radar unit passed over the uneven ground, and slowly the image of a body appeared on the computer screen. Sam felt conflicting emotions hit him, sadness that someone's life had been taken and the corpse callously discarded in the gravel pit and happiness that

Tammy could receive final and conclusive validation for her story.

The forensic team went into action. The immediate area was roped off, and a white tent was erected over it to protect it from the elements and provide shade for the people entrusted with exposing the body and bringing it to the surface. Shovel by shovel, the gravel was removed and sieved to look for any evidence the killer may have unintentionally left behind. Sam wanted it done quickly but understood the need to find any clues which may help track down the murderer. Also, they had to ensure the officers digging didn't damage the body in any way, which might confuse the medical examination that would occur later to determine the cause of death. It was going to be a slow process. The day was warming up, and a minimal breeze in the pit made it hot work.

The dog was led back to a shaded area to rest; though he still seemed agitated, the radar unit continued its scan of the surroundings, and the searchers continued their sweep. Sam radioed his three detective sergeants to advise them of the find and got an update on the interviews, which was also a slow process with nothing to report out of the ordinary.

Rick contacted the medical examiner's office, informed them of the body which was being exhumed, and asked for an M.E. to attend. By the time Ray Bryant arrived, the diggers were close to the depth indicated by the radar and had switched from shovels to trowels.

The lunch supplies arrived, but no one wanted to leave the tented area to go and eat, so Sam asked the food be brought over to them. Sam had not experienced such a mass feeling of sad camaraderie. It seemed no one wanted to leave without news. Fifty officers now stood watching, slowly eating sandwiches while the two experts excavated alongside the medical examiner.

"Here it comes." One of the men called out as he exposed the first glimpse of black plastic. Everyone tried to get a look, and Sam felt a growing sense of excitement in the pit of his stomach. From that point on, the excavated gravel was put into buckets and would be microscopically examined back at the lab later.

What was deemed slow work earlier then became laborious, resembling an archaeological dig as the tools to remove the gravel without damaging the corpse got smaller and smaller.

An hour and a half later, the plastic-shrouded body was exposed and lifted from the hole. A feeling of immense sadness overcame the group. The corpse had been sealed inside two large black bin liner bags, one put on from the top and the other from the bottom. Gray packing tape had been used to join them together and was wrapped around the middle several times.

The searchers went back to their line search in silence, deeply affected by the fact a human being could be treated disrespectfully.

"Inspector," Ray Bryant called from his place alongside the body.

"I'm here, Doctor," Sam replied.

"I think there's a problem. You said this body was buried Saturday night?"

"That's right. What's wrong?" He squatted alongside him and noticed the smell of rotting meat.

"Well, I can't say one hundred percent yet, obviously, but I would bet a hundred dollars this person died quite a bit previously. If it was buried here Saturday, which to me would be very unlikely, death occurred some considerable time prior. I don't think this is the body you are looking for."

"You've lost me. How can it not be the body buried on Saturday night?"

"Even through the plastic wrapping, I can detect the odor of decomposition, and I can tell you it's far more advanced than three days. I'd say this person has been dead weeks, possibly months, but most definitely not days."

They looked at each other as Sam realized what that meant. There was more than one body buried. He took out his phone to call Bob Young and reported the search would take much longer, and there was more than one victim.

The nightmare had only just begun.

****

By nightfall, they had found three more bodies, all wrapped in the black bin plastic liners, taped closed, and located at similar depths. The distance between them was within ten meters and seemed haphazard. When represented by pins placed on a map using GPS technology, there did not seem to be any perceivable pattern.

The plastic-clad corpses had been removed from the ground with the utmost care and kept within their shrouds to preserve as much evidence as possible. They were transported to the morgue, where full postmortems would be carried out, along with forensic testing of clothes and whatever else was found inside the bags. Forensic officers would attempt to identify the bodies using teeth, fingerprints, and DNA and try to piece together some explanation of why and how these unfortunate victims came to their end.

Because he began the investigation, Sam had the authority to investigate the original murders. Now there were five, and it put the scenario in a different light. Officially if the same offender was thought to commit three or more separate murders, they were given the designation of a serial killer. That would get Sam more resources but could also mean he lose control to Bob Young. He had mixed feelings about the possibility, wanting to be in command but worrying he did not have the experience to manage a large team of investigators.

Serial killers, it was always thought, were rare, thankfully. There have been famous cases from all over the world, and Australia was not immune. There were, naturally, a lot of murders in Western Australia, as in other places, and the motivations for murdering varied from domestic violence, jealousy, money, or a situation that got out of hand. With a serial killer, there was often no reason that made sense to any logical mind, only a diseased one. Studies showed the incidence of serial murderers worldwide was increasing at an alarming rate, and because the murders were often random, it could be very difficult to catch them. That meant with the body count at Rolleystone now at five, Sam knew he could well be replaced as the head of the investigation. As much as that would disappoint him, Sam knew, in a way, he would feel relieved.

After the searchers and forensics officers had left for the day, Sam sat inside the mobile unit with the three sergeants in the evening, physically and emotionally drained but needing to go through the interviews they had carried out during the day. None of them had anything concrete to report. The residents all told a similar story; they knew of the pit but had never gone there because they had no need to. They knew kids used it as a play area. Youths took trail bikes, mountain bikes, and four-wheel drive vehicles there. It had never been a place where trouble had been an issue. The closest it came to that was some kids started a fire six years previously, which got out of hand and became a bush fire that swept through the surrounding hills before it could be contained.

Sam told them they were getting reinforcements the next day with whoever could put their caseload aside in the Major Crime unit, even if it was just as a temporary measure. They would be coming to assist with interviewing households, he told them.

"Why the change in manpower level?" Roger asked.

Sam replied, "Before, we were looking for two people who we thought killed one victim and brought the body here to bury it. One offender we know was male by his voice, so safe to assume both were men, though that's not conclusive. They murdered Greg Brady to cover up the burial. That victim could have been killed for any number of reasons, perhaps even an accident, which suggested a certain kind of profile for the killers. Now we have four buried victims. That's a whole different ballgame, and there will be considerably more pressure once the media know about it."

"In what way, Boss? Isn't a killer just a killer?" Beverley asked for the benefit of all the others and herself as she had spent most of her time with Robbery.

"Nobody likes to use the term serial killer in Perth because we have had surprisingly few of them, but with four victims officially, that is what we are looking at here. I'm no expert. Who is? Regardless, one serial killer working alone is unusual, but two killing together?

Wow, that's just freaky and occurs very rarely, with some notable exceptions, such as The Birnies. I'm sure you've heard of them. They were the couple who abducted four young women, raped and murdered them, and buried them in the forest in the eighties. Fortunately, the fifth would-be victim escaped, which brought their reign to an end. Otherwise, God knows how many more they would have murdered. Their motivation was sexual sadism, but it's not always for sexual reasons."

They all nodded. The Birnies was a famous case of which everyone in Western Australia was aware. "Of course, it may not be a serial killer here. Maybe it's just a body dumping ground for some sort of underworld drug dealer organization, and if this were New York instead of Perth, I'd give that a lot of weight. But here, I don't think so. I keep returning to a pair of serial killers working together for some reason.

"Superintendent Young has requested permission for overtime payments for the morgue staff, so they are doing the postmortems as we speak. We will have more information and cause of death tomorrow. The press doesn't have this story yet, but they will soon. Someone will leak it, and we need to hit the ground running and see if we can't knock this case on its head quickly. Any luck with the four-wheel drive?"

"Being small farm holdings, Boss, virtually everyone has at least one. Without a make or model or something to identify it by, there's not a lot of luck there. We don't want to give out the broken tail and number plate lights, so the killer doesn't fix them," Jenny replied.

"Well, there's not a lot left we can do today. Let's get an early night as tomorrow will be flat out. On the way home, Jenny, we should see Tammy and leave her the vehicle book Roger brought with him. We have to hope she sees something which sparks another memory. Otherwise, it's back here tomorrow for round two. It will be another long day."

Chapter 9

The Burial Ground

Once again at the hospital, Sam was impressed with Jenny's handling of Tammy over the picture book of different makes and models of four-wheel drive vehicles. Sam retook a subordinate role, as he knew the rapport between the two was much friendlier than he could cultivate. Clearly, Tammy saw him as the authority figure and Jenny as her friend.

Tammy's mother was present, and they ensured she stayed to hear the news. Sam realized support from her parents would be essential for Tammy's psychological recovery, considering the guilt he knew she felt over not remaining to help Greg on the night.

"Tammy," Jenny began, "we wanted to call in and let you and your parents know what's been happening at the quarry and how important you have been in helping our inquiries. None of this would have been possible if you hadn't escaped the madmen. This case is now a major crime investigation with far more ramifications than anyone could have foreseen,"

"Why, what's happened?" Tammy asked, wriggling to sit up straighter in bed.

"Well, because of your bravery, Tammy, we have a huge search going on at the quarry, and I can tell you we haven't just found the body you saw being buried;

there's more." Sam knew this was not strictly true; forensics had yet to confirm that one of the four bodies was buried on the night, but he supported Jenny in saying it was.

"Our forensics team has uncovered four bodies so far, and they have not finished searching the entire area; there is a lot of ground still to cover. We think this is a burial ground for two serial killers, and it's only because of you we've discovered it. By you escaping them, you've saved untold lives in the future. We can now catch and lock them up. But without you, they would have kept killing and burying bodies there for years."

Tammy was speechless, eyes wide. She stared at them, each in turn, unable to process what Jenny had said.

"Tammy, we also believe Greg died early in the beating. There was absolutely nothing you could have done which could have saved him." Again, Sam knew this wasn't strictly true, but if it helped her from feeling guilty, then the ends more than justified the means. One thing was true; Tammy could not have saved Greg; she would have only gotten herself killed. Had that happened, Tammy would have been buried in the pit too, with the police none the wiser.

"The public owes you a huge debt of gratitude, Tammy," Sam added. "You should feel very proud of yourself."

"I don't feel very proud but thank you very much," she said, looking across at her mother, who had tears in her eyes.

Jenny took the picture book out of her bag and passed it to Tammy, "Tam, what we would love you to do is have a look through here. In my experience, it's best if you don't study it intently. Just feel nice and relaxed and slowly turn the pages. Let your subconscious see if anything seems familiar. I don't expect you to positively pick out a car and say, "That's the one." It won't happen like that, but if you think, *hmm, this one looks like it reminds me of something,* that's good enough for us. Try it a few times if you can, especially just before sleep when you feel most relaxed and not under stress. If it doesn't work there is no problem at all, okay?"

"I will do my best."

"That's my girl. Now we will leave you with your mum, and I will try to pop in tomorrow, but you can call me on my cell phone if you think of anything at all, or just want to have a chat, okay? Get well soon, Tammy."

****

At seven the following morning, Sam and Jenny arrived at the quarry to find Bob Young with an increased contingent from the forensics department and medical examiners, already hard at work.

"Good morning, sir," they both said.

"Good to see you both came in early. I have a bad feeling about this whole saga so I thought I'd come down and see if I can help. You have a knack of being attracted to unusual crimes, Sam, and this one seems to be no exception. Both of you followed your instincts in believing the girl, and it's paid off in spades. I've decided to leave you in charge, Sam, for the time being anyway, but you've got five murders. Granted, it would appear to be the same offenders, but the heat will be on you to solve this quickly. So, what else do you need from me for support?"

"Sir, now we need the forensics reports to give us a steer. We're doing all the preliminaries, but we don't know if the victims are male or female, old or young, or how they died. All we know right now is there are two people, one we know to be male, and they drive a four-wheel drive wagon, probably a diesel with a brake and number plate light out. We think they live somewhere near, or at least did at some point, because they know the area but right now, without forensics we don't have too much at all to get our teeth into. All we can do for the moment is continue to visit homesteads in the area seeking as much information as we can. I'd also like to go to the media. I know it will cause a circus, but we need as many witnesses as we can find while Saturday night is fresh in people's minds. Someone may have seen the staged accident on the highway."

Bob stood silent for a moment, digesting what Sam had said. "Well, let's face it; if you two didn't believe the girl in the first place and raised a storm, we wouldn't have found the bodies. So, I'm sure the rest will follow. I've got faith in you both. I've lit several fires in forensics and the M.E.'s office. The main problem is resources; both departments tell me they are understaffed for normal times, but this many bodies they are struggling. In the interim, the car is being gone over with a fine-tooth comb and you should have a report on that sometime today. You will have preliminary reports on your four buried bodies later too, but obviously, toxicity and chemical analysis will be considerably longer. I must say with five bodies at once, plus their usual load, we have spread them thinly, but they are doing their best. I've got another six detectives coming over, and they will be here by nine. These are all Major Crime detectives which I've taken off other cases, so they are good people and will be a big help in the house-to-house interviews;

I've already briefed them on what to look for, and they all know this is your show. The report on Greg Brady is in, but there's not a lot of help there. He suffered multiple blunt force traumas to the head. The crash and the fire had no effect, as he was already dead. We know that because, as you surmised, there was no smoke in the lungs."

They were interrupted by a shout from the search area. They had found another body, and Sam's heart sank further.

"I think we should give Tammy Reynolds a medal. What has been going on here?" Bob asked incredulously.

They wandered over to the latest hole in the ground, and another bundle wrapped in black plastic and taped across the midriff was lifted out reverently.

"Jesus Christ," Bob growled. "These bastards aren't operating a hobby farm; they are running a fucking abattoir." He turned to Sam and raised a finger to emphasize, "Sam, you make sure you get these bastards. I don't care what it takes or what help you need. You've got it. Do *not* let me down. Take any steps necessary, you get me?"

"Yes, sir," Sam replied, and he meant it.

Bob turned on his heel and left the site saying over his shoulder, "I'm going to see the Commissioner. He needs to be told about this straight away. The shit has well and truly hit the fan, and it God damned stinks to hell."

There was nothing Sam could say in reply to Bob's statement, so he didn't. Instead, he and Jenny walked back to the operations center to prepare for the arrival of the other detectives.

Sam had just finished the meeting and briefing the

additional detectives when word came from the searchers. Another body had been found, taking the toll to six that had been buried, plus Greg Brady. By lunchtime, it was eight, and acres of the pit were still left to search. Sam was going stir-crazy with boredom and frustration and called Jenny to come back. He wanted to personally hurry up the forensics technicians inspecting the car wreck and thought he would do it in person.

****

Sam and Jenny were shown into Jim Laycock's office. He had just completed a thorough inspection of Greg Brady's car and was finishing the report. Sam had met him once or twice before and found him to be a good guy and always willing to help, but Sam knew if you let him chat, he could bend your ear for hours on end about the most minute details. Sam had once been cornered by him at a colleague's retirement party and had almost fallen asleep listening to the latest theories on lividity and calculating the time of death.

"G'day, Jimmy. This is Sergeant Jenny Markham. What do you think of our wreck?" Sam asked on entering.

"Well, hello, Jenny," he said, ignoring Sam. He shook her hand and held on to it far too long, "You can come back anytime and leave your boss back in the office next time."

"Hi, to you too. I might just do that," Jenny replied, winking at him.

"Oh, stop being such a letch, Jim, for God's sake!" Sam said humorously. He was once more impressed with Jenny's people skills. Sam knew she was gay, Jim didn't, but she was wrapping him around her little finger, letting him think she was attracted to him. Sam could see this woman was destined to go a long way, he thought admiringly. "You can swap phone numbers afterward. What can you tell us about the accident?"

Jim comically shook his head and raised his eyes at Jenny as if they were sharing a private joke, and she smiled back. He cleared his throat, turned to Sam, and was instantly professional. "Absolute rubbish, childish, and amateur. Trust me, I've seen lots of staging cases, but this is the worst I've come across. I've read the Incident Report from Major Crash, and the joker who did it should be fired."

"Jesus, don't hold back. Jim, tell us what you really think," a shocked Sam replied.

"Sam, blind Freddy should have spotted this was staged. Sorry for the language Jenny," he smirked, but she smiled back and nodded as if to say she'd heard the word before. "The car was pushed down the hill, the gas tank spiked with a screwdriver for God's sake, then petrol poured all over the inside, and set on fire."

"Any prints?"

"Well, here's the thing. On the one hand, total amateur hour, but on the other, this car was cleaned from stem to stern before the fire was set. I think it was wiped with a rag doused in petrol but can't prove it. No prints and any fibers would have gone up in the flames. Sorry, I have absolutely nothing to help your cause other than inform you I can confirm this car was not in an accident, but someone made it look like it was, and poorly at that."

The three shook hands, again Jim lingered his grip on Jenny, and they left.

"You have an admirer there, Jen," Sam said with a smirk as they headed to the car.

"My mother always taught me you catch more flies

with sugar than vinegar."

"Ah, is that what you call it? Catching flies. Looked more like flirting to me."

****

Sam felt the case, while it was true it was very early on, was stagnating, which dampened his jovial mood. He felt frustrated because he needed a clear direction or leads to follow. But he also knew most cases were solved by diligent, tedious investigations, so it became more of a process of elimination, which took time. They headed to the morgue to see what, if any, news Ray Bryant might have. Ray had taken on the senior role of overseeing all the post-mortems in this case. He was almost jovial and excited when they met in his office.

"Forgive me for sounding cheerful, but this case is something we can get our teeth into and is so far from the normal drudgery we have to wade through. Is that a bad thing?" Ray asked.

"Not if you can give us some information to help catch the bastards, no," Sam replied, feeling confident for the first time.

"I just had a call from the site; you know it's ten bodies now? I've had to borrow a couple of pathologists from Melbourne to cope. They are arriving this afternoon."

"*Ten!* No. It was only eight when we left. What the hell has been going on out there?"

"Well, we've only just begun here, and there is an enormous amount of work ahead of us, but I can tell you what we know so far with the four we've been able to conduct preliminaries on. We have three females and one male. They all appear to be aged somewhere between sixteen and twenty-five years old. The females were naked, the male clothed, which may be significant. They were in different states of decay, so they were killed and buried at different times. It all just educated guesswork for the moment, but we have something like one at around six months, one over twelve months, one at three to four years, and finally, one buried over ten years ago."

"Ten years? This has been going on for ten years? My God," Jenny exclaimed.

"I'm afraid so. We will have to designate numbers for these bodies so we all know which ones we are talking about, and all that information will be in the email I will send you this afternoon. But let's start with the oldest one first. She was buried over ten years ago. The cause of death is not difficult due to the obvious massive fracture of the skull. We have numerous fractures all over the body. Still, some seem to be older with calcification than others, leading us to think the girl was held for some considerable time, tortured, and eventually killed. Deep abrasions to the wrists suggest being chained or handcuffed in a standing position; we think this is because the weight of the body hanging has caused deep and distinctive scarring to the wrist bones. She was blonde, average height, we think around twenty years old, but she could have been up to twenty-five years old. The body was devoid of jewelry, and with the complete decomposition, we don't know about tattoos. The body was naked, as were all the women, so there was no clothing to help us identify them. All we have are dental records and DNA. The plastic bags used to hold the bodies and tape have been sent to forensics; however, the bags are generic so will not be easy to trace. We have taken several good fingerprints from the tape used to hold the bags together, which will help if the killers are on file. We also have recovered hair samples, possibly from the murderers, which will give a good DNA sample."

"It's a similar story for the next two females, except without the skull fractures, but there is the same evidence of prolonged torture. The male, which is the most recent, was stabbed. Once again, I would say he was tortured over an extended period. He suffered forty-three stab wounds, and in my opinion, which at this point is not much more than educated guesswork, the accumulation of injuries killed him from blood loss rather than one major wound. It would appear they occurred over time, as some of the scars had partially healed and scabbed over. Interestingly, the male was stabbed, but the females were beaten. Both have been tortured over a long period, so it is suggestive of the offender doing the same things but in different ways, or of course, other killers. Also interesting to note is that the male was clothed, and the females were not, which along with the sexual torture of women, could mean the killers are not gay or bisexual. I'm no profiler, but for what it's worth, your murderers appear to be heterosexual sexual sadists who derive pleasure from imprisoning, raping, and torturing women over a long time. These women, and to a lesser extent, the man, have been through all kinds of hell before they were brutally murdered.

"We have sent off dental records, and within twenty-four hours, we should have a better idea of when they were killed, which may help you with identification through missing person's reports."

He continued, "Because of the number of bodies and the fact they are all decomposed to varying degrees, we've also requested Silvia Renwick's assistance, and she has agreed to come. She is this country's foremost expert on postmortem facial reconstruction and has been instrumental in developing radical software which can show us a reconstructed face in 3D. She has agreed to come tomorrow. She flies in from Sydney around one o'clock. I hope you guys have a big enough budget because this will cost a fortune."

"That's for the higher-ups to worry about, Ray. I just want to catch these two," Jenny nodded in earnest agreement to Sam's statement. She was pale and appeared horrified at the abuse suffered by the victims. "Thanks for the update. You will no doubt be in touch as developments occur?"

"Oh, you can count on that," he smiled back, trying to contain his glee at such a compelling case.

"We better get back to the coal face, Jen. Thanks again, Doc."

In the car, Sam called Bob Young to report while Jenny drove. "Sir, it's Sam. I'm unsure if you have the latest body count, but it's stretching everyone's resources. They're bringing in pathologists from all over the country to help."

"Yeah, I've been advised of that. This case is a nightmare. The Commissioner is behind us and has pretty much given us an open checkbook. This case will have the eyes of the world watching us, and we need to leave no stone unturned, Sam, get me? You let me worry about the budget. You just catch the fuckers."

"Oh, I get you, and I realize we are being watched. Sir, I want to hold a press conference. I think it's best we lay out what we have here early and set up a special crime stopper's phone number. This number of people can't have gone missing without someone seeing something."

"Yep, I agree. I will get the media involved. Let's do something different and hold it on site. Give them a few pictures to help bring home the scope of what we are looking at here. The weather is good, so I will try to organize that for four to four thirty this afternoon, so they can get it on tonight's news and in tomorrow morning's papers. I will front the cameras, Sam, even though it's your case, but I want you alongside me. This will become a media circus, and it's better if I take the heat and leave you to run the investigation. Are you happy with that?"

"Absolutely, sir."

"Okay, I will let you know what's arranged. See you out there later."

Jenny dropped Sam at the pit and left to continue her list of house-to-house interviews. On arrival, he was informed the count had increased to fifteen bodies raised, with a further three identified by the ground-penetrating radar. He stood with hands on hips and looked out over the expanse of gravel, with exposed trenches dotted all over it, feeling an impending doom and self-doubt. It looked like a crazy cemetery without headstones or a scene from a horror movie.

What if we can't identify the killers? he worried. How could he possibly live with himself if he didn't catch them? All those deaths. Each victim had family, and all would want justice served for the loss of their loved ones. The murderers were monsters who kidnapped, tortured, and killed people chained up in handcuffs over an extended time. Things like this just didn't happen in Perth, not to this extent anyway, but then he doubted mass murders on this scale occurred in many places at all. Never had he felt so minuscule and insignificant. There were so many deaths, so much to do, so many people to coordinate, and so many chances to make a mistake. At that moment, his phone rang. He looked at the display in the sunshine and saw Felix's name.

He answered in a morose voice, "Hi, Felix."

"Hey, hot shot. I hear you are the talk of the police world again. How do you do it? How do you get allocated these amazing jobs?"

"Just unlucky, I guess."

"Unlucky? Did you say unlucky? Jesus, what's wrong with you, man? Any cop would give his right arm for this one. This will send your career into the stratosphere."

"Felix, I don't want my career in the stratosphere. You know the saying, 'The bigger they are, the harder they fall.' This is a career-ender if we can't catch them. You all have me wrong. I never sought the limelight. I just wanted to do my job well."

"Sammy, my boy, now, you listen to your uncle Felix for a minute. You're a good cop; if anyone can stop these monsters, you can. Yes, I know you didn't chase being a hero cop, yet you are one so far as everyone is concerned, so enjoy it. You and I both know the plaudits were well-earned and well-deserved. I remember when you worked for me, you were always whining about the boring side of our job and how you wanted to be out there catching bad guys. Well, here you are, and there are none worse than these."

He laughed a very depressed laugh. "You mean I should have been more careful what I wished for?"

"Okay, Sam. What's wrong? What's really going on here?"

"Felix, it's such a big case. We've got the original killing, plus fifteen bodies now dug up here and another three waiting to be exhumed. I've got no leads or evidence until forensics get back to me, and that could take ages because of the sheer volume of work we've dumped on them. It's spiraling out of control, and there is nothing constructive I can do. I feel like I'm drowning in victims, and my biggest fear is that I will muck it all up."

"Sam, you forget that without you and Jenny in the first place, you wouldn't have those bodies to investigate. Sadly, you and I both know most cops would have gone with the accident report and thought the girl was hysterical. You don't get to work in Major Crime unless you're good, and you certainly don't get to run Major Crime unless you are the best of the best. Bob Young is a great boss, and he won't let you muck up, but he won't be staring over your shoulder, either. Let me tell you this about him; he is the best in the world, bar none, at driving an investigation at arm's reach. He will be there to help, guide, and, when necessary, lead every step of the way while letting you follow your instincts. Don't panic, my boy. Embrace this chance you've been given and do what you're best at, which is being a cop, and a good one at that. If he didn't think you could do this, he would have taken it away from you. Don't stress about the things you can't control. Just do what feels right."

After a lengthy pause, Sam had to agree. This wasn't his first day in the big school. It was the Major Crime Squad, and he had earned the right to work in it. "Thanks, Felix. I needed that shot of encouragement."

"Sam, don't get bogged down in how big this case

is. It doesn't matter how many bodies there are; that just means they will have made more mistakes. The victims were killed by the same men, and they will have made errors. You know that; they always do. These guys have done it for so long they would have become complacent and can't imagine being caught. They think they are safe, but they're not. Supercop is on their trail. And I know you, Sam. You will either find their mistakes, or your gut instinct will kick in, and you will make a leap of faith and *will* catch them. I've never worked with anyone who can understand what's going on or see a problem that everyone else has missed, like you can, hot shot. You will be fine. Just go with the flow."

"Fancy a beer after work?"

"Not tonight. The wife is dragging me along to her book club. We're reviewing the latest Michael Connolly. Tomorrow though, I can fit you in, but it's your buy."

"Book club? Must be a bad line. Sounded like you said you were going to your wife's book club."

"Sammy, if you ever stop screwing skanks and floozies, settle down, and get married, you will realize the beauty of a relationship is sometimes sharing your partner's interests."

"Nuh, not getting it. This is a terrible line. It sounded then like you used the word 'floozies,' but people stopped talking like that in the sixties, so you can't have."

"Get back to work, hot shot. You've got nineteen murders to solve."

"Hey, Felix. Thanks, man. I appreciate the call and the vote of confidence." But the line was dead. Felix had hung up; he could never handle being thanked.

Chapter 10

Identifying the Unidentifiable

Bob Young arrived back on site just before four to bedlam. The rusty entry gate had been oiled and re-hinged so it could be kept guarded and closed to assist in keeping people out. Inevitably news had leaked that a major incident had occurred at the quarry, and hordes of sightseers had descended. The gravel road leading into the pit was clogged with vehicles parked askew, and reporters and sightseers tried to take pictures of the burial ground. One enterprising reporter had brought an aluminum step ladder to stand on to see over the heads of others. A local family sat on a blanket with a chiller box full of sandwiches and cool drinks, as this level of excitement had never been seen before in sleepy Roleystone.

Sam had posted patrol cops around the top rim of the quarry as photographers with telephoto lenses attempted to take pictures of the recovery process going on at ground level. A freelance photographer, trying to get a perfect shot that he could sell internationally, had slipped on the shifting gravel slope and fell, breaking a two-thousand-dollar camera and his left leg. He required a helicopter to lift him from the hill, but the ambulance to take him to the hospital was hampered by the cars parked in the roadway. Sam requested and was given more uniformed police, who issued move-on notices. Slowly, the circus finished, and order was restored, though Sam felt he was more like a traffic director than a Major Crime Inspector, which added to his frustration.

Once the road was cleared, outside TV broadcast vans with satellite dishes on the roofs were permitted to enter the pit and park alongside the mobile HQ; on the strict understanding it would be a temporary situation only for the duration of the press conference, and then they would have to leave.

Medical examiners' vehicles had been coming and going with monotonous regularity, taking exhumed bodies to the morgue. The quarry resembled a combination of a bombed war zone and a graveyard moving many to tears. It was sobering for all who saw the now twenty-three open graves from which bodies had been removed.

It was hard for newcomers to the site to comprehend that number of murders until confronted by the desolation of the open graves stretching out into the distance. The scene made the number of victims more understandable, and many officers were psychologically affected and required counseling.

There was now a definite odor of decay in the still, stifling air. The next day, one reporter called it the smell of death in their headline. To those who were there, it was a very apt description. Whether the smell was real or imagined, everyone experienced it and would be haunted for years.

****

At four-fifteen, Sam assembled the cameramen and photographers and led them to a roped-off area where the bodies had been found. The spot had been examined with the surface radar unit, sifted for evidence, and deemed safe for people to stand. Sam had chosen this spot because the true scope of the number of graves could be appreciated and filmed, and the string lines for the grid search showed areas that had not yet been searched.

One reporter, a veteran from reporting during the Bosnian conflict, likened the scene to a war crimes burial site, and others nodded sagely. As if it had been orchestrated, which it had not, while they were filming, a body wrapped in black plastic was hoisted from another hole in the ground in the distance. The bundle was loaded onto a gurney and solemnly wheeled to the waiting Medical Examiner's van. The picture made the front pages of almost every daily newspaper in the country, dramatically increasing circulation. Such a case had never been seen before, and everyone wanted to read the details, such as were available.

Sam led the reporters back to the awning on the side of the mobile command post, where he had set up a desk for himself and Bob to sit at. Louise Archer, from Police Media, fussed around the reporters and assisted in setting up microphones. To the distant northeast, cumulus clouds were building, making the weather humid. Rain was forecast to arrive overnight, which would slow the searches if heavy, and that was what had been suggested would come.

At precisely four-thirty, Bob Young exited the command post, having used the phone to speak with the medical examiner's office to get the latest information. He had also made courtesy calls to the parents of Greg Brady and Tammy Reynolds and informed them of the press conference, letting them know their names would be released. There could be no avoiding it. Tammy would be in the spotlight, so she and her family needed to be warned.

In Bob's hand was the statement he would read, which had been approved by Louise. Once they were seated, he looked around at everyone to ensure cameras and microphones were turned on. Bob was generally popular with the media, as he always treated them respectfully, recognizing they had a job to do, so long as they understood he did too and had to limit what was released. Once he finished scanning the faces of those waiting, he cleared his throat and began.

"Ladies and gentlemen, I want to thank you for coming out and helping us launch this appeal for help from the public. This is without doubt the most serious case of serial murder this state, this country, has ever seen. I will be reading from a statement, and I would ask there be no interruptions until I'm finished. Then I or Detective Inspector Sam Collins here, who is heading the investigation, will be pleased to answer questions. Is that understood?"

There was a murmur of assent from the twenty or so people hanging on every word.

"On Saturday night, two young people, Tammy Reynolds and Greg Brady, met at a local birthday party and discretely left to come here to be alone. I want to make it perfectly clear this couple has done nothing wrong, and this spot has a bit of a reputation for young people to come to and park. We were all that age once ourselves, weren't we?" He smiled and received some knowing smiles back.

"While they were here, another vehicle arrived with two men. They did not see Greg's car, which he had parked behind me amongst those small hills. Tammy and

Greg observed the two men remove a large bundle from their vehicle and proceed to bury it. The young couple believed they were witnessing a corpse being buried, and when Greg Brady, a courageous young man, went to investigate, he was viciously beaten to death."

He paused to let that sink in before starting again. "The young lady, Tammy Reynolds, witnessed the attack and attempted to intervene to save her friend. I would like it noted this young lady showed outstanding courage and will be recommended for a Premier's Bravery Award when she is well enough to receive it. When the two offenders turned on her, she ran. Luckily, she is a particularly fit woman who participates in cross-country running. Even though she was barefooted, she ran up that slope to my right toward the pine trees you can see up on top."

Everyone turned to look at the slope incredulously, and the sound of cameras clicking filled the air.

"The two offenders chased and hunted her throughout the night, but she eluded capture because of her fortitude, bravery, and determination. Tammy suffered numerous cuts, bruises, and abrasions in her successful escape from what would have been, without doubt, her murder."

Again, he paused and looked around the assembled people to ensure they realized the magnitude of her escape. Once he was sure he had the desired effect, he continued.

"In the early hours of the morning, the murderers gave up their chase of Tammy and returned here to remove Mr. Brady's body and his vehicle. They then took it away to stage a vehicular accident to try to cover up their crime. Miss Reynolds was left to wander through the hills delirious, injured, and exhausted. It was a particularly cold night and by the next day she was suffering from hypothermia. Fortunately, she was found by a local farmer and taken to hospital, where I'm pleased to report she is making a fantastic recovery."

There was a groundswell of comments with that news.

"Due to outstanding investigative police work by Detective Inspector Collins and Detective Sergeant Jenny Markham, the killers' subterfuge was seen through. A search was undertaken to locate the body, which Miss Reynolds said she saw them bury. Unfortunately, we have found considerably more than just one body. We have uncovered twenty-six corpses, of which we have conducted preliminary examinations on eighteen. Of those eighteen, we can say fourteen are young women, while four are young men. All the victims are aged between eighteen and twenty-five."

The reporters could not contain themselves any longer. Some stood and began yelling out questions, all ignored by both detectives, who sat stone-faced until order had been restored.

"Thank you. We understand your shock and horror, but please be patient. Your questions will all be answered with the information we have and are prepared to release now." He looked around at everyone to reassert his authority. He would not be rushed by anyone, and Sam was impressed with his poise and confident air.

Bob continued reading, "Thus far, we have only had time, because of the sheer number of bodies located, for preliminary examinations. We can say the deaths seem to date back over many years, possibly as far back as fifteen to twenty years." The commotion inevitably started again, and Bob sat back in his chair, looked down at his fingernails, and waited. He understood the press's shock and interest. This was a once-in-a-lifetime story they were given access to, and everyone seemed to be morbidly fascinated with serial killers. *TV crime dramas have a lot to answer for,* he thought.

When everyone settled down, he started again, "Our medical examiners and pathologists are working around the clock. We have brought other pathologists and specialists from other states to assist, as no one department is geared up for this many bodies at once. Obviously, there is a lot we don't know, and more information will be forthcoming from forensic testing that should help us identify the killers. We know these young people have been abducted, held against their will, sexually abused, and tortured over a long time until they were murdered." Again, there were raised voices, but this time it was mainly angry outbursts rather than questions being shouted out.

"We would like the public to assist with any information at all to help us capture these two individuals, no matter how insignificant they feel it is. Sometimes it can be something inconsequential to someone by itself, which provides the vital missing piece to the investigators. We are looking for two offenders. One is male, with a gruff voice. We assume the other one is, too; however, it's possible the second one is female. They drive a four-wheel drive wagon, but at this point, we don't have a make or model. They know this area very well, so either they live in or around Roleystone, or they once did. There is also the matter of the staged accident; we would like to talk to anyone who noticed a black late model Commodore sedan, with a four-wheel drive wagon behind it on Brookton Highway, in the early hours of Saturday night or Sunday morning. We would ask anyone who has witnessed anything suspicious in or around this gravel pit to come forward. Once again, I want to stress; sometimes it can be the most insignificant piece of information which helps link other facts we have together. We will now take questions."

"Any ideas at all on why they are killing people, Inspector?"

Sam cleared his throat, "At this point, it would only be supposition, and we don't want to have preconceived ideas that may later turn out to be wrong. We don't know why they are killing people other than the most obvious reason; they like it."

"How is Miss Reynolds' health?

"I'm really pleased to report she is doing well. She was dehydrated and suffered a lot of cuts and bruises, but the worst of her injuries were on her feet. We saw her in hospital last night, and she is in good spirits under the circumstances and is recovering. She has wonderful family support and good friends around her. This is truly a remarkable young woman."

"Should local residents be scared for their own safety, Inspector?"

"People should always be vigilant, naturally, and yes, they should be particularly on the lookout now we know we have these killers on the loose. But, while we don't know too much about the victims yet, we believe they are not local. That number of missing people would have been noticed long before now if they all came from the same area. They are more likely to be transients or backpackers by their apparent age, but we will know more as we start identifying them."

"What should people be watching out for?"

"Good question. Look if anyone has seen any unusual activity around here. We need to know about it. Perhaps a vehicle was seen coming here more than once. We are interested in anyone seen here who drives a four-wheel drive station wagon. We would like to talk to anyone who has visited here for any reason, even if they didn't see anything. Someone else may have seen them, so it's important we can exclude them from our inquiries. Then, of course, there are the perpetrators, two people, and most likely male but could possibly be a male and female couple. Anyone who has seen two people appear to be acting strangely on Sunday or just after. We know that serial killers often appear to be perfectly normal most of the time, but around or after the killing, they can be erratic or seem disturbed. We will soon have times of death, but for now, if anyone knows of someone who at times appears to be erratic, let us know."

"My wife is erratic, frequently," someone shouted out, but this attempt at gallows humor went unanswered, and a pregnant silence followed, which allowed Bob Young to stand up and thank everyone for coming.

Sam's phone rang, and he excused himself from answering it. "Sam Collins."

"It's Ray Bryant, Inspector. We have one victim identified. Her name is Ingrid Stapenda. Twenty years old when reported missing by her parents, who live in Finland. She and a girlfriend, Doria, were traveling around Australia, and she went missing in June two years ago. I'm guessing her girlfriend will be one of the other victims. The MISPER report will be in your email within minutes. One other thing." He paused. "We have found what looks like some sort of pollen in seven of the body bags. We've sent it off for analysis, but that could help you track where they were killed."

"That's good. Thanks, Doctor."

"We could be working together quite a while on this case. Call me Ray."

"OK, Ray, I will, but only if you call me Sam."

"Deal, gotta go. Huge number of bodies to get through, and you people keep finding more. Tallyho."

Sam shook his head. *That guy is enjoying this way too much,* he thought. Next, Sam wondered what the time difference was between Perth and Finland. He would need to contact the parents and deliver the bad news but also question them about the last time they spoke to her.

The reporters were packing up their equipment when Sam found Bob talking to one of the TV journalists. Sam asked if he could speak with him. Bob held a hand to signify goodbye to the well-known TV personality and followed Sam into the HQ van.

"Sir, we have an ID on one of the victims, a backpacker from Finland who went missing over two years ago. Do you think I should call the parents or ask the local police to attend?"

"Hmm. Either way, it's a shit fight. After all this time, they will still be living on hope. I think it best to get the Finnish Police version of victim support to visit personally. Give me the details, and I will make the call for you, Commander to Commander. I will have them ask the basic questions, too but request the parents phone you when they are able. How does that sound? There's going to be a lot of these phone calls to make. The worst part of the job is destroying people's hope," Bob said glumly.

"Thanks, sir. The MISPER report will be emailed

any time now. Any idea of the time difference between here and there?"

"No idea, but with the power of Google...." He pulled out his phone and tapped on the screen while Sam opened his email to look for the report. "Hmm, that's not too bad. We are only six hours ahead this time of year, so it's perfect for making the call straight away."

He picked up a phone on the desk and called his personal assistant, "Jackie, it's Bob. Can you find me someone in authority I can talk to with the Helsinki Police Department? Their version of Major Crime would be good. Helsinki? It's in Finland. Finland is in Scandinavia. Thanks. Call me back, will you? Soon as you can, cheers."

While they waited, they both read the report. Ingrid and Doria had started their working holiday in Sydney, slowly worked their way west, and reached Perth five months into their trip. They hadn't intended to visit Perth but had met two male backpackers from Scotland heading over and tagged along, thinking there was safety in numbers. The boys moved back to Scotland three weeks later.

Ingrid contacted her mother in Finland without fail every Friday, and during the last contact said they had landed some fruit-picking work and had decided to stay two weeks longer. Cheap accommodation was offered with the job as part of the deal, but she hadn't disclosed where. Then nothing further. Her mobile phone never answered again, and when police tried to investigate her disappearance, the phone carrier informed them it had been disconnected, so it couldn't be traced. With such scant information, the investigation wasn't taken too seriously. It was assumed Ingrid had met a boyfriend and would turn up, but she never did. There are so many orchards and fruit farms in and around Perth, then down to the South of the state, it wasn't deemed important enough to send a detective to interview all of them.

There wasn't anything else to go on. The two lads had been contacted in Scotland but could shed no further light. They had not had sexual relationships with the girls. They were just travel companions, they had said, and could shed no light on the fruit-picking job Ingrid had mentioned. The inquiry, such as it was, was scaled back to six monthly reviews.

Jackie called back with the information, and Bob telephoned the Helsinki Police Department. He explained the situation and provided the families' details. They lived in Kouvola, a city apparently north of Helsinki, and he was assured it would be taken care of with the promise to report back once accomplished.

Chapter 11

A Break from Routine

A strange malaise affected the senior officers and investigators collectively that night. Everyone was shocked and saddened by the number of deaths and the disregard for humanity shown by the cold-hearted killers. They left the site, the morgue, or the forensic laboratory that evening feeling dejected at the lack of progress and depressed. At the same time, there was a sense of anticipation the following day could provide the breakthrough which could lead to the capture of what looked to be some of the worst serial killers in the country's history.

It was known most of the victims examined so far seemed to be of a similar age. Young people, primarily women, had left school and traveled around before returning home to start further education or a career. There were many more bodies to study, but that was the investigators' thinking. The thought of two monsters preying on defenseless young travelers sickened everyone connected with the case, especially those with children of their own.

****

Jenny Markham phoned her ex-husband, Mike, who had seen the press conference on TV and heard her name mentioned as one of the lead investigators. She explained she had just finished a horrible day and asked if she could see her son, Josh, and take him out for dinner. Jenny understood it wasn't a night she had been allocated by the Family Court, but this night she felt she needed to hug him.

She gave her ex a brief rundown on the case and told him the targets were young people. Her husband, who had never recovered emotionally when she left him for another woman, could hear the sincerity and anguish in her voice, and his heart melted. Mike took pity and invited her to come around for dinner, so it would be like old times, at least for a while. She wiped tears of gratitude from her eyes as she thanked him. Jenny knew Mike was, and always had been, a very good man and appreciated his kindness.

Jenny arrived early and handed Mike a bottle of red wine, which she knew he would enjoy. While Mike cooked, Jenny sat in her son's room, helping him with homework and talking about his sports, friends, and girlfriend prospects. She basked in the normality of the evening and, at one moment, looked up at the doorway to see her husband smiling back at her.

Since the breakup, Mike had not dated a woman, though he had received offers. He hoped Jenny would return to him one day, and he thought that if he went with other women, she would not do that if she believed he had slammed the door shut on their relationship. Mike cooked lamb chops, potatoes, green beans, and corn. They were superb. The three ate dinner like any other family, and Jenny realized she missed the normalcy of life together. The red wine was enjoyed, shared equally between them, but she drank lots of water, too, so she could drive home.

Jenny had a fantastic night, and after Josh had gone to bed, Mike stood with Jenny at the front door. She looked him in the eye and said, "Thank you so much for tonight, Mike. I really, *really* needed it, and you were there for me. I can't thank you enough."

"I enjoyed having you here. It was like back in the days we were happy. I'm sorry we had so much angst between us when we split. Seeing you tonight with Josh made me realize how spiteful I've been to keep you apart. I was trying to punish you for abandoning me, and that was wrong. I'm sorry for being a jerk in the past. You will always be welcome here. Call in anytime you like. It's time to let bygones be bygones. Josh misses you, and so do I."

A tear appeared in Jenny's eye, and she stepped closer to him and hugged him tightly. He hugged her back, but both felt the awkwardness of the past had left a gulf between them; perhaps that distance could be bridged one day, but not quite yet.

"Thanks, Mike. You're a good man. I'm so sorry for what happened. It was never intentional. I hope you know that; none of it was your fault."

"I've been reading Cosmopolitan and other women's magazine articles quite a lot lately, trying to understand what it must have been like for you. Some days I think I get it, but then others, I just want things the way they were. I'm sorry about that."

"You. Reading Cosmo? Really?" She was stunned. This was not the same man she had married.

"Better late than never, Jen. You can stay the night, you know, and I don't mean in my bed. There is a perfectly good spare room, all made up if you want it. You could be here for breakfast with Josh."

She looked at him. This was a side she'd never seen before. "Do you mean that, Mike, really and truly?"

"Yeah, I think I've finally grown up enough to want you as a friend, a good friend. Even if we can't be together as a couple. You and I created something real special in Josh. He deserves to have his mum and dad, as much as he wants or needs. And you, Jen, you need to see your son more when you can."

"I won't tonight, but only because I'm not prepared for it, and I have to pick up the boss really early in the morning. But I would love to stay over some weekends, and we can both do things with Josh as a family. That would be fantastic, but I wouldn't want to intrude on your life or spoil anything you have going on with, you know, another woman. I'd be happy to sit with Josh if you had a date even."

He grinned lopsidedly, and Jenny saw it was a sad one. "I've not dated anyone, Jen, and I'm in no hurry to. If and when I do, you will be the first to know. When you've had the greatest, it's hard to accept second best, and for me, you were the best."

"Oh, Mike, I'm so sorry." He looked so sad and forlorn. Jenny continued kindly, "Okay, then. It's a deal. How about this weekend? Thank you, Mike."

After a short pause, he said, "This weekend works for me. Jen, can I ask you one thing, you know, about the sex side of things?"

Oh, oh, she thought, *here comes the inevitable 'why' question. Why a woman?* As if she had made a deliberate choice. Jenny had tried to explain it all before, of course, but at the time, he had been so hurt and angry he wouldn't, or couldn't, listen. But, tonight, he had been so sweet; she felt she owed him an explanation if he wanted one. "Of course, you can. Ask me anything."

"I've never stopped loving you and missing you, Jen. I hope you know that. Like I said, I've been reading up on things to see where I went wrong or what I could have done better. Even if I could have been more understanding for you. And well…it seems lots of men now accept their wives' bisexuality and don't mind they have, you know, open relations with other women. Do you think that sort of thing could ever work for us if we tried?"

Jenny was stunned and genuinely touched. "I don't know what to say or how to answer that. I'm not sure anything can be so simple. I've been a mess of conflicting emotions ever since it happened. Some days I don't know myself anymore. But do you know that's just about the most wonderful thing you've ever said to me?"

"Will you at least think about it, Jen? Come and stay for a weekend or two, just as friends, and think about it. No pressure."

"Yes, I promise I will."

She left, thoughtful, and realized deep down inside she still loved the one and only male partner she had ever had. They met at school, and Mike was her first and only love until she fell for Megan. Could she go back? Could it be that simple? Could she be hetero only? Which relationship was real, and which was a fantasy that came to life? She had some thinking to do.

****

Bob Young and his wife Candice had two children. Their son was nineteen and studying engineering; their daughter was seventeen and finishing her last year of school soon. Before he left his office for the day, he called home and told his wife not to cook dinner. He wanted the family to have some fun together and proposed going to their local bowling alley. He suggested eating hot dogs and hamburgers and enjoying some laughs while bowling as a family. Candice had seen the TV reports and knew her husband was suffering emotionally.

The media storm featuring the Rolleystone Murders showed on every TV channel and radio news broadcast from five in the evening. As the true horror of the story unfolded, the phone lines in the Crime Stoppers phone room lit up with hundreds of calls. Bob's mobile phone was turned off, intentionally, so he could enjoy his family time, knowing the next day would be a nightmare. Right then, he needed quality time with the people he loved to help 'ground him.'

Each time he sat down and one of his children bowled a ball, he watched them like a hawk, eternally grateful that one of the bodies dug up at the gravel pit wasn't one of his. No parent should ever outlive their children, especially if they have been murdered.

Bob often thought about how lucky the public was while how unfortunate police officers were. The public didn't have to deal with kids being mugged, attacked, hurt in car accidents, or even murdered; they were wrapped in a cocoon of ignorance, and Bob knew that was how it should be. The suicide rate among police officers was incredibly high for many reasons, but one stood out. Front-line police officers saw the worst ways people can treat each other, while the public just read about it in their newspapers.

That night, he knew how much he loved his children and wife of twenty-six years. It was more than he had the words to describe, and at times his voice broke with emotion. His wife could see he was troubled while having had a fantastic family night together. Rather than put on the flannelette nightie she usually wore on cooler nights, she went to him naked. She knew this man she loved with all her heart needed to feel the closeness and intimacy of her love for him. She approached, took him into her loving mouth until she sensed his urgency, then moved up his body and held him tightly. Afterward, she lay on his chest, soothing him with love and listening to his heartbeat.

****

Ray Bryant was single but married to his work. He kept a foldaway bed in his office for those times when the day had slipped away from him, and it became too late to go to his home in Mount Hawthorn. That night, he went for drinks after work at The Old Baileys Bar with some of the other pathologists. He wanted to show his appreciation to the ones who had come from interstate to help them in what was, without doubt, their most significant and gruesome murder case in recorded history.

June Brookton was a pathologist who had arrived from Melbourne that day and gone straight to work. She had separated from her husband several months before. She was much like Ray in that she lived for her work, and her husband left her for a woman who was prepared to stay home more and didn't smell of death or formaldehyde. That was one of the reasons she had volunteered to come to the West to help. The other was it was a fascinating case, and like Ray, it stimulated her intellectually.

As kindred spirits, they naturally spent a lot of time

together at the pub. After their first bottle of white wine, they discussed unconventional ways of estimating times of death and got so absorbed in the conversation they missed the rest of the party leaving for dinner at eight.

By eleven o'clock, they were back at his home drinking their third bottle of wine, neither having eaten, totally absorbed in each other. They shared opinions about rates of decomposition in tropical climates, different species of maggots and larval development, and other conversations that only two people of their calling could possibly comprehend, let alone find interesting.

Suddenly she stood up, staggering slightly from the wine, and said in a slurred voice, "For God's sake, Ray. What does a girl have to do to get laid in this state?" Without any further words, she began to take her clothes off.

They made frantic love on the couch, then in his bed for a second time. They were both late for work the following day as they dallied for a third time in the shower.

On arrival at the morgue, they suffered knowing smiles and glances from the rest of the staff. Despite their best efforts to hide it, it was obvious to everyone what they had been up to all night.

If two people were destined to be with each other, it was Ray and June. Throughout the day, their eyes would search for each other across the examination room. She was already thinking of requesting a transfer to Perth, smitten with the man who was ideally suited to her.

****

Sam Collins sat in his apartment watching the news for the second time on a different channel while nursing his scotch on ice. Not that he needed to see how he looked on screen in an egotistical way, but Sam wanted to know how the media treated the press conference. He was pleased the TV stations hadn't glamorized or sensationalized the story. The subject matter was serious enough without that. Sam thought he looked serious, intense even, without being miserable.

When his mobile phone rang, he had eaten most of the pizza he'd had home delivered. The number was withheld, and Sam debated whether to answer it but decided he should, though he felt it would probably be a reporter.

"Sam Collins," he said, trying not to sound too annoyed.

"Hi, Sam, it's Caroline Naismith. We met at Didi's wedding recently. I was her bridesmaid and housemate, and I dragged you up on the dancefloor, wounded shoulder and all."

"Oh, hi, Caroline. How are you? It's nice to hear from you!" She had quite a sexy, husky voice, and he remembered her instantly. Had he not been with Felix at the wedding, he thought he could have ended up in bed with her; such was the chemistry between them on the dancefloor.

He cast his mind back to remember her; she was a good-looking girl, as you would expect from a woman who made her living as a lap dancer. She was tall, blonde, and possessed a killer body and a very self-confident air. Her sense of self was very alluring to him, as he had little time for soft women, preferring those with opinions who stood up for what they believed in.

"Well, here's the thing, Sam. I did wonder if you would ever call me, as you promised you would, and who should I see on TV tonight but you? I thought it was an omen. And, if you don't mind me saying so, you look tired and stressed. I thought you needed to hear a friendly voice, and here it is. Not to sound too Muslim, but if the mountain won't come to Mohammed, etcetera."

"I'm glad you called, Caroline; you've brightened up an otherwise awful day. I would have called you, you know. It's just my first day back at work, I caught this case, and it's been very draining and demanding since. Before that, I had no time and needed to get clear from my previous relationship. I honestly haven't had time this week, but rest assured I would have phoned, eventually. Plus, of course, I didn't want to seem too eager and scare you off."

"Well, in that case, I'm glad I called you first, just so long as I don't sound desperate, either. I need to tell you I stopped dancing two months ago. That's just to clear up any misconception you may have of me. I'm not sure if you knew; for all I know, you didn't care anyway." She giggled nervously before continuing, "I didn't really get to talk much with you at the wedding. I know you know I was working with Didi, lap dancing at the Palace, but with all the drama that went on, it opened my eyes to the sort of people we were working for. I thought enough was enough, so I left. By the way, I was never a hooker; I hope you know that.

"I'm glad, Caroline, and no, I didn't think you were a hooker. They are not nice people to work for, and you are far better away from that crowd. So, what *are* you doing these days?"

"I went back to school to finish my degree. Stop laughing. It's true. Since my mum died a couple of years back, I started dancing to help pay my university tuition fees but to be honest; the money was too good at the club.

Studying suddenly seemed too hard, and I wondered what the point was in working my heart out to end up with a degree and earning half what I was when I danced. At first, I thought I would take a year off but then didn't go back when the year was up. But the good thing is I have plenty of savings now, so I've returned and can pay my way until I graduate next year."

"I'm really pleased for you, and I wasn't laughing. You strike me as an intelligent, strong-willed woman who's beautiful and knows how to use it."

She laughed and said, "Maybe not out loud, but you *were* laughing, I bet. I know what people thought of me back then; she's blonde, a bimbo, and works as a lap dancer, which means she can't possibly have a brain, so she must be a hooker. Am I right?"

"I never thought you were a natural blonde." She saw the humor and giggled again, a friendly, genuine laugh. Most importantly, as far as Sam was concerned, she didn't snort at the end, like his previous girlfriend did. "What are you studying?"

"I'm doing a double, Sports Science and Sports Psychology."

"Wow, I'm impressed. Do you miss the dancing?"

"Mostly no, but I've always been a natural flirt, and I enjoyed that side. A normal relationship doesn't usually work too well for me because even though I am one hundred percent faithful, most guys get jealous and clingy, believing I couldn't possibly dance nude and remain true. Besides Didi and Brie, most of my friends are men; women are far too catty for me. I've always been happy with my body too, and I don't think it's a problem to show it off, so I never saw anything wrong with dancing for tips. I never ever screwed a customer for money; just saying, and not because you're a cop. Though I must say, plenty did. You know what Didi said about you and me?"

"Yep. She told me I should lock you in handcuffs and make love to you repeatedly. Just joking. No, what did she say?"

"Oh, my God, she promised she wouldn't tell my fantasy. She told you that, seriously? Nah, I'm kidding, too, now. She said you and I would have beautiful children. She thinks you are hot, and err, I agree with that too."

"What, with me being hot or us having beautiful children together?"

"Both, dummy. Sheesh, men." She laughed again. "So, Sammy, if you don't mind my saying, you looked and sounded stressed on TV. It seems like to me you need a massage, and you'd be doing me a favor by letting me practice my sports massage techniques on you."

"Hmm, well, there's the first problem; I don't have any sports injuries. But I could fake one, I suppose. Let me think about it…okay, I've thought, and the answer is yes. I'm a sucker for a good massage by a beautiful woman. I can fit you into my hectic schedule if it's purely educational and doesn't lead to us having beautiful children together."

"Good job I'm on the pill then. Well, that only leaves one question: your place or mine?" Her voice had become huskier and, Sam had to admit, downright sexy.

"Have to be here, I'm afraid. I've had two rather large scotches, so can't drive, and I have my sergeant picking me up very early in the morning, so cabbing it back here would be a pain."

"How about if you text me your address while I get

my stuff together? Let's see if I can destress you, big boy."

****

That was how the major players spent the night before what was to become the worst day in Western Australia's criminal history. At the end of the next day, each looked back on the night before as the calm before the storm.

In total, forty-three bodies were discovered buried in the pit, all but one wrapped in black plastic. They were each in varying states of decay, but all had one thing in common; they had all suffered horrible, terrifying deaths at the hands of one or more sadistic, sexually deviant sociopaths.

Book 2
Lost in the Depths

"When we remember we are all mad, the mysteries disappear,
And life stands explained."

~Mark Twain

Chapter 12

Evil Dawns

Clancy was a problem child from the moment he was born. His birth took thirty-three hours of pure agony for his mother, so it could be said he was a problem before he was born. His parents, Tim and Lena, should have taken his dreadful drawn-out, painful birth as an omen of things to come and immediately given him up for adoption.

From the first day home from the birthing suite at Armadale Public Hospital, he seemed intent on driving his mother and father insane. Naturally, to them, he was their pride and joy, a beautiful baby boy named after his father's grandfather and would be the last of their three children. They did not intend to have any more, and once they experienced Clancy, Lena had her tubes tied, so it would be impossible. The couple did not have the slightest inkling of what was to come.

Clancy would not take a full feed from the breast,

ever. He would fall into a deep sleep only halfway through and not wake from it no matter what. That would mean he was awake and hungry again every one and a half to two hours. One thing which wasn't wrong with him was he had been born with a healthy set of lungs, and he would not stop screaming until he was fed again, during which he would fall asleep, and the cycle would begin again. Nothing worked, no matter how much they tried to keep him awake to complete a full meal. It was a cycle the parents could not break. Neither the doctor nor visiting family nurse could offer any help, only saying he would grow out of it. After three months of sleepless nights, Tim and Lena were at their wits' end and constantly argued with each other simply because they were so tired.

They weren't the only ones to suffer from sleepless nights. Clancy's brother and sister were woken up constantly throughout the night. This happened so often that his brother, Benjamin, and sister, Charmaine, grew up with an intense dislike for him, which they never got over and didn't let him forget. As the years ahead were to show, their dislike deepened due to the extra attention Clancy received from their parents while they got less. To them, Clancy was *the chosen one*, and they went out of their way to make his life miserable because of the suffering they experienced when he was a baby.

The family lived on a farm in County Narrogin, Western Australia. There were no neighbors within earshot of Clancy's most lusty screams other than the farm manager, who had his own cabin. The nearest property was almost ten kilometers away.

One night, when Tim and Lena could take no more, they decided to let him scream himself to sleep or until his next feed was due, whichever came first. Then, going forward, they would ensure each meal would be when it was due and not one second before. The problem was they had given into Clancy's demanding feeding schedule for three months, and he was not going to take any change without a fight. Even then, his powerfully selfish nature knew no bounds. To the parents' credit, despite Clancy's panic-stricken hysterics, they stuck to their guns.

It took six days. Six long, scream-filled days before young Clancy got the message he would be fed at his parents' timetable and not his. Even as a baby, it seemed he made a conscious decision to make them pay for the power struggle's outcome.

Clancy's brother believed this was the start of a litany of problems that Clancy bestowed on them for the rest of their lives as punishment. Even after he relented and accepted his feeding schedule, he would whimper in his sleep. Clancy's mother thought he did it to remind himself that this was not what he wanted, and Clancy was making sure he wouldn't forget as he got older.

His grandmother said Clancy was a *"contrary and ornery"* child. His grandfather said he was just a "naughty little fucker" and needed a good slapping at least once a week but preferably daily, whether he needed it or not. But his parents never stopped trying to do their best for him. Sadly, in Clancy's opinion, their best was rarely anywhere near good enough.

It wasn't so much that he was deliberately naughty or did terrible things. It was more of a matter of him always wanting his way. Nothing else was acceptable. It didn't matter if what he wanted was right or wrong; he wanted it regardless, and there would be hell to pay if he didn't get it.

One day, aged three years old, Clancy decided he wanted to tie his own shoelaces before his mother took them all to town for a shopping trip and a doctor's visit. He would not, under any circumstances, allow anyone else to tie them for him. When his mother insisted, Clancy punched her arm. While it didn't hurt overly much, she was shocked at the savage look of fury on Clancy's face, which stopped Lena in her tracks. Lena knew he would keep hitting her until he got his way; his steely look of rage and determination frightened her. Clancy had no idea how to tie his laces, but that didn't matter. He sat on the floor for nearly two hours, repeatedly trying and becoming angrier with every failed attempt. He wouldn't allow anyone to show him how to do it; he decided that was the day to tie his own laces and damn the consequences.

Finally, he had a tangle that held together but only lasted five steps before unraveling. Clancy fell to the floor, screaming and kicking with a fury Lena had never seen. While he wriggled and fought like a caged tiger, Lena tied the laces and dragged him to the car. During the forty-minute drive into town, Clancy did not stop screaming.

****

His brother and sister started bullying Clancy even when he was a baby. They simply despised him with a passion that belied their young age. They hated him for all the extra attention he got while they, the well-behaved children, had to take the emotional leftovers from their weary mother and father. They felt the situation was unjust and set out to make his life a living hell in any way they could.

Often, when Clancy was a baby and asleep in his crib, Ben or Charmaine would pinch the skin on his arms and legs or hit him in the stomach. They would sometimes do it, too, when he least expected it while awake. There was no warning. If one of them was alone with Clancy, they would punish him, but never hard enough to bruise or leave a tell-tale mark. The culprit would then act innocent and say Clancy had begun crying for no reason. Later, when Clancy could talk and would tell his mother or father what had happened, they were so used to Clancy screaming for no apparent reason they said he was making it up. Clancy would then be punished for telling lies. It became Ben and Charmain's sport, and they dreamed up new ways of making Clancy's life miserable. They would giggle together at night when one of them came up with an excellent way to get him into trouble, and they would carry out the plan the next day, while appearing to be innocent.

When Clancy turned six years old, he began retaliating and hitting his brother or sister back as hard as he could. Being both older and stronger than him, his attempts to hurt them made little difference, but it didn't stop Clancy from trying. Whenever they hurt him, he responded with as much force as his six-year-old body could muster, which led to fighting. Clancy always came off second best, much to Ben and Charmaine's delight. Occasionally, Clancy's retaliation was witnessed but not the initial attack, and Clancy got into trouble for hitting his brother or sister. It didn't matter that Clancy complained they had started it, which his siblings strenuously denied. Generally, both parents believed their version of events over Clancy's. In his parents' eyes, Clancy was always the troublemaker, always the guilty one, and so was frequently punished for one misdemeanor or another he did not deserve.

Clancy learned early in life to hate his siblings back. One Sunday, Ben cut his finger while playing, and the image of his older brother hurt, crying, and bleeding resonated deeply with Clancy. He started fantasizing about hurting Ben and Charmaine in ways that made them bleed. Sometimes, Clancy would look at them with his deep black eyes when he was in trouble because of their actions and would find comfort in imagining hurting them. He lay awake in his bed when it was dark and imagined horrible fates for Ben and Charmaine, plotting how he would kill them in different ways, each more horrible than the last.

His mother thought, by the grin on his face, he was enjoying whatever punishment she was meting out for that day's trouble his siblings had landed him in. Seeing him smiling incensed her further, making it all the worse for Clancy. If, for example, she was smacking him with a wooden spoon, she would strike him more times than she had intended just to make him stop smiling. She didn't realize he wasn't enjoying being punished; he just wanted to hurt his brother and sister so badly, and it gave him comfort to imagine their destruction in ever-escalating, horrible, and bloody ways.

****

Punishments meted out by his parents varied. They started with slaps on his bare legs, but that didn't seem to work, so it progressed to spankings. His mother replaced that with a wooden spoon, while his father used his belt as he got older. Nothing seemed to make a difference; Clancy misbehaved more, or so they believed. They had no idea that most of his problems arose from retaliation, and Clancy rarely instigated trouble, merely reacting to it. He would be sent to his room, but Clancy seemed to enjoy being alone, separated from his brother and sister. Finally, when nothing else worked, they began hitting him and sending him to bed without dinner. But sometimes, his mother would discover in the morning that the fridge or walk-in pantry had been raided in the middle of the night and food was missing.

When confronted, Clancy denied he had stolen food, which meant he was in more trouble for lying, as his parents never believed it wasn't him. Meanwhile, his brother and sister would laugh at their latest triumph. For Ben, it was a double victory; he got to eat an illicit supper, and his despised brother got the beating for it. Life didn't get much better than that.

****

Eventually, to break Clancy's willfulness, the punishments meted out by Tim and Lena increased in intensity. But it took more and more blows to make him cry, which was the only way they knew he had learned from his mistakes because Clancy would never apologize. Clancy would be sent to bed with welts, bruises, and sometimes even blood on his bottom and thighs, generally for things he hadn't done. Hence, he would not say sorry. In Clancy's mind, his fantasies of revenge and killing his tormentors included increasingly gruesome plots, which included his mother and father.

His parents sometimes found Clancy's drawings depicting people with knives or swords sticking out of them. Sometimes kneeling or sitting in puddles of their own blood. Once it became evident the pictures were of his family, the beatings got worse, so Clancy learned to

165

keep his fantasies to himself. His imagination grew more obscene and violent with the repression.

****

Inevitably, as Clancy grew older, he became bigger and stronger.

For his brother and sister, Clancy being punished with a belt was music to their ears. They enjoyed it and rejoiced in his pain. But as Clancy put on more muscle, he started hitting them back, and fist fights began between the two brothers, and occasionally his sister became a regular occurrence. Clancy began to hurt Ben and Charmaine, and bruises occurred more and more frequently, which Clancy got blamed for. It didn't matter to Clancy when he got injured; it only mattered that he hurt them more. Slowly the tormented became the tormentor.

Their parents were at their wits' end. All they could do was punish Clancy harder and more frequently. Occasionally, Ben and Charmaine were locked in their rooms for extended periods as joint punishments, too, until they promised to be good. This would happen quickly with Ben and Charmaine, but with Clancy, it could take days or, usually, not at all.

To the beleaguered mother and father, Ben was their golden-haired boy who rarely did anything wrong. Clancy was the tormenting black sheep of the family, so his relapses were to be expected.

By the time Clancy was ten years old, Ben feared his younger brother because, in a fight, Ben came off as second-best every time. Clancy had grown in height and bulk, and his punches hurt. He had also learned how to kick, so in a brawl, Clancy would use any means, any weapon, and would hurt Ben much more than he could be hurt himself. Ben stopped trying to get Clancy in trouble, but it was too late for peace between them. Charmaine was petrified of Clancy, too, and avoided being alone with him. She preferred not to speak to Clancy at all unless she had to.

Ben and Charmaine still blamed Clancy for being horrible to them and didn't look inward at themselves and their role in making his life miserable, which caused the retaliations. In their minds, his violent reaction was his fault, not theirs. Clancy had learned that the only way he could be accepted and respected by them was to cause pain, and he took that opportunity every chance he got. He didn't mind being punished by his parents but didn't seek it either. So long as he could hurt his brother and sister first, it was worthwhile. Clancy looked for his opportunities and planned carefully, being smart enough to avoid being punished by his parents whenever he could. Clancy had never enjoyed the pain they put him through and avoided it when he could so often waited patiently and pounced without warning when he saw an opening.

On the day Benjamin moved away from home to go to board at Saint Claire Agricultural School, he left with both eyes blackened and a loose tooth. Clancy had punched him twice because he had called out too loudly to his mother, which had made Clancy jump. Clancy didn't like anything his brother did, but he didn't like being startled by him. So, when Ben yelled, Clancy smudged his homework page and attacked Ben immediately.

Ben couldn't escape the farm quickly enough, and on the bus, after his farewells, he decided he never wanted to go back to live under the same roof as Clancy again.

With Ben gone, Charmaine came under her brother's watchful, cold eyes, exclusively, and her world became a nightmare. He would poke, pinch, and punch her constantly. When she developed breasts, they became his favorite target area, and she endured permanently sore nipples. Clancy's feelings were like a psychedelic painting with conflicting thoughts simultaneously. Clancy had begun to see her in a sexual light, but it was mixed with visions of violence.

Clancy had sex education classes at school, and in general, he was an apt and willing student, so long as he got his own way. Boys talk, and while Clancy had yet to sample a girl's sexual charms for himself, he listened to stories for other lads who bragged that they had. His hormones were raging like it does with all teenage boys. He found a stack of his father's pornographic magazines in one of the toolsheds, so he knew what went where, but he hadn't learned anything about love or romance.

One night Clancy woke after three a.m. and realized he had ejaculated in his sleep for the first time. He tried to remember the dream which had caused it and slowly recalled the details of tying Charmaine to a chair and tormenting her, which made him erect again.

From that moment on, Clancy saw Charmaine in a different light. He wanted her, and dreamed of taking her over and over while hurting her in increasingly bizarre ways. Clancy often fantasized and made intricate plans in his mind for how to bring that fantasy to life. Clancy was smart enough to know he couldn't be brazen about it, he knew his desires were illegal and immoral, but it didn't stop him from plotting and planning.

****

One day Charmaine decided enough was enough and decided to try to make up with Clancy by apologizing for her part in his childhood misery. She was sick of the years of torment on both sides and knew if she didn't take the initiative, Clancy never would; therefore, things would never improve. They were stacking hay bales for their father in the barn, and Charmaine waited for them to take a break.

"Clancy," she began nervously, "I know you don't like me much, and I deserve a lot of that for things I did to you when we were young. I think I was led on a lot by Benjamin, but I want to say sorry for the things I did and ask you if we can start again and try to be friends?"

He stared back with his dark, brooding eyes for what seemed to be an eternity. Clancy nodded and put his pitchfork down on a nearby bale. He then turned, and she could see emotion exuding from every pore of his body, and she ran screaming for the door. He caught her easily and threw her to the ground, holding her down by placing his knees over her upper arms.

He was fourteen by this time, and she was sixteen. He slapped her face several times before bunching her hair in his hands, yanking up and down, so he banged her head on the straw-covered floor. "You wanna be friends?" he screamed, his snarling lips inches from her face, and flecks of spittle rained down. "What's in it for me?"

She wriggled, fought, and squirmed. Somehow, she got free and ran out of the barn. Charmaine swore she would never be alone with him again. Charmaine didn't tell her parents what had transpired because she knew if she did, Clancy would get even with her, and that realization terrified her. She had seen what looked like pure hatred, mixed with teenage lust, in his eyes that day in the barn, and Charmaine knew in her heart if Clancy had a chance to rape her, he would.

Charmaine locked her bedroom door at night from that day on, which infuriated her mother, but she wouldn't stop doing it, no matter what. Charmaine said locking her door was the only thing which prevented her from having nightmares though she didn't say those dreams were of her brother sneaking into her room and forcing her to have sex. She could never admit that to anyone, so she kept the subject of her nightmares vague or sometimes made up so her parents would leave her door locked.

****

With Benjamin gone, things improved dramatically for Clancy as far as his mother and father were concerned. Clancy was given more responsibility and became a very able and willing farm hand, working tirelessly alongside Tim from dawn till dusk during school holidays and on weekends. The extended work hours and Clancy's tiredness at the end of the day kept him away from her, which thrilled Charmaine, and for a while, she felt safe.

If his father had any concerns remaining about Clancy, it was when it came time to kill a sheep or head of cattle, Clancy always wanted to do it. Over the years, Tim had learned it was easier to let Clancy do what he wanted rather than have an argument which could last for days. So, after the first two attempts, where the animal was horribly mutilated, Tim taught his son how to do it humanely and quickly, but he always felt his son enjoyed inflicting pain and death just a little too much.

****

Benjamin finished boarding school and refused to come home. He told his parents he had no interest in farming and wanted to travel for a while, but what Ben meant was he didn't want to be near his brother. Of course, Tim and Lena tried to change his mind, but Ben was determined. He wanted to get away from country WA and see the world while working his way around it.

He got as far as Adelaide and got a job on a freshwater crayfish farm. His hard work and excellent results at the agricultural school held him in good stead. He was offered a permanent position, and he decided to take it, which upset his mother and father when he told them three months later. They took Ben's news hard. During an angry phone conversation, Tim asked his son why he could work on someone else's farm but not his own family's, but Ben refused to answer other than to say he was enjoying his new life. Ben didn't tell them the real reason because he, like Charmaine, realized they had caused the monster which Clancy had become. Ben could not admit that to his parents, let alone apologize to Clancy.

Tim told Ben about Clancy's hard work and what an asset Clancy had become. He then asked why Benjamin couldn't be more like his brother, not realizing that was pushing him farther away by comparing them. Time and distance made Ben realize how dangerous Clancy was, and that it was his and his sister's doing which made him that way. Charmaine had told Ben in letters how Clancy looked at her in a creepy way which made her frightened for her safety. She had not mentioned the episode in the barn to Ben; she preferred not to think about it.

Ben was terrified of returning because the hatred between him and Clancy had not abated with distance, and he knew Clancy would hurt him if he tried. He understood how jealousy worked; with Benjamin gone, Clancy was the top dog, a position he would never relinquish. If Ben returned, he would have to fight to get his status back even though he didn't want it; Clancy would force the issue. Ben couldn't fully rationalize it, but in his heart, he knew if he went home, Clancy would kill him somehow sooner or later. His father had praised the turnaround in his brother, explaining Clancy had left school and taken on the farm manager's role after the longstanding worker surprisingly quit without warning. Ben didn't believe it. It made far more sense to Ben that Clancy had somehow forced him to leave. Ben's mind was made up; he wanted to live and stay healthy, so he was staying away.

Ben thought he knew why the manager, Malcolm, had left; Clancy wanted him to so he could get the job. That would be the only reason, he was well paid, and Ben's father was a good man to work for. Ben had known Malcolm well enough to know he wouldn't willingly leave, so that he had vanished only strengthened Ben's resolve never to return.

Ben hoped Adelaide was far enough from the farm at three thousand kilometers that he would never have to see Clancy for the rest of his life.

****

Malcolm White, the manager, hadn't left the farm and never could. Benjamin was correct; Malcolm would never have willingly quit his job because Tim was too good a boss to work for.

Clancy had become miserable at school. He knew everyone there hated him and made fun of him behind his back. They would stop talking when he neared and start up again once he passed. Whenever he heard a group of kids laugh, he believed they were laughing at him. He had no friends and had been warned that he would be expelled if he was involved in one more fistfight.

He wanted to leave school and thought getting Malcolm's job was the way to do so. When his parents took Charmaine into Perth for a day's shopping, Clancy stayed behind and asked Malcolm to help him fix a fence on a far corner of the farm on the western side. They loaded the trailer with tools and spare fencing and hooked it up to the tractor after securing the digging bucket on the front of it. They set off to make the repair mid-morning.

Clancy parked the tractor under a tree near the boundary, took a treated pine fence post, and hit Malcolm on his right leg smashing his thigh bone and instantly bringing him to the ground. Clancy watched closely while he screamed in agony, deeply interested in the effect of the pain he had inflicted. For Clancy, this was a watershed moment; he had someone in his power, and he could hurt them as much as he liked.

"Why?" Malcolm screamed.

"Because I can," he replied before bringing the fence post down, aiming at Malcolm's head but hitting his arm as he raised it to protect himself. Malcolm begged and pleaded for mercy, which was music to Clancy's ears. He felt euphoric, and a sexual glow tingled his groin as he held Malcolm's life in his hands. Clancy could determine whether the manager lived or died and how much pain he suffered in the interim. He had never felt so happy in his life as he systematically beat Malcolm to death. Even though Clancy had never had an issue with Malcolm, hitting him with the post was cathartic. Clancy felt like he had found his true calling as he dragged out the inevitable death with measured blow after blow, often taking rests to watch Malcom writhe.

He felt incredible when it was over, and the body was a mass of broken bones and bloody pulpy skin. He had discovered the power of delivering a slow, brutal, and painful death. It was like a drug, and he already yearned for his next fix.

While he danced around the corpse lying in the scrub, Clancy wondered who he could kill next. He immediately thought of Charmaine and became painfully erect in his pants.

Clancy used the tractor digger bucket to dig a hole among the gum and eucalyptus trees and buried Malcolm so animals wouldn't uncover the body. He threw in the fence post, which had lost its green tinge and had turned reddish-brown. Before filling in the hole, he went to the shack where Malcolm had lived near the main house and packed his bags with all the clothes and effects he could find. He took those back to the stand of trees and threw them in the hole because he wanted it to appear that Malcolm had left of his own free will. Clancy filled the hole and smoothed the surface, knowing within a short period, the wild oats and grasses would regrow, and Malcolm's grave would be hidden forever.

Later that evening, when his family returned from shopping, he explained to his father over an ice-cold beer Malcolm told him he was quitting because he had been given a better offer from a large station up North. He would be in touch, he said, to let them know where they could send his last paycheck. Malcolm hadn't wanted to hang around to say goodbye as long goodbyes weren't *his thing.* Malcolm had asked Clancy to say he was sorry on his behalf. Better to just move on, he'd said.

Tim Pike was furious. They had shearing coming up in the next three weeks, and with five thousand sheep, it would be so much easier to get it done in time with a farm manager. Clancy acted angry, too; he told Tim he had given Malcolm a few choice words and called him a coward for running out. Father and son ranted and raved while drinking beers long into the night.

After finishing their fourth beer, they agreed Clancy would quit school and work on the family farm full-time. He was sixteen going on seventeen and didn't have that much schooling left anyway, and he wanted to work on the farm. He assured his father that it was all he wanted, and further education would be lost on him. He said he was his father's son, and for the first time, Tim was truly proud of him.

Even Lena agreed it might be for the best, but she had noted the steely, determined look in Clancy's eye and had long since learned not to argue with him once he had decided on something he was determined to do. They also agreed if Malcolm did contact them to ask for his last paycheck, he wouldn't get it. He could take them to the tribunal, but they wouldn't pay him one cent for leaving them in the lurch as he had.

****

For weeks after Malcolm's murder, the memory of Clancy's first kill fueled his fantasies while lying awake at night. It became natural to him to associate torture and death with his own gratification. After a while, he found he couldn't get an erection unless he first thought about causing pain, and his dreams became lurid and in technicolor.

Clancy made several plans to kill his sister, but he wanted to have sex with her first. If the bitch agreed to sex with him in the barn, when she'd tried to become friends, he might have let her live. She had her chance, he decided. Her time had come; her days were limited.

****

Eventually, the memory of killing Malcolm stopped driving Clancy's fantasies. It no longer turned him on as it had, and as each day passed, he became more intent on finding another victim. Charmaine looked more attractive to him than ever, and he planned her rape and eventual murder in intricate detail. Clancy had decided to keep her alive for a long time, so he could have every form of sex with her he could imagine until he got bored, and his imagination knew no bounds. The shack Malcolm used to live in would be her dungeon and sex chamber all in one, and Clancy shivered in delight at the thought.

But first, he had a problem with his parents. After mulling over his options, he decided there was nothing for it. They had to go.

Chapter 13

Patricide

Once Clancy decided to murder his parents so he could be free to torture Charmaine, he needed a foolproof plan and had to determine how he could get away with it. Clancy wasn't dumb. There was no point committing two murders if he was going to get caught and sent to jail. Clancy wanted to stay on the farm once they were dead and have Charmaine all to himself; he had big plans for her. In his bedside drawer, Clancy kept a notebook with page after page of intricate tortures written down, or drawn, which he intended to put Charmaine through. Then there was the section for sex. Clancy had lists of depravities he would make her suffer, which he enjoyed imagining every night in bed. Clancy was working through his thirtieth murder plan when half of his problem was solved out of the blue. When his father died, it was a case of letting it happen, encouraging it even, but he didn't have to do much at all physically.

Charmaine was working at the local pub and was there on the day of the *tragedy*. Lena was in Adelaide visiting Ben, trying to woo him back home to the farm, and intended to use any means, fair or foul, to make it happen. Ben was standing his ground, though he could not tell his mother it was fear for his life at his brother's hand, so she kept trying.

Tim wanted to check the wheat silo and ensure their grain hadn't become moldy and would flow through the hopper for seeding, which they would be doing soon. They had received twelve points of rain recently, and moisture in the air sometimes caused the grains to stick together and form clumps, clogging the flow from the silo so the grains would no longer cascade out of the bottom chute when opened.

The farm's main grain silo was over eight meters tall and stood like a shiny metal beacon on the landscape, which was either brown or green, depending on the time of year. It was common on farms that had been handed down generationally to use poor safety practices. Tim knew only one way to fix grain silos that had become clogged, and that was how his father had shown him. Someone entered through the top of the silo, walked on the surface and trampled through the crust and used a steel rod to break up the lower grains. The job was generally a two-person operation for safety reasons. Once it loosened up, grains could become like quicksand and suck someone down, drowning them in grain and wheat dust. Statistically, three farmers lost their lives that way across Australia every year. The purpose of the second person was to assist the other out using a ladder or knotted rope once the grain clumps were broken up.

Usually, Clancy's job, being younger and fitter, was inside. On this occasion, Clancy asked if he could stay on top as he felt he had a bit of a *funny tummy* and was worried if he got sick, he could vomit and spoil the grain. His father told him not to worry; he had done this job thousands of times. He squeezed Clancy's shoulder with affection and climbed down onto the wheat, holding onto a knotted rope held by Clancy. The other end was secured to the outside ladder as a backup to assist in climbing out once the job had been done. Tim walked around inside, kicking and breaking up the crusty grain. When he wasn't looking, Clancy pulled the rope back up and watched excitedly, stifling nervous giggles while he waited for the inevitable.

Soon, the grain started to suck around Tim's booted feet, and he looked like he was trying to climb a ladder to stay on the surface. It was time to get out, and he absentmindedly reached for the rope behind him, but it was no longer there. He waved his arms around, trying to locate it while his son, lying on the top of the outside looking down through the manhole, felt himself erect at the impending death of his father.

"*Clancy!* Toss the rope down, will you? Why did you pull it back up?" Tim yelled, with no inkling of what was about to occur.

"Sorry, Daddio. No can do," Clancy answered, laughing out loud hysterically.

Tim felt panic set in, but only a touch as his disbelieving brain thought, *He's joking, surely?* Tim looked at the manhole to see his son's grinning face peering down as the grain passed his knees. "Stop mucking about, Clance. Throw it down right now. I'm sinking."

"Or what, Dad? You'll beat me with your belt like all those times you did for things Ben, or my bitch of a sister did but blamed me for?"

"What do you mean, Clancy? Seriously, I'm starting to sink here. Please stop joking and help me out. Throw down the rope."

"No. I don't think so, Dad. It's time I took over running the farm."

Only then did Tim see the pure evil in his son's eyes. He also realized that maybe he had been wrong to beat Clancy. Had Clancy been innocent as he now claimed? When the realization crossed his mind, he knew he would die.

"Please, son," he shouted, echoing up the silo. "I'm sorry if I made mistakes as your father bringing you up. I only ever tried my best. Please, you don't have to do this. It's your farm when I die anyway, with Ben gone."

"Yeah, but I want you to die now, not in thirty years. And Ben, he's the real problem here. All those times he lied to you, Dad, and you never once believed me. Now it's too late."

It took an hour and a half for Tim to drown. He was a strong man, and he fought hard for his life. Tim never stopped hoping his son would relent and free him, his flesh and blood, but Clancy just watched and grinned. Slowly he sank in the grain, deeper and deeper, and as it rose to chest level, he couldn't breathe properly. Before he sank farther, Tim understood something he should have realized before; his son killed Malcolm. Then the inevitable panic set in, and he quickly sank from sight.

Clancy dropped the rope back inside the silo, so it would appear the knot securing it to the outside ladder had slipped undone, and he couldn't climb out. Clancy, of course, would be fencing on another part of the property while his poor father drowned in grain. That would be his story, and no one could prove he wasn't. Clancy wasn't even aware his father was in the silo, he would tell the investigators, and he would be so upset when they found his body. He had been rehearsing how he would behave in his mind all day.

It was unfortunate the grain would be ruined, and

they would have to buy more, but it was a small price to pay as he was sure his dad was well insured, and the money would help with his ideas. Clancy was now one step closer to his master plan of making his sister's last days on Earth; hell.

But first, his mother had to go, and Clancy thought he knew how he would accomplish it.

Chapter 14

Matricide

It's laughable, Clancy thought while in the shower that night, *how easy killing was. Everything went to plan swimmingly. Swimmingly? Where did I come up with that expression?* He laughed while trying to maintain a straight face. He was supposed to look sad, not happy, Clancy reminded himself. Of course, swimming was, in a way, what his father had been trying to do in the grain, and that thought made it seem all the funnier. *Swimming for the surface to breathe.*

He waited until the end of the day until Charmaine was home from her stupid job, in the kitchen peeling potatoes. Clancy was in the shower, scrubbing himself from head to toe. He put on a plaid flannelette shirt and clean jeans and went to the fridge to get a beer. "Where's Dad?" he asked, admiring her ass through her tight denim as she stood at the sink. He could just make out the outline of her panties.

"I don't know, I haven't seen him. Haven't you?"

"Nope. I was fencing in the south paddock. Dad was going to check over the seeder and change the oil in the tractor. He should have been back by now." He flipped the bottle's cap and tossed it into the bin like a mini frisbee, which was no mean feat from across the room. He sat at the kitchen table and opened the newspaper she

182

had brought back from town.

"His truck isn't in the shed, and dinner isn't that far away. Clancy, do you want to go and give him a yell? Make sure he's all right?" She turned and looked at him. Clancy looked up at the clock on the wall, shrugged, and nodded to her while staring at her boobs. *Soon I will be biting those tits until they bleed,* he mused. Clancy got up and went and found his boots.

****

An ambulance was called, and the body retrieved. The police were notified along with the Worksafe Department, as they needed to be for any accident-causing death in the workplace. In due time, the investigation showed, as it always did in that type of farming incident, it was a regrettable accident born of overfamiliarity and unsafe practices. The coroner concluded, "Timothy Pike died when the rope dislodged itself, and he could not climb out of the silo after breaking up the grain." The report went on to say he had the experience and should have known better; someone should have been with him, which would have avoided the fatality.

Charmaine made the painful call to her mother, sobbing and heartbroken, so she could return home with Ben to help arrange the funeral. In conjunction with her grief and sadness at the loss of her father, Charmaine also felt a deep-seated horror he would no longer be there to protect her from her brother. Maybe, she wondered, it was time she moved out of the house. Her boss had previously offered her a room at the pub, but Charmaine realized if she took the offer, her mother would be left alone with Clancy. Charmaine had noticed Clancy seemed to be leering and staring lecherously at her regularly. She was terrified of him, but the thought of leaving her mum alone with Clancy at the farm made her worry more.

Both grandparents had passed away, so the only other family present for the funeral were distant aunts, uncles, and cousins, some of whom were several times removed. The funeral was a well attended event with local townspeople and farmers, who packed the small church and cemetery. Clancy lost count of the number of people he shook hands with who offered help or free advice in running the farm. They correctly assumed he would take over the business because they knew he was close to his father in his final months.

Everyone convened at the town hall afterward, where local families had agreed to bring and share a plate of food for the wake. There was keg beer for the men and cask wine for the women, and both flowed freely. Clancy had something he had to do, which was to ensure Benjamin had no desire to return home, and had devised a plan for how to achieve it. Clancy made it appear he had drunk a lot more than he had, so if needed when questioned by police, Clancy could claim he was drunk. Clancy bided his time and waited for the perfect moment to bring his plan to fruition. Clancy knew for as long as he had been alive, Benjamin was his mother's favorite, and he thought he had the ideal opportunity to achieve several things at once. Clancy could make his mother believe the worst of Ben for once in his life, and in doing so, think the best of him. Clancy would show everyone assembled that he loved his father more than Ben, even though he hadn't, but it was a good ploy to get people to think he had. And finally, Clancy could ensure his stinking lowlife brother would never return and work on the farm again because he would be too embarrassed, ashamed, and scared.

Ben stood with his mother, sister, and three others near the drinks table when Clancy approached from the side. Without warning, he punched Ben's face with as much power as he could muster. Clancy was in his eighteenth year, nearing nineteen, and had put on weight, mostly muscle, through working full-time on the farm and being out in the weather. Clancy could carry sheep, throw a cow on its side, rope and ride horses, and pull strands of five-string wire fencing straight. Clancy planned to hit his brother once to make up for all the years of pain, suffering, and misery suffered at Benjamin's instigation. He also knew one punch would be all he would get in before other farmers intervened and pulled him off, so it needed to be the best he could throw and cause the most damage.

When Clancy connected his fist to the side of Ben's face, it was a devastating blow thrown with everything he could muster behind it. The punch did enormous damage, which would stay with Ben for the rest of his life and would be a permanent reminder to his brother of the saying, *'He who laughs last, laughs the loudest.'* Five teeth were broken, and he would require sixteen stitches at the hospital. His jaw was shattered in three places and would need plates inserted. His sinuses would never completely recover, and depending on future weather, his nose would either be blocked on most days or annoyingly drip like a tap on others.

Ben fell unconscious to the parquet floor like a sack of potatoes, blood poured from his broken mouth, and three farmers jumped in and held Clancy back from following up with a kick or further punches, as he had imagined they would.

Clancy deserved an acting award as he screamed while struggling to get free, *"It's your fault Dad is dead. You killed him. If you were working with us on the farm instead of living in Adelaide, one of us would have been with him that day, and he would still be alive."*

A hush descended over the hundred or more guests present until it was broken by the sound of Clancy wailing and crying as he collapsed with grief in the arms of the three men holding him as they led him away.

Many people thought, *oh, that poor man.* But not one applied the thought to Ben, who was lying in a crumpled heap on the floor, only Clancy. The women wanted to cuddle and comfort him for his obvious grief, while the men nodded in tacit agreement. The fact was undeniable. Tim's oldest son had left home to work on someone else's farm, which was an unforgivable sin as far as they were concerned. They all harbored the same fear that their sons would leave home one day. A family farm should be family-run.

Even Lena, while she would never voice the thought, believed that had Ben not run off to Adelaide, her husband would still been alive. Though she had never consciously thought about it until that moment, she agreed with Clancy. Of course, she didn't agree with Clancy hitting Ben, but she understood the angst which drove one of her sons to punch the other. Only Charmaine saw through the ruse, and her feelings about Clancy intensified. Suddenly, her hatred knew no bounds, but she was also smart enough to know she was alone in that belief. She fell to her knees to ensure her brother was alive and screamed to others for help.

The local men respected Clancy for hitting his

brother. They understood why he had done it, and thought that under the same circumstances, they would have done the same thing themselves. They also respected what a good punch it was and made mental notes not to get Clancy angry lest they suffer the same fate and get hit by him. They could see Clancy was not a man who would be pushed around.

Charmaine went with Ben to the hospital when he came to. He was groggy and badly concussed, so one of the locals drove them to town with a towel wrapped around his face to stanch the blood flow. Lena decided not to go, but to stay at the wake and comfort the one son who hadn't left her, who she could tell, missed his father so terribly and was visibly upset. At one point, she thought life was funny how things worked out. She had always thought Ben was the good son, but Clancy had stayed behind. Clancy had left school to help when the manager quit suddenly, and Clancy would look after her now she was without a husband.

Clancy got drunk that night, deliriously happy his plan was working but outwardly showing misery. As he lay in bed with the room spinning when everyone had left, Clancy thought of the things he would do with his prissy sister once his plan for his mother came to fruition; he just needed some patience.

****

Clancy's plan for his sister was to drug Charmaine with one of his mother's sleeping tablets, which had a weird name. Then, he would take her to the cabin, which used to house the farm manager but now resembled something entirely different. Clancy had been making alterations over time to feed his fantasies. His parents had thought he was decorating it, perhaps to live there or for future farm help, and had given him free rein to do as he wished. But he was really turning it into what would become Charmaine's torture chamber of horror. She was to be imprisoned and become his first victim and slave. He had brought in ropes, chains, shackles, and an assortment of things he thought would be perfect for inflicting pain on her body and kept them locked in a cupboard, for which he had the only key.

For many years, Clancy had fantasized about doing as he pleased with Charmaine. Lurid, colorful dreams of her torment filled his life both when he was awake and asleep. Now the time for her capture was so close Clancy could taste it. Clancy decided she had to be willing to please him and stop more pain from being inflicted on her body. Clancy was sure he would be able to tell if she was acting, and he would wait, torturing her, until she really and truly wanted him as much as he wanted her. Clancy had everything mapped out in his twisted mind. He believed she was a slut, who let boys do dirty things to her in town at the pub she worked at. It was the only reason he could see why she went out some nights or was late home from work on others. That thought alone turned him on as much as it made him jealous. But it would also be payback for all the years she and Ben had made him suffer at the hands of their parents. He would never forgive her for being locked in his room for hours, missing dinners; the list of suffering he was subjected to was endless, and Charmaine was as guilty as Benjamin. While his revenge had been a long time coming and would still be delayed for a while, the wait would make it taste much sweeter when it came.

The last glorious page of his notebook was dedicated to how he would take Charmaine's life when he finally tired of hurting her. The various items he would need to do it were already assembled. He'd got the idea for her ending from his school days when they studied Vlad the Impaler, otherwise known in movie lore as Count Dracula. As his title implied, he was famous for impaling his enemies on stakes and letting their body weight and gravity finish the job while an audience watched. Clancy would be the only audience, but such a drawn-out finish to Charmaine's traitorous life seemed apt.

The crude drawing on the final page displayed Charmaine's hands tied above her head, her body suspended by a rope through a block and tackle, secured to a hook fixed to a joist in the apex part of the roof. Her feet would be held wide apart as far as they could be stretched and secured to ring bolts on the floor. He intended to lower her a little at a time with the sharp tip of a stake bound with barbed wire attached to the floor below her, and his most fervent hope was she would take a long, long time to die while he watched.

Clancy had thought about what he would do with her body and explain away her disappearance afterward. Things had worked so well with Malcolm; he decided not to change a winning formula. He would bury her body in the copse of trees he had used before. Then he would tell everyone they'd had an argument, and she had run off to stay with Ben in Adelaide. If she didn't make it to Ben's, how was that his fault?

Despite endless hours of intricate planning, Clancy failed to see the flaws in his plan because he was blinded by fantasies of how much he would hurt her and the amount of pleasure he would derive. Clancy had mingled obsessive fantasies with plotting, so one clouded the other. Clancy would learn the two are different mental deeds, and this was an area he would improve on significantly with future kills.

****

Charmaine thwarted Clancy's plan and saved her own life. She believed Clancy wanted to hurt her, if not kill her, as he had their father, and she was not going to permit it. Although the investigation found her father's death was accidental, Charmaine believed differently. She'd tried to tell the police officer her dad would never go into the silo alone, but Clancy had shown them the work he had done during the day and pointed out that had his father asked for his help, he could easily have given it, but he hadn't. So, Clancy was believed, and her assertion was labeled paranoia. She had no reply to the question asked of her, why would her brother kill their father? She didn't know. She just knew he had.

Over the proceeding weeks, Charmaine saw how Clancy looked at her, especially when he thought she wasn't aware. It dawned on Charmaine her brother was studying her and daydreaming like a spider looking at a fly. While waiting in town and visiting Ben in the hospital, Charmaine stayed at the pub where she worked until his face had healed enough for him to travel back to Adelaide. Then, knowing Clancy would be working in the fields, they both went to the farm so she could pack and say goodbye to their mother, intending to accompany Ben back to Adelaide. Charmaine had decided she would not stay one more minute in the house with her brother. She had no specific idea of his plans for her but knew he wanted to hurt her and didn't want to hang around to find out how much. Ever since the episode in the barn, Charmaine had convinced herself

190

Clancy was a pervert, and without her father to shield her, she feared Clancy would force himself on her.

Ben and Charmaine tried to make their mother see the evil which had grown in Clancy but failed. Lena was still so deep in her own grief at the loss of her husband she would not entertain the thought that Clancy was anything other than the loving son she believed he had become. Clancy stayed and worked on the family farm while his brother ran away, and now his sister was joining him. In her mind, the older two had shown her their true colors, and Clancy was the one who loved her and was going to look after her.

They persisted, even trying to infer Clancy had killed their dad because he wanted control of the family farm, and moreover, that was why he punched Ben during the wake. This idea was, to Lena, ludicrous and only proved Ben and Charmaine's jealousy had overtaken their common sense. They begged her to go with them, fearful for her safety, but Lena countered by asking if they were so concerned, why wouldn't they stay to protect her? She pointed out that Ben, being the oldest had a responsibility to take over the reins of the farm management, and she was sure Clancy would welcome that. Ben knew better, but despite their best efforts, tears, and pleading, their mother would not leave her family home or believe she was in danger for one moment.

Lena eventually lost her temper and accused them of wanting to destroy the family so the farm could be sold. Therefore, she believed their motives were for selfish monetary gains, while Clancy only wanted to maintain the farm as it had been for two generations. She ordered Ben and Charmaine to leave and never return if that was how they truly felt about Clancy.

****

And so began Lena Pike's dependency on her only remaining son to care for her and the farm, leading to her unknowingly following the path Clancy had laid out for her. Ultimately it would culminate in her death six weeks after her other two children abandoned her.

It began when Clancy came home that evening, and she told him about Charmaine and Ben's visit, what they had said, and they had left for good. Clancy was incensed with rage. All he saw were his twisted pornographic fantasies of the rapes, torture, and death of his hated sister going up in flames, and he turned on his mother and furiously blamed her for them leaving. It made no logical sense for him to blame her, but Clancy was beyond rational thought. In her grief-stricken state, his furious barbs wounded Lena deeply.

Lena was further saddened because, by his rants, she believed it proved he loved his brother and sister and felt abandoned by them leaving, and he wanted them home to help work on the farm and be a family. Her guilt level raised several more notches with his accusations, not realizing her escalated perception of reality couldn't have been further from the truth.

****

Clancy spent the next two weeks poisoning Lena's mind further about Ben and Charmaine. One reason was to ensure that if Ben changed his mind and attempted a return, his mother wouldn't permit it. He had seen how she had reacted to his false accusations, and a plan began to take shape in his mind of how to get rid of her and not get blamed. Hour after hour, day after day, he ranted and raved, "How could they just leave like that? Who is going to do the work to keep the farm going? I can't be expected to do everything, can I? I'm only one man. The farm is too big. I will have to hire some help." On and on, Clancy ranted, never letting up and not giving Lena any respite even though she offered to help take on some of the workload herself.

Lena began to suffer from insomnia and stopped eating with worry. Clancy took her sleeping pills away from her, assuring her it was for her own good. She was in the full throws of the nervous condition Clancy had forced upon her and the grief she already felt from Tim's passing. When the life insurance payout came, he wanted control of it, Clancy insisted, for the farm's best interest. Then Clancy made her change her will, completely disowning Ben and Charmaine and leaving everything to him. Meanwhile, he kept up his psychological campaign of the war. He saw his mother weaken by the day and took advantage of her fragility. She slipped further into depression.

When neighbors visited, Clancy kept them away by telling them his mother was in bed, recovering. Clancy began to infer they might lose the farm because it was only him working it, and if they did, she would be put in a home because it was all her fault. Yes, he could get contractors to shear sheep, seed the grain, and cut hay, but it all took the money they didn't have. Night and day, Clancy kept on at her relentlessly.

When Clancy saw Lena was ready, he planted the final seed he believed would germinate and grow. He asked her how much life insurance she had. The farm could be saved if they had that, Clancy suggested. After all, he reasoned, her life wasn't worth living anyway, without her husband; what else did she have to look forward to with Ben and Charmaine abandoning her too?

By now, in a dark place, Lena agreed her life was horrid, and she had been a terrible mother. If they lost the farm, she and Clancy would be homeless, all because she had forced Ben away, which led to Tim's death, and then she caused Charmaine to run away too. Clancy kept niggling away, and he gleefully watched his mother deteriorate further, eating next to nothing and rarely sleeping.

Seemingly out of the blue, he spoke one night about a friend whose mother had committed suicide but hadn't left a note, and it had caused all sorts of problems for her family. He mused about how inconsiderate it was that in killing herself, she hadn't left a suicide note, so the police never discovered the reason behind her actions. The investigation, he lied, had dragged on and had held up the insurance payout when the grieving family needed it the most. Clancy painted that mother's suicide as the worst thing she could have done to her family, not because she was dead, but because her lack of a suicide note made it so complicated to get paid by the insurance company. If she had *really* loved her family, he complained, she would have left a message for the police. After wiping any of his fingerprints off her sleeping pill bottle, he left it on his mother's bedside table.

Clancy knew he was succeeding with his carefully planned psychological warfare. When he could see she was getting close, he delivered what he considered the coup de grace. He reminded her of the beatings she and his father had bestowed on him as a child when he was growing up. He convinced her that his brother and sister had lied to get him in trouble. He pointed out how much it hurt him, both the physical beatings, and that she had not believed him when he told them he was innocent. Especially now, when they were long gone, didn't that prove he had been truthful all along? They didn't even stick around to help keep the family farm from going under. Clancy often reminded her of his childhood and how he had to spend hours or days unable to sit down because of the welts and excruciating pain. He had been locked in his room for hour upon hour, unable to eat dinner. He had been severely beaten, and it was all because she believed their lies. But they now got to be free while he was in prison, working night and day to look after her in the useless state she was in and run the farm with insufficient money to make ends meet.

And so it was, six weeks from his father's funeral when he returned from a day's work with the sheep to find her dead in bed. She had taken her entire supply of twenty-seven sleeping tablets. To Clancy's joy, he saw she had left a note on the bedside cabinet, blaming herself for the family's disintegration and saying how she was sorry she had taken the easy way out.

Clancy felt as if he had won the lottery and spent half an hour dancing around the house with happiness, waiting to call the police and ambulance, as he knew he wouldn't be able to disguise the glee in his voice. Eventually, he readopted his usual scowling, grim facade, practiced speaking with the even, grief-stricken tone he had perfected from his father's death, and made the necessary calls.

The note made everything easy. Clancy was seen by everyone as the hero once again. Neighbors gathered around, consoled him, and offered help and home-cooked meals, as good people do in the country when a family loses one of their own. The police investigation was cursory at best, and the funeral was quickly arranged, with a suicide verdict made almost immediately.

Ben and Charmaine heard the news from a long-standing family friend because Clancy refused to speak with them. Charmaine had moved in with her brother and found work at a local winery. They came and stayed only for the service and not the wake, much to everyone's disgust. Ben and Charmaine knew Clancy only too well and understood that more violence would flare up if they stayed longer. They vividly remembered the last time, and neither wanted a repeat of that occasion. The two could feel the animosity from everyone in the district, which made it clear they thought Ben and Charmaine had been selfish by leaving to follow their happiness and ignoring their family obligations and responsibilities after Tim Pike's accident. In going, they contributed to their mother's death, and they would never forgive or forget.

In consoling Clancy with his loss, everyone said he was better off without them being there. He was a good man, and Ben and Charmaine were scum. These character portraits further fueled Clancy's inflated opinion of himself and disdain for his siblings. He saw himself as invincible and able to do anything he wanted.

****

The farm's bank manager, Herbert Wilkinshaw, went out of his way to make the property transition to Clancy's name simple. The bank's lawyer helped with probate, and when both life insurances paid out, the farm became debt free with a considerable sum left over. Clancy was suddenly a wealthy landowner and was truly happy for the first time in his life.

Finally, Clancy had achieved all his goals except one. He hadn't got to fulfill his dreams of hurting and screwing his sister. He consoled himself by knowing he now had the freedom to find other playmates, and he knew he would. Clancy turned his mind to decide what else he wanted to do with his future. All he knew was working on the land, but it was a big farm, which would be too much for him by himself. Clancy would need to employ help, such as a farm manager. And if he did, it could restrict his plans for the torture chamber. The one thing he was completely sure of was his future would involve getting as much pleasure in his life as he could. To Clancy Pike, that pleasure would come from finding young women, imprisoning them, making them his sex slaves, and then torturing and murdering them. He couldn't wait to begin.

Chapter 15

Marriage Made in Thailand

Three months after his mother's death, Clancy was invited to a barbeque at the home of one of his nearest neighbors, Kurt and Lindy Boetcher. Clancy had only been seen a little around town by locals when he drove past in the farm truck to get supplies or to the post office. Clancy had never been one for socializing at the town's only pub, preferring to drink his beers at home. Often, Clancy would have neighbors call in to drop off home-cooked meals or fellow farmers offering advice or manpower when they knew he could use it.

Lambing season was about to start, and Kurt wondered if the young'un, as Clancy was now known in the area, needed any help, so he had called by and made the invitation and wouldn't take no for an answer. Lindy, Kurt's beautiful Thai wife, wanted Clancy there for another reason entirely.

Lindy's maiden name was Kulap, and Lindy was her English interpretation, derived from her native name, Maladee. She was from the northern part of Thailand, a farming district. Kurt had met her on one of his trips to Thailand, playing golf with nine other men from the local golf club, which had become an institution for them. For one week, three times a year, the men would stay in luxury, play golf, eat, and drink cheaply, and have enough sex with girls twenty to thirty years their junior to last them until the next trip came around.

Kurt's first wife was from South Africa, as was he. She had died three years before he met Lindy from a nasty dose of the flu which had gone around that winter. Before anyone realized it was serious, her influenza had turned to pneumonia, and by the time she was hospitalized, it was too late. She died within twenty-four hours of admittance. It had taken two years for *the Narrogin golfing gang* to talk him into joining them on one of their debauched trips, but within days of arriving, he fell in love with the country, people, culture, and customs.

Lindy worked as a translator at a small bank in Bangkok by day, but like so many other beautiful women in the city, she hung out at the tourist bars at night. She played pool and bar games, met men, and encouraged them to buy drinks, for which she received a commission. After a hot and humid day of playing golf, Kurt and his friends wandered into a bar to play pool and drink some of the local ice-cold beers, served four to a bucket full of ice, with lemon twists, as it was the preferred way to drink the local brew.

It had been love at first sight for Kurt, and he spent three hours monopolizing Lindy's company. Later, back in his hotel room, it turned into pure lust as she showed him things he hadn't ever dreamt of doing with his wife of twenty-nine years.

To Kurt, she genuinely cared for him, listening to him talk about his first wife and how much he missed her for hours. She seemed so considerate and affectionate, not to mention the sex was out of this world. He was completely and utterly smitten with her, and he genuinely believed she was as taken with him as he was with her. In his mind, it was a match made in heaven. He invited her to his home in Western Australia for a two-week holiday at his expense. Lindy required him to ask her parents' permission, and Kurt respected that and complied. From there, the romance blossomed further. She loved his position in the community, the size of his farm, and his apparent wealth.

They had an incredible holiday together, during which she met the surrounding farmers and wives, who thought she was lovely but also thought she was a *bought wife*. Not that they would dare suggest that to Kurt, as they could tell he had deep feelings for her. Behind his back, though, there were some smirking and knowing looks from the women while the men were jealous, thinking of what Lindy would be doing to Kurt at night.

Before he took her to the airport for her return flight to Bangkok, he proposed marriage and offered her a massive diamond ring, which she delightedly accepted with tears of gratitude. She promised she would be a good wife for the rest of his life and would find ways to please him and make him proud every single day. She stayed true to her word; once they were married and granted a visa to live in Australia. Lindy spent every waking moment pleasing Kurt, who began to look, act, and feel fifteen years younger.

Her family was farmers from the north of the country, near the Cambodian border, and though the farming methods were worlds apart, they had a lot in common. Tradition required two weddings, one in Australia for legality and the other in her hometown, for her family to attend. The Thai wedding was huge, as his wealth decreed it should be, with over three hundred attendees including distant family, every resident of the hometown, and some people imported from surrounding areas. They had a live band with four female singers and three dancers on a stage erected to overlook the crowd. The ceremony was presided over by six Buddhist monks in full regalia, who blessed the happy couple. Everyone partook in a traditional feast of epic proportions with alcohol to match.

The family had arranged an interpreter for the speeches by Kurt and his Australian best man, Lionel, who was one of his golfing friends responsible for luring him to Thailand. Lionel praised the bride and beautiful bridesmaids and spoke of their mutual respect for Thai traditions, while Kurt told them about his love for his new bride. He promised to take care of her, to love and provide for her, which is such an essential promise to a Thai woman, as well as help look after her family, which brought a loud and long-standing ovation. Every mother and father present dreamt of finding such a man for one of their daughters.

Kurt loved the Thai people and their simple and happy way of life. He was head over heels in love with Lindy and enamored with her family. Kurt enjoyed visiting them despite his lack of understanding of the language, but with Lindy's help, Kurt got by, and everyone went out of their way to make him feel welcome. Over time he understood enough of the language to hold conversations with them, and they were delighted that he took the time to learn. They respected him, and he admired them in return.

Lindy, meanwhile, loved Australia and her new way of life. However, she still intended to send money home every week to help support her family, as family responsibility was fundamental in her world. That was another reason Lindy especially, and Kurt by proxy, was keen to help Clancy overcome his grief and pour scorn on his brother and sister for running away. Ignoring family responsibility was abhorrent to any Thai child. Lindy hoped to help Clancy in a way he couldn't even imagine by introducing him to her sister. She eagerly awaited his arrival at the barbeque, feeling a deep sense of excitement in her stomach.

Kurt had invited two other couples from the area he thought might also be able to help the young'un. They were all good people who would go out of their way to help someone they considered worth supporting, such as Clancy, whom everyone saw as a *battler*. Yes, they felt he had a lot still to learn about farming, and yes, he seemed dark and foreboding, downright moody at times, but he'd lost his parents and siblings, so Kurt thought he deserved to be a *little odd*. Clancy seemed willing to listen and learn for one so young, and the community pitched in to help as much as possible.

The locals hadn't seen a lot of Clancy around town because he had been busy working toward his dream. Clancy hadn't neglected the farm, far from it; he had worked like a demon daily and felt healthy because of the workload. At night, he worked on what would become his Torture Chamber, the old farm manager's cabin. He had stripped the internal walls, ceiling, and floors and inserted soundproofing material into the cavities before relining them. He installed double glazing on the windows and internal bars over them. He replaced the door with a solid wooden door with two deadlocks that would withstand a battering ram, so there was no way out.

Clancy enjoyed frequent dreams and fantasies of holding a woman captive in the chamber, using her when and how he chose, and punishing her when he felt she deserved it. In his mind, inflicting pain and suffering had become synonymous with sexual gratification because he had not had sex with anyone other than himself, so didn't know any different.

He had also spent a lot of time wondering where he could find such a victim, abduct her, and remain undetected, so he could enjoy her at his leisure without fearing capture. He had spent three evenings over two weekends in Perth hunting for a candidate. On the odd occasion he had seen a woman on the street alone, he pulled over and offered a lift. But one look at the dirty tray back utility driven by an intense-looking and scruffily dressed man, and any hope of her getting in the vehicle was over. He was annoyed with his run of bad luck because he thought it would be easy to find a woman to play with. Clancy had yet to find his first victim when he was invited to attend Kurt and Lindy's barbeque. He had long admired Lindy from afar because her looks were beautiful and exotic due to her nationality. Clancy was sexually aroused every time he saw her and tried to sneak illicit peeks at her underwear whenever he saw her in town, as she always dressed in a way that invited it, he believed.

Clancy went into town, got a fresh haircut, and bought new clothes for the occasion. He turned up on time, carrying a small ice chest with beers and a bottle of wine which Hank, the manager of the local pub, had assured him Lindy would like.

Kurt welcomed Clancy and took him through the house to the back patio, where Lindy introduced him to her sister, Nadia, who had just arrived from Thailand. She had come at Kurt's expense and Lindy's insistence that she would be perfect for Clancy as a potential future wife. The other two couples in attendance went utterly unnoticed by Clancy, who was hit by a thunderbolt of immediate and utter infatuation with the stunningly beautiful Nadia. Such was the purity of his feelings; he didn't have a single deviant thought of what he would like to do to her; he just stared open-mouthed.

Nadia, whose Thai and English names were the same, was very slight with silky black hair, traditional high cheekbones, and long eyelashes. Nadia didn't wear makeup; she didn't need to and was dressed in a bright purple dress that fit her perfectly. She bowed her head coquettishly when introduced to Clancy and looked at him through the top of her eyes in a manner she had been taught was guaranteed to melt any man's heart. Being so naïve in everyday relationships and attracted to such a woman, Clancy was utterly lost in a wave of infatuation and desire.

When he looked at Nadia, he didn't want to hurt her and force her to perform perverse acts for him. He wanted to hold her. This was the first time Clancy saw a woman in any capacity other than a prospect for his Torture Chamber. With Nadia, he was in awe of her beauty and wanted to worship at her feet if that was what it took for this goddess to take notice of him. He found himself trembling as his breath caught in his chest and began to sweat, beads of perspiration forming on his forehead. Realizing he was sweating only made him more nervous, which made him perspire even more. He was powerless to stop the cycle of embarrassment.

He held out his hand to shake because he didn't

know what else to do. He was incapable of coherent speech, and Nadia took his offering, smiling with her eyes and lips. Her hand, so tiny in his, felt warm and soft, while Clancy's was rough and calloused. Clancy could feel the immediate surge of electricity coursing through his body, starting from her gentle touch, and gathered momentum until it exploded like a firework in his chest.

Though Nadia was only twenty-three, she could see the devastating effect she had on him. She knew he was hooked; her future would now be secure, and she felt her sister's eyes upon them. Neither Nadia nor Clancy wanted to let go of the other's hand as they stared into each other's eyes. It was only Kurt clearing his throat loudly that broke the spell.

Clancy turned around and only then saw the other people in the room. He blushed a deep shade of red as he mumbled an acknowledgment to Lionel, Judy Walton, George 'Bluey' McKenna, and his wife AJ. The two women thought the display was adorable as they watched the two starstruck lovebirds-to-be, while Bluey and Lionel, who were part of the *Thailand Golfing Gang*, knew from experience what young Clancy must be feeling. They knew what he would be doing later, *the lucky bugger,* they both thought at the same time.

Nadia took the portable ice chest Clancy had brought with him and took it out to the kitchen while he shook hands with the men and said hello to the women. Within moments she rushed back with a beer for him and gave her demure, coquettish smile once more. For the rest of the evening, Nadia waited on him hand and foot. When his beer was getting low, she brought a fresh one for him, which she delivered with a little bow. She filled a plate for him when the food was ready and sat at his side while he ate.

Her English was passable, far from perfect, yet Nadia hung on every word he said whether she understood or not as if when Clancy spoke, he was a prophet. Nadia rarely stopped looking and smiling at him unless someone else talked to her. Then it was as if she answered as quickly as possible so she could get back to attending to her man. Like a prized fish, she reeled Clancy in by making him feel, with her little touches and smiles, that he was the most crucial person in the world.

After dinner, the women tidied and cleaned up while the men stayed outside on the patio. Kurt regaled them with stories learned by living with a Thai woman and how the pros outweighed the cons. Clancy listened with rapt attention, picking up pointers, as he had already decided to try to win Nadia's heart but didn't know how. Kurt smiled at his rapt attention, knowing the battle had already been won before they met. Lindy had been correct in her assessment of Clancy and how good a relationship with her sister could be. Kurt wasn't an idiot. He knew a major attraction for Nadia would be that she would enjoy a better life as Clancy's wife than scraping a living in Bangkok, as Lindy had with him. But that didn't make it any less real, and Kurt had never been as happy with his first wife, as much as he loved her, as he was with Lindy. There was no reason Clancy couldn't find true happiness with Nadia. Farming was challenging, working from dawn to dusk, and a man needed a wife to support him.

Once the other two couples left, Clancy remained seated on the couch. Nadia knelt on the floor by his side, a hand on his thigh, while Kurt and Lindy sat opposite them. The two women spoke in their native language while Kurt and Clancy sipped port from Kurt's well-stocked wine cellar. Clancy felt lost. He wanted to be with Nadia in the worst possible way, and he would do anything to make it happen, but what could he say or do? Clancy's mind raced for something to say; he had no idea how to proceed; he only knew he didn't want to let her out of sight. Clancy didn't want to leave Kurt's home because it would mean leaving Nadia, yet he was scared if he asked her out, she might say no, then he would curl into a ball and cry.

"Clancy, hello, Clancy?" Lindy said to him in her silken voice, and he shook himself out of his mental toing and froing.

"Umm yes, sorry, Lindy, I was miles away woolgathering."

She smiled warmly at him. "We understand what you are going through. Nadia says she likes you very much and hopes you will take her home with you. She is here on holiday for two weeks. She will make you a very good wife if you like her."

Clancy swallowed loudly. "Oh, yes, Lindy. I like her very, very much. You mean she wants to come home with me now? Really? But I still need to clean the house up. It's a mess. Since Mum died…" House cleaning, washing, dusting, vacuuming, and such was not his strong suit. He had been too busy. He felt embarrassed that the cleanest, tidiest place on the whole farm was the torture chamber he had made, but he had no intention of taking her there.

Lindy burst into laughter and spoke to Nadia, who laughed too but also smiled at her new man. "I tell her what you say, Clancy, and she is happy to clean house for you. She like that very, very much."

Clancy looked at Kurt, who nodded before adding, "Nadia has come from Thailand just to meet you because Lindy arranged it that way, not for a holiday with us. Nadia wants to stay with you for two weeks, and if you like her and she likes you, which I know she will, Clancy, have no fear about, then we can work out how you can be together more. Just treat her well, and she will do anything you want, just no violence, Clancy. Don't ever raise a hand to her. Thai women won't stand for that. It is their culture to please their man, and you will love Nadia as I came to love Lindy."

He stood up and crossed the room, hugged Lindy, and whispered his thanks in her ear, his voice quivering, then stood and shook Kurt's hand. "I promise I will never hurt Nadia."

Clancy had never felt more nervous as he returned to where he had left Nadia to find her gone. Moments later, she was back with her suitcase in hand, head bowed, waiting for him to take her home.

He had no idea how to make love to her because, up until that point in his life, he only had pornography and fantasies based around kidnap, rape, and torture. That first night, Nadia showed him how to be gentle, realizing he was nervous and inexperienced but wanted to learn. She undressed before him, reveling in the adoration of his eyes on her naked body. Then Nadia slowly undressed him. When Clancy tried to rush, excited, she gently but firmly slowed him down while at the same time teaching him where and how to touch her. Nadia showed him when to be soft and harsh with her.

That first night together, they could not get enough of each other. She mounted and rode him, her hands on his chest, watching his eyes so she could see the moment he ejaculated. She loved how excited he was with her. She took him higher and higher until he reached a peak he could not have imagined possible.

When Clancy recovered after their first time making love, Nadia brought him back to life with her hands, lips, and tongue. He had never imagined how good oral sex would feel in real life, even though he had seen it in magazines. Clancy had no idea lovemaking, as opposed to violent sex, could be that great, as she brought him to the brink time after time before urging him to finally finish. She swallowed as she gazed into his eyes and saw the total devotion he now had for her. If Clancy wasn't totally mesmerized and lost before that moment, he certainly was after.

The two weeks together flew by, every day bringing wonder for Clancy in every imaginable way. The house had never been so clean. It sparkled, his clothes were washed and pressed to perfection, and the food she cooked was incredible. Slowly Nadia increased the chili content, so by the time she was packing to return to Thailand, he was totally converted to Thai cuisine. She was also open to helping him with jobs on the farm, offering to spend the day with him on the tractor, working with the sheep, cleaning out the chicken coop, and showing she came from a farming family background.

****

All thoughts of rape and torture left Clancy's mind, and the chamber he had spent many hours creating stayed locked. When Nadia offered to clean in there, he told her it was one private place he did not want her to enter. She respected his request with a bow and a smile.

There was no doubt in either of their minds that he

would want to marry her. Clancy could no longer imagine a life without her, and Nadia desperately wanted the stability and lifestyle Australian citizenship, and marriage would bring. Kurt was there to advise Clancy on how to proceed, having been through it himself.

When her two weeks were up, Nadia had to return to Thailand, and Clancy was miserable without her. But he had to apply for a passport and wedding license in two countries, which took time. When his passport arrived, Clancy booked a flight to Bangkok. Nadia had promised to meet him at the airport, and Clancy feared she wouldn't be there, but he needn't have worried. Together again, they took a connecting flight to the northern border town closest to her family's farm. She had arranged for her brother to meet them at the airport and drive them in a hired vehicle, paid by Clancy, to her home so he could formerly ask her parents' permission to marry her. Not surprisingly, they agreed.

Like Kurt, he soon fell in love with the gentle way of life of the Thai people. He had already been converted to the food, and he had missed Nadia's home cooking while they had been apart. Kurt had readily agreed to be his best man, and for the second time, the family enjoyed another colossal wedding ceremony. The family was the envy of everyone because they had one and now two wealthy men to look after their daughters and provide money to support the family. They were rich beyond their wildest dreams.

Kurt and Lindy's house was built on the farm by then, and Clancy and Nadia stayed with them for two weeks, during which they had the ceremony. A complete change had come over Clancy since being with Nadia. He seemed taller as he no longer walked with a stoop, and he was rarely seen not smiling. Life was good. In fact, it was better than he ever could have imagined it.

When they returned home to the Narrogin farm as man and wife, Nadia was carrying their child. The sexually perverted fantasies he used to enjoy were a thing of the past. Clancy felt he had changed to such an extent he considered making peace with his brother and sister, but after much self-debate, he decided that was just a bridge too far to cross.

Chapter 16

The Spawn of an Evil Mind

On the fourth of May 1983, Joel Timothy Pike was born, and unlike his father, he was a dream baby. With his shock of black hair, coal-black oval eyes, and slight build, he was a gorgeous baby everyone wanted to cuddle. He had inherited his mother's olive skin and looks and his father's deep thoughtfulness, even though later it would be judged to be a moody temperament.

Clancy was absolutely smitten at first sight of his son and cried tears of joy, which was a new emotion for him. He vowed to himself never to hit his child or even raise a hand to him, as he had been beaten. He doted on Joel every chance he got, and his love for Nadia grew even more than he thought possible. He thanked her for coming into his life, changing him for the better, and giving him a son he idolized.

Clancy Pike was a different man to the one who lay on the top of a wheat silo, watching his father drown in grain. He was calmer and more self-assured. Now he could be found whistling a tune or singing a song while he worked around the farm, which he had certainly never done before.

While he mellowed and became a better man over the next few years, Clancy noticed Nadia slowly changed for the worst. It started with small things; she would appear to be angry with him over trivial things, and when she was angry or moody, she wouldn't want the sex which he had come to think of as a regular part of their relationship. After numerous arguments, Nadia said it was because they lived remotely from anywhere, and she felt isolated. Other than occasional social gatherings with other wives she met through Joel's school, her entire life revolved around the farm. Nadia said she was bored and pleaded with Clancy to sell the farm and buy something else closer to the city so she could have friends and things for her and Joel to do. Even for Nadia to visit her sister, their nearest neighbor, without a driver's license was a major organizational nightmare. Nadia wasn't used to being away from family and friends for long periods.

Clancy agreed; the farm was too big for him to run, and he had been thinking of selling it for a long time. Clancy had to employ more people than he wanted to run the place efficiently, and he had been unsuccessful in finding a good farm manager. The farm was profitable, but it occurred to him that Nadia was right; almost every waking hour was spent working. It had always been his desire to downsize anyway, but he just hadn't been able to commit to doing so. Clancy realized Nadia was echoing his own secret thoughts, and it would be good for them as a family to have more free time to spend with Joel.

Of course, when he had harbored dreams of a torture chamber years before, selling the farm was out of the question. But now his life was so different; his priorities had changed. Since Joel had been born, he wanted to spend more time with him first and Nadia second, so he had no problem putting the farm on the market and moving nearer to Perth.

Clancy had long since restored the torture chamber back to its original status as a cabin and removed all the gruesome items of torture and imprisonment he had collected. He couldn't imagine returning to those dark and morbid thoughts. He had turned it into a guest cabin for when Nadia's family came from Thailand for short holidays, which they had on two occasions. He assured Nadia he was happy to give her what she wanted, but to maximize the sale price, they needed to do some fixing up around the place first, which would take a little while.

She seemed to cheer up again, the arguments eased, and she helped as much as possible, desperately wanting to escape her isolation and loneliness. Their sex life was great again, and with the tap turned back on, Clancy was happy once more with life.

****

What Clancy did not know, or would ever know, was that the sex was far from spectacular for Nadia. She knew Clancy had never been with anyone before her, and she had patiently, but unsuccessfully, tried to coach him to think of her needs too. In their early days, Nadia had gone out of her way to make things memorable for him so he would want to marry her, but that had set the tone for Clancy to think he was the world's greatest lover. Clancy had never taken criticism well, and when she tried to make him help her enjoy sex, he wouldn't, or couldn't, do it. She became more frustrated as time passed, which added to her loneliness.

****

Five months later, the agents were called out to value the property, and word traveled like wildfire throughout the Narrogin area that the Pike farm was up for sale. There was a healthy market for good quality farming properties of their size of operation, and within short order, offers to buy were rolling in.

Kurt and Lindy were dismayed to lose Clancy and Nadia but understood it was better for them as a family to bring up their son closer to the city, especially if it would make Nadia happy. When the two men were alone talking privately, Kurt asked Clancy if everything was all right at home. Clancy replied, "Yes, everything is fantastic. Why do you ask?"

"Listen, Clancy, don't take this the wrong way, okay? But you must try to understand how some Thai people think and guard yourself against it."

"What do you mean, Kurt?" Clancy was not angry but instantly became wary. He did not like the way the conversation was heading. He respected Kurt, but if he thought he would allow his soon-to-be ex-neighbor to insult his wife, they would fall out in a hurry.

"I'm not saying Nadia is like some others but let me just say this; Lindy believes my farm and money are tied up in family trusts, and she can't get her hands on half of it if we broke up." He stared pointedly at Clancy.

"Are you saying Nadia only wants me for my money and will take off with half of everything once I sell? Kurt, you, and Lindy introduced us. How could you have done that if you thought that was true?"

"I'm not saying she is like that, son. I'm just saying to be careful, just in case. You've heard the old saying 'forewarned is forearmed?' Well, once you sell the farm, if she took you for half of your money, she and her whole family could live like kings for the rest of their lives in Thailand. That's a big temptation for anyone, but family responsibility is such an important consideration for any daughter in Thai culture. Also, consider this: Nadia has an Australian child, and she doesn't need you to stay here as a resident. She can get citizenship easily because she married an Australian. Now, if she is delighted with her marriage with you, then don't worry about it and forget I said anything, but if you think she might not be happy, be careful when the farm is sold, and don't give her the opportunity to take off with Joel."

Clancy's blood turned to ice in his veins, and his hands formed fists. Were it not for a deep friendship bordering on affection for Kurt, he felt he could not stop himself from hitting the much older man. No one, not then and not ever, would take his son away from him. He would die before he allowed that to happen. Whether it was Nadia or anyone else, he knew he would kill them if they tried it.

"Calm down, Clancy. I'm just asking you to be careful because I care for you. You've been like the son I never had, and I don't want to see you hurt. Please just remember what I said and be wary. In my heart, I think if Lindy thought she could get half the farm, she would have left me long ago because her obligation to herself and her family is so much stronger than her obligation to me. Look at me; she is eighteen years younger than me. I'm not stupid; I know what she sees in us being together. She is happy because she has a good life here, far better than she would have had back in Thailand, but I never forget she would be off in a flash if she could get her hands on half of my money."

Clancy didn't reply. Instead, he turned on his heel and left, taking Nadia. Kurt thought Clancy would calm down and understand his warning was not malicious, but he never did.

At first, Clancy refused to believe Nadia would do that to him. She loved him, and that was all there was to it. Kurt was out of line to infer Nadia would run off with his son and half his money. It was too late when Clancy suspected Kurt had been right all along. Clancy had chosen another path, and pride would not allow him to tell Kurt he had been right from the start.

The seed of Nadia's discontent had been planted in Clancy's brain, and the worms of doubt grew slowly. It festered, and Clancy began to see Nadia in a light he never would have if Kurt hadn't opened his mouth. He began to recognize fault in her when before he thought she was perfect. When she didn't want sex with him, Clancy wondered if she was getting it elsewhere. After all, Clancy reasoned, he spent many hours in the fields; how would he know if she had a lover call around when he was busy? Clancy further speculated if she wanted to move closer to the city because she was bored or to fool around with other men. Once the green god of jealousy turned its evil eye on Clancy, there was no stopping it from turning from suspicion to conviction.

From that day forward, he never felt as happy or content with life as before, except when he was with Joel. Joel could do no wrong, and as father and son, they became closer by the day. They went fishing and shooting together, and Joel was a quick learner. Like his father, he had no compunction with killing animals, especially when praised for doing it. Joel's world revolved around pleasing his dad, and he was never as happy as when he and Clancy were off on the Quad bikes or shooting rabbits, which his father explained were vermin but tasty to eat. They both loved Nadia's version of Thai Green Rabbit Curry. Joel never gave cause for

Clancy to yell at him in anger, let alone hit him. They were as close as two people could be, so close Nadia felt excluded from their secret *boy's* world.

From a very early age, Joel was taught to kill farm animals for food and wild dogs, which threatened the sheep, rabbits, kangaroos, and even wild pigs roaming their land. By five years old, Joel was a perfect shot and could kill most animals he aimed at with only one bullet. He also learned to butcher them and though he didn't admit it, derived a lot of pleasure from using his father's razor-sharp knife on any animal living only moments before.

The farm's new owner, who was taking over at the end of the financial year, was a mining magnate actively expanding his business into farming properties. Just before the farm settled and they were to move out, Clancy went up to the copse of Gum Trees, where he had buried Malcolm, the farm manager, long before to ensure there was no visible sign of the grave.

There was no tell-tale dip, or rise, in the lie of the land, and if Clancy didn't know where he had buried the body, he could not tell because of the undergrowth and new trees which had taken over the grave. The trees were ancient but healthy, and he ensured it was deep when digging the hole. The area was too undulating for practical farming, so the new owner would be unlikely to rip up the trees and seed for grain. Malcolm's body was as safe there as anywhere, he thought. Clancy said a silent farewell, without nostalgia, because since he had made his first kill, he had never lost one minute of sleep over it. As Clancy looked around, he knew he would be safe. No future owner would want to do anything with this small piece of land because it provided shaded shelter for the sheep and assisted with the rising salt level, a problem for all farmers.

****

While awaiting settlement, Clancy purchased a hundred-and-eighty-acre property in the hills around Perth he and Nadia found, which had vast amounts of almond, peach, and plum trees, along with enough sheep to keep him busy and room to grow grain to feed them. It was scenic land with a large, five-bedroom federation-style house and three cabins for staff to live in when fruit pickers were needed. A beautiful creek ran through it, fed by an underground spring. Water was abundant with several large dams, and Nadia wanted to use one to grow fish, as her parents did in Thailand.

Over the next few years, they settled into everyday family life in their new home. Joel seemed happy, as did Nadia, though deep down, she still felt isolated, bored, and sexually frustrated. Since they had moved, Clancy had seemed colder to her. In some ways, though he had never raised a hand to her, she feared him. It was in his eyes, she realized. They were the eyes of the dead when he didn't get his own way. One night, after Joel was in bed when she genuinely had a headache and did not want to perform for him, his look was cold and distant, and she felt fear for her life. Because of her fear, she succumbed despite the headache, hoping this would be one of the times Clancy was finished quickly, but of course, he chose that night to be a stayer, not a sprinter.

Since the falling out with Kurt and Lindy, Clancy had actively discouraged her from contacting them. The trips to Thailand and back to see her sister slowed, and eventually, with Clancy insistently pushing, they stopped. If they tried to call on the phone, Clancy would either say she was out, didn't want to speak to them, or was away on holiday without him and wouldn't be back for days. He never used the same excuse twice; over time, it had the desired effect; she spoke much less with her family.

Since the fateful conversation with Kurt, Nadia noticed Clancy looked at her in a different light though she never found out why. At first, he slowly became more demanding, jealous of her movements, and more controlling. The changes in him came so slowly Nadia barely noticed them, but she saw his demands for sex and how he wanted it to become more domineering, even at times, bordering on callous.

Clancy barely noticed the change in himself, but because he was wary of Kurt's warning, he became suspicious of even the most innocent things. When she became close with Len, the man from the brown trout fish farm, his jealousy knew no bounds.

****

Nadia had always wanted to branch out into fish farming. She investigated which were the best fish to breed. Her studies made her think trout could be viable, and conveniently, a trout farm was only fifteen kilometers away. Joel was in school when she went to see the fish farmer and got some advice on whether her plan was viable.

She was immediately attracted to Len, the owner, and believed he was toward her. Nadia knew she was still an attractive woman whom the years had been kind to. She noticed the spark ignite in each other, as did Len's wife, Ann, who made sure she didn't leave them alone, knowing full well of her husband's penchant for casual sex with any woman he could seduce with his good looks and rugged manly nature. She had threatened to leave him on previous occasions, but there was a lot to love about him; Len never made any secret of how he was, and finally, he always returned to her.

When she came home to Clancy that first day after meeting him, she talked incessantly of trout. It was, "Len told me this," "Len showed me that," or "Len offered to help stock the dam." Everything was "Len, Len, Len."

Nadia saw Clancy was troubled, even jealous, and calmed him, telling him he was being silly. She made love to him, knowing that was the easiest way to ease his worried mind and stop the inevitable cross-examination of any future meetings with Len. Nadia knew if Clancy's sex life was good, his world was good. When she seduced him, it was purely for his benefit and to show her love for him because Nadia imagined it was Len making love to her, and for the first time in years, Clancy nearly made her quiver in orgasm. Nadia continued her visits to the trout farm for advice, and Len visited to look at their dams and water supply.

Where Clancy was stocky, dark-haired, and moody, Len was blond, well-tanned, built like a bricklayer, and happy. He rarely wore a shirt, so when Nadia was talking with him, she could see the beads of sweat on his skin, and she fantasized about him taking her in his big strong arms and making her scream in orgasm, which she hadn't done with Clancy for a very, very long time.

Once, three years earlier, she had taken Joel into Perth to have his tonsils removed, which made Clancy distraught as he didn't want to leave his son's side. But they were right in the middle of shearing the sheep, and he had to stay behind on the farm. For the first time in their marriage, once her son was settled for the night in his hospital bed, she went to a bar in the city, like she used to in Bangkok. She had a great night out and allowed herself to be picked up by a man whose name she couldn't remember. The one thing she could remember was how he made her scream in the throes of a massive orgasm in his hotel room. Nadia hadn't looked for an opportunity since, but when she talked to Len, she remembered how good sex could be and wanted him to take her and make her scream like she had before. When Len delivered the first two hundred fingerlings and released them into the dam, Clancy was out spraying the plum trees, after which he would pick up Joel from school. Len and Nadia stood side by side, watching the fish swim in their new home.

She brought him a cold beer from a small, insulated container she had thought to bring with her from the house to reward him, followed by another and then another. They talked for what seemed like ages in the afternoon sunshine, and Nadia felt the attraction for each other growing. After an hour and a half of watching the fish and drinking beer, she turned to him, "Thank you for bringing the fish, Len. I will have Clancy pay you for them." She said, looking up at him as he towered above her and stared into his eyes.

"That's fine, Nadia. He can pay for the fish, but there was another way I was hoping you could pay me for the delivery fee." He reached out and cupped her breast in his right hand while he put his left hand on her buttocks. She gasped in shock and arousal when he squeezed and rubbed with both hands. She froze like a rabbit in headlights and closed her eyes, unable to stop him and not wanting to.

Nadia felt mesmerized as Len caressed her. He

undid all her shirt buttons, yanked it out of her jeans, down her arms, and tossed it onto the grass. She wore a pink bra, and he pulled the straps off her shoulders and down her arms, exposing her breasts to the cool breeze. He dropped to his knees at once, sucking, licking, and biting each of her nipples in turn while at the same time undoing her jeans and jerking them and her panties down. She had yearned to be taken by a big strong man and she felt her pulse racing. He was stripping her naked in the open air, and she so desperately wanted it.

"We can't do this," she cried breathlessly, her hands on his shoulders steadying herself as his fingers found her wetness and delved inside her, firmly, almost roughly, like he wasn't going to take no for an answer.

"Yes, we can. You want it as much as I do." Len pulled her down onto the grass and ripped one of her shoes off, followed by her jeans and underwear over the same foot, leaving them coiled around the other.

He knelt between her thighs, looking down at her naked body, with obvious hunger, making Nadia pant with desire. He was savoring the moment, she knew. He undid his jeans and pushed them down over his hips, and Nadia felt a shiver run through her entire body as she looked at his huge, throbbing manhood, knowing it would be inside her any moment.

"Tell me you want it," he said, "tell me you want me to fuck you."

His dirty words only turned her on more, and the last of her willpower departed, and she moaned, "Take me, Len."

Nadia wrapped her legs around him so he could go deep into her body. She turned her head to the side and moaned out loud, and as she opened her eyes, feeling more excited than she had in years, she saw Clancy and Joel, watching them and standing just a few feet away.

She gasped loudly and froze in shock, and in an instant Clancy was upon them. He kicked Len viciously in his side; his steel-capped boot connected heavily. Before Len could respond or do anything, the breath was knocked from him. Clancy punched him to the side of his face, a damaging blow that cracked bone, and caused him to fall to the ground, clearly dazed and confused. By then, it was all over, but there was no stopping an enraged Clancy. Nadia watched helplessly as Clancy dove on Len, and they rolled until Clancy knelt on top of her near-unconscious lover and pummeled his face with punches from both fists.

****

Joel watched with a faraway look in his eye. His fists were clenched because he wanted to help his father and hurt the man, hurt him severely for what he had done to his mum. Joel watched as his mother jumped to her feet, naked except for the jeans around one leg, and tried to pull her husband off the other man. She screamed for him to stop, that he was killing Len, and slowly her voice appeared to break through the red veil of anger that seemed to drive his father.

Seeing the unbridled violence and his mother's naked body aroused Joel in a way he had never felt before. Far from being horrified, he was excited. Like his father before him, in his mind, he now associated violence with sex.

****

Clancy stopped punching, his knuckles bloody with two of them broken. His victim was unconscious, his face battered, broken, bleeding, and Clancy realized he was panting and could barely catch his breath. He looked down at the fish man, his face now unrecognizable, and thought: *you won't be fucking another man's wife anytime soon, will you, fish-man?*

Eventually, his breathing and strength returned. He still knelt over Len when he looked up at Nadia, crying and repeatedly sobbing about how sorry she was. This was a side of her husband Clancy knew she had no idea existed, and she looked terrified, which pleased him.

Clancy pushed Nadia away, and she fell over on the grass as her feet tangled in her jeans. He slowly stood up, still angry, but now his focus shifted to her. He undid his leather belt, and when it was unbuckled, he pulled it through his denim jeans belt loops and wrapped the buckle end around his hand. Clancy could feel he had become his father in a way he couldn't comprehend. Nadia needed to be punished, and he was the man to deliver the punishment. Clancy wanted to hurt her as he had been punished as a child.

"You see, Joel? You see what your mother is? She doesn't love you or me." He stood over her and brought the belt down on her bare skin with a loud cracking sound, which left a bright red stripe. She screamed and raised her arms to ward off further blows, but it was useless. A mental image flashed into Clancy's head of himself cowering when his father had done the same to him, but rather than make him stop; it urged him on more as if it were his father he was punishing and not Nadia.

"I do love you both," Nadia shouted, but the belt came down again and again as she screamed louder and turned over, trying to crawl away, which only gave an easier target for Clancy. He continued to rain blows on her bare skin until it glowed red. Eventually, Clancy's arm ached. His adrenalin was used up, and he had to stop, tired and breathless. He slowly put his belt back on and walked back to Joel, kneeling in front of him, "Son, this is how a real man treats his woman when she's been bad, do you understand?"

"Yes, Dad," he answered in a hushed voice. Clancy thought Joel seemed disappointed it had stopped as if he wanted to join in.

"Good boy. Dad loves you; you know that don't you?" Clancy asked, and Joel nodded eagerly.

"Remember when we talked about rabbits when we shot them? What did we say they are, Joel?

"Vermin, Dad."

"Good boy. That's exactly what rabbits are, son, vermin, just like women. Let's go and have some ice cream. We'll leave these two to say their goodbyes to each other, shall we?" He took Joel by the arm and led him to his whimpering mother, face down in the grass. "Tell her what she is, Joel."

Joel stood shaking his head. Clancy noticed his son's dark black eyes were a mirror of his own. "Vermin," he said. He bent at the waist and slapped his mother's bare bottom.

****

Nadia knew it was bad enough she had done what she did and been caught and whipped for it, which was no more than she deserved. But that her son had witnessed her being punished, hated her for her actions, and then joined in was more than Nadia could bear. Nadia could not have imagined such shame, and she cried with a staggering depth of despair. She wanted to crawl into a ball and die. Nadia had breached the most important family values, and amid her world of pain was the real fear that if Clancy told her family what had happened, they would collectively disown her. While she hadn't spoken to them very much recently, she couldn't bear the thought of never being able to again.

"You better help your boyfriend, little rabbit, Clancy muttered. "When he wakes up, you tell him if I ever see him here again, I will kill him, and if you ever see him again, I will kill you both. Oh, and if he goes to the cops, I will kill him and then his wife. Things are going to change around here now that you've shown your true colors, little rabbit. You mark me well. Come on, Joel; let's leave the two love birds to it. I feel like some chocolate sauce with that ice cream. What about you, champ? Strawberry or chocolate?" Nadia felt sick at being called a rabbit in the demeaning way Clancy had, but knew she deserved his anger.

"I want to be like you, Dad," Joel replied, looking up with a smile. Nadia could see Joel didn't just mean about the ice cream. He wanted to *be like his father,* and her heart sank lower.

"That's my boy. Chocolate it is. Race you back to the car, *go!*" And Joel took off, laughing, with Clancy jogging behind: father and son, two peas in a pod.

****

Len had always considered himself tough and didn't feel any guilt in trying to seduce other men's wives; it was just sport so far as he was concerned. Most almost begged for it. But Len knew he had crossed a line with Clancy. If he ever tried again with Nadia, Clancy was capable of a ferocity and level of violence beyond him. When Nadia told him, what Clancy had said, he believed the threat implicitly.

For the first time in his life, Len felt fear of another

man. So much that he knew if he ever walked down a street in the future and saw Clancy approaching him, he would cross the road to avoid coming face to face. Len also knew his wife would not be stupid enough to fall for any explanation for his injuries other than the truth. She knew he screwed around. Ann had always accepted it so long as he went home to her and was discrete. No doubt she would be pleased he had got his just desserts. Len took the risk knowingly with married women; he'd rarely been caught in the past, and when he had, the husband had been too much of a coward to confront him. Now he had gotten caught by a husband who wasn't scared; *that's life*. As he climbed into the cab of his utility, his tongue was worrying two adjoining, loose teeth, and he had trouble seeing out of his left eye due to the swelling which had forced it nearly closed. Len finally accepted he was the problem, not Clancy, and would not report the assault to the police.

****

Three hours later, Nadia got back to the house. It wasn't too far from the dam, but it had taken that long to walk because she was in so much pain. Nadia knew she could not have left Len as he was, for fear he might die. She cooled him down and cleaned the blood off him with his own T-shirt dipped in the dam water until he eventually regained consciousness and could return to his farm, as dazed and concussed as he was. Nadia would not leave the farm to drive with him. If she had, and Clancy found out, she knew there would be hell to pay, more than she had already experienced.

Nadia returned to the house to find Joel had showered and eaten dinner. He was sitting watching the TV with his father in adjoining armchairs, and she noticed, not for the first time, just how much like his father Joel was. They sat the same and had identical expressions, and now she knew they also thought the same. The slap Joel had delivered out of his disgust with her was a testament to that. Watching Joel was like looking at a smaller, younger version of Clancy.

Neither looked up to greet her, and she stood momentarily, not knowing what to say to them. Their disdain for her was painfully obvious. She knew she had to try to find a way back in with them, no matter what it took. "I am ashamed of what I let Len do today. I am sorry. Please, I beg you both forgive me."

Neither Clancy nor Joel spoke, looked up, or even acknowledged she was there. Slowly and silently, she walked away to the main bedroom and the adjoining bathroom to shower her poor, painful body. Nadia felt dirty, ashamed, and lost. She could not run away because she had nowhere to go, and despite Joel despising her, he was her son, and she would not abandon him. Nadia would bring untold shame upon her family if she left, as they would disown her once they found out what she had done to cause the breakdown of her marriage. Her only hope lay in trying to make it up to Clancy and Joel and showing them that she was genuinely sorry.

Once showered, she got ready for bed and returned to the family room, where they were still sitting in the same position, except Clancy now had three empty beer bottles by his side and another one in his hand. She knelt at Clancy's feet, her chin touching her chest, and whispered, "Please forgive me. It never happened before, and I was so wrong. I beg you both; please forgive me. I do love you, and I know I made a terrible mistake. Please let me make it up to you both. I am so ashamed."

"Your mother, my wife, made a mistake, Joel. Did you hear? What do we think of that kind of mistake?" Clancy replied, not moving his gaze from the TV screen.

Joel shook his head, his eyes dark and hooded, his brow furrowed, precisely like his fathers was when he was angry. Deep down, Joel was confused and conflicted, but he loved his dad more than anything and, even before today's disgrace, much more than his mother. His mother had never mistreated or laid a hand on him, but she was frosty compared to his dad's outpouring of love and affection. His dad was angry with his mum; therefore, he was too; that concept was simple to him. There could be no doubt she had done wrong; he knew what she had done with the man was dirty and disloyal to his father, and his dad's anger made it even more dirty. The other thing which made him feel conflicted was that he liked watching his dad beat his mum. In fact, Joel enjoyed it for reasons he couldn't understand. Joel loved the cracking sound of the belt on her skin, her begging and screaming for it to stop, and the red welts which appeared. He felt in awe of his dad's power over his mum and the pain he inflicted on her naked body. Her nakedness was another guilty pleasure Joel felt. He knew he shouldn't be thinking of his mother that way, but the combination of her being naked and the whipping she received reached into his soul and flicked a switch on.

He knew his father had been proud of him for smacking his mother as she lay on the ground and pleasing his dad meant more than anything else to him in the world. That was the only reason Joel tried so hard at school, not because he liked studying, but because he needed to please his dad, whom he idolized.

"Bad, dirty, mum," he said, not bothering to disguise the disgust in his black hooded eyes as he looked at her.

"Good boy, Joel. She says she never did it before with the fish man. Do we believe her or is she telling lies? What do you think?"

"I promise you. I never did it before." Nadia pleaded, "I am so sorry. I will never do it again. I don't know what came over me."

"What did mum do to you when you did a bad thing when you were a kid, Joel?"

"She punished me."

"That's right, son, she did. When she did the bad thing with the fish man, she disrespected me, and I punished her with my belt because she deserved it. You watched me do it, and when I was done, you smacked her, too, and I was proud of you for that. But that wasn't really your punishment to her; it was because you were angry like I was. My father used his belt on me when I was a boy, and sometimes he would do it so hard he made me bleed, and that's what punishment should be, Joel. My dad did it even when I was good; he just thought I was bad. I think you need to punish your mother, too, don't you?"

His voice trembled with expectation and excitement as he replied, "Yes, I do, Dad. I want to punish her."

"Nadia, go over to the couch and bend over. Put your face into it, deep into it. Joel is going to punish you now too. That's what you deserve."

"No. You can't mean that? He's my son, Clancy; please don't make him......Ahh!" As she pleaded, Clancy leaned forward, slapped her hard, interrupting her words.

"I told you. Things are going to change around here,

little rabbit. You brought this on yourself, not Joel and me. We thought we were all happy, didn't we, son? But you, Nadia, you wanted the fish man all along. Now you do as you're told or pack your things, get out of this house, and never return. Make your choice and be quick about it. Perhaps you could go and move in with your boyfriend, the fish man. I'm sure his wife would love that. Yeah, don't bend over for a spanking. Go and move in with the fish man and his wife. Boy, I'd love to be a fly on the wall if you did."

Nadia held her hand to her smarting face, wide-eyed, totally despaired, and ashamed. Clancy had never hit her before, but she knew he would in the future if she didn't do everything he wanted to fix the mess she had made for herself. She gave one last sob knowing she had no choice. Nadia turned and waddled on her knees across the room to the couch, folded her arms on the seat, and buried her face, crying deeply. Nadia had no idea her husband could be so cruel. To make her son watch and join in her debasement was unthinkable. But she had done wrong and brought this upon herself. She thought this might be an Australian tradition when a wife was unfaithful. All Nadia knew was she had nowhere to go, so whatever Clancy was going to do to her, she deserved and had to accept. She prayed he would forgive her one day and she could return to her previous life, which she now realized wasn't as bad as she believed it was.

Clancy stood up, took off one of his slippers, and handed it to Joel. Clancy lifted Nadia's cotton nightdress, so it was bunched up on her back. Nadia's shame sunk to new depths. "Please," she begged, "Don't do this to me; I promise I will never do anything like it again." To be exposed like this to her son was not right, but she could hardly lecture them about what was right or wrong.

"Joel," his father said. Twenty should do for today. You hit her as hard as you can on her bottom while I count them out, son. It's okay. It's a punishment, so she knows never to be a bad little rabbit again.

The next few minutes were the worst moments she had ever experienced. It wasn't just because being spanked on her bare behind with a shoe was so painful, which it was. But that it was her son delivering the spanking made her feel sick to her stomach, and as she sobbed in pain and humiliation, she swallowed bile and took big gulps of air to stop from vomiting.

When it was over, she made to get up, but Clancy stopped her with a hand on her back. "You just stay there until I get back. I'm going to take Joel to bed, and then we have some more business to attend to," she groaned, knowing what that meant.

When Joel got into bed, Clancy stroked the hair from his forehead and gently said, "You know I love you, Joel, and you know I would never do anything to hurt you, don't you?"

Joel nodded back.

"I don't want you to worry about what happened. Your mum was naughty, and we punished her because that's what we do when someone is bad. I hurt the fish man, and we both spanked mummy, and there is nothing for you to feel bad about. Do you understand, Joel?"

"Yes, Dad. I don't feel bad. I liked it. Is it bad to like doing it, Dad?"

"No, son, it's not bad. In fact, it can be a very good thing. You're a good boy, and I'm proud of you. Now you sleep tight. I love you, lots."

"Love you too, Dad."

He left the bedroom, turning the light off and softly closing the door as he passed through. He was looking forward to continuing Nadia's debasement. He knew she had no choice but to take what he dished out. She couldn't return to her family in shame. After what she had done to him, the love he had always felt for her had died in the very instant he heard her tell Len to take her. Clancy now despised Nadia and saw her as no better than his sister. When watching TV earlier, Clancy remembered everything he wanted to do to Charmaine. Now, at long last, it was time to realize some of those dreams and fantasies. He reasoned it wasn't his doing; it was all her fault.

First things first. Clancy was erect, and his new slave was on her knees waiting. He was going to teach her for wanting to play with other men. Nadia wanted more sex? He was just the man to give it to her. And that was just for today. He would come up with many more exciting things for her in the days, weeks, and months to come. Clancy felt at last as if he had *come home,* he had reached the place he was always destined to reach. He had his very own slave.

Chapter 17

Transition and Bonding

Nadia was strong. She fought them mentally for as long as she could. Her willpower lasted almost a year. For the first few months, Nadia thought if she worked hard and did everything expected of her, Clancy would eventually forgive her and accept her back into their everyday lives. She lived on hope and tried hard to please him. She cooked, cleaned, and worked at any task he gave her like a whirling dervish; she was keen to atone for her sin with Len.

She dressed and used makeup to look attractive and let him have any form of sex he desired, in any position, anytime, and any location. She acted as if it was the best sex she had ever had when for her it was the worst. Nadia would perform oral sex on him whenever she thought he was getting excited to show she was sorry but also because he would usually hurt her less if it was over quickly. Nadia eventually realized her husband looked for ways of causing pain to heighten his own pleasure, and gradually, the pain he inflicted became more extreme.

For Clancy, the sex Nadia offered willingly, and with seeming, pleasure only confirmed in his mind she enjoyed being hurt, which meant he could escalate the next time. But for Nadia, there was no way around it. It wouldn't have made a difference if he had realized she didn't like it or was acting. She came to understand all he cared about was his perverse enjoyment. That meant treating her like a slave and using her body however he saw fit.

Nadia tried to talk to Clancy about her fall from grace many times, to no avail. He either stared at her blankly like she was speaking another language, stood up and walked out of the room or worse, yanked her over his lap and spanked her behind until she begged for it to stop. Because she felt the need to apologize to Joel as well, she tried to apologize to them both, and eventually, Nadia realized it was those occasions when Joel was in the room when Clancy would spank her bottom harder as if to show their son who was in charge.

****

Some nights Joel lay awake in bed and listened to his parents. The smacking sounds, her crying out, and moans of pleasure sounded like she enjoyed it. Having seen the sex act between his mother and Len, the fish man, and the pictures boys shared at school, he knew what was happening, but not being able to see them doing it heightened his imagination, and the sounds of the violence made his visions more lurid. Even when his parents weren't having sex, he began to fantasize, thinking how his dad treated his mom was typical between all men and women. He hoped one day he could experience hurting a woman too.

Clancy installed a series of ringbolts in the center of nearly every room in the house and bought a chain length, a throat collar, and handcuffs. It had been six months since the fish man incident when he told her, out of the blue, as he could no longer trust her, Nadia would be chained to the floor with enough slack to clean the room and no more. Nadia begged and pleaded for him not to lock her up. She told him, to no avail, she would do anything he wanted and never leave the house if he told her not to, but Clancy's mind was made up. While Clancy was working on the farm and Joel was at school, Nadia remained a prisoner in her home. She hoped Clancy would change his mind if she worked hard and acted obediently, ensuring the room she spent the day in sparkled when he returned.

The worst thing for Nadia was that the chain length would not permit her to get to the bathroom. She had to use a bucket if needed, which made her lose what self-respect she had left. Eventually, Nadia began to realize things would not get better and suffered pangs of depression when alone. Somehow, she managed to cheer up when Clancy was there for fear of him thinking she was unhappy and so punish her more. She felt it was essential to put on a brave face because she still hoped he would one day decide enough was enough and would permit her to return to a normal life with him.

No matter how hard she tried, there always seemed to be something she did wrong. She would be lucky if she escaped by being spanked; at other times, it was worse. Sometimes two weeks or more would pass between punishments, and Nadia thought she was slowly clawing her way back. These times of peace would end on an inevitable night when she would be spanked and sometimes raped after Joel went to bed. Clancy enjoyed the bare bottom spanking he would bestow upon her.

One night Joel left his bedroom to watch his mother being hurt. He had decided listening was no longer good enough; he wanted more. He wanted to watch. Joel got out of bed, silently opened his door, and inched his way down the passage on his tiptoes toward the family room, the sounds of his mother's cries getting louder the closer he got.

As he peered around the corner, he couldn't help but gasp loudly at the sight in front of him. Clancy heard the gasp, stopped what he was doing, and turned to see Joel watching them. He smiled at his son to let him know he wasn't in trouble, crooking his finger to let him know he could come closer.

"Mum's been naughty again, Joel. I'm sorry if we woke you."

Joel moved closer. His mouth was wide open; this was much more exciting than when it was played out in his imagination. He lowered himself to the floor, sitting cross-legged.

His father smiled knowingly. *Like father, like son,* Clancy thought, with immense pride, deciding right then to let Joel get more involved with Nadia. He turned back to Nadia to continue.

This became their ritual. It didn't happen every night; there were often long gaps when Nadia would recover and regain hope. But when it was time, she would cook the meal for them and then clean everything up while they played a game or watched TV. Then she would go into the family room where they waited for her, kneel before them, and await her fate.

Slowly, Nadia's spirit was broken, her depression deepened, and as each day passed, her willpower to keep trying weakened.

The pretext of Nadia doing something wrong to deserve her punishment had long since passed; the enjoyment of delivering pain and suffering now provided ample cause for their treatment of her. When the mood took him, Clancy liked to get started straight after Nadia cleaned up after dinner so he could include Joel in whatever he had dreamt up for her. Then, he could get their son into bed, especially if the next day was a school day.

Nadia was worn out, sick of being used and abused, but trapped, chained up like a dog when alone, so escape was impossible. After Clancy invited Joel to become involved, Nadia knew her torment would never end. This was to be her life, for however long that lasted. She was eating less, her skin was loose on her bones, and her long, straggly hair falling out. Her bouts of depression were getting longer, and she was always miserable. Both her husband and son didn't seem to notice or care.

Over time Joel had, like his father, lost all feelings of love and emotion for his mother. She became a plaything to him and nothing more, and he looked forward to the special evening's entertainment. Joel had become a clone of his father and was proud to be so. Sometimes he and his dad would have long talks about women or little rabbits, as his dad liked to call them. He taught his son they should never be trusted and their only purpose was to serve men and suffer when they fell short of delivering satisfaction. Clancy had successfully brainwashed his son into his own perverted way of thinking. He had also convinced Joel their world of degradation was secret and couldn't be shared with friends at school. Joel didn't correct the error in that statement; Joel had no friends at school.

Nadia's final day of incarceration was a Wednesday. Joel was in his last year at school, and Clancy had been back to have lunch made by her. He had been working on the farm, it was a hot day, and he was careless when he shackled her back up. Nadia was so morbidly depressed she didn't notice his mistake right away, and after he left, she just lay on the couch and slept, wishing she could die so her torment and misery would be over.

She awoke with a start and noticed by the sun's angle through the window that time had gotten away from her, and she needed to make a start on dinner. As she walked past the ring bolt on the floor, she noticed the padlock had sprung open. *She could unhook it and run away.*

Nadia had been cowed and imprisoned for so long she froze for minutes, uncomprehending. Finally, Nadia plucked up the courage to crouch down and unhook the chain from the lock. *She was free!* Nadia went to the tin cup on the top shelf in the kitchen cupboard; there were usually some odd notes and coins there for emergencies. Nadia pulled out the princely sum of forty-two dollars. It would be enough to get to her sister's where she would throw herself on her and Kurt's mercy and show them the scars on her. She prayed her sister would take pity and help her.

Nadia quickly dressed in a T-shirt and jeans with soft shoes, which would serve her for the cross-country walking she knew she had to do to escape. There was no way she could stick to the roads. If she could get across the hills and into the city, she could catch a train or bus to her sister's town and phone her so she could be picked up. She grabbed one of Joel's old backpacks and put some food supplies in it. Then she took a light jacket and ran out to the tool shed to find a way to get the chain from around her neck. She doubted she could drag it too far, and getting on a bus would get unwelcome stares.

Using a pair of pliers in one hand holding the ring and a small hacksaw in the other, she sawed at the clasp, nicking her skin several times, which coated the blade and ring she was trying to cut through with blood. Eventually, it came free. She yanked open the leather strap and ran out of the shed straight into Clancy's arms.

****

Clancy had returned to the house before getting Joel from school as he had cut his finger. He'd wrapped a piece of rag over it, but the blood seeped through, so he returned home and got a sticking plaster. As soon as he entered, he saw Nadia was gone. In a panic, he ran to the shed to get one of the four-wheel Quad motorbikes he kept there. Clancy thought he could track her down if she didn't have too much of a head start.

Nadia blindly ran into Clancy's arms and screamed in shock and frustration that her bid for freedom had been so short-lived. She lacked the strength to fight him and knew it would be useless even if she did, but she let out a long, drawn-out scream, hoping someone might hear her and come to her rescue. To be so close yet so far was heartbreaking for Nadia, but she was not going back to being chained up and whipped without screaming as loud and as long as she could.

Even afterward, when Clancy examined his feelings about killing her, he didn't know if he meant to commit murder or just shut her up. Either way, he didn't care once it was over. He was getting bored with her constant whining and moodiness anyway. He could have punched Nadia to quieten her, but instead, Clancy put his hands around her throat and squeezed as hard as he could. He didn't think anyone would have heard her scream, but he wanted to shut her up, just in case. When she raised her fingers to try to break his hold, he shook her violently, forward, and backward, and didn't let up until she stopped moving. She was so light it took no effort at all.

Clancy stopped when she was a dead weight in his hands, and he realized he had killed her. He dropped her lifeless body into the dust. Clancy panicked for a few seconds; shit, *shit, shit, what do I do now?* Joel had to be picked up from school, and he could hardly leave Nadia's body there. With a grim smile, Clancy suddenly realized he wasn't upset about ending Nadia's life, only what he would do about it. He picked her up in his arms, noting she had lost weight, and carried her back into the shed. There was an old rug rolled up leaning against the wall. *Perfect,* he thought. He dropped her on the concrete floor and then rolled out the carpet, placing Nadia's body inside and rolling it back up.

After one last look to ensure the rug didn't look too much like it was concealing a body, he left her in the shed. As he closed the door, he noticed his cut finger, which he had covered with a torn rag. Now, the rag was missing, and his finger was bleeding profusely. He raced back into the house to clean up the blood, hoping he wouldn't be too late for Joel. Clancy changed his shirt, which had red stains on the cuff, and put a Band-Aid over the gash. He would worry about disinfecting it later. It would have to do; Clancy had to pick up his boy.

He worried about where he could hide the body while driving the truck to the school. The idea hit him as he pulled up at the gate to see Joel sitting on the flower bed brick retaining wall waiting. The old, disused gravel pit would be the perfect spot which was only a few kilometers away.

The difference between when he buried Malcolm

and where he decided to bury Nadia was, he had well over nine hundred acres to hide the body on the old farm. The nearest neighbors were a long way away, but in the hills, it was different. He had much less land, and there were no tree-filled copses he could use other than the orchards. The neighbors were a lot closer and might take note if something sinister was going on. Clancy's property predominantly lay in a long, deep valley so anyone could see him from the surrounding hills. Unlikely as that was, he could not take the chance. Clancy also couldn't risk burying Nadia on the property in case some nosy cop found her if her sister complained long and loud enough to make them carry out a search. *Nope,* he thought, *it would be much better to bury her somewhere else.* Clancy had reasoned that if anyone asked after her, he would say she had left him for another man. He could even say she told him she wanted Len, the fish man, back, even though the episode was a year earlier. *That could be fun*, he thought, but then dismissed it because the cops might think it gave him a motive.

He had heard about the disused, blue metal quarry pit just a short distance away some months before. Clancy had taken Joel there, quad biking, on several Sunday afternoons and had a lot of fun. It was where all the local trail biking youths went to let off steam. The quarry was spread over several acres and comprised numerous dips and swirls, making it ideal for mountain bikes or trail bikes. Father and son enjoyed it while Nadia stayed home, chained to the floor, Clancy recalled. *Surely, buried three feet down Nadia's body would never be found because no one would dig there, and the place is totally unsuitable for development?*

The land was nondescript. There was nothing but

gravel for miles. It was an enormous hole in the hills, like a giant dessert spoon-shaped depression, surrounded by towering cliffs and hills. Being gravel, it should be easier to dig a grave in than the bush, Clancy decided.

With the problem solved, Clancy knew the only issue remaining was Joel. He had to convince Joel his mother had run off and hoped he wouldn't be upset. Clancy needn't have worried; Joel barely batted an eyelid. The only disappointment Joel felt was that the evening fun and games with his mother wouldn't be happening anymore, but he wouldn't miss her for anything else. The preceding year's nighttime fun and games had seen Joel's devotion to his father increase as respect for his mother decreased at the same ratio.

He had increasingly become his father's son: cold, calculating, heartless, and save for the bond he felt for his dad, uncaring about anyone or anything other than his own pleasure. He had become a tear away at school. Joel hadn't become a bully, but he enjoyed a fight when one came along, and when the opportunity for a brawl did present itself, Joel was relentlessly ruthless in inflicting as much pain as he could, often having to be pulled off the other boy.

****

A little after midnight, when Clancy was sure Joel was asleep, Clancy quietly loaded up the body in the back of the utility with a pickaxe and shovel and took off for the gravel pit, with lights dimmed until he was far down his driveway. He didn't see a soul on the drive there, though he had smeared mud over the number plates on the truck just in case he did pass someone on the road. Clancy was dismayed to see the gate across the driveway padlocked because it had always been open on the weekends when he had visited before. The local council may lock it during the week, Clancy assumed, though he couldn't figure out why.

Clancy got out and examined it. The hinges and assembly were rusty and looked like a good shove would break through quickly enough. Clancy slowly edged the Toyota up to it so the steel bull bar on the front touched where the two gates met in the middle. Clancy drove forward slowly until the chain snapped off the clasp, and both gates flew open on screeching, corroded hinges.

As expected, the place was deserted and as quiet as the grave at that time of night. Clancy smiled at his humor because a grave was what it would be shortly. There was nothing except for the sound of the breeze through the pine trees on top of the hill and an occasional owl cry. Clancy drove where he thought he couldn't be seen from the road, parked, and turned the lights off.

He waited, listening, and letting his eyes adjust to the dark. Then, when he was sure it was safe, he dug a big hole deep enough to contain the body. The gravel was easy to shovel, Clancy was fit, and before too long, he thought he was deep enough that animals wouldn't dig Nadia up. As an afterthought, he dug a bit deeper to be safe.

With one last look around to be satisfied he was still alone, Clancy manhandled the body, wrapped in the rug, off the back of the tray, dragged it to the edge of the dug grave, and then using his foot, pushed, and let it roll in. Within minutes he filled the hole back in with gravel and scraped the excess around so that there was no more than a minor bump, which he knew was no more or less discernible than any other of the thousands all over the quarry.

He was back home, sitting on the armchair by one-thirty, sipping a brandy, feeling happy with the outcome. Clancy peeked in on his son, who was fast asleep. He stood for a while, leaning against the doorframe, sipping from the tumbler of neat brandy, thinking about how life would be with just the two of them. Clancy figured it could be fun. Sure, he'd have to take on cooking and cleaning chores, but Clancy felt Joel was old enough to help more around the house; he would talk to Joel about a division of labor over breakfast in the morning.

****

With Nadia gone, they became close to being inseparable. Other than when Joel was at school, father and son always found things to laugh at and do together. They also enjoyed their serious times. If there was work to do on the farm, Joel wanted to help, and he became as well-tanned and fit as his father as they worked side by side in the orchards or working the sheep. Joel also helped in the kitchen, preparing meals, and cleaning the house. He even became an expert with the vacuum cleaner; neither missed Nadia at all.

The occasional phone calls from Lindy slowed and eventually stopped as Clancy continued with barely disguised excuses to make her believe her sister no longer wanted contact.

****

To his father's surprise and delight, it was five months after Clancy buried Nadia when Joel suggested, in a conspiratorial whisper, who their next victim should be. It was just after the completion of stone fruit harvesting season, and Clancy had taken in a young couple from Denmark to help. They were traveling around Australia for a gap year from university and had driven up the driveway one sunny afternoon looking for temporary work. They were blond, fit, and healthy in their late teens or early twenties. Like most Scandinavians, they were beautiful, especially the girl, Dyna. Both spoke good English and were very polite, explaining they had left Perth to head toward Albany but were hoping for some work to get cash to help them along the way in their battered old hatchback.

Clancy gave them some work for two or three days and offered them the cabins to stay in for free. He set Jens to work stacking the hay bales which had been recently cut while he had Dyna clean the house from top to bottom. It had been a long while since it had a spring clean, but that wasn't why he had hired them. Clancy wanted to see Dyna naked, and he thought if he could watch her and Jens having sex, it would be even better.

While she cleaned, Dyna wore cut-off jeans with frayed hems so high her bright red panties could be seen underneath if she moved a certain way. She also wore a cotton T-shirt without a bra, so her small but firm breasts moved freely as she did. It was a highly erotic sight for both father and son, who was nearing his seventeenth birthday.

Clancy had installed the three cabins with spy holes, which he used whenever he let casual workers stay in them. Dyna was the prettiest girl, with the best body, who had visited so far. She could have easily been a model with her deep blue eyes, high, firm breasts, and legs that went on forever. Clancy eagerly awaited that first night when he planned to spy on them. He had no interest in looking at men, but he did like pornography and hoped to see a *live show* of them together later that night.

She cooked, Dyna had told him, so Clancy let her have free use of the kitchen to prepare dinner for them all, which he admitted, and Joel agreed, was the best meal they had eaten in months. Once they had finished the fresh lamb casserole with vegetables cut from the garden, they shared a couple of beers, and then the travelers returned to the cabin, at which point Clancy sent Joel to bed. Clancy then crept out the back door and, hugging the shadows around the house, headed toward the rear of the cabins.

Joel knew his father too well; he had seen how he had looked at Dyna all day, undressing her with his eyes as Joel had himself. He was also aware of the spy holes as he had used them, though previously, he had not told his dad that. When his father sent him to bed and closed the door, Joel jumped up and went to the window to watch and wait. Sure enough, within a few minutes, Joel saw Clancy cross the lawn area to the line of lemon and lime trees, which led down to the cabins. Joel decided tonight was the night to tell his father he knew of the spy holes, so he dressed and followed.

Clancy had oiled all the doors in the cabins, so they opened silently. The light was on in the middle, and Clancy entered the left-hand door. In the darkness, he crossed the room and took the print of a waterfall off the wall to peek through the hole, which looked into the other lounge area. The room contained an imitation leather couch which the Scandinavian couple was sitting on. They were kissing. Dyna's T-shirt was lifted, and Jens caressed her bare breasts. They were, as Clancy had imagined, stunning. He rubbed himself as he became stiff and eagerly awaited Jens to remove her shorts.

He was so engrossed in watching the young lovers.

Clancy didn't hear Joel enter and very nearly gave the game away by almost jumping with a yell when he felt his shirt being tugged. He turned his head and saw his son looking at him with a grin and an evil look. Clancy raised his finger to his lips, took him by the arm, and led him out of the cabin. He was angry for the first time ever with his son, not because he wanted to spy too, but because Joel had spoiled his pleasure.

Halfway back to the house, Joel pleaded, "Dad, why can't we play with her like we did with Mum?" Clancy stopped midstride, astounded, and immediately wondered why he hadn't thought of it himself. "I want to hurt her, Dad, slap her, spank her, make her scream, just like we used to with Mum. I want to fuck her as well."

Clancy turned, staggered to hear his son speak that way before answering quietly, "It's not that simple, son. I wish it were because she would be fun, wouldn't she?"

"Why isn't it easy?"

"Well, Joel, to hold someone against their will is illegal, so if we did it, and she went to the police, we would go to jail. Not to mention hurting someone like we did Mum is also illegal. We could go to prison for a long, long time. Then there is Dyna's boyfriend; what do we do about him? Jens won't let us play around with her and keep quiet."

"You got rid of Mum. She didn't go to the police."

Clancy stared at his son and suddenly saw a reflection of himself staring back. It dawned on Clancy it was like looking in a mirror, and he didn't just mean physically. Clancy had told Joel his mother had run away, which was the first and only time Clancy had told him a lie. If he repeated it now, he would regret it because Clancy now thought Joel had never believed him. His own flesh and blood deserved to know the truth. Clancy said in a very soft voice, "Your mother died, Joel. She couldn't go to the police."

"I know she did; you killed her."

Clancy's blood turned to ice with fear. Joel saw his father's face turn dark and hastily said, "I heard you drive out that night and noticed you didn't have the headlights on. When I looked out the window, the rolled-up old rug was on the back of the truck. What was inside it was obvious because I didn't believe you when you said she had run off. I waited for you to come home, and when you did, the carpet was gone, so I know you got rid of her body. I knew she hadn't run off, but I understood you said she had to protect me."

Clancy retook Joel's arm. They headed back to the house. The garden wasn't the place to discuss, "Let's go and have a hot cuppa and talk some more; it's getting cold out here."

Inside, when the mugs were filled with steaming chocolate, they sat at the kitchen table and sipped. Clancy saw how cold and black his son's eyes were for the first time. He was sixteen years old, but most times, he acted like he was twenty, which, Clancy thought, came from spending so much time with him and not children his own age. Joel seemed to have few friends his age; he preferred his father's company. Sometimes Clancy had worried about that but ultimately decided he also enjoyed his son's company, so it worked well for them both. He took his time thinking and decided to know how far his son was prepared to go to have Dyna as a plaything. "So, if we did want to keep Dyna, what would we do about Jens?" he casually asked his son.

"Kill him," Joel answered, so matter of fact, it was

as if he was talking about killing a sheep for food.

"And the body, Joel, what would we do with that?"

"What did you do with Mum's?"

Being someone who had never stopped to worry about a murder to get what he wanted, Clancy found he was amused, but also a little shocked, to hear those words coming from his sixteen-year-old son. But then Clancy remembered when he was Joel's age; he fantasized about killing his entire family and had for years. So, why should he be too surprised? Clancy realized the old saying was true: *the apple doesn't fall far from the tree.* Clancy continued, "Have you thought about killing someone, Joel? Have you considered what it would be like, to take someone's life and how you would feel afterward?"

Joel shrugged, unwilling to admit he had thought many times about taking a knife to school and stabbing several people who annoyed him, including his math teacher, who treated Joel like an imbecile. "Dad, I want to play with Dyna, and so do you. I was talking to her earlier. She told me no one knows they are here because stopping in here was a spur-of-the-moment decision."

"You've thought a lot about this then, haven't you?"

His son just nodded. His eyes were jet black and ice cold.

"But, Joel, could you take Jens' life yourself just to get to play with Dyna?"

"When you were hitting Len, the fish man, I didn't want you to stop. I wanted to help you kill him. I wanted to hit him, stab him, and rip his insides out. Yes, Dad, I could do it, especially if you were with me, helping me. Let's kill Jens together and then play with Dyna as much as we like."

Chapter 18

The Beginning of an Era

They talked for another hour, father and son, cold-heartedly planning to murder one person and turn the other into a prisoner sex slave who they could torture and rape until they tired of her.

Clancy grabbed a writing pad to make a list, to teach Joel that planning would be everything if they didn't want to get caught and spend years in jail. Item one on the list was the killing of Jens. Clancy pointed out Jens was young and fit and would fight hard to stay alive. He wasn't concerned, but he wanted Joel to understand the ramifications of what they were going to do and to calmly plan things so they didn't make any mistakes in the heat and emotion of the act. He also wanted Joel's input and for him to be a willing, active partner in their crimes, not just an underling. This had to be a partnership. It was vital to Clancy they sank or swam as a team.

"We need to separate them, Dad. Tie her up first so we can take care of Jens together.

"Good thinking, son. Do you have something in mind? Because I do if you don't."

"Well, I was thinking about another problem we would have, and the solution to that problem also solves this issue."

That sounded confusing, but Clancy loved the passion in his son's voice. "Go on. I like the way you're thinking."

"Well, I was wondering, once Jens is out of the way, where would we keep Dyna? Sometimes if the breeze is right, I can hear the Samuels next door if they make a lot of noise, so they might also hear her screaming when we play with her. Mum never made that much noise when we played, not *really* screamed like Dyna will. Plus, I want it to last. You have to work the farm, and I have to go to school, so we need somewhere we can keep her quiet when we aren't here."

"You're thinking of the fruit cellar, aren't you?" Underneath the house was a large cellar used to keep fruit cool and store preserves. These days they had a large, refrigerated cool room in one of the sheds, so the basement wasn't used for much, but it would make the perfect prison and torture chamber. Clancy had to hand it to Joel; he had put a lot of thought into his plan. There was no bathroom down there, so they would have to give Dyna a bucket. No big deal there. They could bring her up to the house to shower so she didn't stink too much, or they could just lower a garden hose down, but other than that, it would be ideal.

"That's what I thought. If I stay here with Dyna tomorrow, and we get her to help me clean it out, I could then pretend to come up here for something and lock the trap door on her. She would be trapped, and then I could get the quad bike and come to where you're working with Jens."

"Okay, champ. Yeah, that sounds great. High five." They clapped their hands up high. It was one of their *things* their mother had never understood.

"What was your plan, Dad?"

"Well, I thought we would get one more day's work out of them, get Dyna to cook us dinner again, and then ask them to stay back after for a couple of beers. I will keep them talking while you get the beers and put your mother's old sleeping tablets in theirs. You put, say, two in each bottle. That's four pills, enough to knock a horse out if they finish both. Clancy laughed suddenly, "Just make sure you don't get the bottles mixed up and drug me instead. We then put Dyna in the cellar while we kill him. We could wrap him in two big black plastic bags taped together, then bury him in the gravel pit. When we return, Dyna will still be out of it, but we can still have fun with her. The next day, when she wakes up, the fun will *really* begin."

"Wow, that's a better plan than mine, Dad, and safer too 'cos he won't be able to fight back. Let's do it. We can still get her to help clean out her own prison first. That's only fair."

Clancy burst out laughing again. He just loved his son's sense of what was *'fair.'* Even though he didn't get the joke, Joel laughed along. "How do you want to kill, Jens?" Clancy asked when they stopped giggling.

"Well, we could shoot him, but there's no fun in that." Like most farms, they had weapons; two rifles and a shotgun. "We don't want to make too much mess unless we make Dyna clean it up."

"That would be fair." Clancy joked, and they laughed all over again. "It will be more fun if Dyna has no idea what happened to Jens. It may give her hope if she thinks he escaped. With hope, she will be willing to do more for us if she thinks she will be freed by him."

Joel thought about that and nodded. "How did you

kill Mum?"

That question stopped Clancy's jovial mood straight away, and he paused. "I strangled her. She somehow freed herself, and I caught her trying to escape. She was outside by the shed and started screaming when I grabbed her, so I choked her to shut her up. Guess I don't know my own strength," Clancy shrugged, and Joel nodded again.

"Bitch," they both said simultaneously, which set them laughing once more, which called for another high-five.

By midnight they retired to bed, their plans complete, and they felt they had covered all the possible outcomes. They also felt the excitement of knowing they would have a plaything to control, degrade, and suffer as of the next night.

The following day was cloudy and threatened rain from the Northwest. Clancy was up early to cook breakfast of pancakes and boiled eggs with toast for everyone, and the smell of toast brought Jens and Dyna from the cabin. She looked beautiful, with her gorgeous smile and long, blonde hair tied in a ponytail. Clancy noticed she wore a pale-yellow T-shirt and didn't have a bra underneath. She was wearing the same cut-off denim shorts from the day before.

Clancy smiled and welcomed them in. He poured a coffee for them, spooned the eggs out of the hot water, and put them in a bowl so they could serve themselves. While he worked, all he could think of was her purple colored underwear. He had a glimpse as she sat down.

After breakfast, they separated. Joel stayed behind with Dyna, and Jens went off with Clancy as the rain looked like it would hold off. The four worked through the day and reconvened after showers for another fantastic dinner prepared by Dyna with eager help from Joel.

Everything went perfectly to plan. By nine o'clock, both guests were unconscious, and father and son high-fived each other, grinning like Cheshire cats. Just in case Jens woke up early, Clancy handcuffed him with his hands behind his back. Then they half dragged Dyna through the open trapdoor and down the stairs. Once there, they lay her on a large sorting table, tied her ankles and wrists to the legs, then stood back and admired their handiwork.

On cue, they took one side each and ripped her clothes off until she lay naked, with only one or two tatters left, still dead to the world. Clancy and Joel admired her nude body and wanted to play with her, but their fun would have to wait. They had work to do before they could relax. Dyna would not wake up anytime soon, and they had an appointment with Jens and the gravel pit.

Clancy tried to get Jens at least semi-awake because he was well-built, tall, and fit. He would not be as easy to move as Dyna had been. They shook him, yelling they were taking him back to bed because he had drunk too many beers. They got some cooperation from him in his drugged state, and somehow, they manhandled him through the front door to the veranda where they had earlier left a wheelbarrow.

They lowered Jens into it, and he passed out again, so it was easy to take him to one of the small sheds, which housed a freezer and a cool room with a concrete floor with good drainage. Inside was a large stainless-steel sink with a long, flat draining board. It was the shed where they cut up sheep and the occasional head of beef for meat for home consumption, and they had decided it would be the ideal place to end Jens' life. Inside, with the fluorescent lights on and the door shut, they manhandled his body out of the wheelbarrow and onto the draining board, face down, so his head lay in the sink. Then they took a breather. "He's a heavy bugger," Clancy told his son, but they were in such a good mood it was a minor inconvenience and nothing more.

Clancy picked up a small bladed, sharp boning knife, but Joel stopped him with his hand on his arm. "Let me, Dad. Please?" he asked, his voice quivering with excitement.

"Okay, Joel. But only if you're sure, mate." Clancy handed over the knife and stepped out of the way.

Without hesitation, Joel lifted Jens's head by his curly blond hair, effortlessly slid the knife underneath, from right to left, and cut his throat. Joel dropped his head and stepped back as the blood poured out but not quite quickly enough to avoid his hand and wrist being coated with blood. Unruffled, he turned on the tap, washed his hand and arm, and looked up at his father, grinning.

"I'm proud of you, Joel," Clancy whispered. Joel had indeed become his father's son.

By the time they got his body wrapped in the black plastic bags, taped up, and loaded onto the back of the truck with the help of the wheelbarrow, it was late enough to make the trek to the gravel pit. When they arrived, the gates still hung off their hinges to the sides. No one had bothered to repair the damage from Clancy's earlier visit. Once more, the place was deserted, and with two men digging, the hole was complete, and the body was deposited and buried within thirty minutes. They high fived each other for a job well done, loaded the shovels and picks, and headed back to the farm and their captive. It was going to be a long night.

Back at the house, after a celebratory beer, they both went down to the cellar, their excitement palpable. As it had all been Joel's idea, Clancy let him enjoy the spoils first, feeling a sense of pride. He sat on an old orange box, sipping a second beer, and watched as his son used Dyna, urging him on, offering tips and advice.

It didn't take long before Joel stepped back and grinned at his father, who stood up to take Joel's place.

****

The next day Clancy drove Dyna and Jens' beat-up old car to Midland train station and parked it in the car park. He left it unlocked with the windows down and the keys under the sun visor, making it easy for any thief who wanted it. He had worn gloves for the entire trip, so he didn't worry about leaving prints, though he doubted the car would be there more than a few hours. Clancy caught the train back into Perth City and then switched to another train to Armadale station. From there, he called a cab and was back home only two hours and forty-five minutes after he left. During the trip, he had been thinking about what he intended to do to Dyna on his return, as she would be awake by then.

She had been still very much out of it when they had returned the night before from the pit, so while they had fun, she was almost comatose, which spoilt their enjoyment. Today would be much more fun.

Clancy had been impressed with Joel's cool, calm, and collected behavior and the way he had dispatched Jens; he was a son to be proud of. He was growing up, and Clancy felt immense love for him. Clancy was happy to be able to further his education.

****

Dyna's hell on earth lasted sixteen days. Clancy and Joel had not one ounce of conscience, compassion, or mercy, and their only focus was to inflict as much pain upon her body as they could while laughing and high fiving. Finally, Dyna's broken and battered body could take no more, her heart gave out, and she passed into oblivion.

****

After Dyna was laid to rest in the pit, father and son began planning for a replacement. They realized they had made mistakes with their first victim and rationalized it was only natural that they would. Joel had been too eager and drunk on the excesses which Clancy had permitted because he got caught up with Joel's enthusiasm. Clancy felt that they would take their time with the next victim.

Clancy made them analyze what they enjoyed the most and ranked each depravity with a score out of ten. That way, they knew which things to do in what order to maximize their pleasure next time. Going forward, he pointed out to Joel they needed to plan better to ensure the experience lasted longer. They had hoped the once beautiful Dyna would last months rather than just over the two weeks they had shared with her. They blamed themselves for being too violent too early. They never forgot that early lesson, much to the horror of future victims.

They decided that backpacking tourists looking for casual work were easy prey and could be made to disappear quickly and without too much danger of being caught. The risk increased later with mobile phone technology, but early in their seventeen-year reign of abductions, it was all too easy to find playmates. Once found, there was no escaping. The men had become highly efficient in their vocation.

Backpackers were generally young and attractive, though, to the father and son duo, looks were less important than the body. Anyone too fat or too skinny they would ignore. Often, backpackers traveled in pairs, thinking there was safety in numbers, but as Clancy and Joel finessed their skills, there was no safety to be found. None of the people they abducted escaped the farm or their eventual death. If the travelers were a pair of women, so much the better; they had double the fun and could make it last twice as long. If it was a male and female, the man would be dispatched quite early, as Jens had been, leaving his female traveling companion to experience a long, lingering, drawn-out, and painful death.

They became familiar with the hostels in the areas and the coffee shops and bars nearby where backpackers would hang out. Clancy and Joel never went to the same hostel twice in the same year for fear of being recognized, but there were so many to choose from it was never a problem. Once they found a suitable victim or pair, they would offer those travelers fruit-picking work on the farm, with wages payable in cash. They promised to pick them up from their hostel, provide free accommodation, then deliver them to their next hostel on their travels. Clancy bought a four-wheel drive wagon to help as the farm truck was too old and ugly. The girls were so trusting they would generally agree and never knew which orchard they were being taken to; therefore, friends or hostel owners couldn't tell anyone who might search for them later. The backpackers simply trusted they would be safe and looked after.

Clancy and Joel got very good at picking out potential victims. Clancy would work alone if they chose a bar until Joel became old enough. If it was a tourist destination, cheap eating place, or coffee shop that was different, then they would work as a team. Joel became good-looking as he got older, which became added bait for similar-aged girls.

They killed six times in the first year. All were pairs, mainly two girls together rather than boy and girl. They murdered nine the following year but only five the next year. The longer they went on, the better they became at keeping their victims alive.

Joel's eighteenth birthday was spent with two young women from England. They hailed from Liverpool, and Clancy left him with them all night as his gift to his son. In the morning, one was dead, and the other had gone insane, watching her best friend being tortured and murdered. When Clancy went to the cellar in the morning, he saw the bodies and blood. Even though they had agreed they would never kill in the basement, he couldn't be angry with his son, as it had been his birthday. The surviving woman never stopped mumbling incoherently and meekly allowed herself to be led to the shed, with the chain around her neck, where she killed.

****

During their seventeen years of terror, Clancy and his son Joel made forty-two successful trips to the gravel pit. While disposing of their forty-third victim, the fateful night it all ended, they were discovered by Tammy and Greg.

In the aftermath and the raging debates, it was easy to discount Joel's role because he shared the same genes as his father. Most believed that his insanity must have been hereditary, a defective gene, some theorized. When the story became known in full detail, others wondered if his mother had not been unfaithful on that day with the fish farmer and had not been discovered by son and father, might he have led a *normal* life? Some pointed out that while Clancy had murdered before his marriage, he had a twisted motive for doing so. But his wife's infidelity tipped him over the edge into a world of madness, perverted sex, and murder for pleasure. The debates would be discussed back and forth for years, never receiving a complete resolution as to why the horror came to be.

Book 3
Climbing Toward the Light

"I have my own little world, but it's okay – they know me here."

~Author Unknown

Chapter 19

Putting the Jigsaw Puzzle Together

While he was addressing the assembled detectives, Sam's mobile chimed. He noticed the call but didn't answer because the ID was blocked. *Whoever it is can leave a message and wait. I'm busy,* he thought.

They were still operating out of the transportable Command Centre and using its extended awning, but the sun made it unbearable inside, even with the air conditioning. It was nearing the end of the day, and Sam was listening to reports from the interviews of surrounding homeowners, which essentially amounted to *nothing new*. No one saw anything. No one heard anything besides the usual kids who went to the pit to have fun, generally on weekends, when the sound of racing trail bikes resounded through the hills.

One local suggested that some years previously, the pits had gotten a reputation for men to meet other men for casual gay sex. The location was promoted on a website as a place for men to *cruise*. But it seemed, after due investigation, there hadn't been enough *action* there, and it lost favor to other, more popular, areas in the hills, mainly parks with public toilets.

While the rumors momentarily caused a flutter of interest, it was felt that even if those clandestine meetings were still going on, it was likely irrelevant because most of the victims were females who had been sexually abused as part of their torture. That logic didn't stop the newspapers from suggesting that, as men who meet other men for casual hook-ups are undoubtedly perverts, it wasn't much of a stretch to say they shared some commonality with the murderers.

Once each of the detectives reported their lack of success, it was Sam's turn to respond. "Okay, listen up. I'm afraid I have the latest body count, and it's still climbing. The latest tally is thirty-four. They seem to be primarily young women, with only a few males, though the men don't seem to have been tortured. About forty percent of this horrible pit is still left to search, so God knows when this body count will end. We now have seven victims identified, and as we initially thought, they appear to be overseas backpackers. From what we can gather, the victims all have similar profiles, and all went missing with no suspicious circumstances at the time. They just vanished. According to missing person reports, most were staying at backpacker hostels, YMCAs, or similar locations and reported nothing suspicious to families back home. Four said they were going fruit picking, and that's possibly our link to this area. We need to look hard at any local properties with fruit trees or orchards, especially considering the pollen found on some of the bodies." Sam paused and sipped from his can. "Something interesting about one of the unidentified bodies is that she seems to be one of the early kills, if not the earliest. She was fully clothed, so I think this victim is significant. It could well be this was the first one, and possibly this death started our killer, or killers, on their path."

"Why do you think this one is significant, Boss?" Jenny asked.

Sam perched himself on the edge of the desk while Bob Young stood in the background, listening, "If you want the truth, it's not much more than some logic and gut instinct, but here's what I think. First, understand we don't have the full PM yet, but I've asked them to prioritize this victim. It's not much more than a skeleton, but there appear to be significant differences apart from the clothes. There are no scarring wounds to the wrists, so if she was held captive, she wasn't suspended by handcuffs like the others were. At first glance, there appears to be some minor evidence of fracturing but nothing like the horrific injuries on some other victims. She wasn't wrapped in plastic bags but rolled up in what was left of a rug. And then there are the clothes. Every other female victim was naked, and we have extensive evidence of sexual trauma to the less decomposed bodies. So, if you want to know what my gut tells me…?"

Everyone nodded and listened; rumors had reached the squad about Sam's instincts and that they should be heeded.

"Well, I've got a hundred bucks that say this victim was known to the killers. And, while she may or may not have been held captive and may or may not have been tortured, it wasn't anywhere near to the same extent as all the victims who followed, so it begs the question, why? Though we do not know her age, initial thoughts are that she was considerably older than the average age of the other women. The plastic bags the others were wrapped in tell me they were premeditated, while using a rug seems, how shall we say, like it's a body disposal of convenience? So if we can identify this victim, we may well be able to identify the killer because he knew her, some way or somehow. Anyone want to take that hundred-dollar bet?" No one put up their hand.

"Tomorrow, I want backpackers, hostel owners, and staff interviewed and any cafes or bars where the victims might have hung around close to them. These guys have been snatching young girls for over fifteen years. Someone somewhere must have seen these men regularly stalking victims; they may have been offering cash money for work. Some of the girls said they got jobs fruit picking, and we know they use a four-wheel drive type wagon; these kids were lured somewhere, and some sort of farm orchard seems to be our best bet. We now have pics of some of the victims provided by families. Show them around; I know some of these disappearances date back a long time but keep pushing."

"Jenny, you and your team stick with the house to house. We know they live around here, somewhere, so it's up to you to find where. Remember: pay particular attention to orchards. Thanks to forensics, we know there is pollen in some of the bags, and stone fruit such as peaches, plums or similar are likely candidates on some of the bodies. I've requested a list of local registered growers of those fruits from the Department of Agriculture, but, and this is a big but, people, the pollen doesn't necessarily mean our killers are registered or commercial growers or orchards. It could just as easily be a property with a few fruit trees for personal consumption. Also, pollen can be wind-blown or even carried by bees, so pay attention to small hobby farms and neighbors of those properties. We also assume these victims were held captive for some time as the pathologist tells us the torture lasted weeks in some cases, so they were secured somewhere neighbors couldn't hear them scream. Watch out for places you think could be a possibility."

Sam glanced at his notes. "Mark, you take your team and cover the backpacker accommodation places; I want action from your guys tomorrow. Let's get to work and make it count."

All the detectives agreed that they would by nodding and muttering assent. Some stood to leave, while others stayed in small groups chatting and staring at the whiteboards which had gathered information displayed on it. Sam went to talk to Bob Young, who told him he had arranged for a clinical psychologist to visit the site in the morning to give an opinion of the kind of person capable of such brutality.

Sam nodded, not overly enamored with such opinions. To him, the psych profiles were like Nostradamus' obscure prophecies; they only made real sense after the event and were rarely helpful during an investigation. Still, Sam was willing to try anything different which would bring a rapid close to the case, so despite his prejudice, he thanked Bob for arranging it.

Jenny came in from outside, where she had gone to take a mobile phone call, and headed over to Sam and Bob, "That was Tammy, Boss. She is being discharged from the hospital tomorrow. She still needs a lot of rest and recuperation, but she's responded well and is good to go. I thought I'd drop in on the way back and see her. She's been through the car book a few times but hasn't picked anything out which could help us, but I thought I'd share some relaxation exercises with her to see if that helps. I'm also going to strongly suggest they get away for a few days. The press is staking out the hospital, and she needs a break, not to be hounded by the media."

"Okay, Jen, that's a terrific idea. You take the car, and I will get a lift back with one of the others. It's time I got my own set of wheels anyway, so I'm not restricting you. No need to pick me up in the morning."

"Goodnight, Sergeant. I'll drop you back at HQ if you like, Sam, so you can pick up a car," Bob said.

Sam's phone rang. Once more, the screen displayed there was no caller ID. "Thanks, Bob; I'll take you up on that offer. See you tomorrow, Jen," Sam said, then turned away to answer the call. "Sam Collins."

"Joe Pike. Accident Investigation, Inspector. I just wanted to apologize for my poor judgment. Boy, I really stuffed up with that wreck investigation, didn't I?"

Sam was shocked and momentarily off balance. Of all the calls he might have expected, this wasn't one of them. "Well, I appreciate you taking the time to call and say that. Fortunately, it didn't affect the outcome, and we are now knee-deep in recovered dead bodies."

"Well, that's good to know. I've learned from my mistake, but I've been suspended; I just wanted you to know I'm sorry for making a wrong assumption, and it's likely to cost me my career."

Sam moved the phone away from his ear and stared at it. The call was becoming more bizarre by the minute. It sounded as if the cop held a grudge for Sam doing his job when the man hadn't done his. "Senior, why are you calling me, really?" But there was no reply. The phone was dead.

Jenny spent over an hour with Tammy and her mother. She had stopped during the drive at a hamburger drive-through and bought three soft-serve ice cream sundaes to take in as a treat. She took a chance that Tammy would like one, and one of her parents would be with her to take the third. Tammy was delighted to see Jenny and grateful for the sundae, but her mother declined, saying she hadn't yet had dinner, but Tammy insisted she stays and eat with them. Jenny thought the girl looked remarkably well. Being young and fit had made her resilient, Jenny realized. *Oh, to be that youthful again*, she wished.

They chatted briefly about the case, and Jen told them the latest body count. Once more, she reinforced the importance of Tammy surviving her horror in the hills. Jenny pointed out that families worldwide could get some closure because their loved ones were being identified. By now, Tammy had taken the time to come to terms with and forgive herself for leaving Greg, understanding there was nothing she could have done for him except get killed herself. At least by running away, she had provided a chance that his murderers would get caught.

While Mrs. Reynolds went off to find dinner for herself, Jenny stayed with Tammy. Only then did Jenny bring up the picture book of cars and ask if they could go through it together one last time, just in case.

"Sure, we can try, but I can't promise any improvement; the pictures don't look familiar; I'm so sorry, Jenny."

"Hey, no need to be sorry, you've been fantastic,

and I understand Tammy; it's just one last shot, is all. Remember the last time I talked you through that dreadful night? I helped you relax? Well, I'd like to try it again if that's okay, nice, and slowly now that you're over the trauma of the night. Maybe there is something there I can help you find. Are you game?"

Tammy nodded, a faint smile on her lips, and held out her hand. Jenny took her spot on the bed beside Tammy, took the offered hand, and stroked it gently, almost like a tickle, while Tammy relaxed back into her pillows after Jenny dimmed the lights. "Tammy, love, I want you to turn the pages in time with me stroking your arm. Can you do that?"

"Okay." She propped the book on her thighs, then Tammy slowly turned each page while Jenny watched the young girl's face closely.

On one page, she paused and imperceptibly stiffened, and her eyes narrowed slightly. Jen didn't mention it; she wouldn't have noticed had she not been watching for it. Only when they finished the entire book did Jenny return to the one picture, which had caused a reaction that Tammy wasn't aware she had made.

"Tammy, I'm so pleased with all the amazing help you've been to us," she said softly, still stroking her lower arm. "I want you to look at the picture in front of you. Just keep looking like you're seeing through it, not at it like one of those *magic eye* pictures. It's just sitting there in front of you. You're aware of the image but not studying it. Do you understand what I mean, Tammy?"

"Yes," she replied in a calm, almost dreamy voice.

"That's perfect, Tammy. Now just listen to my voice, nothing else. Just listen to me and stare at the picture while we talk about that horrible night. You are perfectly safe; nothing and no one can hurt you. I'm here with you, protecting you, and we're just chatting. Do you remember it, Tammy? You're with Greg in the car's back seat, and you're having fun, aren't you?"

"Mmm, yes. He wants me, and I want him. He's so good looking."

"Just remember that, Tammy. You're safe and feeling good, and Greg wants to make love with you, but another car has just driven in. Look at the picture, Tammy. Is *that* the car? Take your time. Just listen to my voice and look at the picture."

Tammy's eyes narrowed again, and her body stiffened as Jenny continued, "You've both sat up and are watching the car as it drives away. It's dark, I know, and it's hard to see clearly. But you can see the car, can't you? It's a dark color, or is it, Tammy? What color is it? Is it black, dark blue, or green, maybe?"

"It's gray. It's very dirty. It's kind of dark silver or gray."

"That's fantastic, Tammy. Okay, so it's silver or gray, but it's dirty. Does it look like the car in the picture?"

"Ye-ess, it's that kind of shape."

"Brilliant. Well done, Tammy. Now keep looking and remember how it parked. The two men got out and buried a big bundle, didn't they? Then, they filled in the hole and put their shovels and stuff back in the rear of the car. Can you see the car as they are getting back into it, Tammy?"

"Yes."

"Good girl. Now it's turning back toward you and heading your way again, but you're safe with me. Just keep looking at the car. I know the headlights are on, but just at the last moment it's turned. Can you see the car, Tammy? Does it look like the picture? Look at the picture, Tammy, now."

Tammy had tears in her eyes and looked up from the picture to Jenny. She nodded frantically, "Yes, it looks like the one in the picture."

The team had interviewed sixty-nine homeowners and left business cards in the mailboxes of numerous others. The cards were left when the owners were not home when called upon, with the officer asking to be notified when they could speak with them about a series of bodies found at the quarry. Some had called back already; others were away, while a few were known to live in the city and only occasionally enjoyed their *weekender* homes. Slowly they were eliminating people from the inquiry, but it was slow going.

****

Clancy sat on his veranda, sipping from an ice-cold beer bottle, with Jenny Markham's calling card in his hand. He was wearing shorts, work boots, and a blue singlet. Deep in thought, he was drinking his second beer of the day as the sun was going down over the hills. It was his favorite time of day as the last of the sun's rays peeked over the Western ranges bordering his property. While waiting for Joel to come home from work, he remembered *the bitch.* The nosey parker woman he had chased through the hills and lost. She had ruined everything, and he wanted to make her pay.

Clancy wasn't dumb. He knew it was only a matter of time before he was caught now; the cops would be closing in soon. They had to be. It stood to reason with forensic science what it was; they would find Nadia, and the game was up once identified. If he had any choices about anything, it was how he ended it from that point forward. Sooner or later, the cops would come, so as he saw it, his options were limited.

His first choice would be to run for it. He could take off to Thailand before they froze his passport and use what money he had to try to buy a visa. Even without one, he could hide and live for as long as possible in a country where his money would go a long way.

Clancy remembered a case in the papers a few months before where a major drug dealer was found living in Bangkok, having fled while on bail. After spending months in a Thai jail fighting extradition, he was deported by the Thai government, brought back to Australia, and jailed. In an interview, the dealer said he should have returned sooner, as life in the Bangkok jail was hell on earth. So, Clancy figured if he ran overseas, all he would do was buy some time, and sooner or later, they would find him. Caucasians tended to stick out there, especially if they were not residents. A tourist visa must be renewed from outside the country every three months. Clancy knew from discussions with Nadia often ex-pats crossed the border to either Cambodia or Laos by a bridge across the Mekong, paid the fees, and returned, and that was how fugitives were caught. Without renewing a visa resulted in a waiting game, as without one, he would have to resort to bribery, which, while rife in Asian countries, meant it worked both ways. Often the police offered rewards for information which meant informers got paid twice. Clancy figured even if it didn't happen, someone would see him in a bar or sitting on a beach and report him. Then he would have to rot in a Thai jail for months while waiting to be deported. *No, thank you, sir;* he didn't like the thought of that one little bit.

Being the mass murderer he was, and Clancy was fully aware he was precisely that, there was no point denying it; the hue and cry for his capture would be relentless. His picture would be in newspapers and on TV, and people would shake their heads and call him a madman. In fact, Clancy was willing to bet that while he was on the run, there would be sightings of him all over the place who wasn't him. Such would be the public outrage; a massive number of people would be looking for him, all wanting to be the one to bring him down. He would be seen in the oddest of places. That was how it would go, for sure. One thing was undeniable; they would remember him long after he was gone from this mortal coil.

So, the question he had to ask himself was, did he want to buy that time for as long or as short as it was? Clancy knew he was a down-home country farm boy, not some world-traveling entrepreneur. He would be caught in no time flat because he would stick out like a sore thumb.

He took another long sip of his beer and resigned himself to the thought that if he did run, he would have three to six months at best. Once his identity was known, police would check with immigration, realize he had left the country, and know where he went. So, he thought he would have less time than three months, possibly much less. So, if that was the case, why should he even bother? What would be the point? Yeah, back when he had been happily married, he loved going to Thailand with Nadia, but as soon as his wife had shown her true adulterous colors, he lost his taste for all things Thai. As far as he was concerned, the women were just money-grabbing sluts, so why would he want to live amongst them for three months, especially if it would be the last three months of his life?

The next option he considered was going on the run but staying within Australia. But, again, with his picture plastered all over every newspaper and television screen in the country, how long could he possibly hope to evade capture? And, if that was a given, why even bother? *Really, what is life even for?* He mused. *It's for taking whatever enjoyment you can while it lasts?* There were two types of people in the world, so far as Clancy was concerned; givers and takers, or as he preferred to think of them, sheep and shepherds. The strong always overcame the weak, survival of the fittest…and all that stuff. He had enjoyed his life to the full, even though others suffered for his enjoyment, but he didn't give a hoot about them. So, if it had to end early, and there was no doubt about that now, then it had to be all about how it ended, which was Clancy's choice to make.

Clancy had two options if he didn't run and stayed right where he was. First, he could let himself be arrested and held up to face a mockery of a trial, where he would be called a madman; and Clancy knew he wasn't. They would call him a psychopath, a sociopath, and other long, intricate psycho-babble names, and he didn't want to give the mongrels the opportunity to mock him. Clancy knew it was one of those situations where the more he explained he wasn't insane, they would use his words to show he was. And for what, anyway? To spend the rest of whatever life he had left in jail. No way, Jose.

The second option he could take would be to fight. If he chose that, he had more options again. He could have a shootout with police at the farm and take as many of the fuckers as he could with him, *shootout at the OK Orchard.* Clancy grinned at his sparkling wit. Or he could take the fight to them. The second option held some natural appeal to Clancy. But maybe there was a third? *How about taking it to them and having a shootout? Now that is exciting,* he thought.

As Clancy saw it, things had gone wrong for him and Joel because that *fucking bitch* outran him up the side of a gravel pit. Who would have thought that would have happened with her wearing no clothes? She had to be taught a lesson; that was priority number one. If she had just taken her punishment for being an interfering rabbit, he and Joel wouldn't be in the mess they were now. They could have buried the pair of them and hidden the car somewhere, and all would be fine and dandy.

No, the interfering woman had to pay and pay dearly for mucking up the perfect life he and Joel had going. Joel was already taking care of finding out where she lived, so they could pay her and her family a visit and kill them all.

Next on his hate list were the two cops. Why couldn't they just believe it was a car accident which killed the boy like they were supposed to? Why couldn't they have accepted the drunken girl had imagined everything? Was that too much to ask of them? Apparently, it was, so they would have to pay, too.

Clancy looked down at the business card in his hand, which he held between thumb and finger on opposing corners, and turned it over and over like a revolving sign. *Detective Jenny Markham* and her mobile phone number were written on the plain white front with the Western Australian Police logo. She was one of the two cops that ruined his future, and she had called at his home, perfect.

The cop who got shot at the Marina some time back taking down that biker drug dealer Mallory. Collins was his name; he was number two of the dynamic duo. Both had to die.

He revolved the card around again and saw the handwritten note, neatly written on the back, for the homeowner to call her so she could set up an appointment to ask some questions about a spate of murders at the old gravel pit. *Hmm.* He asked himself, *could she make it any easier for me to kill her?*

A plan was coming together in his mind, and he liked it. Clancy smiled broadly to himself and took another sip of his beer. Clancy tried to think back; of all the women he and Joel had played with, was one of them named Jenny? He didn't think so, admitting to himself, *after a while, who remembers names anyway?*

His plan could be fun and a great way to go out on a high note. To strip naked, some stuck-up bitch of a female cop who was used to giving orders, not taking them. To play around with her a bit, make her scream and bleed. *Mmmmm, yes,* Clancy loved the idea. When the police eventually raided the place, it could make going down in a shootout with them even more fun if they had Ms. Markham to play with for a while beforehand and have her as a hostage during their final stand.

Clancy saw Joel's headlights and heard the tires on the gravel driveway at about the same time. His smile grew bigger with love and pride. No matter how old his son got, Clancy still loved him as much as he did when Joel was a baby, and Clancy knew because of their special bond, his son felt the same about him. And hadn't Joel done well for himself out in the big wide world?

He'd risen to a position of authority and respect with the police force, and Clancy took comfort in knowing that he had brought him up well as a single father. Yes, he was a boy to be proud of. Joel being a cop had other benefits too. Like for getting information about the women they abducted and making sure missing persons officers didn't link them all together. Any time in the past when Joel thought there could be even a hint of an investigation, and there had been the odd time or two, they shut up shop for a few months until the dust settled.

If Clancy had any regrets at all, it wasn't for himself. No, it was that his son wouldn't get to live out his allotted years as a free man. It would be Joel's choice whether to run, give himself up, or stay alongside his father and fight it out, but they were still so close he thought he knew what his son's choice would be. Yep, there was no doubt about it; he was a son to be proud of.

****

Back at headquarters, Sam and Bob had a beer together but did not discuss the case, as there wasn't much to say which hadn't already been said in the car driving back. Bob had to leave shortly as he had agreed to participate in a live interview for the national TV's seven-thirty news bulletin. Bob would bring the public up to speed on the body count and progress of the investigation thus far. The country watched with morbid fascination; they simply couldn't get enough of the evolving story, which had gained the headline in the papers as *The Rolleystone Burial Ground*. Bob didn't enjoy the TV limelight but had done it for so long he was seen to be generally unflappable and photographed well. Louise was going to meet him there, and he hurried to finish his beer so he wouldn't be late.

Sam had a date planned with Caroline, so he was in a hurry too. He couldn't shake the feeling that the following day would be significant. He felt they were on the verge of discovering something which would break the case wide open, and he said as much to Bob as they both took the last sips of beer.

"Jesus, I hope you're right, Sam. We haven't started coping flak from upstairs yet because they know we are still uncovering bodies and won't have full forensics and postmortems for days yet, but the media are like baying dogs at my heels, wanting an arrest."

"Yeah, I get it. Let's face it is one hell of a sensational story. I've always hated it when newspapers say, ' *Police still have no new leads in the so and so case,* ' when they don't have positive things to say. Like we spend all day sitting on our hands."

"They call that negative reporting, Sam. They can still write it and make a story when they have nothing new to say. In a case like this, though, it's fascination by the public trying to understand the killer. People are naturally sad for the victims and families, but they want information about who and why."

"True, very true. Oh, Bob, I know what I meant to mention to you. I had a weird call from the guy who botched the crash investigation earlier. It seems like he's been suspended, and he half apologized, and half let me know he was annoyed with me. The weirdest phone call I've ever had, to be honest. Then he hung up without warning, just to reinforce he thinks I'm an idiot for not taking his report on face value."

"The fuckwit should be sacked not suspended. He's probably off on full pay while he sits as home scratching his ass. Then before you know it, he will go on 'stress leave,' so we have to keep paying his wages indefinitely."

"I completely agree. Okay, Boss, that's it for me. I've got a hot date, and forgive me for saying, but she's a lot better looking than you. I'm out of here. See you tomorrow."

Bob smiled and waved his hand, "Goodnight, Sam. See you tomorrow."

Chapter 20

Building Bridges

When Jenny left the hospital after Tammy's mother returned from dinner, she thought about calling her boss to tell him Tammy had been able to identify the type of car the killers used. But checking her watch noticed it was close to eight o'clock, and she thought it could wait until morning. After all, Jenny reasoned, she still didn't have a registration number, only a make and model of vehicle, and even then, that body shape ran over several years. To make matters worse, silver or gray were common colors. *So why,* she asked herself, *should I interrupt Sam's date?*

Before Jenny left the hospital, she'd tried to impress Tammy's mother that getting Tammy away for a while would be best for the family but, most importantly, for her daughter because the media were rabid for details and would not stop pestering them all until they got their scoop. Tammy would be stronger for a few more days of respite and more able to cope with the relentless questioning from the reporters who were desperate to interview her. Tammy glanced at her mother, and they nodded and said they would discuss it, but Jenny had the feeling, possibly due to their financial constraints, they would just go home and not open the door.

Even though Jenny didn't yet have a registration

number, she knew it was a giant leap forward for the investigation and one she was delighted to have made, not just for her benefit but also for Sam's. Jenny liked Sam more than all the bosses she had worked for in the past. He talked to his people, not at them, and best of all, he was intuitive and wouldn't get bogged down in a *just-the-facts* mentality. Jenny believed Sam could and would trust his judgment or gut feeling, permitting his detectives to follow their instincts too. Finally, he was trying to be not only a good cop but a good boss, too. It couldn't be easy to suddenly be thrust into the position of managing a task force, especially when she knew one or two detectives thought Sam didn't deserve the promotion. Sam was running the operation under Bob's watchful eye, which was true, but it was likely to be the most significant murder inquiry ever in the country's history, with now thirty detectives on board. Yet, Sam took the time to talk to each detective, to make them all feel they were contributing, even when they thought they weren't.

Some of those who came aboard had resented Sam's meteoric rise in stature within the police force, and the Major Crime Unit in particular. But even they soon came to appreciate he was very good at his job. He cared about the case, and his staff and everyone got credit and his congratulations when they deserved it. Of course, Sam was adept at delivering a verbal kick up the ass when merited, too. She thought he was not, and never would be, a political animal, no matter how high he climbed. He would always want to have a beer with the boys. Jenny thought Sam would never forget he came through the ranks, and every ounce of the success was earned with blood, sweat, and tears.

Jenny drove, tiredly heading toward her home. She was looking forward to a long, hot bath and a microwaved frozen dinner with her cat in front of the TV. Her mobile phone rang, and Jenny fumbled in her bag at the bottom under tissues, makeup, breath freshener, and other assorted stuff which resided in the chaos. She smiled when she saw it was her ex-husband calling, and she hit the hands-free button to answer.

"Hi there, Mike. Is something wrong?" she asked.

"No, not at all. I, umm, just wanted to call and invite you over for dinner if you don't have plans already. I've cooked a roast chicken with all the trimmings, and well, look, it's going to be way too much for just Josh and me, and I know how busy you are with this mass-murder case, so I thought you deserved a home-cooked meal, intrepid police officer that you are."

She smiled. Mike was being so sweet and trying hard to get them to reconcile, which was fantastic for her ego. Ever since the night when they had *the talk*, he had phoned her once a day. He didn't do it to pester or hassle her, just to chat. When they had been together, Mike was never much of a talker and an even worse listener, so she was enjoying this new side to him. If she was busy when Mike rang, he would get off the line quickly, but only after asking if he could ring back later, which he always did at the appointed time.

Mike would ask after her and make sure she was feeling okay, as he understood it was a very stressful case she was working on. She realized with every conversation they had, it had become more comfortable and less awkward for them to talk openly. His sense of humor was back, and Mike made her smile and feel better about herself and her job. In fact, yesterday's call had been at ten at night, and when she hung up, she was shocked to see they had been talking for over an hour. When Jenny stopped to think about her feelings, she was confused and torn, which was as nice as it was confronting. Jenny liked to be in control, but her attraction to women, well, one woman in the past, conflicted with a resurrection of her feelings for Mike for fear she might get that temptation again. If only her complex life could simplify, somehow.

"Boy, Mike, you sure know the way to a girl's heart, especially after a long day like today; your timing is perfect, as I've only just finished work."

"I'm trying," he said quietly.

Jenny knew he was. *Oh my God,* she thought. *He is trying so hard to win me back for good.* With the realization came several conflicting emotions. She needed time to analyze them and sort them out in her head, but whenever she tried, she only ended up more confused than before. Jenny found herself smiling, like a schoolgirl, because she knew deep down, he was succeeding, and her defenses were coming down. Mike was courting her, and she was slowly falling for him all over again.

It seemed as if, at that moment, while he waited for her reply, a hundred thoughts raced through her head. Was she gay; was one lesbian relationship just a one-and-done infatuation? Was she bi and not gay at all? Could it work with the new and improved Mike? If she was bi and went back with him, what if she fell for another woman sometime down the track? Or was she just reading too much into things? Should she just go with the flow and see what happens? Another consideration was their son, Josh; she must consider his feelings. He had been overjoyed his mum and dad were talking again. "Shall I pick up a bottle of wine?" she asked, to give herself time to sort out the jumble of feelings racing around her head and heart.

"Only if you share it with me. The chicken will be ready in about twenty-five minutes or so if that suits you."

"But, Mike, I should drive home after dinner, so I won't drink more than a glass of wine. There will be lots for you to share." Jenny bit her lip, knowing what was going to come next.

"Jen, you can drink as much as you like if you spend the night, which you can if you want." She could tell the nervousness in his voice, and she felt a thrill run through her body from her chest to her toes. With dawning shock and inner excitement, she realized she felt an urge, one she was unfamiliar with. She wanted to spend the night in his arms, naked, wrapped around the body she used to know so well. If not for the sex, the intimacy, and the closeness of a human being who cared for her. Maybe the case had affected her, or perhaps it was something else, regret? Loneliness? Desire? *Maybe all three,* she decided.

"Red or white?" she asked, equally as nervous.

****

Just after eleven later that night, long after Josh had gone to bed, a kneeling Mike lowered Jenny's panties and kissed her lower tummy at the top of her pubic hair. Jenny thought that he intended to kiss lower to show her he wanted to be able to please her, and she was quivering with excitement. While Jenny held his head gently but firmly, she looked across to the dressing table mirror, which showed the lewd sight of her standing nude and him kneeling about to lick her most intimate place. Jenny softly moaned encouragement.

In the final years they had been married, Mike hadn't seemed to be bothered about her feelings, pleasure, or happiness too much. It seemed to her now like they had been stuck in a rut and took each other for granted. But Mike seemed different now; he had grown up, matured, and even studied how to be a better husband, the least she could do would be to try to be more of a woman for him. There was a lot of truth in the old saying that you never knew what you had till it was gone.

They had necked like kids on the couch after Josh had gone to bed, with soft music playing on an FM radio station. In the past, after dinner, it would have been TV sport for Mike while she did the dishes and tidied the kitchen. But then again, maybe her marriage only seemed so bad after Jenny fell for another woman. She knew she had been guilty of her perception being skewed by the passion and eroticism that another woman awoke in her.

Mike had delighted in taking her top and bra off and had spent ages holding, kissing, and licking her breasts, and she enjoyed that he was taking things slowly. It had not been like that for her in a long time. They had become complacent when they had been together: stuck in their roles of her being a bored housewife, albeit a working one, with him as a self-centered alpha man. Sex had become regular, uninspired, and boring for her, and that made her open to a woman's soft, gentle, and passionate lovemaking.

Within moments, she clenched his head in her hands tighter, holding him against her as she orgasmed deeply.

Her breath caught itself in her chest, her body twitched, and she bit her lip to not shout out and wake Josh. Mike stood, hugged Jenny as she trembled, and helped her lie on the bed. She watched as he took the last of his clothes off, his desire for her obvious. When he entered her, Jenny hugged him back and moaned, wondering, with utter amazement, if maybe she wasn't as gay as she'd thought. This was so very good, and Jenny still loved him dearly.

****

Sam fumbled his key in the lock of his apartment door, which wasn't easy to do with Caroline pinching his behind with one hand and fondling his crotch with the other while telling him to hurry up so he could get her inside.

They had been to the *Windy Bar* in Northbridge because they had an outstanding soul band playing, which both loved. They had danced with extravagant twirls and dips between drinking beer with tequila shots, which they loved to do. In their own individual ways, they were very much alike; they had big egos and liked to be looked at. In fact, they made a fantastic-looking couple. Didi had been right; they would have beautiful-looking children if they got that far.

When they danced, they held center stage. The men looked lustily at Caroline, dressed in white jeans, a crimson satin shirt open enough to show a sexy cleavage but not enough to be slutty, and four-inch stiletto heels on her feet. The women watched Sam in his faded denim jeans, white boat shoes, and a white T-shirt. His look was simple but manly, and he looked like a well-built male model with a muscular frame. The saxophone and electric guitars played, the tequila flowed, and every time they looked at each other, the sexual tension and wanting hung between them like a curtain.

They didn't make it to the bedroom. Once inside Sam's apartment door, they were pulling at each other's clothes, kissing, and frantically touching each other. With her jeans and panties down around one foot and his jeans pushed down to his thighs, Caroline jumped into his arms. They kissed, devouring each other, her legs wrapped around him and arms around his neck. Sam held her buttocks and lowered her body until he was inside her. They stood, enjoying the moment, then Sam carried her to the couch, where they fell on it laughing.

****

In the Roleystone Hills, father and son Clancy and Joel sat around an old-fashioned laminate table in the kitchen. There were fifteen empty bottles of beer sitting between them, along with a notebook where they had written a well-constructed plan for murder.

There would not be any prolonged, drawn-out arrest and trial for them. They had spent seventeen years with only one thing on their minds, their own hedonistic pleasures, and they weren't about to stop now.

They intended to make the people responsible for the end of the lifestyle they had become accustomed to pay with their lives. Their plan was to go out in a way that would help ensure the legacy they left behind would long be remembered.

****

The crime stoppers' phones had run hot for the first three days following the press conference and had logged hundreds of calls. It didn't matter that most of those calls would amount to a waste of time; each would be checked out. Naturally, they lacked the manpower to work through that number of reports immediately, so Sam had allocated a senior detective to conduct a triage system to prioritize the calls a detective needed to investigate straight away, and which items needed a uniform to check out when they could. Ones he deemed minor could be put on the back burner until time and resources permitted.

In his latest pile of reports from the phone operators was a single sheet, a third from the bottom, which made for interesting reading. It would be only one day before the report was seen and acted on, but it would be too late by then.

TIME OF CALL: 14.35

NAME OF CALLER: LEN OR COULD BE GLEN (NO SURNAME GIVEN)

RETURN PHONE NUMBER: NOT GIVEN

CALLER COMMENTS:

LEN ADVISES OFFICERS SHOULD CHECK OUT THE OWNER OF WINTER SUN FARM. ROLEYSTONE. CALLER SAYS THAT APPROXIMATELY 18 YEARS AGO OWNER OF FARM'S WIFE DISAPPEARED AFTER BEING CAUGHT BY HER HUSBAND WITH A LOVER IN THE ACT OF HAVING SEX. HUSBAND TOLD NEIGHBORS WIFE WENT BACK TO THAILAND. LEN SAYS THE OWNER IS CAPABLE OF EXTREME VIOLENCE AND, IN HIS OPINION, MURDERED HER.

THE CALLER HUNG UP THE PHONE AFTER REFUSING TO SAY MORE OR ELABORATE FURTHER

OPERATOR NAME AND NUMBER. CHRISTINE 0415

Chapter 21

The Last Day by the Numbers (1)

0600 to 1200
06.00 a.m.

June Brookton gazed into Ray Bryant's eyes from her position straddled above him as he reached release inside her. She had woken him up with her lips and tongue earlier and mounted him, wanting to please him, as she had decided this was the day that she would ask him if she could transfer from Melbourne to Perth permanently and, hopefully, move in with him.

She knew it was fast, most would say too fast, but they had both been *around the block* before. Neither of their marriages worked because their partners didn't understand pathology and didn't want to try. Ray and she could discuss the most fascinating topics, like decomposition, for hours. He was stimulating intellectually; they were a similar age, and if she was honest, Ray was good-looking. Not that looks were in any way vital to her; however, the fact that he was, was a decided bonus. They weren't getting any younger, and June had never met anyone with whom she had so much in common.

They could discuss dead bodies and the latest scientific ideas for diagnosing causes of death, and both wanted to work in research fields. They had a similar repertoire of jokes about body parts and organs, and they could make each other laugh, dripping in blood while reaching into a gaping chest to remove a lung. Where else was she going to find another man like him? Nowhere was the answer to that question; she knew that well enough.

June liked him. In fact, she had fallen in love with him, and she hoped he had fallen in love with her, too. Medical Examiners needed balance in their lives, and June had never felt so even keeled since meeting him. She took a deep breath, astride him, and psyched herself to ask him if he wanted her to move over from Melbourne. Her heart fluttered terribly, wondering what she would do if he said no.

****

06:01

Sam and Caroline exited the lift to go for a jog. She had spent the last three nights at his place. "Moving in by stealth," Sam called it, but he smiled when he did. For the first time in her life, a relationship felt so *right* for her, and she hoped it would last.

They took off at a good pace toward the river, and Caroline became lost in her thoughts. Caroline's mother had always told her to remember it was the accumulation of little things which counted most in relationships. Her reasoning was if you both looked after those, the big things would take care of themselves. The way they jogged, Caroline realized, was one of the many small things which showed how suited they were to each other. They didn't like to talk while running, preferring to be alone with their thoughts. Fitness was important, and they wanted to focus on it, so idle chatter while they ran was not their way. *Really,* she asked herself, *how rare is it to find a guy who wants to jog? And that Sam likes to do it as I do? Wow.*

Caroline mused that if she had a whiteboard, she could list all the good things about Sam and how fantastic they were as a couple. But Caroline knew it would have to be a big board because so far, she hadn't found anything she didn't like about him. The closest Caroline could come to a fault was his ego, which was a touch more than healthy. He did like himself, but then, so did she. Conversely, his ego gave him an air of self-confidence, which was good. Caroline wanted a strong man who knew what and who he wanted and was confident enough to get it. She couldn't stop her secret dream of them being together as a couple, permanently. Caroline mentally ticked some things off as she ran, loving the feeling in her muscles as they started to warm up.

So, where to begin? I know I am, in some ways, relatively shallow and like to look good myself. I like his looks and that he is comfortable with himself. He is fit and strong, and I like being out with him and knowing other women envy me. Some women would feel threatened by that, but not me. He seems to enjoy the natural flirt which I am, and I think he is comfortable knowing I will always kid around with other men, but no one else will ever touch me while I'm with him. He takes me seriously and respects that I am studying at university. Sam knows I spent three years as a lap dancer, and that alone makes him unique because he values me even though I did it for so long. Most men in the club wanted to screw me, but all the time I was dancing, that was all it was: wanting. Sam knows I wasn't a hooker, and I never even dated a man I met there. Sam is different from anyone I've been with; he asks my opinions and listens to what I say. Oh, my God, I think I love him.

The sudden realization both shocked and warmed her soul. Caroline knew Sam was intuitive and went with his feelings, which she liked. A logical, look-at-all-the-angles kind of guy wasn't an attractive trait in a man for her. Instead, she needed spontaneity in her life, and he gave her that by acting on a whim. Suggesting they go out for a drink at the bar last night, for example, then getting her to drink goodness knows how many tequila shots, and could the man dance? She had an absolute ball out with him. It was, in fact, the best night out she had had in years.

And Sam didn't just look good; he was great in bed, too. Sex was important to her, and he took her to unbelievable heights because he genuinely cared that she enjoyed it.

The list continued as she felt the warm burn in her legs. She felt safe with Sam; she knew he was brave, proven by the lengths he went to save her best friend, Didi, including getting shot. She loved that he was a senior detective with the police. She knew a lot of women, especially in her former job, who hated cops on principle like they were the enemy. But she couldn't get why it was the case. He was a good, honest man who wanted to make a difference. How could anyone not find that a good thing?

Caroline had no idea how long the relationship would last because she knew Sam had been married before, albeit too young, and had no desire to rush into marriage again. Sam had been clear on that, another quality she admired in him: emotional honesty. But

Caroline believed he *really* liked her, which brought…possibilities for hope. Not that she wanted to influence him to choose her for the long haul, but she hoped Sam would make that call in his own time. He seemed to be comfortable with her, so time would tell. In the meantime, life for her had always been about the journey, not the destination, and so far, Caroline was thoroughly enjoying the ride.

On a whim, Caroline decided to pick up the pace as they turned onto the walkway alongside the river. Of course, Sam kept up with her. Thirty seconds later, he increased his speed again to push her. *That's another thing, Caroline* thought; *we like to challenge each other.* It wasn't about being better, faster, or stronger but about challenging and rising above the challenge.

****

Jenny kissed Mike at the front door early in the morning. He had gotten out of bed to make her a coffee while she showered and was there to say goodbye. The farewell kiss turned into several, and Jenny had to drag herself away from him breathlessly. She wanted to get to her computer at work to get more details of the killer's car, print off some pictures, and do registration checks to see how many four-wheel drive wagons of that make and model were registered to Rolleystone Hill's residents. Jenny knew Sam and Bob Young would be delighted with her, and her place in Major Crime would be permanent if it were her efforts that were responsible for bringing two mass murderers to justice.

The previous night had been a first for Jenny; she had reached orgasm during intercourse with Mike, and she still wore the glow from it like a velvet cape wrapped around her. She wanted to experience making love with him repeatedly, not just because of the climax but because his level of caring and intimacy astounded her. If he could keep doing that to her. *Hello, brave new world,* she thought while washing her body earlier. Not that she had left Mike for sex reasons alone. Her justification was far more profound than that. Still, she felt happier inside than she could ever remember after one of the most enjoyable nights of her life.

Jenny still couldn't quite comprehend Mike had forgiven her for the affair and waited for it to end. He had faced the indignity of her leaving him for another woman, and she understood how he had suffered. She forgave Mike's anger, bitterness, and even his fighting her in the Family Court for custody of Josh to punish her; she deserved that and more for being unfaithful and falling in love. She was a police officer; she understood people's need to punish the wrongdoer better than most. But, despite his angst, Mike had waited. He had never dated anyone else but chose to focus on two things. First, they brought up their son, and Mike had done a superb job. Secondly, he studied women's needs, in particular, bisexual women. And then he bided his time and waited, hoping she would give him another chance. She knew Mike was remarkable, truly remarkable.

Jenny had a lot of thinking to do; boy, did she have a lot of that ahead of her. Nothing could ever be so simple; nothing in her life ever was. Jenny spent months thinking she was gay and believed the only way she could ever find emotional and sexual happiness was in another woman's arms, and now she knew that to be, well, if not wrong, misguided.

The question she had to ask herself was, could she go back? Could they have a second chance at a life together as a family? Mike had told her if ever she felt the need to be with another woman, he would be willing to accept it was a need, not a want, and he would understand. Never could she imagine anyone loving her so much and being so considerate of her needs, and he seemed genuine. Not that Jenny could see it working in practice. Jenny wasn't even sure if she would want to because she wasn't the sort of person to go to a gay bar and pick up a single lesbian for sex. What had happened before was a friendship which grew into mutual attraction, and the sex grew out of it. Would that be likely to ever occur again? Jenny didn't know, but if Mike was sincere, to know if it did happen, she could *experiment* meant a lot to her. *She possibly mused that they could have a threesome so Mike could be a part of the experience. Maybe our breakup may have been the best thing to happen to us. Maybe we can be better, stronger, and happier because we went through it?*

She had lots of things to think about, for sure. But she looked forward to returning to Mike's after work that night with a smile. She intended to stop at her place, grab some things and her cat, then go to the house they used to own together. They had agreed it would be a trial for a few days to see how they fared. Mike had promised to cook her a *special* dinner, and Jenny couldn't wait.

****

07.01 a.m.

Jenny parked her car at the gravel pit as the forty-second body was exhumed and logged. The crew had worked through the night under brilliant portable lighting towers provided by the hiring company. The ground penetrating radar detected the forty-third and final body, and they were digging down to it with their

296

usual slow and deliberate method. They hoped to have the corpse out of the ground before lunchtime.

The grid search had been completed, and the final tally was known, but the work was far from over, as the number of bodies had exhausted the Western Australian Coroner's office staff beyond their means. It would take pathologists many more days, if not weeks, to complete all the autopsies, DNA testing, and forensic investigations. Meanwhile, they were doing everything they could with preliminary inspections to be able to give the most information possible to assist the police with the investigation as quickly as they could. The doctors understood the pressure was on to find and stop the murderers.

Forty-three murder victims were an incredibly high number to work on in such a short period of time. It was obvious that each victim's wounds and torture were beyond horrific. Words like *animal, sadistic,* and *monster* seemed to stop having all meaning after the tenth body was found. Pathologists generally were hardy souls, but the volume of bodies and the extent of the mutilations was dulling to the senses and making them immune to the brutality and violence. Therefore, workplace psychologists forced them to take time away from the case to not succumb to the inhumane callousness and sheer volume of work. Even though more than anything else, each member of the crew wanted to work longer and harder to help catch the two individuals responsible, it was not possible, nor was it permitted by Sam in conjunction with Bob Young.

****

07.15 a.m.

Jenny spent some time with the digging crew and

was told the search of the pits was over; she was given the final body count of forty-three. Even though she had been a part of the case from the start, she was staggered to discover so many young people had been abducted, raped, tortured, and murdered by the two unknown individuals. She stood shaking her head for a few minutes; it was unbelievable they could have gotten away with it for so long.

Jenny entered the command center, sat at a terminal, and logged on. Once she was in the database, she typed in the make and model of the vehicle from the page of the printed book and the years in which that body shape was sold. Once Jenny found one in a gray color, she sent it to the printer to run off thirty color copies. Jenny then logged into the licensing area. This would take longer, as the search capabilities were less helpful than she would have liked. In the end, Jenny pulled up each year individually, starting in 1998 through to 2004, and requested a list of registered owners. From there, she could reduce it by postcode, transferring that list to a spreadsheet. While printing out her spreadsheet, she made herself a coffee while she waited for the rest of the team, feeling very proud of herself.

07.48 a.m.

Sam drove through the gate and parked, still smiling as his mood was good. He had completed a good run with a stunningly beautiful woman, which always set him up for a great day. Sam then showered with her and made love under the cascading water. Sam loved looking at Caroline, clothed or unclothed; she was, without a doubt, spectacular. Then, he had breakfast of muesli with fresh fruit and almond milk with the same beautiful woman. What was remarkable about that, other than being with a beautiful woman, was she enjoyed, yes, enjoyed, the same breakfast as he did, which was a first. Most women pulled a face at the mere thought of drinking almond milk. Caroline loved it and even thanked him for introducing her to it.

Sam knew he had to watch himself. *I could fall for this one,* he knew. But then, at odd times, Sam found himself thinking maybe, just maybe, that wasn't such a bad thing. He even suspected it was too late; he might have already fallen for her. Sam dared not tell Felix. He would send out the wedding invitations, as Felix had been telling him he should settle down for years. Well, Sam wasn't sure how Caroline felt, but for him, this was different, and he believed Caroline was exceptional.

He entered the transportable office. "Good morning," he said to everyone, then noticed the *cat that got the cream* look on Jenny's face. *She either had some great sex with a woman last night, or she has made a breakthrough on the case,* he thought, not knowing he was almost right on both counts.

Most of the other detectives doing the door-to-door interviews with Jenny had already arrived and were waiting for Sam's blessing before starting their day. Sam noticed they all had an expectant look and realized Jenny had asked them to stay back for her announcement. Knowing she had gone to see Tammy the night before, he knew it had to be some identification of the four-wheel drive. Sam could have spoilt it for her but chose not to.

"Boss, I've had a mini breakthrough," she said and could barely contain her enthusiasm.

He sat on the edge of her desk and smiled back, waiting while the others gathered around, "Go on, Jen.

We're all ears."

"Well, I spent well over an hour with Tammy last night and did some relaxation techniques with her while looking through the book. When she was going at the pictures, I was watching her and thought she had a little flinch when it came to one page. It was so slight she didn't know she had done it herself, but I think her subconscious saw something familiar. So, I got her to look at that picture closely and then took her back through the night, nice and slow. I got her deeply relaxed and calm, and she confirmed it was a silver, or light gray Jeep Grand Cherokee, an old one. The model ran from 1998 to 2004, just like this one." She held up a picture of the Jeep.

"That's fantastic work, Jenny. Well done." Sam was impressed. She had excelled, once again, and had done it after hours. She was undoubtedly an outstanding detective, and Sam was lucky to have her as a partner.

"Well, it won't stand up in court. They will say I planted the thought in her head, but I'm convinced it's genuine, and once we catch these guys, we hopefully won't need this as evidence."

"Oh, I think we will have more than enough DNA, so we won't need to raise how we got the vehicle, Jen, which is good enough for me. Have you done a data search?"

"Yes, Boss, I've got twenty-one possibilities registered in this postcode. Tammy thinks it was gray or silver, but I've left all colors in the search criteria just in case it's a red or other color that had a paint job or covered in primer, which made her think it was silver."

"That many? That surprises me. It must have been a popular four-wheel drive with farmers and hobbyists.

Right, let's get to it then. Let's see if we can't get to all these today. Let's meet back here at five and see what we've uncovered. Jen, have you handed out lists?"

"They're right here." She stood up, grabbed the spreadsheet pile, and handed the lists to the other investigators. They all left with a purpose and a spring in their steps. They could all feel it; they were closing in.

****

08.03 a.m.

The support staff arrived and took seats as Sam updated Bob Young about the suspect vehicle. He also explained how Jenny had used a relaxation technique bordering on hypnosis to get the information from Tammy, which was an extraordinary gift Jenny had. Sam assured Bob that Tammy would not have remembered the vehicle details without Jenny's unique talent.

Bob groaned, "Sam, its great news, but you must be careful with that stuff. Some smart lawyer can use hypnosis to get the case thrown out of court. Please be careful that your arrest doesn't hinge on identification from it alone."

"We will, Bob. If you want my opinion, it won't matter because when we close in on these guys, there will be so much forensic evidence the prosecutors will be jumping with joy."

"I hope you're right. Boy, I hope you're right, but remember that too much science can confuse a jury; we need this ironclad. Keep me posted, Sam."

****

08.43 a.m.

"Sam Collins." He answered the ringing phone.

"Ray Bryant, Sam. How are you?"

"Hey, Ray, I'm good. You?"

"Well, I asked a woman to marry me this morning, and she said yes. So fair to say I'm very happy. Enough about me, though. I have something for you."

"Congratulations, Ray. Is she the woman who accompanied you out here the day before yesterday, the one you could barely keep your hands and eyes off?" Sam smiled as he recalled Ray's usually stiff, formal manner, which had been blown out of the water around the woman he had with him on his last visit to the *burial ground,* which everyone was now calling it.

Ray cleared his throat before saying, "I have no idea what you are talking about, Inspector. If you are referring to the assistant medical examiner who accompanied me, yes, she is the lucky one. Do you want this information or not?"

"She's cute, Doc. Gorgeous, in fact. I only have one question. What does she see in you?" Sam laughed but quickly added, "I'm just kidding. I think she is lovely. Yes, I do want to know what you have for me. Please go on."

Ray ignored the joke and cleared his throat. "Victim number one is from Thailand. We called her number one, not because she was found first but because, from what we can tell, she was buried first."

"Jeez, you guys are good. How can you tell from a skeleton what country she is from? Doc, I'm impressed."

"Do you understand anything about genetics and genealogy, Sam? No? I didn't think so. Nationality is relatively easy. However, we don't need to wait for the DNA result in this case because she suffered a broken leg as a child and had a titanium pin inserted. Prosthetics and the like have batch ID engraved on them, and from the number, we can track the country, hospital of origin, and patient's identity. I've emailed you the details. You can contact them and request information so you can identify her.

"Thanks a heap, Ray. I appreciate it. I still don't see what such a gorgeous woman sees in you, but thanks for helping. You've done amazing work." He laughed, and Ray laughed too, and after a few more pleasantries, they hung up.

****

08.56 a.m.

Sam forwarded the information to Bob Young, who promised to contact the Thai police and pin manufacturer to request assistance. Bob had volunteered to do all the overseas work, including conversations with victims' families, to free up Sam's time to be more hands-on at the site and help with the number of detectives under his command.

Sam walked over to the whiteboard, picked up one of the pens, and wrote *VICTIM #1: THAI.* Then he stood before it, as he often did, and looked through the accumulated information. His eyes were drawn to the picture of Greg Brady's burnt-out car. Every other time he looked at it, something bothered him. Whenever he thought the answer to his niggling doubt came tantalizingly close, it shot out of reach again like a genie disappearing, leaving him annoyed and frustrated.

****

09.22 a.m.

Sam was looking at the list of items in evidence bags with the forensics department turned up by the grid search for the hundredth time, hoping to see something which made sense, when his mobile phone rang. One look at the display and all feelings of frustration were quickly replaced with a warm glow.

"Hi, beautiful," he answered.

"Hi, hunky man," Caroline replied. "Guess what I've been doing for the last half an hour?"

"Hmm, that's tough. Did it involve touching yourself?"

She burst into happy laughter, "No, dummy, when I think of you, it doesn't take me anywhere near half an hour. No, I've been on the phone with Didi. She and Nicky are back from their honeymoon in Mauritius. Bree told her I've not been home for three days, so we had some girl talk about our men."

"Is that what I am? Your man?"

"I hope so."

The silence hung. Sam felt they both wanted to say more, but through habit, Sam held back, not wanting to be the first to commit, but he hoped Caroline would.

"So, how was Mauritius?" he finally asked.

"Oh my God, she said the three of them had such a good time. They had a cabin on a jetty over the water in this beautifully secluded bay, and they just swam, ate seafood, and after Siobhan went to bed, well, you can imagine that part." She giggled. "They are so much in love, Sam. You did such a great thing by saving them."

"All part of the service, ma'am." *If only you knew just how much I saved Nicky, but you never will,* he thought. That secret will stay buried forever.

"So, anyway, she was thrilled to hear that you and I were seeing each other. They want to take us out to that cute Chinese Restaurant, with the amazing Alan Chan, for dinner, just the four of us. Are you up for it Saturday night, or should I take one of my other boyfriends?"

"Hmm, let me just check my diary." He rustled

papers on his desk near the phone for effect, "As you know, I have other girlfriends to consider too, but no, it seems you're in luck. Looks like I'm free on Saturday."

"Okay, that's good. I will tell them it's a date. Bree is going to their place to babysit Siobhan. Do you want to meet them there or at the restaurant?"

"Hmm, look. Can we leave that part open and confirm on the day? I have a feeling this case is going to break wide open at any tick of the clock, so it's always a possibility I might have to cancel last minute, and you will have to go with one of the other men you have on the side. Don't think I don't want to go, because I do, but sometimes the job will get in the way. I hope you're going to be okay with that in the future?"

"Sammy? If you're saying we have a future, I won't have any men on the side, just so you know."

Before he could answer, knowing he wouldn't be comfortable, she pressed on, "So yes, babe, that's fine. I will always understand and will explain it to Didi. Okay, I will let you get back to making the world safer for people like me. See you tonight?"

"Can't wait."

****

09.28 a.m.

Joel broke the window in the back door of the Belmont home with his elbow, then reached through the hole with a gloved hand and undid the latch. Stepping over the glass on the floor, he entered and closed the door behind him.

He knew no one was at home; he had seen the mother and father leave earlier, driving out of the garage while he was parked fifty meters down the road. He knew they were going to pick up the daughter from the hospital because he had called the nursing station earlier. She was being discharged that day. They would find him waiting when they returned home as a happy little family. *This will be fun,* he thought.

Joel wore his uniform in case he was seen entering or leaving. Easier to talk his way out of a situation dressed as a cop; that much was obvious. The first room he entered was the kitchen. It was clean and tidy, and as he looked around, it looked like it had been renovated within the last few years.

He crossed over to the electric kettle, picked it up, and shook it. Once Joel confirmed there was water, he put it down and turned it on. Then he opened the cupboards until he located a mug he could use. Joel knew he had time to kill, so why not make himself at home and make a cuppa? *Undoubtedly, the homeowners won't mind; even if they do, they won't live long enough to worry too much. Joel* found the makings and took the milk out of the fridge. While he waited for the kettle to boil, he searched through the drawers. He wasn't looking for anything to steal; he was just nosey, and you never knew what you could find until you looked.

Once the coffee was made, he walked through the house, looking for the girl's room. He had no interest in the parents; they were insignificant. But the girl; was different. If all went according to plan, he intended to kill Mum and Dad and then have some fun with the daughter before murdering her, too. He was angry with her for escaping, and she deserved everything which was coming to her.

Joel and his father had decided she had to pay, so she would suffer before her inevitable end; strangulation, probably though he hadn't decided. Joel knew he wouldn't have the time he usually took when he played with a woman but was sure it would be enjoyable.

Over the years, the father and son duo developed ways to increase their victims' suffering while keeping them alive for weeks. What they had found most interesting was if their prey thought she had some chance of survival, she could last a long time. If she had the merest inkling, she could escape; she would receive great pain and perform any abomination. Conversely, when she lost her last ounce of hope, she lost her spirit and will to live. And then, inevitably, the fun was over.

So for Joel and his father, the challenge was to keep letting them hope. They had come up with different ways to deliver hope. Sometimes one would be the tormentor while the other befriended the victim, offering to help them escape soon. They would laugh to themselves when they relived it over supper after their latest victim had passed out from pain and exhaustion.

Today, though, was less about pleasure and more about revenge. The bitch had ruined their fun and had to pay. He opened her wardrobe and sipped his coffee while running his other hand through her clothes. *Typical, like all young girls these days, her clothes are all too short, too thin, and way too slutty* he thought. *Is it any wonder women get raped when they dress like that?* He shook his head and shut the wardrobe.

He opened the top bedside drawer and saw her filmy, colorful, and tiny underwear. He held a minuscule pair of see-through pale blue panties to his nose. They were clean, but he still hoped to catch something of her. All he had was his imagination. He put his coffee on the bedside cabinet, sat down, and then lay back on her bed, putting his head on her pillow. He closed his eyes, smelling to try to catch her scent. With his other hand, he unzipped his pants. He had lots of time before he killed her. *I have to amuse myself somehow.*

****

11.17 a.m.

The final body was loaded into the medical examiner's van and taken away, and Sam watched it go. He stood alongside Ray Bryant, who had come out for a final look around. Both were silent for a long time as they surveyed the scene of open graves stretching into the distance. It resembled the most bizarre scene from the goriest horror movie either could imagine, but this was real.

"I'm not one to get emotional about death," Ray said. "Well, I can't in my profession. I must stay detached, but I find this scene incredibly sad."

"I know what you mean. I stare out here often and just think one word: how? How could two people be so depraved as to do this? And how can it be two of them? One would be bad enough, but how can you possibly get two people so twisted?"

Sam shook his head sadly. "I've just had the psychologist here talking to me about sexual sadism, the sociopathic psyche, and the sort of childhood these people had which could lead them to become psychotic. He thinks it's a pair of brothers who were sexually abused as children, which all sounds a bit too pat to me. Anyway, it's not as if it makes catching them any easier, but I still can't get my head around the why."

"Do you think we'll ever know that? Or will it be one of those cases where they won't talk?"

"I'd certainly like to ask them when we catch them. Ray, and we will catch them. You can bet on that."

"Well, when you find out, let me know. I suppose for me, this whole affair has been good for one thing. I'm going to marry one of the medical examiners who came over from Melbourne to help us. So, if we didn't have this case, we never would have met. Go figure. That brings me to why I came; I thought I'd tell you personally because of what we've found on one of the victims, which is the one most recently buried. You may not understand the true horror of it simply by reading the postmortem result."

"Do I want to hear this?" Sam asked, not wanting the gory details.

"No one normal would want to hear about it, but the fact is, as you know, the decomposition of virtually all the other bodies has made it almost impossible to understand the true picture of all the injuries they sustained before they died. With the other victims, we had to surmise a lot of what was done to them; most of it was soft tissue damage, and the soft tissue had decomposed away."

He was silent for a long time, remembering the extent of the wounds the poor young woman suffered before finally giving in to death. "Sam, it's like these two monsters have made an art form of causing pain. She was whipped, bit, punched, burnt, cut, stabbed, and some things even worse."

Sam stared at him, wondering: *What could be worse?* He didn't want to know his question's answer but had to ask. "What could be worse, Ray?"

"Well, it's like they tried to infect her deliberately. They cut her, put dirt in the cut and sewed it back up, then let it go septic. And as if all that wasn't bad enough." He stopped to shake his head and swallow back down the bile which came up. "Let's just say identifying the killers won't be too much of a problem. We have a ton of DNA which has gone off for testing, recovered from different places on, and in, her body."

"Oh my God. Do you mean what I think you mean?"

Ray nodded, not wanting to detail the sexual abuse on the badly mutilated body. Instead, he cleared his throat again and said, "I can't even talk about it; sorry, Sam. I thought I could, but I just can't. Do me a favor, please, when you catch them?"

"What's that?"

"Don't bring them in. Do us all a service and shoot them dead. I better get back to the lab. Good hunting, bye."

Sam watched him go, stunned. This was the same man who was delighted with the body count just a few days ago because it made his work more enjoyable, yet today he was sickened. That alone told Sam just how badly the victims must have suffered.

****

11.50 a.m.

Jenny and her partner Jamie Byrne drove through the gate with a badly faded sign announcing it was The Winter Sun Farm. This place was on her list for a callback as no one answered her previous call when she had left a card. It was also on her second list because Mr. Clancy Pike owned a dark gray four-wheel-drive wagon that matched the description. She drove down the long, twisting driveway with an observant eye toward the home and other outbuildings, past the hay on the right and rows of fruit trees on the left that disappeared into the distance.

****

11.53 a.m.

Where the fuck is she? Joel screamed inside his head. He was frantic with boredom. He had run out of ideas to amuse himself and was far too focused on adrenalin and excitement to sit down and watch TV, but he was *B-O-R-E-D*. He had finished three cups of coffee, searched the house from top to bottom, ejaculated in the bitch's underwear, and urinated on the mother's clothes hanging in her wardrobe.

That last thing had brought him enormous pleasure and made him giggle outrageously. He'd love to be a fly on the way when they discovered that little gift he left for them. Though if everything went well, they wouldn't find it because they would die before it happened.

Out of sheer frustration, he took out his mobile phone, looked up his recently dialed calls, and found the hospital number he rang earlier. Joel tried calling again. When it answered, he asked to be put through to the girl's ward.

"This is Senior Constable Joe Pike, WA Police Department. I know Tammy Reynolds is being discharged today, and I have a statement I need her to sign. Can you tell me what time she is getting out, please?"

"I'm sorry you've missed her. They left about forty-five minutes ago."

"That's all right. I will catch the family at their home, then. Thanks for that." He almost hung up and, in fact, had the phone away from his ear when he heard some words spoken but couldn't quite hear what those words were. "I'm sorry. I dropped my phone. What did you say?"

"I said, Constable, you won't find her there. They've

311

all gone down south for a few days to hide away from the reporters who are hounding her for a story."

He nearly threw his phone across the room in a rage. *That fucking, fucking, fucking bitch has got nine lives,* he thought. He struggled to reign in his anger and keep his voice calm as he asked, "Ah, right, I don't blame her. I don't suppose they mentioned where specifically, did they? I really do need to get this signed."

"Not to me, she didn't. Hang on, though. Let me ask the other nurse who looked after her."

After what seemed like twenty minutes but was a lot less, a different voice came on the lines. "Hello, this is Nurse Harmon. You want to know where Tammy has gone, do you? Who is asking, please?"

"Yes, please, if you could assist, it would be a big help. It's Senior Constable Joe Pike here. I can give you my badge number if you like."

"Well, forgive me for asking, but her dad, lovely man he is, is trying to keep her away from all the reporters who have been driving us nuts here trying to get her story. So, they made me promise I wouldn't let on where they were going. How do I know you are from the police and not just some reporter lying to me?"

Joel was struggling to hold his temper. *How hard can it be to kill one fucking woman?* He asked himself before taking a deep, calming breath and continuing, "Look, nurse. I don't want you to break any confidence, but here's the thing. I was given this statement last night to get her to sign, but on the way there, I got caught up in a bad accident on the freeway. I wasn't in it, but I witnessed it. And this guy was badly hurt, so I gave him first aid and kept him alive till the ambulance arrived. Anyway, by the time I got done, it was too late to get there to see her, and I was covered in blood, too, so I left it till today. I will be in real trouble with my boss without it signed. Oh, well, not to worry. Thanks anyway."

"I see, look, all right. I shouldn't be doing this, but The Reynolds family has gone to The Abbot Beach Resort for three days. Apparently, her uncle has an apartment there, but I don't know exactly where."

"Thanks for the information. If the boss doesn't want me to drive there, we can send it by fax through the resort management or get a local cop to see her. Thanks for your help. I owe you one."

The Abbot Beach Resort? Well, that puts paid to my plan; the bitch has escaped again. There was no way he was driving there and searching for her. There would be way too many people around. *Fuck it.*

****

11.55 a.m.

Jenny left a second note on the back of a card for the farm owner, stressing the matter was urgent, and tucked it under the front door. As she squatted down, she picked up a faint dusty, dirty, and unpleasant smell inside the house, seemingly from under the door. She shook her head, thinking it wasn't very nice at all, as she stepped back to get distance from the scent.

Jenny and Jamie stood in the veranda's shade, silently scanning the farm. There were no vehicles to be seen anywhere, though they could see tire ruts in the gravel. There were several outbuildings where tractors were undoubtedly housed, and the Jeep could be in one. But they all appeared locked; they had no warrant and no reason to go peering into locked sheds without the owner being present.

****

They were being watched from one of those outbuildings where many people had been killed over the years. Clancy stood in the dark shadows looking at them through the window, deep in thought. They had come earlier than he would have liked. He wanted Joel to be with him so he could share the fun. He watched the female cop slide something under his door, which meant they would leave. *Excellent,* Clancy thought. *I can call her and arrange for her to return later when Joel is back from killing the bitch and the other cop Collins.*

Chapter 22

The Last Day by the Numbers (2)

1230 to 1430
12.16 p.m.
"Sam Collins." He answered his phone, welcoming the distraction of reading through the latest reports from the Crime Stoppers phone calls.

"Bob Young. Sam, I've got something back from Thailand and a name for our first victim. Her name was Nadia Putenhaminas. I've done a check, and that surname doesn't appear on any immigration visas other than a two-week holiday visa from twenty-odd years ago. Which only leaves two alternatives. Either she was an illegal immigrant when she was murdered, which is a possibility as the rules were a lot slacker back then. Or possibly she married in Thailand and came over with a different surname. I've requested a check through the Thai government marriage records, but it could take a while. I thought you'd want to know."

"Thanks for that, sir," Sam answered, troubled at the thought she might have been married for some reason, though he didn't know why. They chatted about the case, which they both felt was getting closer to solving by the hour. Sam told him Ray Bryan's comments about the most recent victim and the horror she must have suffered over an extended period.

"Sam, are you okay? I mean in yourself. No matter what, don't let these murderers' lack of humanity destroy your own. As hard as it is, don't let their savagery get on top of you."

"No, I'm fine, sir; it bothers me, but only because it makes me angry and more determined to catch them." Sam felt a steely calm but took Bob's warning seriously.

"All right, let me know if you need a break, and keep me posted on any developments."

"Will do, and thanks for the consideration."

****

Roger Kincaid phoned Sam from a noisy pub, where the team working the backpacker hostels had met to catch up for lunch and compare notes. Unfortunately, he had nothing positive to report, which wasn't surprising. They knew it would be tough with the volume of young, fit, and healthy tourists traveling through the state. But it had to be done as they now had seventeen backpackers identified, and the list reads like a roll call of nations for the UN Assembly.

Once he hung up, Sam thought back to the call from Bob Young, and he realized there was an anomaly there. Nadia, with the unpronounceable surname, was the key. She was the only one, so far as he could see, to not be a backpacker.

He sat back in his chair and let his mind run over that in more depth. Nadia, whatever her name was, had been in the ground the longest, so clearly, she was the first victim. She was fully clothed, not naked. She was not wrapped in plastic but a rug. She was not a backpacker and had not come into the country under her own name. What did it all mean?

He made one of his leaps of faith and realized she

wasn't an illegal immigrant. He could see only one explanation that made sense; the killer married this woman in Thailand and brought her back as his wife. She had first come to Australia as a tourist for two weeks, met her husband-to-be, then returned to Thailand. He followed, they married, and the happy couple came back to live in WA. They had a life together until something went wrong, very wrong. Maybe she wanted to leave him and go back to her country, and he killed her in such a way that affected him emotionally, and that started the killing spree, which lasted over fifteen years.

The pathologist estimated her age at her time of death to be between thirty and forty, so Sam assumed thirty-five. Further, Ray said she had been in the ground eighteen years, give or take, which would make her fifty-three if she were still alive today. So, the original killer was, he guessed, between fifty-five and sixty-five years old now. He had read those men usually married younger Thai women, so those sums felt right to him.

Sam left his desk and wrote the information on the board, then stood back and looked at the notes as the mental image of the man became more apparent. Fifty-five to sixty-five-year-old, gruff Australian voice, who drove a four-wheel-drive and was formerly married to a Thai woman who would be, if she had lived, fifty to fifty-five years old. Thanks to Ray's colorful comments, Sam knew they now had definitive DNA of the killers, so there was no doubt in his mind they would catch the sick son of a bitch and his accomplice soon.

He smiled as he remembered how nervous he had been only a few short days before when Felix gave him a talking-to. Once this case was wrapped up, Sam decided he would take Felix a bottle of single malt to say thanks. As always, Felix had been right; Sam had been doing just fine.

****

12.46 p.m.

Jenny Markham called Sam from where she and her partner were having their lunch break. She had made sure her team texted her directly with any farm owners who had sufficient alibis or any other substantial reason to remove them from the inquiry. The team only had fourteen remaining to discount. As a team, they would discuss it later when they got back to the office see why some should be discounted, but for now, she wanted to pass on the results.

Sam stood by the list on the whiteboard and checked off the names which had been cleared as she read them out. His opinion of Jenny as a detective grew every day they worked together. Her ability and work ethic continued to astound him.

"Good work, Jen. One thing I can tell you is the original victim was from Thailand, and I think she married an Aussie over there. It looks like she came into this country on her married name using an Australian passport. Bearing in mind she has been in the ground for anything up to twenty years, she could have entered something like thirty-odd years ago when the immigration laws were a lot easier than they are now. We are checking to get her married name. Once we get it, I think this case will be over as it will lead straight to her husband, who I think murdered her in perhaps a fit of rage and then started his killing spree."

"Like you, I've had a feeling all day we're getting close, Boss. We've got the car and now a Thai wife. It's all falling into place, isn't it?"

"Yes, Jen, it is, and we also have a bucketful of DNA from the most recent victim. Identifying the offenders is not going to be hard."

"Thanks, Boss. That's a visual I didn't need while eating lunch."

"Sorry, point taken. Talking of lunch, I'm here alone, besides the officers manning the gate. Everyone else has gone to get their lunch since the mobile canteen packed up and left, so I better go and grab something myself. See you back here around four."

"Will do, Boss."

****

12.52 p.m.

Sam climbed into his vehicle, about to drive out of the car park, when his phone rang. There was no caller ID showing. "Sam Collins."

"Joe Pike. Inspector, look, I'm sorry about the other day. When we were talking, my phone dropped out of range, which happens when you live in the hills quite a lot. You probably thought I was just being rude."

"That's okay, Senior, I get it. What can I do for you?" Sam's hackles stood to attention. He did not like this man one little bit. Something about him made his skin crawl, though he could not tell why.

"Well, I was apologizing to you the other day for being slack and not doing my job properly, and I was saying I had been suspended, you remember?"

"I remember. Go on."

"Well, they bounced me out of there so quick and took the wreck away that I forgot all about the evidence bag I had with all the stuff I found in the car. So, I wondered if you'd like me to drop it off this afternoon. I take it you're out at the old gravel pits manning the command post?"

"Let me get this straight. You've got evidence that hasn't gone to forensics?" Sam was angry evidence had not been logged. Anything useful could now be tainted due to the compromised chain of evidence trail.

"Yeah, well, like I said, they got my ass out of there the minute I walked in that morning. The wreck had already been picked up while I was off shift, so I didn't know differently. I was told to go home when I arrived, so I just assumed someone else would have given your people the evidence bag. But I went to work this morning for a meeting, and it was still there. I'd like to make up for my earlier poor attitude, so I grabbed it, thinking I could drop it off to you and apologize personally at the same time. It's no hassle. I live in the hills at the Winter Sun Farm, so it's not out of my way at all."

"Yeah, okay. I'm going for lunch right now but will be back in an hour." Maybe Joe wasn't as bad as he first thought, Sam wondered and hung up.

His car spewed up gravel from his tires as he drove away to find somewhere which did a half-decent ham and salad roll; he was hungry.

****

13.22 p.m.

Detective Sergeant Beverley Maddison stood at the desk of the Rolling Waves Backpackers Accommodation in Northbridge, talking to Mandy Myers, the owner. Mandy was a larger-than-life character who looked like she was still living in the sixties. Beverley thought the woman would have been fifty, if not sixty years old, yet wore a tie-dyed purple T-shirt and a long, yellow gingham checked skirt with the buttons undone. Her faded and bleach-blotched denim jeans seemed to be held up by a lime green head scarf knotted at her waist. Her unkempt, straggly bleached blonde hair was a sight to behold. But the hippie look didn't stop there; her broad Australian accent sounded like she had moved to the city straight from a Northern Territory bush camp only the day before. She also loved the sound of her own voice.

"Jeeze Louise, we get some real grouse young people thorough here, from all over the bloody world, no worries. And the clothes they wear? Crikey near gives my poor hubby Stan a bloody heart attack, especially in summer. But they are beaut people, and I love 'em all to bits. I like to make friends with each and every one of them. I'm like the mum they never had but wish they could, know what I mean, doll? And do we have some laughs? You bet we do. I love all my young travelers, and nearly all of them stay in touch and write to their Auntie Mandy when they get back home."

Beverley took an immediate liking to this wonderfully colorful woman and had to stifle a giggle at the same time, as her accent and choice of words were hysterical. She could have listened to her all day, as once she got wound up, there was no stopping her.

"Corse, Stan the man, still thinks he is God's gift to the Sheila's, so he thinks they all fancy the bejesus out of him, but you know what I reckon? I reckon, to these young blonde Scandinavian women he lusts after like a dog with a bone, he resembles their grandfathers back home. Laugh, do I? He thinks they fancy him, but really…" Mandy leaned forward in a conspiratorial way. "Well, let me ask you. I mean, you look like a woman of the world. Would you fancy a nookie with someone who looked like your grandad?"

By now, Beverley couldn't stop the damm wall from bursting, and she laughed outrageously, as this was the funniest conversation she had ever had. And the amazing thing was it just kept getting funnier. Beverley suddenly realized she hadn't even asked a question yet; the woman was like a verbal steamroller. Beverley had just introduced herself then Mandy hadn't stopped except to take a breath. With this realization, her laughing fit took off anew.

"Exactly, I knew you'd agree," Mandy turned her head to shout to the back office. "You see, Stan, you old codger? Even this lovely Sheila out here from the bloody cops agrees with me you're as useless as tits on a bull, and she hasn't even met you." She turned back to Beverley, "Well, that's done it. He will be sulking for the rest of the bloody day now, so it's not a total loss, is it?" She burst into her own cackling style of laughter, which set Beverley off again.

"I mean, seriously, what would he do if one of these gorgeous young things said 'yes' to his silly, bloody pandering? Probably run a mile, then have a bloody heart attack. I mean, Jesus, please. Anyway, what did you want to ask me, love?"

It took a few seconds to bring herself under control, but even then, it was challenging as Beverley wanted to laugh every time she looked at her. "Umm, well, Mrs. Meyers..." she began.

"Cripes, doll. Call me Mandy. Every other bugger does."

Bev had to bite her lip again, bringing herself under control. "Well, Mandy, it's a very serious matter, but I seem to have a fit of the giggles. I'm so sorry. You've undoubtedly heard about all those bodies found in the gravel pit in the Roleystone Hills?"

"Yeah, every mug and his brother have. I've tried to warn all my young travelers, but do they listen? Course they don't, just like you and me didn't at that age. Jesus, I was like a blue heeler chasing sheep when I was a teenager."

It was no good. Beverley laughed again, doubled over with tears in her eyes. All she could think of when she looked at Mandy was a blue heeler dog chasing sheep. *This woman should be doing stand-up comedy,* Beverly thought. It took a minute for her to calm down enough to ask the next question. "Well, most of those victims, it seems, were backpackers who were lured somewhere, possibly with a promise of cash work, like fruit picking. So, we are doing the rounds asking if you've seen anyone offering work to girls who seemed a bit suspect if you know what I mean. We don't have a description, but this guy has been preying on young backpackers for over fifteen years, and we're hoping someone remembers something which they thought was odd at the time."

"Well, you know what, doll. I reckon I did see someone like that. Oh, must be six weeks ago? I can look up the date, 'cos the girl was staying here. Julie, her name was, lovely English Sheila with skin as white as clean sheets on the washing line."

Beverley became very serious. Six weeks sounded about right from the initial report of the most recently buried victim. "Please, Mandy, go on. What can you tell me?"

"Let me think about this because you know what? Cripes, now I think of it, I know why it bothered me at the time, because the same thing happened once before.

Okay, its coming back to me, doll. So, Julie, I can look up her last name, but off the top of my head I don't remember it for the mo. Cute little thing, she was. Came to me on a Sunday evening and said she'd scored a week's worth of fruit picking for cash money, and the guy was coming to pick her up straight away. She'd been at the Rancho Café where most of the young'uns go, and this guy approached her. Apparently, this farm had free on-site accommodation so she could stay there for nothing and get fed as part of the deal, and she could begin work first thing in the morning. So anyway, Julie had booked and paid for a week to stay here but had only been with us a couple of days. She asked me if she could have a credit and use up the other days after she worked there for a week. Well, Crikey, she was such a bloody cutie, I said, yeah, she could do that, no worries, and she hugged me and then went on up to grab her stuff."

"Did you actually see the man, Mandy?"

"You bet I did, doll, and I'll tell you this for nothing. He looked like he was as crooked as a dog's hind leg. His bloody eyes were too close together, know what I mean? I reckoned at the time he was as mad as a sack full of snakes."

Beverley was becoming immune to Mandy's beautifully funny way of speaking, as the *sack full of snake's* comment only raised a smile. Also, Beverley smelt the scent of closing in on their prey. This sounded very promising. "Do you still remember him, Mandy? Can you describe him to me?" She took out her notebook and turned to a fresh page.

"Well, the canny bugger only stuck his head in that door and asked if Julie was coming down. He didn't come right inside. He had this old cowboy-style hat on.

Looked like it had been ten rounds with Mike Tyson; he probably was as old as the hills. He had gray, untidy hair that stuck out at the sides under his bloody hat. You could tell he worked on the land or out in the sun. His skin was, what's the body word, leathery? Wore a red checked shirt and dirty jeans, oh, and boots which were as scuffed as a pine floor in the front bar of a busy pub. If I had to guess, I'd say he was a farmer or rodeo rider, but he was too old to ride broncs, but that's what he reminded me of."

"This is brilliant stuff, Mandy. If I put you with a police artist, do you think you could help come up with a decent pic of him?"

"Yeah, no worries, doll. The thing is, I was looking at this bugger, thinking, *I know you, my bucko,* but it didn't come to me right off the bat. I said, "Yeah, she's getting her stuff." He said something like, "Thanks Missus," and walked back outside and got into his wagon, which he parked right in front of the window. It was bugging the whoopsies out of me, then Julie came back down, all out of breath like, gives me one of her best hugs, thanks me for being so kind, and says she'd see me in a week, 'cept, I never did. She didn't come back at all. Is Julie one of those bodies you found out there?"

"I'm not sure, Mandy. We must wait a while for it to be confirmed by DNA or dental records. There are a lot of bodies that haven't been identified yet."

"But you think it is, don't you, doll?"

Beverley nodded and softly said, "The timing is about right for one of the victims, and if you think she intended to come back… Well, I can't say any more right now. I hope you understand."

Mandy shrugged sadly, and a tear ran down one cheek. "She was a bloody lovely girl; make any parents proud, she would. That's just so sad. Do me a favor, doll, when you catch these buggers? String them up in the sun by their balls over a termite hill."

"Do you remember where you'd seen him before, Mandy?" Beverley asked gently.

"Yeah, as it happens, I do. As I watched Julie climb into the car, one of them four-wheel drive Jeeps it was. She was only short, and it was quite a step up for her; that's when it came to me. About two years or more before, I watched Hilde climb into the same car in the same way. I recall she had on a short skirt showing her legs all the way up to her bum. I remember thinking, *thank gawd Stan isn't watching. His eyes would have bugged out.* I could just about see her fanny."

"Can you tell me what happened that time, Mandy, please?"

"Hilde was traveling with her boyfriend, Jorgen. They were German and an awfully nice couple, very affectionate with each other. He adored her, and why wouldn't he? Stan, as he always does when we have Germans staying, kept telling me not to mention the war. Jeez, Louise, he thinks he's a bloody comedian. Anyway, they had been out at the coffee shop and got dropped off right out the front again in this Jeep wagon. Hilde and Jorgen run in. She looks happy and says they got two weeks' fruit picking for cash and free accommodation if you don't mind. So, they're off, she said. But she assured me they would return when they finished traveling around WA 'cos they wanted to stay with us again before heading to Sydney. "Okay," I say, "that's great, Hilde," and they rush up to pack while the old codger waits in his Jeep for them. I remember looking through the window and thinking he was a sleazy-looking dude wearing a filthy cowboy hat. I remembered his hat the second time, and it was the same guy. No worries about that.

"Mandy, do you remember what color the Jeep was?"

"Yep, gray, but it was grubby. You know, red dust and mud down the sides? It looked way overdue for a wash."

"Did you happen to notice what model it was?"

She rested her elbows on the counter and bent at the waist. "Doll, I know what you're thinking. You're wishing if only women noticed car makes and models just like the men do, aren't you? It's all right. No need to answer. I'm from the bush, doll. I can change spark plugs, clean a distributor, and plug a hole in a radiator with mustard powder, all before I've had my breakfast. Yeah, I know what bloody model it was. It wasn't one of the new boxy shape ones; one of the old ones with curves like Marylyn Monroe."

"Wow, Mandy, I'm impressed." And Beverley was, the woman was a gold mine.

"Are you now? Well, how impressed would you be if I gave you the rego number?

****

14.10 p.m.

"Detective Markham," Jenny said, answering her mobile phone. She and Jamie were conducting an interview with a retired accountant who had a hobby farm in the hills. She excused herself and walked away to take the call.

"Hello, Detective. This is Clancy Pike from the

327

Winter Sun Farm. You left a card for me to give you a call."

"Thank you so much for calling me back, Mr. Pike. We are conducting interviews in the area regarding the bodies found at the gravel pits and would like to catch up with you to ask you some questions. Would you be home this afternoon if we were to call back?"

"I've got a farm to run. I can't wait around all day, can I? Maybe, if you give me a definite time."

"How about two-thirty, give or take five minutes?"

"All right, I will be here."

****

14.25

"Stan, where's my bloody notebook gone, the one I keep in the drawer?" Mandy yelled out at her poor, long-suffering husband.

"I've not seen it, Mandy," Stan yelled back from the depths of their residence.

"Really? Is that what you're saying, you big galah? You mean I didn't see you with it last week when you wrote down the measurements when you replaced the bloody fly screens."

There was a long pause, during which Mandy comically and exaggeratedly raised her eyes to the heavens before whispering, "Honestly, doll, he's as useless as a fart in a sandstorm."

This time Beverley didn't laugh. She was far too excited as she knew she was on the brink of a monumental discovery. At any moment, she could have in her hands the means to identify the men who murdered forty-three people.

"Hang on a minute. Maybe I left it in the shed. I'll go and check now."

****

14.27

"Sam, it's Bob Collins." Sam heard when he answered his phone. "I've got some news for you. The Thai Department of Immigration has got back to me, and the woman's married name was Pike, Nadia Pike, husband Clancy and the address given was Crackerjack Farm in Narrogin. I've done a check, though, and they moved from there years ago. Not sure where, but I've got records looking deeper and hope to have something later this afternoon or in the morning at the latest. I've also got the local Narrogin cops talking to neighbors."

"That's great, sir. Thanks for letting me know."

"Seems like your gut feeling was right, Sam. We're getting close."

"Yes, I think we are."

"What's wrong? You sound miserable."

"Sorry, no not miserable, distracted. That name rings a bell, and I'm trying to remember where I've heard it."

"Well, I'll get off the phone and stop distracting you, so you can remember."

Sam stood, walked over to the board, and studied it but could not see Clancy Pike mentioned. *Maybe it was from one of the farm interviews,* he thought.

He heard a car drive in through the gate as the gravel crunched under the tires. Sam sat back down at his desk, knowing it would be the accident investigation cop. He was not looking forward to this meeting. He idly turned to the next page of the crime stopper call logs reports as he heard the car door slam and footsteps approaching the command center.

His eye wandered over the sheet before him, still

distracted, and stopped at three words: Winter Sun Farm. Suddenly, in a blinding flash of understanding, he got it all. Clancy Pike and his Thai wife, Nadia, had a son. They named him Joe, Joe Pike. He grew up and joined the police force and somehow wound up in the Accident Investigation Squad. The same Joe Pike who said he lived at the Winter Sun Farm...*Oh fuck.* Sam suddenly realized why the accident was staged, why the killers thought they could get away with it, and why the investigation was botched. Because the murderer was investigating himself. The murderous twosome was a father-and-son combination.

The office door flew open, kicked almost off its hinges. Joel Pike, in uniform, stepped through with a gun in his hand, his body turning, looking for Sam.

***

14.29 p.m.

Jenny Markham and Jamie Byrne stepped out of the police issue vehicle stretched as they closed the doors and walked toward the veranda of the beautiful farmhouse. Before either of them could step on the rickety wooden stair, the front door opened, and Clancy stepped out with a double-barreled shotgun, cocked, and raised. If both barrels fired, it would instantly kill them both at that range.

"That's far enough, fuckers," Clancy said with evil menace. Jenny had no doubt whatsoever he would not hesitate to pull the triggers. She realized this was one of the killers and was hit with a sharp pain in her chest akin to a heart attack.

They both raised their arms as Jenny tried to calm the situation, "Mr. Pike, it's Detective Sergeant Jenny Markham and Detective Byrne. I spoke to you on the phone."

"I know who you are. I saw you and your boss on TV. Now I want you both to take your guns out and toss them over at my feet. Do it very, very carefully, or I might accidentally shoot."

It was hopeless. Jenny knew they had to do as they were told but feared that by disarming themselves, they were at the mercy of the killer of forty-three people, a man who knew no mercy. "Why are you doing this, Mr. Pike? It's only some simple questions we have for you," Jenny asked as she took a step away from Jamie, thinking if they could separate, they may have a chance.

Taking a step away saved Jenny's life, or at the very least, a severe wounding. Clancy jerked the gun from aiming at them both to just Jamie and pulled the left-hand trigger. The blast hit him squarely in the chest, with stray pellets hitting his neck, shoulders, and arms. He was killed instantly, his body picked up and thrown backward like a rag doll to lay twitching and bleeding.

Before Jenny could breathe, the shotgun was leveled back at her chest, and Clancy spoke again, "You will soon learn, little rabbit, when I say do something, you do it immediately, or there will be consequences. People don't usually like my consequences, so that's your last warning. Now take your gun out and toss it at my feet."

Terrified to her very core, Jenny held back panic by a thread. She raised her arm to reach for the holstered gun at her hip and realized some pellets had hit her arm, which only now hurt. Her arm was bleeding freely. "Please, please don't do this, Mr. Pike," she whimpered as she threw her gun away from her to clatter at his feet.

"That's what they all say, little rabbit. That's what they all say," Clancy replied and grinned, then stepped back and beckoned her inside the house with the shotgun.

****

14.30 p.m.

Beverley saw quite a dapper little man stepping through the doorway. He was slim, gray, and impeccably dressed, with what she thought of as an old air force mustache, twirled and waxed. He had a writing pad in his hand. "Here it is, my precious. I found it for you."

"Oh, that's a freakin' laugh. You found my notebook for me when you're the galah who lost it." Mandy snatched it from his hands, but she was smiling as she did, so it was done more in humor than malice.

She flipped through the pages one at a time until she triumphantly found the one she was looking for. "There you are, you bugger," she yelled, and with a flourish, she tore the sheet out and handed it to Beverley. There was scribbled *1OUF 912*. It stood out with a big circle and little doodled flowers around the ring. *The flowers are so typical of the woman*, Beverley thought.

"Thank you, Mandy. Excuse me, I need to ring this in straight away. She turned away, dialing Sam's mobile number. She felt like she had won the lottery. *Oh my God, we've got him.*

Chapter 23

The Last Day by the Numbers (3)

0230 On

Sam's phone was set to ring a nondescript soft ringtone for obvious reasons. He could hardly have a rock song raging while interviewing a witness or suspect. It was also switched to vibrate, so if he didn't hear the tone, he could feel he had a call or message coming through his pocket as it shook, rattled, and rolled. When he was on the phone with his boss earlier, he had gone to the whiteboard to look for the name Pike. Distracted, he absentmindedly put his phone down on the aluminum ledge, which held the different colored marker pens and an eraser.

As Joel stepped into the transportable office, Sam sat at his desk, frozen in shock to see a man he now knew to be a serial murderer walking in, dressed in police uniform, with a gun waving from left to right and murderous intent in his coal-black eyes.

Three months prior, Sam had been shot and wounded while in the cold and murky waters of the Swan River late at night, and the psychological trauma had never left him, even though he thought it had. Sam had also come away from the episode with a short-term phobia of water, so his psychologist had focused on that as well as being wounded. Sam spent several sessions with June Faraday, working through it, and both thought Sam was over the mental anguish and trauma from his brush with death at the hands of criminal drug dealer Jimmy Mallory. The second he saw Joel Pike enter; Sam froze in complete shock as he stared at the gun.

When Sam replayed it later in his mind, there was no doubt that if Beverley had not phoned him at that precise moment, he would have been shot dead at his desk, frozen in time, unable to move. Beverley was calling to tell him her great news that she had discovered the registration plate number for the four-wheel-drive used by the killers, and her timing was perfect. Sam shook himself out of his Malaise with the phone's vibrations on the ledge full of whiteboard marker pens, which made an awful, jangling noise. The sound galvanized Sam, jerking him back to reality, and he reached for his own gun. The sudden clatter at the whiteboard distracted Joel, who was scanning for Sam. He turned toward the sound and fired his weapon instinctively.

Joel had killed many people over the years and never lost one moment of sleep. For all the deaths at his hands, he had never fired his police-issued gun at a person, and he had never been shot at himself. So, being in a gun battle was a learning curve. Not so for Sam, who had twice shot at men; killing one but missed the other.

Before Joel could realize his mistake and turn to where Sam sat behind his desk, Sam yanked his automatic pistol from the holster at his hip, leveled, and fired four times in rapid succession. The noise was deafening in the command center, and his bullets hit Joel Pike three times: the fourth hitting the wall behind him as he fell backward. The triple hammer blows made by the hollow point rounds drove Joel through the doorway to fall onto the same gravel where he had buried so many bodies. The murderer lay, bleeding while Sam followed at a run and saw the three wounds were fatal; Pike would not survive his wounds. He lay on the gravel, staring at the sky, shot in the upper chest, stomach, and neck, each hole pumping blood in rivers. Sam later thought it was hardly perfect grouping, but using hollow point rounds made each hit devastating and deadly because of the mushrooming effect on impact.

Sam kicked Joel's gun out of Pike's reach, unwilling to take any chances. He was trembling and breathless, high on adrenalin, and feeling close to vomiting. Sam took deep breaths and swallowed continuously as he squatted alongside Joel Pike as blood sprayed from the neck wound onto the dust and stones.

Sam was suddenly joined by the two staff who had been working in a separate office entering data at the far end of the command center. The woman, Brenda, screamed, and the man, Jeremy, vomited in the gravel, both having never seen anyone shot. Sam had no time to counsel them. He yelled for them to call an ambulance, knowing it was useless. But he knew that's what should be done in the situation.

Sam looked down at Joel, and their eyes locked. He had to know. "Why?" he asked, "Why did you kill all those young people?"

Joel tried to answer, but all that came out of his mouth was a gurgle and a spurt of blood. He turned away from Sam, looked to the sky, and died.

****

14.48 p.m.
Jenny Markham wished she was dead. No nightmare

could ever be as bad as her life was, and she knew her torment was far from over. She had been led, docile, crying and begging down the steps into the cellar, and when the stench hit her, she was sick to her stomach. It was the smell of decay, blood, feces, and death. Nothing had ever smelt so horrible to her in her life. After Jenny vomited everything which she had in her stomache, she stood weak and sweating, with her hands on her knees, bent at the waist.

"You know, when you rabbits make a mess down here, I make you clean it up, but I guess it doesn't matter much anymore. You and your boss have seen to that. Well, little rabbit, around about now, Inspector Collins is dead; my son went to kill him. What do you think of that?"

"Why are you doing this?" she pleaded, eyes frantic, hoping upon hope he was wrong about Sam being dead, but knowing he probably wasn't.

"Because I can. Now, shut up with your whining and show me the goods. We have time and can have some fun before Joel gets back."

She didn't know what he meant by *showing him the goods*. Her brain was slow and muddled from fear and being sick. He held the gun in his left hand, picked up a long thin bamboo cane from the bench with his right hand, and brought it around in an arc. It swished through the air and connected with her hip. The pain was searing and sudden and would have cut her to the bone were it not for the business skirt she wore over her pantyhose.

"Here's how this works, little rabbit. I tell you to do something, and you do it. Now, if you do it quickly I might hurt you, but then again, I might not. But if you don't do what I say straight away, I most definitely will cause you pain, and bad, *really* bad pain. Now show me the fucking goods. Get your fucking clothes off."

Jenny's heart sank. She had only one hope of survival, to hold out long enough for help to arrive because it had to come; the only question in her mind was whether she would still be alive when it did. As slowly as possible, crying in fear, she removed her jacket and dropped it on the dirty floor. When she was naked, the old man led her to what looked like an ancient, solid low bench or coffee table. With increasing horror, she saw handcuffs fixed to the legs at one end.

"Lay face down, little rabbit, and put one of them handcuffs on. I'm sure you know all about handcuffs, don't you? Don't keep me waiting, now."

He still held the shotgun in one hand and the cane in the other. Jenny knew she had to do as she was told. The wooden top was hard, cold, and unforgiving as she lay down, put one cuff over her wrist, and clicked it closed. Pike put down the cane and shotgun, squatted, put her other wrist in the remaining handcuff, and tightened it.

He stood up and started to undress, talking to her in a strangely perfectly normal voice. "So little rabbit, we have ourselves a bit of a dilemma here, which I'm sure you can appreciate. Normally, when Joel and I bring a playmate down here, we know we have lots and lots of time, so it means we can start off nice and slowly. But, you know, don't you, little rabbit, we don't have long before all your mates come around and want to arrest me. And whose fault is that? Why, I do believe it's yours and your idiot boss's fault for not believing the accident site we set up. So that's not good for me, but it's also not so good for you, is it, little rabbit?"

Jenny had been a police officer for years; she had

endured twenty-three hours of childbirth to bring Josh into the world, seen dead bodies in car accidents, and interviewed murderers, gang members, and cold-hearted killers. Nothing had prepared her for Clancy Pike. He was a completely cold and psychotic murderer. Yet he was functioning calmly as if this was normal behavior, which terrified her soul because she knew the horror the previous victims had been through. There was no escaping what was about to happen, and she sobbed. She didn't want to die, and she didn't want to be tortured. She bit her lip so hard she tasted blood in her mouth.

"So we don't have enough time to break your heart and soul slowly and have some fun along the way, do we? But, and here is the dilemma, little rabbit, Joel isn't here. I don't want to make too much of a mess of you before he gets to have some fun, too, so what's a man to do, little rabbit? We don't want to just wait, do we? Oh, no, there's no fun in that. Is there?"

Slowly, she turned her head to him, frightened of what was to come, and saw he was now nude.

Over the years, age had caught up with Clancy, causing a drop in his sexual desire and ability. He had also become so used to inflicting pain and torturing young women as a prelude it would be useless to try without some suffering first. Besides, for him, that was where the fun was, hurting the little rabbits. Clancy walked back to the tool bench along the wall, with all their utensils scattered over it, and put down the cane after inspecting it. That one would cut too deep and wouldn't do. He wanted something which would give an old-fashioned thrashing but didn't cut the skin too deeply. Clancy loved it when they begged for it to stop; it was music to his ears. He found a thicker bamboo cane, flicked it through the air, and thought it would do the trick nicely.

****

14.53 p.m.

Sam stood before the whiteboard, still shaking, his nerves frayed. He was sweating profusely, and his chest felt tight. Sam looked down at the list of officers due to call on the Winter Sun Farm and saw it was Jenny and Jamie. He phoned Jenny's mobile number with a sinking heart and a feeling of inevitability. It rang out and went to her message bank. He had the same result with Jamie's, so either they were out of range, in a dip in the hills, maybe, or incapable of answering. He knew it was the latter.

Sam knew he should not leave the scene. He had shot someone dead, and protocol insisted he stayed there, made a statement, and handed his weapon in for testing. That was what Sam should do, what the rulebook demanded, but Sam knew when the rulebook was written it didn't envisage the current situation. So, that wasn't what Sam was going to do. There was no fucking way he could sit on his hands waiting while Jenny and Jamie suffered God knew what.

He realized if he left the scene then, when investigated later as it had to be, the Internal Affairs Investigator would say Sam was emotionally unbalanced at the time, and no matter what, he should have stayed put. But Sam's only thoughts were with Jenny and Jamie, ensuring they were safe and getting them help if they weren't. One maniac was dead, and the other was with them; if his detective weren't dead now, they soon would be. He just knew it.

Fuck that for a game of skittles, he thought. *Jenny*

and Jamie are in mortal danger, and no matter which rule book you want to quote, I am the closest officer who can respond. Sam told the support crew what he was doing as he changed the magazine in the Glock for a full one and then ran to his car and started it. Sam rang Bob Young using his hands-free system as the vehicle fishtailed through the gate.

Before Bob could answer by stating his name, Sam let fly, "Bob, it's Sam. I'm on my way to the Winter Sun Farm. The killers are a father and son team, Clancy and Joe Pike. Joe Pike was the police officer who performed that crap investigation of Greg Brady's wreck. No, please don't interrupt because I don't have much time, and the signal could drop out at any moment. We need TRG to go to the farm ASAP. Jenny Markham and Jamie Byrne are not answering their phones, and the Winter Sun was on their list of farms to visit this afternoon. I am very concerned for their safety. I have just shot dead Joe Pike, who came to the Command Centre with the intention of killing me. He kicked open the door with gun drawn and fired but missed me. I didn't miss him."

The car skidded around a corner, siren blaring its warning to other road users, and almost lost control, swerving with Sam's over-correction, but he got it back under control. "An ambulance has been called, and the support crew is reporting to Internal Affairs, Firearm Discharge Branch. I know I should stay at the site, but again, I am frightened for my officer's safety, and I am the closest to their location. Every second counts. Please send TRG and any armed police officers who are anywhere near that farm urgently. We will also need an ambulance with paramedics, as I'm positive we have officers needing medical attention."

"Sam, do not, I repeat, *do not* enter the property until backup and TRG arrives. I will send them immediately. Do you understand me? You must not enter in the frame of mind you are in."

"Bob?"

"Yes, Sam. I'm listening."

"What do they do with women on the farm?"

Bob paused. "Sam, you *must* not enter without support. That is an order. If we have lost two officers, we do not want to lose a third."

"Not sure if you are getting me, Bob. The reception is horrible, the signal is dropping out, and I can't hear you." Sam hung up the phone. He had no intention of spending precious minutes arguing with his boss, which would delay Bob calling an ambulance and TRG. In his heart, he knew, he absolutely knew, they would need an ambulance.

If, by some legal loophole, Clancy Pike walked free because Sam entered without a warrant, then the whole legal system could take a hike, as far as Sam was concerned. Jenny Markham was one of the best detectives he had ever come across. She worked for him, and he would crawl over hot coals to save her if he could. Not to mention Jamie Byrne, a young married detective with a new baby and his whole life ahead of him, was with her. The rest would have to take care of itself; Sam was past caring about the consequences; he was beyond rational thought other than saving his detectives.

His mobile phone rang, and he looked at the display. It was Bob Young again. It would be obvious what he would say, so he ignored it and put his foot down harder on the accelerator.

****

In the cellar, Clancy manhandled Jenny from the bench to where a chain was bolted to the wall and handcuffed her with arms above her head. She was now upright, though she lacked the strength to stand, so hung by her wrists. Her body weight ensured the cuffs dug deeply into the skin and slowed circulation to her hands.

Clancy felt good. He had enjoyed himself. The rabbit was less pretty than other backpackers they had lured to the farm, but that didn't matter. *It's nice to have a mature woman for a change, and being a cop makes up for* her looks, he thought. Clancy crossed to the bucket of water with a ladle sitting in it; he took it from the water and filled it, then walked back to her and threw the water in her face. Jenny flinched, shook her head, and realized where she was. The pain in her wrists was excruciating, and she shuffled her feet to take some weight to ease it.

Jenny's world was a combination of different pains, all fighting for supremacy. Her back, legs, and behind felt white hot, and she fidgeted from one leg to the other as her body tried to ease the excruciating agony and failed. She shook her head again, trying to focus on anything but the pain, and opened her eyes. Clancy's face was within inches of hers. His breath stank and made her gag. Then she saw the long-bladed knife in his hand.

"We've had our fun, little rabbit. Soon, either Joel will come to take a turn with you, or your lot will arrive. Joel should have been here by now, so I think maybe they got him." Then he stabbed the long sharp blade into her stomach. Jenny was beyond feeling more pain. She was in shock, she vaguely realized, or perhaps it was because the rest of her body was busy dealing with various agonies it tried to ignore the knife entering her skin.

Jenny believed she was dying and welcomed anything which permitted her to escape her world of horror. She tried to scream, but no words came out. Her breath was stuck in her lungs. The cellar spun around with vertigo, and she wanted to be sick.

Slowly, while grinning, he pulled the blade out of Jenny's stomach. "Shush, shush, shush, little rabbit. If Joel turns up soon, that little nick won't kill you; I've had lots of practice at this, trust me; I know what I'm doing. We will patch you up so he can have some fun with you. You'll like that, won't you? Good-looking boy, my son Joel is. You'll like him, trust me. But if Joel doesn't turn up soon, then I'm afraid your punishment will be that you'll probably bleed to death. Sorry about that," he grinned at her, then shook his head as she slipped back unconscious and sagged against the handcuffs. He walked away, back to his clothes, to get dressed.

****

As the cellar was below ground, Clancy didn't hear the car arrive at the front of the house and stop next to Jenny's. Sam had turned the siren off so he wouldn't announce his arrival. He leaped out before it stopped fully and saw Jamie Byrne's body and the flies buzzing around the gaping wounds to his chest and face. Sam was on autopilot, incapable of rational thought, and could see Jamie was dead at a glance. He gritted his teeth in rage. Sam had one thing on his mind, to save Jenny. He hadn't been in time for Jamie but prayed he wasn't too late for her.

San ran to the verandah, pistol in hand, and noticed the steps looked rickety. He used the outside edges to avoid creaks. He turned the handle and pushed open the front door, ducking to one side to avoid being shot if someone lay in wait. Sam noticed the smell wafting out and gagged before swallowing and stepping through the doorway. He looked around the large family room, which was empty. Sam saw the open trap door and hurried over but was dismayed as the floor creaked underneath him. Sam stepped onto the first rung, which groaned heavily, and heard the voice coming up from below.

"Is that you, Joel? Did you kill the bastard cop?"

Sam could tell the direction of the voice, so he hurried down the rest of the steps and was facing Pike when he saw the old man pulling up his pants. With a sinking heart and horror, he noticed Jenny hanging from her wrists, blood streaming from the knife wound in her stomach, and the mass of red welts on her skin. He thought he was too late.

They stared at each other. "Joel?" the old man asked and then glanced at the shotgun only two steps away.

"Dead."

Clancy nodded and shrugged. "We had a good run."

"Why did you kill all those kids?"

"Why? Why? There is no why, you fuckwit. I did it because I wanted to." He sprang toward the table with the shotgun but only got halfway.

Sam had no recollection of pulling the trigger. He didn't consciously shoot Clancy Pike dead, yet his gun discharged time after time while he watched as if in a daze. As Sam told investigators afterward, it was like someone else pulled the trigger repeatedly. He could only stand by and watch as each bullet found a home in the body of the sick, perverted psychopath. Clancy spun as he was shot, stumbled, and fell on the concrete floor, tangled up in his pants. Even with the erratic movement, every shot Sam took found its mark in the torso.

Sam looked down at the gun in his hand. He noted the cordite smoke in the air, and the slide had locked because the magazine was empty. He realized then he had shot Clancy Pike nine times in cold blood. Sam dropped the gun to the floor, ran to Jenny, and felt for a pulse. Relieved, he found one and was thankful she was unconscious; he thanked God silently, glad had arrived in time.

"Jen," he shouted, "don't you dare die on me. Don't you die, you hear me?" He looked around frantically for the keys to the handcuffs and couldn't see them anywhere. He searched the bench, talking nonstop to her to try to let her know she wasn't alone. She was finally safe. But there were no keys anywhere he could see. Sam recoiled at the thought that they could only be in one place. He ran over to the crumpled bullet-ridden body and rifled through the pants pockets around Pike's knees. Sam felt a ring with keys, breathed a sigh of relief, and yanked them out; they were wet with blood.

He dashed to Jenny, reached up, undid one cuff, and lowered her arm around his neck. Then he inserted the key into the second slot, wrapping one arm around her naked body to take her weight as he released the other lock.

She collapsed into his arms, a dead weight. Sam continued to speak to her, "You're ok, Jen. I've got you. You're safe now; I've killed him. Please don't die. Please don't die."

He held her, looping one arm under her legs, and carried her to the steps. "C'mon love, let's get you out of this stench into some fresh air. C'mon, wake up now. You're okay; just stay with me."

Back upstairs, Sam kicked the trap door closed to keep the smell down in the depths and gently laid Jenny on the couch. He frantically looked around for something to cover her up and stop the bleeding. Sam wanted to preserve her dignity and keep her warm and alive. Desperate, he yanked the tablecloth off, scattering dirty dishes and beer bottles all over the floor. He wildly shook dirt and dust off it.

Next, Sam ripped his own shirt off, sending buttons flying everywhere, and balled it up in his hands. He placed it over the stab wound, then covered her with the tablecloth to keep her warm. He sat by her side on the floor to wait while maintaining pressure on the shirt over the stab wound to minimize her blood loss as he talked to her, trying to reach her and keep her alive.

Epilogue

The West Australian police force had never faced a situation like what followed the killings of the father and son murderers. Debate raged in the hierarchy for a long time about what to do. As protocol demanded, Sam Collins was suspended while Internal Affairs conducted investigations into his behavior by leaving the command center against specific orders not to do so and then shooting the unarmed Clancy Pike dead. By far, the popular point of view hailed him as Jenny Markham's savior, while the IA investigators saw Sam as a murderer.

****

Jenny underwent emergency surgery. The doctors thought they were successful, and the stab wound had caused no significant damage, but Jenny wouldn't wake up once the anesthetic wore off. She had retreated inside her own protective cocoon. Her body had shut down, and Jenny was unreachable no matter what doctors tried, so they consulted with the senior psychiatrist on staff, Dr. Henry Babbington. He spoke with Sam to understand what Jenny had been through and diagnosed her problem as self-induced psychological catatonia to escape the sheer horror of her torture. He believed without her consciousness cooperating, all they could do was wait and hope she chose to come back from wherever she was hiding.

****

Sam didn't move from his apartment for six days after he was suspended following the interview with the hostile Internal Affairs investigators. He was mentally, emotionally, and physically exhausted. Were it not for the loving care from Caroline twenty-four hours a day and repeated visits from June Faraday, his old counselor, he may have jumped from his eighth-floor balcony to the sprawling traffic below; to escape the horror movie his mind had created.

The newspapers and TV reporters resembled a pack of feeding sharks once the story broke. Of particular interest was that a policeman had been one of the serial killers. Much to the Commissioner's anger, the media were drip-fed information of the investigation led by Sam by *informed sources* or *a police spokesman who didn't want to be named*. The true story of Sam's behavior was leaked to them daily, ensuring public support for Sam Collins grew.

Despite an internal inquiry to find the source of the leaks, it was never discovered the culprit was Bob Young. He intended to build and grow support for Detective Inspector Collins, who could otherwise be hung out to dry for the killing of a serial murderer. Bob knew if he couldn't succeed, Sam would be arrested and taken into custody. Should that happen, Bob couldn't imagine a jury would convict him, but the Internal Affairs officers might feel compelled to charge him anyway to save face. Such an arrest would end Sam's career, which would be a terrible shame as Bob believed he was the finest police officer Bob had ever encountered.

One night, he lectured his wife in a drunken stupor

caused by his frustrations at how Internal Affairs treated Sam. "The law is a fucking ass." He then cited many of the things senior police have thought for years about the judicial system. Like how soft they were on criminals and how hard they were on police who made a mistake or an error in otherwise good judgment and paid a higher price than the person they arrested.

The undeniable fact IA had to consider was Sam had shot an unarmed man. Not just once, but nine times. There was no escaping that, even though Sam believed Clancy Pike was reaching for a shotgun. That Pike had murdered forty-four people, including Detective Jamie Byrne, was largely unimportant under those circumstances. Also irrelevant, in the eyes of the law, was how Detective Markham was tortured, raped, stabbed, and left to bleed to death. She would have died were it not for Sam's intervention, which was not in dispute. But Sam had shot the man repeatedly while he had been putting on his pants. That he had been reaching for a shotgun was considered, but the number of bullets fired showed a different story, they believed.

Bob hoped the Public Prosecutors Office realized there was no way they could find a jury that would convict Sam. He believed the public agreed with the execution Sam had carried out, no doubt while under enormous emotional stress and shock. There could be no question he was affected psychologically when Sam pulled the trigger. "Who the fuck wouldn't have been in the same circumstances?" he yelled at his wife, who calmly nodded and agreed for the twentieth time.

In Bob's opinion, the police force was about to lose the finest two officers he had ever worked with. One was comatose, and the other was about to be kicked off the job. He believed that were it not for their determination, the burial ground would not have been discovered at the gravel pit, and the killings would have continued for God alone knew how long. *Surely that must count for something?"* he raged at his wife, who naturally agreed.

Bob had personally pleaded with the Commissioner and urged him to direct the Internal Affairs Department to find no case to answer for and no charges to bring. He shook his head and said while he agreed with the situation's blatant unfairness, he couldn't intervene, fearing such interference could blow up on him someday. After all, the Commissioner pointed out, he could well be charged, or at least lose his career, for pushing a blatant cover-up of one of their own. He impressed upon Bob that due process had to be done and *seen* to be done by the public.

There was nothing for it, Bob decided, but to wait to see what action internal affairs would push for and what the Public Prosecutors Office would do. The police themselves could not be seen to meddle in a case against one of their own Detective Inspectors who had killed and not been arrested. However, there was one thing he could do to help, and he began that night.

****

Two things occurred on the seventh day following the shootings. The first started around nine a.m. when the apartment intercom was buzzed by a visitor from the main entrance. Sam was sitting on the balcony, sipping a coffee which Caroline had made for him, staring out across the Swan River toward South Perth.

On a clear day, sometimes he could make out the roof of the apartment block where he had fought and subdued the Domin8 killer some months before, but not that day. It was too overcast. Rain was threatening, but he still liked being out on the balcony as often as possible. It was where he relaxed the best, which he needed to do to fight the boredom of sitting at home, day after day.

Caroline went to the intercom to see who it was, expecting yet another reporter, but she saw a middle-aged man and a young boy on the monitor. "Hello," she asked, "can I help you?"

"Hi, I'm Mike Markham, Jenny's ex-husband, and this is Josh, her son. I wonder if we could speak to Sam Collins for a few minutes, please."

"Of course, you can. Come on up." She pressed the unlock button, permitting them to use the elevator to climb to their floor. Then she went to the front door, opened it, and awaited their arrival. "Hi guys, I'm Caroline. Come in. Is the press still waiting around the front door? There's never less than three or four of them on any given day."

"Umm, no, we didn't see any, did we, Josh?" Mike answered.

"Sam won't talk to them. I wish he would. It might help him come out of his shell, but the fact that he got suspended was the last straw for him. He doesn't seem to care much about anything anymore, not even me," she shrugged, very close to tears. "He believes he is going to jail for murdering that maniac."

Mike shook his head. "I'm so sorry to hear that. We've come to ask his help with Jenny."

"Well, he's on the balcony. Whatever it is, I'm for it. He is just wasting away in here, feeling sorry for himself." She led them to the glass sliding door, opened it, and introduced them, "Sam, Jenny's husband and son, are here to see you."

He stood up immediately and shook hands. "How is Jenny? I've phoned the hospital daily, but because I'm not immediate family, they won't tell me a thing other than she is still in a coma. The press has me under siege here, so I can't get to visit her."

Josh burst into tears, and his father hugged him. Over Josh's shoulder, Mike said, "We're losing her, Sam. She won't wake up. The doctors can't help her anymore. They say there isn't anything wrong with her physically; she just doesn't want to come back because of what she went through in the cellar. She's in a coma being fed by a tube."

"Oh God, I'm so sorry," Sam hung his head.

"We would like to ask you to come and talk to her and see if you can reach her. No one else can."

"Me? I'll try, but why would you think I can help?"

"The night before it happened, she spent it with us. She stayed over with me, and um, she said she was happier than she had been in years. We stayed awake most of the night, just talking, and Jenny spoke a lot about you. She said you inspired her; you were the best boss she ever worked with, and she wanted to spend the rest of her police career working with you. If anyone can reach her, down in the depths of wherever she is hiding, it's you, Sam. Will you come and try, please?"

"Of course I will, if you think it will help."

****

Mike and Josh led Sam into the private room, which housed the shell of the person Jenny once was. She lay on her back, looking peaceful as if she might wake up from her slumber at any moment, though Mike had said Jenny hadn't moved in seven days. The drip tube hung from her arm, and an oxygen line fed air through her nose while the monitor beeped out her heartbeat. Sam had never seen a sadder sight.

"We, err, will leave you alone and wait in the cafeteria for you. Take your time, Sam. There's no rush. And thank you for coming to try." They left quietly and closed the door behind them.

Sam stood by the bed, looking down, not knowing what to say but knowing he wanted to try. Suddenly he remembered what Jenny had done with Tammy, and the more he thought about it, the more he knew it was what he should do. Sam pulled the chair over and sat by her bedside, very close, facing her. He reached under the bedclothes, gently pulled Jenny's hand out, and held it in his, then with his other fingertips, he slowly stroked the back of her hand and lower arm the way he had watched her do.

He took a deep breath and began. "So, Jen, I want you to know you are safe now; no one can hurt you anymore. I killed them both, father and son. They're gone and they cannot come back and hurt you. I promise you, they're dead." Sam kept stroking softly, up, and down, up, and down.

"They tried to kill Tammy. The son Joel went to her house. He would have killed her and her mother and father, but you saved them. You said they should go away for a few days to escape the press, and they did, Jen. They are so grateful to you for suggesting that. Tammy wants to come and see you as soon as you wake up. She's desperate to thank you herself and thinks it's only fair after you visited her so many times. Can you please come back to us, so Tammy can see you?" Sam watched her closed eyes and thought he saw some movement of her pupils.

"I won't tell you what Joel Pike did inside their house, but they took your advice and went away, so they weren't home when he went to kill them. Tammy is back running again, and she wants you to come and watch her compete in her first triathlon. Will you do that, Jen? Please?" There was no sign she was aware he was even in the room, let alone stroking her hand. Jenny looked the same as when he had arrived.

He bent his head so he was closer to Jenny's ear. He decided to take another direction. "I need you, Jen. I need you to wake up and tell them what happened; otherwise, I think they may send me to jail. They are going to charge me with murder, Jen. I saw what he'd done to you and shot that bastard nine times. But he was unarmed. They don't believe he made a lunge for his shotgun; they think I executed him, but you know what? I'd do it again if I could. He hurt you and all those others, and we are all better off because he is dead and can't torture anyone else. But I need you, love. I need you to wake up and help me. Help fight for me. With you by my side, I have a chance. Without you, I think I'm going to lose."

He looked up and noticed she had changed. In the corner of her eye was a single tear. It trickled very slowly down the side of her face.

"Please, Jen. Come back to work with me. I need you. I honestly need you. There is no one else I want as my partner, and if you don't come back, I will be charged and tried for murder. Jen, please, come back."

Suddenly, she was crying, sobbing, and awake. Sam stood, bent over, and hugged her tightly. She whispered with a croaky voice, "He hurt me so much, Boss."

"I know, love," Sam replied softly, "but he can't

hurt you anymore, Jen. He's dead."

****

The second thing that occurred that day was a phone call by the Commissioner's personal assistant, asking Sam to be in his office at two-thirty for a meeting. Sam agreed he would attend.

He'd left Jenny with Mike and her son, sitting up, hugging each other. She would undoubtedly have many nightmares ahead and need much help and support. But Jenny was awake again, and the rest could follow. Jenny would fight her demons. She promised Sam she would.

Just before he left, Jenny beckoned him to her bedside and then even closer, so she could whisper in his ear, "Boss, you fight them. Don't you dare give up. Fight them, or you'll have me to answer to." Then she hugged him and whispered, "Thank you for saving my life."

****

Sam showered, shaved, and put on his best suit and tie, resigned to the fact he was about to be formally arrested. *At least I can look good when they do,* he thought. He turned to leave when he saw Caroline was dressed up too.

"Are you going somewhere?" he asked her.

"Of course I am, dummy. I'm going with you."

"No, you stay here. They're going to arrest me. Best you don't see that."

She had tears in her eyes as she said, "Don't you dare send me away. Don't you fucking dare, Samuel Collins. You are the best, kindest, and bravest man I've ever known, and I love you, you dummy. Where you go, I go. If they dare arrest you, I'm going to fight for you. In fact, I might just shoot them myself."

"Oh, babe," he said, sighing, "I'm so sorry how

things turned out. I'm so sorry I've not been good company for you this last week."

She punched him in the arm hard, and he looked shocked, "I said I love you, and I said I'm going to fight for you, and I am. You are always there for other people, saving lives, helping them. Now I want to be there for you. Don't you even dare think for a moment you can stop me doing that. Now I want you to fight for yourself. Stop apologizing. You've done the world a favor. I love you, Sam. Now let's go and face the bastards together."

****

They entered the Police Commissioner's office holding hands and saw Bob Young and Michael Winters, the head of the Public Prosecutions Department. He nodded at them both, knowing because the PPD was there, it confirmed he was about to be arrested for murder.

"This is Caroline, my fiancée, though she didn't know that 'till right now. I haven't asked her to marry me yet, but I hope she says yes when I do," he said.

Caroline was as shocked as anyone, but her face showed she wanted to scream, *"Yes, yes, yes."*

Sam continued, "As my fiancée, I want her here to witness what happens. I hope's okay with you, Commissioner." Sam made the introductions, not waiting for his request to be denied, and sat where they were directed to sit.

"Inspector," the Commissioner began, "I'm not going to beat around the bush. The fact is I think even you would agree you very much overstepped the bounds when you shot Clancy Pike dead. We all know he and his son were the worst serial killers this state, in fact, this country, has ever seen. That is not in dispute. However, we cannot have police officers shooting unarmed suspects, no matter how much they may feel it was justified."

Sam nodded. He understood the situation all too well. "Commissioner, if you want the truth, I had only one thing in mind when I went to their house, and that was to save the life of two officers under my command, who I believed were in danger. Further, I knew there was insufficient time to wait. Jenny could easily have died if we had waited, and Jamie Byrne was already dead. I did not go there with the intention of killing Pike."

"That may be Inspector, but he was unarmed when you shot him nine times. *Nine times,* that's hardly an accident."

"I had just escaped being shot myself by his son, and but for my phone going off at the wrong time, or the right time for me, I would have been murdered by him. Three months prior, I was shot by Jimmy Mallory, and when Joe Pike arrived to kill me, I mentally blacked out. I have no recollection of shooting that animal in the cellar. I have no memory of making any conscious decision to fire. I believe I was in shock and under severe stress, and I do not believe a court would find otherwise."

The Commissioner nodded, "Your belief has been confirmed by the report compiled by June Faraday, Inspector. But it's not that simple, and you know it." He then turned to Bob Young and held out his hand, "Superintendent, please?"

Bob held out a buff manila folder with papers overflowing the sides, and the Commissioner took it from him. "It seems the superintendent here, despite giving you a direct order not to enter the house..." he held up his hand to stop Sam from interrupting and continued, "please, inspector, don't insult our intelligence by telling us your mobile phone signal dropped out. It's the oldest trick in the book."

Sam sat back in his chair, knowing when he was beaten. Caroline took his hand in hers and squeezed it for moral support.

"As I said, the Superintendent here has been garnering support for you. I know, for example, he has been feeding the press with positive stories about you, and please, Superintendent, don't you insult our intelligence either by denying it. But, Inspector, you should know the Superintendent didn't stop there. He has got a petition signed by virtually every single police officer on the force. Not only did they say they don't want you charged, but for the first time anywhere in the world that I am aware of, each and every one of them has agreed to go on strike if you are. Can you believe the utter chaos if every single police officer went out on strike at the same time?"

Sam was stunned and sat with an open mouth. He turned to Bob Young, who smiled back and nodded imperceptibly. "Commissioner, I had no idea," Sam said, still confused.

"No, of course, you didn't. Now the next thing is the Internal Affairs Department report is in, and they do find you culpable and negligent in your duty to arrest a suspect. However, they are of the opinion you should only be reprimanded. They have considered the enormous mental and emotional stress you were under at the time, again confirmed by your psychological assessment by Mrs. Faraday. They believe you are guilty of nothing more than poor decision-making when incapable of making the right one. But wait, there's more. The Director of the Public Prosecutions Department has recommended they feel it is not in the public's interest to take you to trial for murder; they feel the public would be better served by not charging you. No doubt that's mainly because of the public support your boss has raked up on your behalf."

Sam was incapable of speech. He couldn't believe what he heard, let alone comment on it. He was, quite simply, stunned.

"So, what's to do? We must absolutely punish an officer, who shoots dead an unarmed suspect nine times, but a trial is out of the question, and the entire force goes on strike if we arrest you. So just before you arrived, the three of us formed a disciplinary committee and reviewed your case. Inspector Collins, you have been found guilty of dereliction of duty, and we have decided to suspend you, on full pay, for sixty days. During which period you will be under the strict supervision and care of June Faraday, and only she can release you back to duty when she believes you are fit. There will be no loss of rank, so after your suspension and clearance by her, you will resume your duties with the Major Crime Squad. Do you have anything to say?"

Sam gulped. He wasn't being punished. He wasn't going to jail for twenty years. "Sirs, I'd like to thank you all for your support. It is truly humbling, and beyond that, I don't know what else to say."

The Commissioner stood up and said, "Sam, the official part of this meeting is now over. I'd like to shake your hand and tell you this, completely off the record, and I will deny it if ever asked. I don't know a single police officer who wouldn't have done exactly what you did under the same set of circumstances. I'm not saying it was right because it wasn't, but what I am saying is it was understandable. We need to stand by our officers who make the wrong decision but do it for the right reasons, especially when they are under the kind of stress you were under. Personally, I commend you. Publicly, I must reprimand you, and I hope that's clear. I want to see you back on duty in two months with your sergeant. Now I propose the five of us go down to the pub. It's my first buy, and we can celebrate your engagement to this beautiful woman here who, so far, hasn't said a word, but I can tell she is happy by the smile on her face and the tears in her eyes."

Authors Note:

Hello, dear ever-patient reader.

I hope you enjoyed *Burial Ground*. As dark as it is, the story means a great deal to me and has taken a few years from the first draft to what you've just finished. Read on if you are even remotely interested in how such a horrific behemoth came to be. If not, you can ignore my rambling about this story's beginnings as useless self-indulgent trivia and find something much more worthwhile to do.

As an author of seventeen books, I can say, with authority, that the number one question readers ask is: *"Where do you get your ideas from?"* Mostly, they ask with an incredulous, even interested look, but occasionally, after reading my darker stories like *Glimpse, Memoir of a Serial Killer*, it is with barely concealed horror. As anyone familiar with my *Glimpse* series will know, my *'thing' in this genre* is to try to get into serial killers' heads and show why. Why did they do it? What drove someone to take another life, not just once, but over and over again? Trying for realism in *Burial Ground* took me down some very dark laneways and left me with nightmares from which I woke in cold sweats. I promised myself I would leave serial killers alone for a while when this *BG* was finished, and I did. The next book I wrote was called *Winter at the Light,* a romantic thriller set on a lighthouse in the 1950s, which is as far away from serial killers as I could get.

Burial Ground completed my Sam Collins trilogy, a story I envisioned as the rise through the ranks from detective to detective inspector of a *Good Man*. He is not a bulletproof superhero cop, but a 'normal' decent human with many faults, just like the rest of us, doing a shitty job and trying his best to make a difference. We first meet him in *Domin8* as a partner to his mentor, the prude-ish Felix Milanski. Next, he was the lead detective ordered to hunt down a vigilante in *The Dancer and the Vigilante* while a crime war erupts between two rival biker gangs to control the drug trade. Finally, in *Burial Ground*, Sam gets to head up a task force to find a serial killer pair who have murdered forty-three victims over a seventeen-year reign.

I recall reading an interview with jailed Ivan Milat while trying to develop a plot for the third book. This *'gentleman'* was one of Australia's most notorious mass murderers. I was stunned to read that despite overwhelming evidence, he never admitted to the killing and burial of his victims in The Belangalo Forrest in New South Wales, Australia. Police believed he murdered as many as twenty more victims than the seven he was convicted of. Yet, he took his secrets to the grave, denying many families their desperately needed closure. Such was his complete disregard for humanity. I tried to capture that sense of brutality and a total lack of regret in my antagonists in this story. Did I succeed? That is up to you, dear reader, to determine. I can tell you that trying to get into the mire and describe Clancy Pike's evil personality affected me deeply, so I hope I conveyed that.

I've cut over twenty-five thousand words from the original first draft manuscript to this version you have just read during the many rewrites and editing rounds. That might not sound like many when you say it quickly, but to put that number into perspective, it is almost a quarter of the finished novel gone. Most of the deleted scenes were just too dark and depressing, but I found, like any good method actor, that I got so far into the character that I had to shower in hot water several times a day to wash the filth off.

I must say that despite the months of work in writing the original manuscript and through editing, the finished book is much better off without those words. They say, *'less is more,'* and in writing terms, it means the fewer words used, the more impact they have. There is one exceptional and vitally important person in my life to thank for teaching me that and so much more.

If, dear ever-patient reader, you enjoyed this story, please spare a thought for my amazing editor, the fantastic Melanie Billings. Mel has put up with me through ten books, and she not only deserves a medal for continually correcting my grammar but also a HUGE round of applause. Her work helping and guiding me through *Burial Ground* is astounding, so Mel, THANK YOU from the bottom of my heart - I could not have done this without you. For me, *Burial Ground* came from my heart, soul, and imagination, but for Mel, it was her job to wade through the quagmire. I say job, but I know it's far more than that for her; it's a vocation and her unwavering desire to help people like, me. I love you to bits, Mel.

My next release is called, *A Love to ~~Die~~ Kill For.* Mel hasn't read it yet, but it is coming soon, Mel. This is the first time I've written a story based outside my home state of Western Australia. It's set in New York, where my incredible publisher, The Wild Rose Press, is based.

~ Steve
Perth, Western Australia

A word about the author...

I was born in the UK, what seems like an epoch ago, and moved to Australia at age 16. I was a long haired rock guitarist and poet/songwriter, before real life got in the way, and I gave it all up for love.

I've always felt I had tales to tell and won short story competitions and published poetry in my wilder, younger days. More recently I've written and published five novels. While they have all been Police procedural thrillers, mainly focusing on Serial killers, they all have a love theme running through them.

I believe love, and family are everything. Anything else you gain in life is a bonus.

I live in Perth, in Western Australia and am fiercely patriotic, and parochial. My wife is amazing in that she not only puts up with living with a writer, but encourages it. I've been blessed with five children, and I adore them all.

http://stephen-b-king.com

Thank you for purchasing
this publication of The Wild Rose Press, Inc.

For questions or more information
contact us at
info@thewildrosepress.com.

The Wild Rose Press, Inc.
www.thewildrosepress.com